OTHER BOOKS BY PETER FARB

Man's Rise to Civilization as Shown by the Indians of North
    America from Primeval Times to the Coming of the
    Industrial State

The Land, Wildlife, and Peoples of the Bible

Face of North America: The Natural History of a Continent

The Land and Wildlife of North America

The Atlantic Shore: Its Human and Natural History (with
    John Hay)

Living Earth

The Forest

Ecology

YANKEE DOODLE

BY

PETER FARB

SIMON AND SCHUSTER · NEW YORK

First printing

SBN 671-20676-1
Library of Congress Catalog Card Number: 74-130196
Manufactured in the United States of America

For Mark and Thomas

"It's good to be shifty in a new country."
— *Some Adventures of Captain Simon Suggs*, 1846

YANKEE
DOODLE

BENJAMIN PENNYMAN, ESQ.
ATTORNEY-AT-LAW

A TOURNEY! OUTLAW! Prisoner Pennyman, are you sworn? Yes, judge, cross my words and hope to be. Prisoner, are you represented by a lawyer? Yes, jedge, ah got mah liar right aside me. Prisoner Pennyman, you are guilty of wordploy and shall be sprayed with verbicides until didst. Have you anything to say? Laddies and gentilemen of the jury, I admit that I am quilty of this unpardonable scion.

All ye Pennymans. Pennymanies. Dry moths impaled by memories. Memory alone survives. Here lies. That is true. A youth who bore. Excelsior! Thus spake Henry Wordsworth Lungflow. Life is but an empty dream. Things are not what they seem. Pinch the Pennymans no more. Gone. All gone. Noah more Pennymans to come. Washed up. Times changed. End of the loin. Last stop. Get off, Pennymans. All out. Terminus. Pity the Pennyman. Pity-pity-pity-PITY.

My Black Book. My Blah-Blah-Black Book. It's the last word. From me. Formerly me. It's every Pennyman's genealesis. Read by each of their regenerations. Looking backward. Write finis to it. ti ot sinif. Byebye, Pennymans. Good night, ladies, good night, sweet ladies, good night. Three hundred years. Old. Vellum mellowed, yellowed, and hellowed. Ink faded. Folio. Bible black. No ribbon to mark where they fell to sleep or drooped dead. Pennyman in gilt. I am quilty. Isaiah Pennyman began it.

Selfrighteous. Full of Old Testymeant wroth. He never doubted God was the tenth man on his team. Page the one. The beginning, which I will end.

We determin'd to make this Strange Schore to Blossom & to Yeeld uppe ites sweete Bountie, to Create a Neue Jerusalem in a hideous Willdernesse fulle of willd Beastes & willd Salvages. As the Lord surround'd His chosen Israell with dangers to make His Miraculous Diliverance famous throughout alle Time, so here oure Handfull of chosen People struggle through a forlorne Willdernesse that they mighte achieve the Glorie of being discover'd by Christe Jesus. We remember'd Sion . . .

The redd Salvages present'd themselves to oure Viewe as if they had emerg'd from Some Eden, bringing with themme Giftes of Featheres, Quiveres, Shelles, & the Privie Partes of Beastes, which they worre as Adornement for their Personnes. They were without Clotheing otherwise, but shew'd no Shame at ites Lacke. The Childeren are verie Innocente of Harme, and the Woemen verie Comely & Virtueous and resist'd the Debaucheries of oure Sailores . . .

The Grande Unfoulding of God's Designe for us in this Promis'd Place shalle be like a Floure waxing from the Budde until it openeth to reveel ites fulle Glorie. Go forthe, mine owne Seede, and plante ye in this Neue Sion the buddes of a Neue Jerusalem. Thou shalt calle this Chosen Place by Neue Salem & shalt Namme everiething in thy kenne as Adam namm'd the Beastes of Creation. All shalle be welle in this Neue Founde Eden where the Gouvernours shall Adore the Gouvern'd, the Masters theire Slaves, the Riche the Poore, the Fedde the Hungrie.

The Great American Unfolding. The promis'd place, a new Eden. Primeval. Memory pines and hymnlooks. Old Isaiah would be lost in New Salem today. Isaiah Van Pennywinkle, Esq. He would wake up to whats and whiches. Witches sneaked into Neue Jerusalem. And then they all came. The blacks and the Polacks. The Irerish and the Eyetalons. Yids with their kids. Now the Poor Reekans are coming. That was the prime evil, Mister Henry Willsworth Lordfellow. All aboard to New Salem! No stopping them. Prepare for the tourney! Outlaw! In mine own land.

The Unfoulding of a Neue Jerusalem in the Willdernesse deserveth to be Commemorat'd to future Posteritie & so I commission mine owne Seede to sette downe in this holie Blacke Book the common Experience so that God may have his due Praise & the Nammes of His Servantes be knowne as Stewardes of His Neue Sion.

The burden placed upon the Pennymans. Poor Pennymans. Old Isaiah wrote in the Blah-Blah-Black Book in 1663. The year before he died. Then his owne seede Zechariah. But waited until he was near ninety. A patriarch also. Pushed his luck. Then Obadiah, grandson of Isaiah. He didn't take any chances. Wrote in Black Book when only twenty-five. Good he did. Killed by Indians in 1742. We burned the Indian villages. Eye for eye. Killed the verie Innocente Childeren. End of Indians around New Salem. That was the original sin. Hosea was next Stewarde of Neue Sion. Fought with Israel Potter in Revolution. Then Jonathan, grandson of Obadiah. Switched to Episcopal Church. Pennyman children no longer named after the prophets. Because of an argument with Congregationalists about a stove. Stubborn Yankee. Episcopalians were being persecuted then. Family fortunes fell. Lands sold off. Great-grandfather Gideon opened law office in 1828. They didn't need lawyers at first. Jehovah was their lawgiver. The Bible their statute-book. Next came Grandfather Samuel the Just. Then a blank. My father gone. Where is Sam's son? Eyeless in Gazer. Then my brother. Another blank. He ran also. A man without a country. Thus spake Mother. I'm the last Yankee Doodler. No more begots. Close out the book? Burn the Blah-Blah-Black Book?

One. Two. Two bells. Good bongs still left in the Episcopalian bell. Old Annie Bell belongs in an institution. Well, it was many and many a year ago. Tolls the knell of Old Irish Annie Bell. Bong. Bong. Pity. Pity. Poor Pennyman. Lost somewhere between sunup and sunset. Two golden hours. Each set with sixty diamond minutes. No reward offered. Because lost forever. Lost a life. A misplaced life.

The Polack is late again. What does he want? First Select-man-to-be, Polack-hath-been. Should I wait? Why bother? First Selectman Gladinski. A very select man, our Poleass. He'll get the minority voters. Select-select-select-SELECT. Damn! Listen to that! Windows closed. Still the hammering comes in. Stifling in here. Damn! It goes on all day. Freudenthal building on the common. Restoring the old Bellamy place. Ruination of the restoration. Freudenthal in Bellamy. Gladinski in Town Hall. Joy in Mudville. All's wrong with the world. In the beginning, that was the end. Forgive us, Izzy Pennymensch, Esq. We never should have let them into your Countrie. God was your tenth man. And he struck out for the home team.

■

IN THE BIG INNING. Yessir, folks, we're beginning. This is big-league bushball at its behest, the beth baal. Ha-ha-ha-HA. Come on ott & root, rue it, ruth for the hohum team. And don't forget that now is the time to crock up with your favorite beer. It's good for what ails you, & if nothing ales you, it's gut for that too. It's a premium peer. Costs fifty pennies the class. That's two pennies for the grain and forty seven for us knowing how. The leftover penny? He's the Pennyman. A taste temptation. I tell you true. We provide the taste and you do the rest. So be ready for the big inning with your payforit beer. Peewee-nuts, popcorn, crackerjackies!

Kill the umpire! What a day, what a do! A doubledeader day, a doubleday. Weather sunny on ole terra firm. The sun is sheening bright on this flivvered land. Hot & humid. Hey, look at them toss that apple around! Lots of pepper out there. Now for some color on the players we hand the mike over to our sidekick, Barefoot Hyde, a gentleman of choler. Ah sees we iz most raddy to begin commencin'. Dere he iz now cummin' out, dat Polish pitchur. Yo' look right close. He iz a seelect man. He iz de king kong killer. He iz de hunk greenburr. He iz de man til now. Ef yo' tink dat evers de chance come your way to museyalong to de ballpeck, yo' better come. Else Mumbo-Jumbo will hoo-doo you. Boomlay. Ah sware dat pitchur iz eight feat tale, least a spahn wide, a body dat iz puffectly slant-indicular, en arms dat reach to de ski. Ah neber seen a Poolish feller so rampagious as he. He strides toward de mount like an intergoddampendant person. Yessuh, it's shure gonna be a jubalee today! Omen, Omen.

Like we were saying, folks, roturning to the mound today for the New Salemites we have the Yankee Doodled League's leading latecomer and bitcher. He awe to be here any moment. Every aye is watching for hum. Your favorite fellow and mine, the parttime Poleite. A lefty, he throws em fast, throws em slow, dips and doe with a hay and a hoe. He's well known for his doster which has beaten many a batter. But he claims he's nod going to pitch that one today. Instead he'll relie on his armsnal of knicklers, slighters, and screwballs. He's supposed to be a spitboiler, but he swears he never true one in his life. He may, though, be a reasonable fakesimile. Dizzhe or didn't he? Dickey or doesn't he? Mickey or might he? Christy or can't he? Sandy or sinned he? Wee, will he or won't he? We tell you tris, when the Pole spits he rings the spittune. He's for he, himself & Companie. Years of experience behind him, he gives stellar promise of big, big years ahead. He tells everyone that New Salem is the greatest little town in Connecticut and he's happy for the opportunity to be a part of it. All of us say that the feeling is musial. Aymen, Aymen. He's our very own candidote for the Hill of Fume.

Allrightski, here we go! Pay Paul! Qu'il the umpoor! Let there be! The first battler is coming up to the plight now. But before he lightly doffs his cap in response to the jeers, here's a signlit on our pitcher, folks. They say he's a very honorable man, but they all, all got an honorable mine. Yessir, we're all counting on the perfect Pool today. He's the won gonna win the lorels for the home team. Be it ever so hubbell, there's no place like hum. Play poor! Fill the himpire! Yessir, our Pole can tie up the batter into more nots than a preacher knows the name of. He makes him blight the dust. The stomp of his personality is indelibly pressed on the whirl of buzzball. A battler standing against him couldn't hit a strait lick with a crossed stick. If he don't wynn, it's a sham. He's a veritable immutal. Amen, Amen.

So come on out to the game, cause this is woeman's day. The bellepark is still unfilled and it's a grandificent day. And a special sirprise for the ladies. I'm not ribbing you. Oops, we done forgets to tell yo' what hopenning. Now lemmesee. Ah iz gettin' a li'l obflusticated. Dat wuz stroke five. Ah done counted damn. Dere wuz one en tree en more. Dey is multiplicatin'. Dey hacks at de ball like it wuz a rattlesneak. De pitchur done Polished de batter off. He's morticaied! Databoy, pitchur, yo' tell 'im! Hit 'im on de head! Yo' can't hurt 'im none dere. Hit 'em where dey ain't. Hski-hski-hski-HSKI. Hit 'im agin. Boomlay! Now we gots Merde's Rue comin' up. Hit's a merkle he trows dat ball so fast. Hit's a-maysin'. Yo' tell 'im, pitchur! Yo' tell 'im, cause mah tongue's in mah shoe. Yo' tell 'im, toothache, yo' got de nerve. Yo' tell 'im, snow, cause ah ain't got de drift. Yo' tell 'im, postman, cause you're de man er letters. Yo' tell 'im, tree, cause yo' got leave. Yo' tell 'im, fireman, cause yo' know hose side you're on. Yo' tell 'im, window washer, cause ah got a pane. Yo' tell 'im, policeman sir, cause yo' can do hit in de pinch. Yassuh, yo' tell 'em all! Boomlay! Heah come de singer to lead de meetin' in our natcheral anthem.

> Dis whirrl wuz made in jest six daze,
> En finished up in varyous ways,
> Den dey made Salem trim en nice,
> En Adam culled it Paradise.

Dat shure tells what iz in de hurts uv all us. Oops, wait de minute now. Dere iz gonna be sumpin spoken ober de lipspicker.

"Le tris now batting for la joy. Stock market crashes. All runners fall down. Groundkeepers Thorn and Thistle, pick up the pieces. Keeper Kane, are you abel to find your brother? Is Old

Chief Wundawucker in the grandstand? Umpire, please dust off the plate. At the conclusion of our game we will play our national anthem, 'Old Folks at Home.' Play ball!"

Folks, you heard it straight from the liespeaker. You can beleave that. We don't know why it told the ruiners to advance one base, but while we're speaking to you we're thumping as fast as we can through the paiges of our rule book. This game sure is one for the book! Just a minute! Here is an utter word from the lordspeaker.

"Kindly emendate your scorecards. Stock markit rises. All ruiners must retrite one price. Oomphire, please desist the playette. Old Chief Wundawucker has been scene in the gruntstand. We will now play our national anthem, 'Blest Be the Whys That Blind.' That is fall for now."

Can you beat that! You heard it as well as we did, with your own two hears. Erin is believin. We don't know who that is announcing, but you can be certain we'll try to find out his name for you. Wait! Hear this! "All runners are rout." Did you fear that? All ruiners are right. That is distinctly what we heard him say. What is the mutter with him? What an inning this has been, folks! Yessir, it sure has been the Big Inning. That's the word. Allmen, Allmen.

Now just a quick recap on the action so far. We're seeing a pitcher who's riding the crest of a fablous winning streak and who's cheered the hurts of every New Salemite. Whoop! He does it again! He touched the far side of the blight and successfully aspired the tip of the order. Hellstone! How ard the mighty fallin! Yessir, we're seeing some pretty positive pitching by our Pole. Just you watch him step down off the firmamound. He's a feller who doesn't waste time out there. He really makes the game move along. No nodding in this grandsland.

The Pole has endowed us with a legacy of devotion to our national spurt that will not soon be forgotten. The cheery fans who come here today know that he has already richly bestowed on the town he loves a record of accomplishment that will shine as long as the waters of the Housatonic bubble on to the sea. He was still a bright-eyed, rosy-cheeked, freckle-faced immigrant from east of where the Oder rises when it was clear that he was going to join all the stars in the firmament of our nurturnal pastime. His sturdy pitching arm carved its own chronicle in the books. His feets have made secure his standing in leg-end. May the years fail to doom our memory of him. The pomp of hymaldry. The toast of pyre. The baths of gory lead.

Wait! They're positing the score now and we'll give it to you in joust a minuet. Aye-aye-aye-AYE. Yes, here's the sore.

NEW JERUSALEM	0
THEM	5724

The Mudville nine is in there battling to stay alive! There's a roisting tumult! A banned is playing somewhere! That's all, folks. They're going to pull the Pole. He's gone sauer. They're ribbing him for eveing the score. Aid 'im! What insinuendos against him! Throw hymn out! He stinks like dead frisch! They knocked the Pox out of the box. Moses out of the poses. Simon out of Sion. That's all for him. Let him be! Into the showers with him. Naked he came and nicked he goes. Dust thou ist. They got his number in that big scorebored in the ski. Nothing like this has been seen since America in the days of gore. There he goes, walking out past the blitchers, past the booed row. Head bowed. The big bull of dustiny. Send your dolors to him at Levity, Conn. All commisserations greatfully reseized.

Suddenly there's a darkling sky! You can hardly see the sinlight. It has gotten as cold as the north side of a gravestone in Dissembler by starlight. Tongue and teeth are as tight as a frozen oyster. It's like a reshiverator in this pressed box. Old Soul has left us! There's a strong wind blowing off Mount Noname! Lightning flushed three times in the east! The waters of the Housatonic are freezing over! They say a whale swam up the Naugatuck! We hear the Quinnipiac is rising o'er the people in rowboats! Tell us it ain't so, Noe! Omen, Omen.

We'll have a new pitcher to get the Pole out of the hole. Can he thame the tide? Whose he gonna be? That's the question all the fans in the palldark are asking. There's a Mystery Man our pilot has warming up out yonder in the bullpen. Wait a sec while we don our spec. Yes. No. Perhaps. We think we can seize him now. It's Mastery Man! There he is, combing out the flowing locks of his white beard. He shear needs a haircut. The honus is on him now, folks. Listen to the lietongue.

"Mustery Man now pitching for the Palled Ox. Stock mockit swindle reviled. Groundsmen Whistle and Worn, please go to the flowers. Keeper Kine, where is your brooder? Umpure, please dost the plaåt. Old Chief Wundawucker, come out wherever you are. We will now play the New Salemite anthem, 'Long, Long Ago.'"

Folks, we're trying to see if that's Big One. Let me look. It peers to me. That's he! That's thee! The splitting image! Yessir, that new pitcher is a branch off the old tree. He's a righty. Dio-dio-dio-DUM. Listen to those fans chant! The Big Won has decleared that he is now going to throw one for old Gip. We know that wearever he has gone the oiled Gyp is watching us now. Big One has taken up the mantle. May he wear it with dextinction.

Here we go again, folks. Play fall! Fill the brimfire! There's Big One getting ready. Let's see if he can emulate those heroes of your in today's cliffhanger. Let us watch him stride toward immutality in the whirl of sportsdone. No sir, he's nothing like that poor Pole! This one is all Hamerican and a mile high, with a heart as pure as the snows of Mount Washington and a drawl as long as the Connecticut River. He's a regular attentive at the Episcopalian church and his twelve little boys are in the preacher's Bubble Class. He's a man you can trust. His whole life is devoted to idylotry.

Our ace nitwork broadkisser Connie McGillicuddly has just gone onto the field with his remote mick to get Big One to say something to all you fans confided at home in your sexbeds. Here now the words of Big One!

"Yessiree! I can out-fight, out-jump, out-run, out-yell, out-drink, and out-wench anyone. I'm the scion of distinguished pedigrees in both branches of my blued line, cause I'm a well-connecticked Yankee. Yessiree, on my momma's side I count as kin cancer and influenza, and on my good old dud's I'm related to strokes and epilepsy. I only got to glance at the Litchfield Mountains and they quake. I got a meat-axe disposition, and don't no one forget it! When I'm relaxin I push abut two hunred pounds, but when I'm mad I weigh a ton. That's cause I'm a runaway locomotive, a howling jet engine, an exploding rocket shell. When I'm hungry I gather the nuts from an acre of spreading chestnut-trees and when I'm thirsty I lap up the Connecticut River and when I'm sweaty I fan myself with a hurrycane out of the Hotlantic Ocean. For exercise I race up Niagara slick as a wildcat up an oak, and when I'm feeling poorly with hemorrhoids I massacre a score of injun villages to put spirit back into me. With each swing I make a gape in the crowd that lets in an acre of sunshine. The whole state of Connecticut is my private graveyard for them what doubted these facts. Yessiree, I'm a regular corpsemaker! If you think I'm tough, I got a daughter that wears a hornet's nest trimmed with wolf tails for a bonnet and my boys use lightning to spark their dollar cigars. Tornadoes and hailstorms follow them around like pet animals, so when you catch their scent, you better run. They're reeking with meanness, and just naturally they can't help it, cause they're all mine. Yessiree, I'm the giant in these days! I wear iron for shoes and hitch my britches with a living rattlesnake. I can pitch a ball faster than fire, harder than hail, straighter than a pine tree grows—and some folks declare the spiral staircase was fashioned after my curve ball. The foxx learned me how to run and the lynxx how to slide. I can swim like an otter, fight like a bobcat, and bellow like a bull moose. There's a sprinkle of all creation in me. I'm the scion of a whole zoological society. Yessiree, I'm Bigun, and don't you forget it! (Braggin is cheaper than advertisin.)"

Well, folks, you heard him, we say you nay. Scion will be redeemed! Cockalorum, cockledo. Now for a few vitale straight-

istics on Big Won. Religion: Amenostic. Philosophy: Too soon
oldt undt too late schmart. Language: Homerican with a Big
A, A, A. Favorite tree: Bearer of bidden bruit. Favorite personality: Houdini. Favorite trick: Making loafers into fishers. Favorite book: Wrathchild's bankbook. Favorite poem: Murmuring puns and homelyks. Favorite hobby: Collecting foist
editions. Favorite season: Winter of discontent. Favorite state:
Chaos. Favorite time in history: Any time before the present
eerie. Most recent address or domusile: 5724 Numbers Strict,
Kings Country, Isaiahoway.

Folks, we can't revile his name to you, but we do want to say
that Big Chief is a full-bloodied salvage, untouched by the
syphilizing influence of western civilization, one of the ten trip-
ulations miraculously transported to the Pains of Abraham
where the New Salemite scouts spotted him, signed the May-
follow Comepicked covenant with him, & brought him here for
your commandation. Fierce in bottle, forgiving in victory, he
stands for all the red nobility that made America zing. The
notable salvage.

Folks, hit's aweready de sabbenth inning en de score iz all
tidied up. De Big Chief iz better dan de Polecat. He iz de king.
Der King uv Sweat. He has successivefully retried moss uv de
mans he has phased. Dey jest kin't ketch holt er 'im. De mag-
giority er de batters kin't stan up to de man. Hail de King!
Oops, heah come de big news agin.

"Big Noise speaking. Game called on account of rain.
Groundkeepers Pourin and Pisstle, watch out for floods. Keeper
Kahn, vhere ist ein brutter? Water rising on Wail Strait. Old
Chief Wundawucker, you are excommunicated from the tribe
with pill, puke, and kindle. Play brawl!"

Folks, we hear there is pandemoney on Wild Script. The
stock market is falling! And in our stedium every fan is trying
to escape the rinsing waters of retribulation. We are now trying to get you the word. You must beleave us! You must have
fate in the Lored! We will try to get onto the playing filled,
but the noisy crowweds are blocking our way. Let me through,

kind sir. Grand pardons, grandpa. Out of my way, mack. Excuse me, you cheery bums. Madam, I'm not backward about being forward! MADAM, I'M ADAM! So solly. Scusi. Squeezi. I lament that. Ho. Say! Er. Thank you.

Folks, that took a bit of doing, but here we are with our hayro of the day, Big Wind from Mount Noname. We are having just a wee bit of difficultry locating his mouth obscured by his bushy beard. I think I hear a noice. What's the mutter? Where is his myth? I think I may have found his mouth now, folks. You me scuse bigfellow Chief Big One. Im bigfellow just want-want movum hairs outum mouth so get-get face. Belong what name you pitch-pitch im dis bigfellow? (We always try to convoice in native tongues, folks, but I'm innocent of feeding the pidgins.) Sorry it's taking so long, folks, but we think we've found an eye or a tooth. Wait! Hay, what's this? His beard is coming off in handfills! I've got a fistful of Big One's beard! And the rain is washing the rest of it away. It's loose fur! Well, I'll be a Conned Yankee! Ah'm flamigasticulated. He ain't de Big Man at tall! He's fake-believe! Folks, we're sorry to tell you it's the same told story. The psalm ole psong. There's lyin' in Zion.

◾

PAPYR YELLOWED. Gelded blinding rubbed. Nothing left but the awefull pages. Of the Black Book. Pro patria and progeniturs. Unholt me, ye begots! Let me live life alive! Pity-pity-pity-PITY. Free me! Suffocating in past participles. And genealesis. Salve me! Knuck-knuck-knuck-KNUCK. Fatale hammering on the door. In, Miss Maggiore. Come.

— I know you asked me not to disturb you, Mister Pennyman. But the First Selectman's secretary phoned.

— Mister Gladinski? He hasn't been elected First Selectman yet.

— But he's running unopposed, Mister Pennyman.

— It still isn't the same.

— Anyway, Mister Gladinski can't keep his appointment. He's terribly sorry he can't come over now. But he couldn't break away from one of the vice presidents down from Hartford.

— I hope he doesn't run his insurance business the way he keeps appointments.

— Well.

— That's twice he broke appointments in the same day. And he's the one who wants to see *me*. I'd say that's rude.

— Well. He did say he'd like a raincheck for later in the day, about four thirty.

— Thank you, Miss Maggiore.

— Your letter to the French Tourist Office is ready for signing.

— Just let me glance at it a moment. Oh, oh. You misspelled "Belle." That should have the feminine ending. La Belle France Budget Tour.

— Oh. I'm sorry.

— Well. You have to retype it anyway. So let me add something I thought of. Put in another sentence right after where I ask if there is much rain in April. "Also, kindly send a list of approved antique shops where I might purchase one of the gold-painted souvenir models of the Eiffel Tower, with the little hole in it revealing a view of Paris, which were so popular earlier in this century." That goes right before "I would appreciate hearing from you at an early opportunity. Sincerely yours." No, better make that "Very sincerely yours." They're touchy about politeness. I think that should do it. I'm sorry you have to type it again.

— That's all right. I had to anyway. Because of my misspelling. Is there anything else I can do?

— No, I guess not, Miss Maggiore. When you took this job I told you things wouldn't be very lively. Most of the old clients are dead or have moved to Phoenix.

— Yes, Mister Pennyman, you did. But that's all right.

— I guess you can start cataloging those inactive files. We'll have to arrange storage for them this winter.

— Yes, I will, Mister Pennyman. I wonder.

— You wonder?

— Well, I was just wondering why Mister Gladinski used the expression "raincheck." I'm not sure I understand what it means.

— Baseball. It's from baseball. If it rains, then you can come back and see a game some other time. They give you a check so you can get into the park again without paying.

— Oh. But what if it rains the next time also?

— I suppose you would just have to bring your rainbrella.

— Pardon?

— Just a poor pun. From Benjamin Punman.

— Of course it doesn't rain every game.

— No, Miss Maggiore. Not anymore. My Grandfather Samuel the Just claimed it used to rain a lot more in the old days. But that was long ago. Our climate seems to be changing.

— I meant to ask, Mister Pennyman. Is that his portrait?

— Yes. He was as much a man of integrity as this town has ever known. He had a sense of history. "Memory Survives" it says on his headstone. But the epitaph failed to discourage Mother Nature. The rain has nearly washed away the letters. My Mother got cheated on the quality of the stone.

— I'll do this letter now, Mister Pennyman.

— Pardon? Oh, yes, the letter. Thank you.

Withdraws. Wets her draws. Probably had to take a piss. All the time I was dictating. Waters of babble on. Sighin for Zion. Probably what made her say raincheck. Pit-pit-pit-PATTER. Let it rain, let it pour, Pennymans ain't no more. Pity. She's not too smart. Nice girl, though. Polite. Considerate. I wonder. Why doesn't it rain as much? Maybe atomic-bomb tests changed the climate? Wish it would rain. Maybe stop that damn hammering at the old Bellamy place. But Freudenthal would keep the men working anyway. He wouldn't give them time off in a hurricane. He starts to say doughnut. And it comes out pretzel. Complicated man. Mister Facing-Both-Ways. Freudenthal's bank. And Gladinski's insurance. And Rappaccini's hardware. All the new people. Rain, rain, come again. Wash them all away. Start over again. Rebuild Neue Jerusalem. In our own image. Put up fences to keep them out. We never should have killed off the Indians. Torts. Ancient wrongs. Murmuring pains and hardlucks. Their country first. New people swamping us now. First a trickle of them. Little Black Sambos. Italian stonecutter. Irish bricklayer. Jew peddler with pack. Polack grocery store. Soon a flood. More and more. Faster and faster. Rapids, falls. Lakes of ski-blue waters. Gootchy gloomy. High water, Hiawatha! Roll on, roll on! Sweep all away!

I, Zechariah Penniemanne, son of Isaiah, this Dayye take Delight that God hath sente to Helle one hundrede Heathen Soules which have menac'd Neue Salem. God hath withdrawne His holie hande from the Salvage villages & hath allow'd themme to be Extirpat'd from the Promis'd Eden which was prepar'd for us. The redd Salvages are more Abominations in His Eyes thanne the Venomous Serpentes in oures. These heathen People shalle suffer the Floode of the Lord's Vengeance.

The settlers. They first fell on their knees. Then they fell on the Indians. The Great American Dream. Eden lost before it was found. They killed for God and country. New birth of freedom. Shots heard round the world. Embattled farmers stood. But my brother ran away. A man without a country. Thus spake Mother. He tore the tattered ensign down. Shem, shem on him. Let it rain, let it pour. Ain't gonna cry noah more. Indians understood rain. Noah more Indians. Noah did view, The Old World and New. We need a flood again.

■

LONG AGO when Earth was new, Sun was nearer to us than he is now. That was when the animals and men talked to each other. There was no winter, there was no summer. Nor was there autumn, nor was there spring. It was never cold, it was never hot. The people did not wear clothing. The animals wore no fur or feathers.

New people came from the directions of Four Winds to build their lodges near Old Man. Old Man did not stop the new people from coming into the land of his fathers. He was happy to welcome them because he had no one else. His father had gone away, possibly to become a great chief in some other land, and his cowardly brother had shown the white feather in battle. His mother he had laid to rest on the hill. But the new people were not grateful for the welcome they received from Old Man. That is why it soon grew cold. The animals put on heavy fur because they knew a hard winter was coming, but the new people killed them to steal their pelts. Old Man was saddened.

He stopped talking to the new people. He talked to himself. He went every day to a quiet pool of the river where he watched his lips move. He spoke also to his penis, his little brother, taking hold of it in his hands so that it seemed a live thing that listened to him. It was such a large member that he had to keep it wound up under his breechcloth. Sometimes he talked also to the animals of the forest, posing them puzzles and asking them riddles which they could not answer. Of all the animals, She-Wolf listened to him the most.

She-Wolf decided that she wanted Old Man for her husband. Each night she pattered outside Old Man's lodge and sang to him the songs of our people.

> *A loon*
> *I thought*
> *It was*
> *Caressing*
> *The waves.*
> *But*
> *It was*
> *My love*
> *Making water.*

Old Man, though, had no need for a woman. He gratified his little brother with deer's liver which he shaped into a vulva, hollow gourds, mud holes, the flowers of lilies of the field, the furry ears of Moose, and other cunning devices. So She-Wolf decided to travel far to Great Spirit to ask his help. She ran for many days through the forest, and she swam across many rivers.

Finally she found Great Spirit in the Land of Northern Lights. She told him about Old Man who did not want to have intercourse with her. Great Spirit promised She-Wolf he would help her. Then he thought and he thought until finally he developed a plan which he was very proud of. He said he would drown Earth and kill all living things so only She-Wolf and Old Man would be left. Then, he said, Mother Nature would take her course. All the animal spirits listened politely to the plan Great Spirit promised She-Wolf, but they did not like it. The animal spirits did not like the plan because all their innocent relatives would be drowned just so Old Man would have intercourse with She-Wolf. Great Spirit admitted that was a big price to pay. But he said he had made his promise to She-Wolf and he could not change it. That's the way Great Spirit was.

So Great Spirit made it rain all over Earth. It rained in the forests and on the mountains and even in the rivers which everyone thought already full. She-Wolf stood outside Old Man's lodge and sang to him every night about the danger from the rising waters.

> *I hear*
> *The clouds coming*
> *The winds wailing*
> *The ground grumbling*
> *The sky shaking*
> *The river running.*
> *Aaaay!*

She-Wolf did not sing to the new people or to the animals about the danger because she wanted all of them to drown so that Old Man would have intercourse with her.

At last Old Man came out of his lodge and saw that it was

too late to build a canoe. But She-Wolf showed him how to flee the rising waters by running up High-Mountain-With-Noname. They were safe there and She-Wolf wanted to have intercourse with Old Man right away. But Old Man was busy making good medicine to cure the tightness in his bowels, and so he did not unwind his little brother out of his breechcloth. Instead he held it gently and spoke to it. "My little brother, you must wait to have intercourse, for I am distressed in the bowels." Thus spake Old Man.

Soon the waters rose even to the top of High-Mountain-With-Noname. So Old Man and She-Wolf climbed onto the broad back of Turtle. There She-Wolf sang to Old Man.

> I am ashamed when I lie down.
> I am ashamed when I wake up.
> I am ashamed before Sun.
> I am ashamed before Moon.
> I am ashamed before Stars.
> Because you do not have intercourse with me.

At last Old Man thought it might not be a bad idea, and so he said, "My little brother, the time has now come for you to have intercourse." Thus spake Old Man. But just as he was about to unwind his little brother he saw some animals of the forest who were trying to stay afloat in the water.

Old Man invited the animals onto Turtle's broad back. She-Wolf was very disappointed to have missed intercourse, so she complained that Turtle would sink from all that weight. But Old Man rescued the animals anyway. In that way Old Man saved Eagle, Beaver, Porcupine, Turkey, Deer, Bear, Skunk, Rabbit, and the many other animals that we know in the forest today. By and by they heard crying in the water and Old Man pulled Loon to safety on Turtle's broad back. But Loon was so scared that he could not stop crying. And that is why Loon cries to this day.

Old Man heard Moose bellowing from the top of High-Mountain-With-Noname. He told She-Wolf to swim there and save

Moose. She complained that Turtle already had too many passengers, but finally she dove off Turtle's broad back and swam toward the forest at the top of High-Mountain-With-Noname. After a while Old Man could no longer hear Moose bellowing. By and by She-Wolf swam back to Turtle. She said she had looked everywhere for Moose but she could not find him. Old Man was saddened at the loss of Moose, but he was very grateful to She-Wolf for trying to save him. So Old Man decided that after the other animals had gone to sleep his little brother would have intercourse. But She-Wolf told him that she had fallen off the roof. That did not worry Old Man. He said he would make good medicine to take the curse off her. All night he sang and sprinkled tobacco, but by the time morning came and the animals awakened, the medicine still had not done its work. "Be patient, my little brother, and soon you will have intercourse." Thus spake Old Man.

Then the animals felt hunger in their stomachs. Beaver and Porcupine said they should look for floating logs for food, but Turtle, Turkey, Deer, Eagle, Bear, Skunk, Rabbit, Loon, and She-Wolf all said they did not like to eat wood. So Deer and Rabbit said they should look for leaves for food, but Beaver, Porcupine, Turtle, Turkey, Eagle, Bear, Skunk, Loon, and She-Wolf all said they did not like to eat leaves. So Loon, Bear, Turtle, and Eagle said they should look for some fish, but Deer, Rabbit, Beaver, Porcupine, Turkey, Skunk, and She-Wolf said they did not like to eat fish. So Skunk, Turkey, Bear, and Turtle said they should look for some insects, but Loon, Eagle, Deer, Rabbit, Beaver, Porcupine, and She-Wolf all said they did not like to eat insects. So She-Wolf, Eagle, and Bear said they should look for meat, but Skunk, Turkey, Turtle, Loon, Deer, Rabbit, Beaver, and Porcupine all said they did not like to eat meat. The animals could not agree what to eat, and that is why today they eat different food and that is why people prefer to live with their own kind.

Then one morning the rains stopped. The sky held up a big rainbow as in the old days when Sun was closer to Earth, when the animals spoke to men, and when there were no new people. Old Man told Loon to fly off in search of land. Loon flew to the north and to the south, but he could find no land. Loon flew to the west and to the east, but nowhere could he find land.

Old Man then told Eagle to fly off and search for land. Eagle flew to the north and the south and the west, but he saw no land. Eagle rested and then he flew to the east. He was gone a long time. Finally Eagle appeared in the distance and sharp-eyed She-Wolf said that he carried something in his talons. Old Man looked deep into the waters and prophesied, "Eagle carries a twig he plucked from some spreading chestnut-tree." Thus spake Old Man. Then they all saw that Eagle was not carrying a twig but the skull of one of the new people. Old Man never had much luck as a seer.

Turtle had grown very tired from paddling, but his energy was renewed when he saw High-Mountain-With-Noname rising out of the water. As soon as Turtle's broad back touched the mountain, Old Man set off into the forest to explore. Old Man looked to the left and to the right. He looked in front of him and behind him. Everywhere that he looked he saw the carcasses of the new people who, his medicine told him, had been punished by Great Spirit for some sin or other, or perhaps to teach them humility. But as he looked closer he saw that each of the new people bore the marks of Bear's claws. Old Man felt a pain of sadness deep in his heart, for it was clear that the new people had not been taught a lesson by Great Spirit. They had been killed by Bear's sharp claws just for their meat.

Old Man returned very angry to Turtle's broad back and he wanted to kill Bear. But Bear escaped by climbing into a tree. To this day Bear climbs because he is afraid that Old Man will try to catch him.

Once again Old Man set off into the forest. He looked to the left of him and to the right of him, in front of him and behind him. He walked farther than he had the first time. Then he saw that Beaver had built a palisade of logs around Gray Lake to keep it for himself. Old Man felt a pain of sadness deep in his heart.

Old Man returned very angry to Turtle's broad back and he wanted to kill Beaver. But Beaver escaped by slapping the water very hard with his tail and sending up a great splash that hid him. And that is why to this day Beaver slaps the water with his tail when anyone comes near.

Once again Old Man set off into the forest. He looked to the left of him and to the right of him, in front of him and behind him. He walked even farther than he had the second time. Then he saw that the tops of all the plants had been eaten by Deer. Nothing as beautiful as grew in the old days could ever grow again. Old Man felt a pain of sadness deep in his heart.

Old Man returned very angry to Turtle's broad back and he wanted to kill Deer. But Deer stood absolutely still and his coat looked so much like the leaves of the forest that Old Man could not see him. To this day Deer stands still in the forest because he is afraid that Old Man will try to catch him.

Once again Old Man set off into the forest. He looked to the left of him and to the right of him, in front of him and behind him. Everywhere he saw all the evil things that Porcupine, Turtle, Turkey, Eagle, Skunk, Rabbit, Loon, and the other animals had done. Old Man felt many pains of sadness deep in his heart.

Old Man returned very angry to Turtle's broad back, but all the animals ran away. Porcupine shook himself and sent a rain of arrows at Old Man. That is why to this day Porcupine shakes himself. Skunk and Rabbit dove into dark holes to escape Old Man. That is why to this day Skunk and Rabbit live in dark holes in the earth. Turkey ran off to hide in the darkest part of the forest, and that is why to this day Turkey lives in the darkest part of the forest. Eagle flew high into the sky to escape Old Man, and that is why we always see Eagle flying high. Turtle dove to the bottom of Gray Lake where he lives to this day. Old Man nearly caught Loon around the neck, but Loon pulled away. To this day Loon wears a ring of feathers around his neck to show the place where Old Man grabbed him.

So Old Man was left alone with She-Wolf, which is the way the wise Great Spirit had planned it. They built a lodge along the shore of Gray Lake and Old Man started to tell She-Wolf stories about the old days. She-Wolf wanted to have intercourse right away, but Old Man's organ was sore from having chased after the animals. "Wait, my little brother, and soon you will have intercourse." Thus spake Old Man.

Old Man made many trips into the forest to find good things to eat. But whenever he set off in the direction of High-Mountain-With-Noname, She-Wolf asked him to do something else. One day, when She-Wolf was not watching, Old Man went to the mountain. He climbed and he climbed. He looked to the left of him and to the right of him. He looked in front and he looked behind. Soon he reached the top and there he found the pieces of Moose. Old Man remembered that when he sent She-Wolf to rescue Moose, Moose suddenly stopped bellowing. Old Man remembered that by and by She-Wolf swam back to Turtle. Old Man remembered that She-Wolf claimed she was unable to find Moose. Old Man felt a pain of sadness deep in his heart.

She-Wolf scented the anger in Old Man's heart, and that is why to this day she can smell a man many miles away. She ran into the forest and Old Man was all alone. The new people had been torn apart by Bear and none of his other animal brothers had lived up to expectations. Old Man had no one to tell stories to about the old days. His little brother was angry because he had not had intercourse, and so he lay lifeless in Old Man's hands. Because Old Man did not use the big member given him by Great Spirit, today our people have only a little member. So Old Man sat by himself by the shore of Gray Lake and he was very lonely.

Then a plan came to Old Man. He dove into the lake until he reached the bottom. He brought up as much mud as he could carry in his arms. Again and again he dove to the bottom of the lake for mud. Old Man then fashioned the mud into Great Earth. He made The Great River of the Connecticut and The Great Mountains of Litchfield. He made the mountains and the prairies and the oceans white with foam.

When Old Man had finished making everything from sea to shining sea, he shot arrows into Earth and they grew into trees. He blew at Earth and made Four Winds. He made his water on Earth and all the rivers flowed again. He shat on it and made the soil out of which everything grows. Then he cast his seed onto Earth, and from it came corn, beans, squash, potatoes, and the other good things we eat today. Then he made a time for sowing and a time for harvesting, summer and winter, heat and cold, day and night. In this way Earth on which we now live was remade.

Old Man looked about him at all the things he had created and he gave them names. Most of these names have been forgotten, but others have been preserved for our children by The Great White Father who established parks for that purpose on our lands. Some of the places Old Man named for us are Devil's Punch Bowl, Widow's Veil Falls, Window Rock, Garden of the Gods, Painted Canyon, Wall of Windows, Fairy Temple, Cathedral Rock, Queen Garden, Seal Castle, Island in the Sky, Newspaper Rock, Needles, Angel Arch, Dead Horse Point, Phantom Ship, Gumbo Limbo, Painted Pots, Vulcan's Throne, King Arthur's Castle, Great Thumb, Dragon Head, Cock's Comb, Hanging Lake, Bumpass Hell, Devil's Kitchen, Frozen Niagara, Giant's Coffin, Echo River, Rainbow Forest, Avenue of the Giants, Monte Cristo Palace, Pearly Gates, Minerva Terrace, Old Faithful, Artist Point, Sleeping Giant, Elephant Back, Cloud's Rest, Great White Throne, Twin Brothers, Angel's Landing, Weeping Rock, Craters of the Moon, Devil's Postpile, Fiery Furnace, Jewel Box, Devil's Garden, and many others.

Then Old Man went to High-Mountain-With-Noname and put together again the pieces of Moose that She-Wolf had torn apart. It was like doing a difficult puzzle, and so there was one piece Old Man could not make fit. Finally he just hung it around Moose's head, and that is why to this day Moose has a dewlap.

Then Old Man went to the bodies of the people mutilated by Bear. He breathed on them and they came back to life. But there were so many of them that Old Man grew weary before he could fix all of their bodies correctly. And that explains why today there are many people who are crippled or hunchbacked, or who lack an arm or a leg, or both arms and both legs, or one arm and one leg, or two arms and one leg, or one arm and two legs, some who suffer from loss of vision or speech or hearing but are otherwise hale and hearty, and some who are paralyzed from the waist down and some who are paralyzed from the waist up, a few who are dwarfed and others who are giants, some who suffer from wasting diseases and others from fattening diseases, those who have game legs or withered arms or cauliflower ears or arthritic hands or spatulated fingers, or those who possess all their faculties except their minds, and those who damage themselves during fits of despair or ecstasies of exaltation.

The animals came to see the Earth that Old Man had made. But they did not bring their Sunday manners with them. Woodpecker drilled oozing holes in the new trees. Porcupine started eating the forest from the top down and Wood Rat started eating it from the bottom up. Moose rubbed his shag against the trees until the bark fell off. Raccoon stole the fruit of the trees, but it already had been ruined by Wasp and her sisters. Bear dug his heavy claws into the wood when he climbed to steal honey. The new forest did not wear well. It was the same old song.

And so Old Man grew white from many winters. He took to drinking rum, the white man's milk. His eyes clouded over and soon he could no longer hear the birds sing. The skin on his arms sagged and he walked with a crooked back. His voice became harsh and he developed a deep cough. He even began to smell a lot.

Now I must tell you how Old Man went to Other World. He

was plagued by tightness in the bowels and so he went into his lodge to make his famous good medicine. But the medicine was bad, and the cure made him break wind with the force of a hurricane. The wind raised him so high into the air that he hit his head against a tree branch with a noise like a thunderclap. Old Man lay between the lands of Life and Death for a long time. He awoke once and sang his famous medicine.

> *The odor*
> *Of death*
> *I smell*
> *In front*
> *Of me.*
> *A warrior*
> *I have been.*
> *Now*
> *It is over.*
> *Life is a swindle.*

Thus spake Old Man. The new people thought he was just complaining again.

But one bright morning the new people noticed by the stench that Old Man had been taken to his fathers several weeks before. They renamed him Old Settler, said they would try to honor his name in the future, and pushed his body into a cave. Then they sprinkled some tobacco around the place so that Old Man would not be an inconvenience to them in death as he had been in life.

That is the story of Old Man, and now, my friends, you understand everything about the world.

■

THUS SPAKE the Old Chief. Memory pines. Tales of the timberlost. The notable salvage. Gone, all gone. Indians plus Rum. Equals Extermination. The Great American Equation. Gone are the living, but the dead remain. As memories. Constant memorizing increases the power of memory. That's what Mother always said. Benjamin has memorized everything. Thus spake Mother. Benjamin can tell us anything. Benjamin is an exemplary child. Benjamin does very well at school. He writes poetry and someday he will grow up to be. Benjamin, par example, tell us. What then is the American, this new man? He is an American, who, leaving behind him all his ancient prejudices and manners, receives new ones for the mode of life he has embraced. C'est très bien, mon enfant. Tell us, Benjamin, tell us. Tell the ladies about the Indians, mon petit. (You may take off your glasses when you speak.) Benjamin, name the tribes of primeval Connecticut for the ladies. Mahican. Pequot. Nipmuc. Some Narragansett. Very good, Benjamin. Benjamin, why did the Indians have so many tribes? Confusion say. Of tongues. Benjamin, we are waiting for an answer immédiatement. Because not everyone spoke the same language, Mother. Then tell us, Benjamin, how many language families existed north of Mexico. Fifty-eight. Alors, Benjamin. Tell the ladies which language family was composed of the largest number of tribes. Athapaskan. How many tribes spoke Athapaskan, Benjamin? Fifty-three. Which language family was composed of the fewest number of tribes? Beothukan. You may pause for one breath, Benjamin. Thank you, Mother. How many tribes spoke Beothukan, Benjamin? One. How many Beothuks survive today, Benjamin? None. C'est dommage. How many Yahi survive today, Benjamin? None. Very good. Now, Benjamin, tell the ladies whether or not the Natchez Indians, baptized so fervently by the French, are still found in Mississippi. They are not. C'est terrible, for your mother, as you know, has always loved the French people. Tell us, are the Alabama Indians still found in Alabama? They are not. Benjamin, are the Miami Indians still found in Ohio? They are not. Are the Peoria Indians still found in Illinois? They are not. Are the Delaware Indians still found in Delaware? They are not. Benjamin, where are all these Indians now? Gone, Mother, gone. And all their innocent little children? Gone, Mother, gone. And their comely & virtuous wives? Gone, Mother, gone. Par malheur, Benjamin. Now tell us, where is your father? Gone, Mother, gone. Thank you very much, Benjamin. (You may put your glasses back on.) That is all, Benjamin, for we have now finished our tea. Good night, ladies, good night, sweet ladies, good night. Byebye ladies. Byebye. Byebye Pennymans. Byebye Beothuk. So long Sacagawea. Shit you Sitting Bull. Wack off Wovoka. Suck off Sequoyah. Gone, all gone. Offpolished. Offcast. Offfinished. Gracedecoup. Goneall.

I never could understand you. She said to Father. I wish I knew what you were getting at, mon mari. What do you mean by that? What a strange remark. Pardon? I never heard of such. Comment! I really can't understand you. The Blah-Blah-Black Book is la malédiction of the Pennymans. Thus spake Mother. Please stop your stuttering this instant. She threatened to burn it. Byebye Black Book. He ran away. Father ran away. The son of Samuel the Just. Sam's son fled. Far-far-father. Brother too. He was a man without a country. When Duty whispers low, Thou must. Youth replies, I can. He couldn't. All gone, like the Beothuk. Byebye Pennymans.

Father might have gone anyplace. Maybe become a king among the savages. In Tahiti. Or black alleys in Chicago. He might still be alive somewhere. No, he would have to be over a hundred. Hundred and one. Might, though. Where did he go? How did he leave? Bumming it? Flagging a freight? Argots of purple sail. Cant. Can't understand. Beachcomber? Bones bleaching on beach. Blowns blitching on blitch. Or maybe. Maybe a chief in Africa. Fat black bucks in wine-barrel rooms. Where? *On shush a Dayye of Winde & Raine, in the fifthe monthe & in the twentie first dayye of the Yeare of oure Lord sixteene hundrede and sixtie foure, we Laide to Reste my father Isaiah Penniemanne. We laide him in the Earthe above Neue Salem where he establish'd a Domaigne for his owne Seede that they mighte Unfoulde God's glorieous Planne in this bountiefulle Newfounde Worlde.* What was the plan? It should have been fulfilled. In me. One more place on the hill. For me. Formerly me.

What will happen to our old house? To be bought by new people? Strangers? A desirable property. Ladies of the hysterical society. History is bunkage. Once a year traipse through. Tee-hee. Pardon me, where is the? You know, the? I have to use the. Tee-hee. They come to pee in the Pennyman pot. Worth a dollar. They tell their friends they peed in the old Pennyman pot. Herstorical society. Missus Abraham Freudenthal, president. A Shebrew. Fifty years ago she had no history. No society either. No Freudenthals in New Salem then. Now Freudenthal in Bellamy. Gladinski in Town Hall. Joy in Mudville. Foreigners swamping us. Swamp-swamp-swamp-SWAMPUM. Benjamin Pennyman, his story. That's history, Missus Freudenthal.

■

BELL. Phone ringing. Where Miss Maggiore gone? Oh, yes. Down the hall. To pee. Let it ring. Let freedom ring. No. Don't bother. Yes. Answer. Hello. Hello! Yes? What? You must have the wrong number! Wait a moment! I can't understand. Confound your babel! Can you please speak more distinctly? What language is that? Pliz spicka mas slowly. You sabee me? Parlez-vous? ¿ Habla? Sprechen Sie? Chinook? Esperanto? Pidgin? Sabir? Swahili? Taki-Taki? Creole? Lingua franca? Basic English? Cant? You can't!

— Kann ich bitte Herrn Old Chief Wundawucker sprechen?

— Tiens! La belle ici.

— Qu'il t'y! Telefonista! Deu-me o número errado!

— Que voulez-vous dire?

— Quero falar com o Belshazzar cinco-sete-dois-quatro.

— Kindly stop bellowing, bel ami, but that is an unlisted number. What bailiwick are you balling for?

— Baile Atha Cliath.

— Verziehung.

— Oh, balls! Il lore numero di telefono è Baal cinque, sette, due, quattro!

— Bells cinquante-sept, vingt-quatre? Le bordel?

— Tout le monde est un bordel. Tu comprends, ma bellotte?

— Tiens! La belle ici! Montez et voyez-moi tôt ou tard.

— Posso parlare con il signor Old Chief Wundawucker?

— ¿ Que? La puta aquí.

— Kann ich bitte Herrn Old Chief Wundawucker sprechen?

— Ah, je comprends! Le mauvais numéro. La putain ici.

— Bizaad aldó' t'áá sahdii ya'?

— Bizaad t'áá sahdii. Al'ąą ádaat'é dóó al'ąą át'éego kéédahat'i.

— Senhor Old Chief?

— Buon giorno. Qu'il t'y?

— J'accuse une belle.

— Alexandre Gréhomme?

— Non, fou!

— Say th't agin an' oi'll belt ya.

— This is Old Irish Annie Bell, your operator. Why do you ring the bell? Un coup de bélier?

— Ba subailceać na rioġna iad sùd!

— Posso parlare con il signor Old Chief Wundawucker?

— Einen Augenblick, bitte. Qu'est-qu'il y a?

— Rien. I belched.

— Der alte Chief Wundawucker? Chuaid se asteać ġo tiġ De.

— Adoni, Laab al Adonai chonem ral.

— Non, la bellotte ici.

— Sie haben mich falsch verbunden.

— Diné bizaad bóhoosh'aah. Aspetti un momento. La linea è occupata.

— Sprechen sie Yiddish?

— Sí. Viví en Nuevo Salem por cinco mil setecientos vienticuatro años.

— Usted habla bien el Yiddish.

— No entiendo, mi belleza.

— Mirabelle? I'm sorry, Belleau Wood sheer-cuts are disconnected.

— Belldamn! La féette, we are dear!
— ¿ Me entiende ahora? Ma belle, ma belle!
— Ich kenne das Wort nicht.
— Belle!
— Ich kenne das Wort nicht.
— Belle! Belle!

■

— Oh. You're back, Miss Maggiore.
— I just went down the hall for a moment, Mister Pennyman. Giggle. Not smart. Nice girl, though.
— I sheer have to be shorn.
— Pardon?
— I mean I'm going to get a haircut, Miss Maggiore. Excuse an old man's humor. It gets less funny with increasing age.
— Oh.
— I ought to be back in an hour or so. I'll probably stop by the bank for a few minutes. Then I have to get something at the drugstore.
— I could get it for you, Mister Pennyman. I'm not busy right now.
— That's very thoughtful of you. No, I'd better get it myself.
— Don't forget that Mister Gladinski is coming. He said about four thirty.
— Well, it's only about three now. Anyway, I was the one who waited this afternoon and he didn't show up. And this morning also. There's not much certainty he'll come at four thirty either.
— But. But it sounded as if it might be something important.
— Not as important as the fact that Jim's Barber Shop gets crowded later in the afternoon. I'd better go now. If I'm a few minutes late Mister Gladinski can wait. Give him a book to read. Broaden his mind for the future challenges of the office of First Selectman.

— Well, I'll find something to keep him here if you're delayed.

— Thank you. Bye now.

Soon as I'm out. She'll rush down the hall. Chatter with other sexytary. So he said. Then she said. But he said. And you know what she said? Well she said. And what did he say? Then he said. But she's a nice girl. Considerate to an old man. Down we go. Yankee Doodle goes to town. Town-town-town-TOWN. Be careful of the steps. Should put in stronger bulb. Three. Four. Five. Six. This one squeaks. Eight. Eight more steps. Thirteen. Fourteen. Fifteen. Excelsior! Got down from the mountain. Now cross the street? No, better go right. Shadier.

Where was Moses when the lights went out?
Down in the bushes with his shirttail out.

Dam-dam-dam-DAMN. Damn banging. It's louder in the street. Freudenthal in Bellamy. Oh, oh. Dog. Mongrel cur of low degree. Like this town. Said one flea to the other. Shall we walk or take a dog? That's a shabby-dog story. He's been barking at me for five years. Still doesn't know me. I pity his owner. Travails with Charley. Will he bite someday? I should carry a walking stick. Outstare him. Make him back down. Stare. Doesn't work. Get away fast. Better take it slower. I'm not young anymore. Which way? Stop by Myer's Drugs first? No, get it on my way back. Go right. Shadier. Lincoln Building. This nation under God. No, a different Lincoln. Always wondered if this Lincoln was guilty as charged. Said he stole town funds. He practiced financial ledger-de-main. Died before trial. Historical society noncommittal. Locusts whine in elms. Saw-saw-saw-SAW. Blight. Dutch elm disease. A parasite on native growth. Disease brought to this country. Like chestnut trees. Blighted, all dying. Spreading chestnot. Gone, gone.

Post office. Shingles warped. Glass cracked. Eyesore. Next Great Depression build another one. They last from depression to depression. Plan it that way? Gives work to unemployed. I'd better check my box. Plastered with posters. "Getting A VA

Check?" "Fair Labor Standards Act." "Benefits." "Now ZIP Speeds." "Federal Government Supports Loans For." "Welfare Program Provides." Bend to box. Should get one higher up. Key? Here. 1242. 1243. 1244. One letter. Looks like an ad. Nothing else. Throw it away. Wastebasket over there. Oh, oh, here hies Hamilton. I'll do it later.

— Hello there, Ham. What are you looking so upset about?

— Upset isn't half the word for it, Ben! See that new notice I just tacked up? It came today from the postmaster I'm responsible to in Hartford. By name, Aaron Rabinowitz. And a new Postmaster General was named today. Gronouski. He replaces J. Edward Day. The names tell the story of what's happening in our country. I'm forced to tack these up. Lose my job if I didn't, even after forty years of service. It's another one of those new Kennedy welfare programs being announced. About the tenth this year. The liberals sure know how to be liberal with other people's money.

— Well.

— Ben, the Kennedy brothers are buying off the coloreds. There's no question about that. Like the way we had the whole city of Washington thrown open to that march. That fellow who led it—what's his name again?

— King?

— Yes. King. The whole country is becoming one big whorehouse, Ben. I tell you, I'm fed up to here. The sooner they learn there's no gravy wagon hitched to the stars, the sooner they'll go out and work. A hungry dog runs faster, everyone knows that. I supported a drunken father and worked nights to get through high school. I got up so early to work that sometimes I met myself going to bed. No Mister Rabinowitz or Mister Gronouski ever offered me anything for nothing. Hell, Peter was a fisherman and Jesus a carpenter. There's nothing wrong with honest work.   ·

— Well.

— Hell, Ben, I've spent my whole life working in the bureaucracy, a servant for other servants who serve others, until no one knows what he's doing. Now coloreds that can hardly read are getting into Yale, free on government scholarships. Despite the fact that everyone knows their brains are smaller than ours. They just can't handle all that information. It's known that their bodies are more adapted for enduring the outdoor heat than for being cooped up in libraries. And where it'll all end, I just don't know. What'll happen to those coloreds when they get out of Yale? They'll be too high-and-mighty to take an ordinary job like I did. Any psychologist can tell you that. As the missus always says, never wash more than you can hang out. Things like this always end badly. Everyone knows that. It's plain common sense.

— Well, Ham, I admit that these times do try the soul a bit.

— Ben, the day of reckoning is coming faster than you think.

— It's always one crisis after another, Ham. Panic of 1894. Bust of 1907. The Great War. The Great Depression. All trying to tear the tattered ensign down.

— Ben, the Republic can't take much more of this without toppling.

— That's what Grandfather Samuel the Just said about Reconstruction. But the Good Lord looks after little children, drunkards, and the United States.

— Ben, this country sure needs looking after right now. I can see the changes here in the post office. I see the names on the letters. New names. Most of them you can't even pronounce. And boy, are those people touchy when you mispronounce their names! If you don't call one of them Mister, he rushes home and sends off a letter to the state discrimination office.

— Well. I admit, Ham, it looks as if we may soon need a visa to walk around our own common.

— And now we've got that new Puerto Rican family that moved onto Patriot's Ridge. Sure, sure, I heard he's supposed to be some college professor from New York. But you know the way these Latins think only about love-making. They'll ruin the morals of this town. One comes, they all come. Anyone can tell you that when one gets in, the rest of his tribe follow. I hear there's an organization in New York that picks out nice towns to bust. They send the most diseased families they can find in Harlem to move there. A lot of people have told me that. And another thing people say is—

— Ham, excuse me, but I've got to be moving along.

— Sure thing, Ben. Say are you going to Malachy Murphy's burying? I'll walk over with you later.

— To the Sign of Hopalong Chastity?

— Haw-haw. That's a good one, Ben. I guess we oughtn't to be sacrilegious, though Malachy would have been the first to enjoy a good laugh. Yes, that right—it's at the Church of Our Lady of the Lame.

— No, I guess I won't be going. Malachy will have to meet his Maker without my support. Don't worry about him, though. He'll alter heaven to his advantage. And get himself the best pair of wings.

— He was a sharp trader all right.

— So I once learned, since I was a commodity he traded in for a time. I can forgive but not forget.

— Hell, Ben, that was long ago. He's in heaven now, at any rate.

— His loss is our eternal gain.

— Say what you will about him, Ben, he sure was a character. Steady in his work too. Not like most Irishmen. Ben, you know you could stop by just for a short time. You don't have to go to the cemetery.

— No, Ham, I'm not going.

— Still. Oh well, I'll be seeing you, Ben.

— Bye, Ham.

■

EVERYBODY KNOWS. Scientists say. Anyone can tell you. It's a fact. A sure sign. People say that if your nose itches, it's a sign of nosey company coming. Lots of people know that since the atomic-bomb tests the weather has changed. After a haircut you should have the ends of the hairs singed to keep in the vital fluids. Every schoolteacher knows that lots of memorizing increases the power of memory. It's a fact that more boy babies than girl babies are born just before a war to make up for the men lost in battle. You should always let a baby cry to make its lungs stronger. Blind people develop a sixth sense to guide them. The artistic temperament can't be trusted to act as honestly as other people. And it's been shown that these precocious artists pay for their gifts by early deaths. Some people say that being buried near a church increases your chances for salvation. Most folks know that no one is poor except through his own fault or circumstances. When animals grow a heavy coat of fur in the fall, it's a sure sign of a hard winter coming. People who've lived in the country can tell you that unusual activity by bees is a sign of rain. A drowning man is lost if he goes down for the third time—and as he's drowning, his whole life passes before him. It's been shown by the fall of ancient civilizations that nations are weakened by soft living. Oysters are poisonous in those months that don't have an R in them. Town drunks live so long because the alcohol in their blood makes them immune to infection. It's a plain fact that the kind of food you take into your body determines the kind of person you are. Frenchmen are light-headed and pop off quickly because of the bubbly champagne they drink. The heavy food eaten by Poles and Germans makes them slow and stubborn. The Irish diet is so poor that they are forced to drink a lot of whiskey to keep up their body heat. The greasy food eaten by Jews makes them oily.

A lot of people who have studied the Negroes know that they don't mind working on road gangs and in the fields because their bodies are better equipped than ours to endure heat. Their skulls are thicker than ours, so when a policeman hits one over the head with a club, it's the club that's likely to break. Because they work out in the sun so much, scientists believe that the heat has overstimulated their sex glands. They're also the most superstitious people on earth, having lots of foolish sayings about the weather and keeping your health. If Negroes really are our equals, then why weren't they the ones to invent automobiles and airplanes?

Anybody can spot the Jews by their hooked nose, frizzy hair, and swarthy skin. It's also been observed that their tribe is born cleverer than other people, which is why you got to skin them before they skin you. Anyone who has had dealings with them knows that they're real miserly and will Jew you down on a price. And if you see someone flashily dressed in a restaurant, asking for the best table and overtipping the waitress, he's likely to be a Jew.

It's known that Indians are plainly different from us. For one thing, anyone who has spent time around them knows that they have a sixth sense of direction. And they have a sign language because they can only communicate by grunts and a few verbs in the present tense. Their bodies are known to be particularly susceptible to alcohol because liquor affects them much more than it does us. If your church charity sends them clean clothes, they'll immediately dirty them up because that's their preferred way of living.

It's been said that Italians are capable of making love more than other people because of the wine they drink. Everyone knows that Irishmen like a good laugh, but they are not steady in their work. The Germans are the best organizers in the world.

People who plain don't know anything are speaking more drivel and twaddle today than ever before. Look at what they mistakenly call The Great Depression. No sir, that's baloney about the factories, mines, and banks closing because of some flaw in our system! People in the know say the whole thing was planned by some pretty important philosophers Herbert Hoover secretly brought to Washington. Mister Hoover was smarter than people give him credit for. He had put his finger on one of the most important problems of his administration—the need to encourage camaraderie in a population that no longer socialized because it spent every free moment at home listening to the new radio invention. You've got to admit that Mister Hoover turned the tide—even though he never got any of the credit —and soon folks were socializing everywhere, on street corners, park benches, railroad freight cars, and mission houses. Before you knew it, both the poor and the best society, who never would have had the opportunity of mutual introductions, were sharing the common experience.

And another thing you'll hear a lot of fiddle-faddle about is child labor, particularly in the mines. Those with access to the inside dope can tell you that child labor enhanced the health and personality development of our Nation's future leaders. Anyone can tell you that those fortunate youngsters who won the jobs of playing in the mines for sixteen hours a day had no trouble enjoying a restful repose the other eight hours, which is the amount of sleep doctors say you should get. Aside from which, you know it wasn't real work those kids were doing down there. You think they didn't have a whale of a good time riding those elevators up and down the shaft? And below they had all the rare sport they wanted in hauling those cute little trucks around. Why, the little devils even held contests to see who could pull the biggest loads. But they did it fair and square, holding two separate categories of contests, one for the younger fellers aged five to seven, and a completely separate one for the grown-up boys, aged eight to ten. And the management, bless them, joined in the spirit of fun and awarded the winners—in each category, mind you—an extra ration of rum with which to celebrate. Yessir, our ancestors were a lot smarter than we are. They knew youngsters had to be allowed to give vent to their natural destructive tendencies, so they let the little fellers grab a pick and pound away at the walls of the mine until the high spirits had been worked off for the day. The youngsters entertained themselves down below in lots of other ways too, such as playing with those little canary pets the miners kept. Well, it certainly was a paradise for children down there, the likes of which our youth will never see again, no matter how many playgrounds we build.

Most of us are sick of being bamboozled by all the hokum and bunkum we keep hearing from the bleeding hearts about our Nation. We sure hear a lot of malarkey about the institution of slavery because most people don't know the true story. It all began with an excursion to South Carolina made in the seventeenth century by the famous Great Emperor Blooz of Boomlay in the Congo. Great Emperor Blooz promptly became a conversation piece among the hard-working planters, not only for the feats of strength he was always delighted to demonstrate without remuneration but also because he, like all his tribe, was born naturally musical. Everyone knows that the aristocratic planters of South Carolina cultivated the fine arts, having brought over at great expense French dancing masters to instruct their children. Well, when they heard the singing performances of Great Emperor Blooz and his brethren—the style of which they named after him in his honor, even though they could have stolen the idea from him since he wasn't nothing but a nigger—every planter's wife just had to have a family from the Congo so her children would not be deprived of their rightful education in singing the Blues. It was no more morally reprehensible than paying a dancing master to come direct from Paris. The planters, to satisfy the yen of their culture-hungry wives, had to pay good money to Yankee impresarios who sailed their ships all the way to Africa and provided passage—free of charge, mind you—for Great Emperor Blooz's people to get to our shores, where everyone knows opportunities for advancement are unlimited. Sure, a few of the coloreds died on these cruises, but that wasn't the fault of their Southern patrons or of the Yankee impresarios. It was due solely and completely to the coloreds' hoggishness. You see, some of them wanted to get the edge over the others in emoluments once they reached Charleston. These were the ones who spent so much time practicing the songs and dances of their Blues that they wore themselves to a frazzle to the ultimate detriment of their health. Well, the Blues craze spread out from Charleston all over the Southland and the planters were forced to provide increasingly extravagant benefits to attract these talented people, just so their wives could hold up their heads in the best society. You know how these country wives are. If they don't get some frill or other, they fret for a month. All good things eventually come to an end, and that's just what happened to the institution of slavery when the avaricious New Englanders, who were trying to parlay symphony orchestras at the time, misused federal power to halt the concerts. Even so, you couldn't keep Great Emperor Blooz's tribe down. No sir, not them, for it was just as natural as typhoid that they had to sing and dance. So, during the trying times of Reconstruction the coloreds continued to present musicales to which the leading citizens were invited. But these inspired concerts had to be performed in the privacy of the forest, to avoid prying Northern eyes, and the distinguished guests had to endure the humiliation of masking themselves. Which is how the fraternal organization of Klans originated, which was somewhat like The Friends of Italian Opera and other fan clubs. But that's another story most people don't know about.

■

WE KNOW what we know. Every man's opinion. Good as another. We'll fight for it. The right to be wrong. Let me make the superstitions of a nation. And I care not who makes its laws. Thus spake Pudd'nhead Wilson.

Optician. Mine lies have seen. Damn-damn-damn-DAMN. Damn banging! Moderne's Men's Store. Mirror in window. Shows my shapeless suit. Should I get another? Maybe for France? Some people say they're cheaper over there. "Next To Myself I Like B.V.D.s Best." Corner. Wait. Look both ways. Speeding kid. Caution—Weird Load. He almost hit me. Guilty of manslaughter. Man's laughter. No consideration for others. School is open too. Ought to take his car away. Lock him up. Fine his parents. Here comes a truck. Rumble and bang.

Whew! Stinks. They shouldn't allow it. Old tin lizzie ain't what she used to be. The wonderful one-hoss shay was built in a logical way. Yankee Doodle rode on a pony. The state should build a bypass. Exhaust smells. No fresh air anymore. All clear? No, not yet. Oh, oh. No escape. Here he comes. Constant complainer. A man of sorrows.

— Hello, Mister Myer. I agree, that exhaust smell is terrible. I know there aren't enough parking places. No, I walk to the office. But if I drove I would complain also. Yes, I would. I know. I've been trying to get across Pennyman Street myself. Yes, it is as difficult as parting the waters of the Red Sea. You're right, the heat doesn't make it any easier. It is a shame that we have to pick up our mail instead of getting it delivered. I'm sure they lose most of the letters too. Do you really think they steam them open and take out checks? Ham's been our postmaster for forty years and I don't think he'd do that. Well, no, I have no authority for doubting your statement. Possibly one of his newer postmen does it. No, I can't attend Malachy Murphy's funeral. I have some rush work to do for a client. Yes, very important. Has to be done this afternoon. Of course I'd go to his funeral otherwise. I'll be stopping by your store later. Yes, I need something. Yes, I do hope we should all live so long. Bye now.

Left. Right. Left. Right. Do right. Do right. Dum-dum-dum-DUM. Damn! Walk this side. Keep common to the left. Shadier this side. Go across and then down the block. Pattern of sun and shade. Go around the square. Damn! Never heard such banging on a house before. Old Bellamy place didn't need making over. By any newcomer. Looks all right to me. Scaffoldings around it now. Italian workers running on them. I better move away. They might drop something. They drink too much wine. It's a good house. Forthright. Symmetrical. Two windows on each side of the door. Five windows facing front upstairs. Timbers look sound. They built to last in the old days. Most things are best left alone. It didn't need saving by Freudenthal. A peculiar people.

How odd
Of God
To choose
The Jews.

Birds are gone. Scared away. Except the starlings. They're newcomers too. No more bluebirds. No more orioles. Silent. All
gone. Gone are the chirps and chatters, chants and chortles,
whistles and warbles. Diseased elms. Decapitated trunks.

Freudenthal's bank. Next to the church property. It's not
right. Pity, pity. Missus Petichek coming out. The new people
use his bank. Smile to petite Petichek. Chuck little Master Petichek on petichin. Now laugh avuncular. Now make pleas-
antry. Now leave. Smile at Missus Goldhaber. O daughter of
Zion. Swarthy. You can always tell one by. Carrying her greasy
groceries. That's what makes their tribe oily. Her twin boys.
Everyone having boys. Like those quintuplet boys yesterday in
Venezuela. Born of a grandmother too. Maybe it's a sign another war coming. Oh, oh. Poor Reekans. Señora Alegria.
Smile. A flood of them. They're coming, they're coming! To
arms! Spread the alarm through every Middlesex. Smile to the
ladies. Hello, ladies, Look out, here I come. Look out, there I
go. Gone. Gone are the days. Watch the dago by. Left. Right.
Do right. Do right.

Tourists taking pictures of church. Famous steeple looks like
a witch's hat. They take pictures, use up film. Kodak gets rich
on our church. Does taking a picture take anything away from
the church? Would taking a thousand pictures make it any
thinner? A million? Foolish thought. Sign in front. Churches
getting like highway billboards now. Have to coax you in. "The
Fifteenth Sunday After Trinity. Celebrant: Dr. DuMont. Sermon: The Undying Wisdom of Solomon." He'd be wise not to
preach that old chestnut. Doctor DuMont must be running out
of sermon topics. "Newcomers' Coffee Hour Each Thursday.
Meeting of Nutmeg Festival Committee Will." One of oldest
Episcopal churches in New England. Greek Revival architec-

ture. The Pennymans might have stayed Congregational. If it wasn't for the stove. Jonathan, grandfather of Samuel the Just. He wanted a stove during winter, congregation didn't. "If Brother Jonathan needes a fiere, he will soone finde one year around when he goes to that Place appointed for him." That's what it says in the Black Book.

— Oh, hello there, Tim. You're right, summer doesn't want to call it quits. Say, Tim, you're going to have to do something about those hot-rod kids. One of them almost blasted my glasses off a few minutes ago. Yes, it was that good-looking Marvelli kid. Oh, I know their parents are well-meaning people. They're also new people in this town. New Salem isn't their private racetrack. And I'll tell you something else, Tim. We've got laws against indecent exposure and it's high time you started enforcing them. Don't forget you've still got the authority under the lascivious-carriage laws. I just saw Missus Petichek with her breasts hanging out. No, I don't think they enhance the landscape. I realize styles change. But decent standards don't. And another thing, I—

Walked off. Fondling his stick. He doesn't care. More voters among the new people now. They're organized. Only one Pennyman vote. The last. Member of one. He's a member of their club. Their tool. Irish too. Oi'll loin ya. Thinks he's a ladies' man. Irish Mafia in Washington now. Kennedy may have gone to Harvard. But he's still shanty Irish. His grandfather was a saloonkeeper.

Main Street. Wait for cars. "Welcome to New Salem, Conn— *the* Growing Community." Growing by leaps and bums. We're being conned. Don't trip on broken curb. Two years ago, when a truck skidded. Never fixed. All right now. Cross. There! Up and over. Excelsior! For they shall rise again. Now turn left. The hundred block. Now this crossing. Oh, oh. Who let that one in? Droopy pants. Ingratiating smile. The Wandering Jew arrives. Don't smile back. Not a friendly town. The welcome sign only a formality. A rootless people. Dresses shabby. But he probably has millions stashed away. Or in diamonds hidden

50

up his rectum. Better remember to stop by Myer's Drugs later.

The Hundred and One—Everything Electrical. Tommy's Place. He means Tomaine's Palace. Custard's last stand. It's all right to eat oysters this month. A mirror. My feeble shadow. It's hard for an empty sack to stand upright. Thus spake Bendyourmind Franklin. Number one forty-one. New Salem Fine Wines & Sprites. No, that's Spirits. "God Is My Senior Partner." Does he split the profits? Ye Countrie Shoppe. Phoney. Factory-made clothes. Grandma Moses copies. Next store vacant. Being refurbished. Someone said it'll be a bookshop. Gladinski Insurance Company. Sticker on door. "Our Nation—Love It Or Leave It." Truebluepoleamerican. He might be in. Then I don't have to watch the time getting back to office. Anyway, he'll be flattered I stopped by.

— Hello, Whit. Is Mister Gladinski in?

— Well, hi there, Mister Pennyman. Golly, no. He had to go out to consult with a client.

— I thought he was tied up with some big executive from Hartford.

— No. I mean. The vice president was in. But Mister Gladinski finished his work with him. And then he was going to see you. But something came up with this new client. It was important.

— I'm sure. Evidence conclusive. Either way.

— But he said he was planning to stop by your office later, Mister Pennyman. Along about five.

— I thought it was four thirty.

— It may have been four thirty, Mister Pennyman. I'm not certain.

— Well, Whit, I'm positive he'll get to my office when he gets there. I was just passing by. How's business?

— Growing by leaps and bounds. New records every year. We just heard we'll get another achievement award from the company. That's seven out of the last ten years. It's not just the records and the new business, though. Sure those things count. But it's a real satisfaction to know we've protected the people who sign with us against calamities. The Great American Accident Company paid off in excess of fifty thousand dollars in claims in the New Salem area alone last year. It's impossible to alleviate human misery, Mister Pennyman, but our policies try to take some of the financial hazards out of it. Why insurance is one of the

■

ONE OF THE great endeavors of mankind. Know that, and in the future you will examine the world differently. You will realize that a paraplegic, rolled along the sidewalk by a white-starched nurse, is not an object of pity but an ambulated advertisement for the profits to be made from this noble institution. Oh, the good works that an accident policy in force performs! An entire family—the consumptive mother, the wastrel father, and the six yellowish children, all under the influence of malnutrition—can pull themselves out of poverty by the simple blessing of the father toppling off the curb. Hardly a crippled man in New Salem neglects to raise a crutch in enthusiastic praise of this beneficent institution. The human face knows no expression so joyous as that of the bright-eyed lad who learns that his mutilated father has hit the jackpot—or so downcast as that of the son who learns that his old mother's cracked skull went to naught because she had been remiss about reading her accident raffle. The Great American Accident Company is the eleemosynary institution with which to place your bets. People who used to patronize other companies switched their trade to Great American and now they walk around in happy affluence with bandaged heads, crutches, or faithful seeing-eye dogs. Great American lays out before you a choice sweepstake of hazards, including (but not limited to) Riots, Volcanoes, Earthquakes, Floods, Tornadoes, Explosions, Lightning, Hail, Blizzards, Atomic Radiation, Chemical Pollution, Murder, Drowning, Assaults by Robbers and Civil Disobedients, Falls, and Acts of God, all of which offer sundry prizes for Fractures

(Simple, Complex, and Chip), Dislocation, Concussion, Burning, Insect Sting, Stab Wound, Gunshot Wound, Intentional Poisoning, and various Infections which are itemized in the policy itself. Everything is so finely calculated that top dollar is paid for the loss of one foot and two hands, or as an alternative, one hand, one eye, and three fingers from the right hand. Anyway, the lottery grades down from that in equitable stages. You can hedge your bet by placing your wad on loss by removal of one or more entire toes and the entire phalanx of one finger, which would pay seventy-five percent of the pot. The wild joker in the pack is the word "complete." A complete fracture of the shaft of the thigh pays much more than a mere chip of the coccyx. The agent may let you up the ante somewhat by trying for a combination. One client raked in the whole pot by being bitten by a rabid dog, which was owned by a civil disobedient, during a hurricane, and in the process of fleeing from said beast fell down and smashed his forearm between wrist and elbow. Or you might buy a chance on the gunshot-asphyxiation-insect-sting parlay, which also pays top dollar. Gladinski Insurance states in its tip sheet that Great American Accident has seventy-five million dollars of policies in force, and that last year it paid off on nearly one million dollars in winnings. But it seems that except for a few customers with the inside track who get mangled, most people don't earn back their investment. They are life's unfortunates who never seem to be where the rivers are rising or the earth quaking. These unlucky bettors are a plague to our profession because they maintain that insurance is, essentially, a swindle.

■

— IT's an important service that signing up for an insurance policy performs, Mister Pennyman. I mean, it relieves anxieties about the unexpected. Well, I could go on for hours. Guess I'm just a natural enthusiast.

— I guess you are, Whit. Sorry, I've got to be getting along.

A haircut. If the First Selectman-to-be comes back, tell him he can catch me at Jim's for the next half hour or so. And my regards home to your parents.

— Thank you, Mister Pennyman, I'll be sure to tell them. Can I speak to you professionally for just a moment? I was going to call you at your office this week.

— Of course, Whit. What is it?

— Well, I'm getting married.

— That's good news. Who's the fortunate girl?

— You don't know her. She's from Omaha. I met her at the big June Dance at the Country Club. She was visiting here.

— I look forward to the opportunity.

— I'm sure she'd like to meet you, too. Anyway, I'd better have a will drawn up. Not that there's much in the way of assets. I'm afraid I belong to the shabby genteel.

— Happy to, Whit. There's no charge of course. The Pennyman firm had three generations of business from your family. I guess we can throw in a will as a wedding present.

— Golly, that's real white of you, Mister Pennyman.

— Have you found a place to live yet?

— No problem. We're going to live in Omaha. Her father is the biggest insurance agent there. He's taking me in. She doesn't have any brothers.

— What does Mister Gladinski say about that?

— Well. I haven't told him yet.

— Oughtn't you to soon? I bet he'll be sorry to lose you.

— I guess so. Sure our firm is prospering, but I don't see much future for me with Mister Gladinski. It's a different kind of clientele from the people I grew up with.

— I bet it is. Well, I have to be moving along, Whit. When you call, tell my secretary I said to give you an appointment at your convenience.

— Thanks again, Mister Pennyman.

Save me from the unexpected. Come ye and covenant with The Great American Swindle Company. I never noticed before. Safeway Market. It's next to Gladinski Insurance. A combination. Chainstore money is forcing the little man out. Breakfast of. Chases Dirt. When It Rains It. The Skin You Love To. Litter basket at the corner. Throw out the ad letter. Letter to the litter. Not now. Don't break stride. Here come the ladies. Smile at the ladies. Drop it in the next basket. Oh, oh. Trapped anyway.

— Can I help you with your packages, Missus Novak? Oh no, just an old-fashioned gentleman. I'm too old to have ulterior motives. But if I did, you're the one I would be ulterior with. Ha-ha.

Wears sunglasses you can't see into. They reflect me. Do I look same to her as I see reflected? Probably not. Curved surfaces distort. Some physical law or other. Don't remember. Goodbye, ladies, goodbye, sweet ladies, goodbye. Took long way around. But it was shadier. Peri's Buttons 'n' Things. Homos. Middlesex. Got them all in this town. It's another country. Ambisexterous. What's Tim doing in there? He's got time to talk to homos. But he walks off on me. Maybe the homos have been causing trouble. Good if we had an excuse to clear them out. Jonathan's Glass, Shades & Wallpaper. His boy running the store now. Running it, ruining it. Jonathan built it up. His son weakened by soft living. That's a pretty insect. Flying to flowers someplace? Somewhere in this favored land? Not here. Was it a beetle? A flutterby? A cant? A myth? A flee? A wisp? A nat, a nit, a naught? A me.

Oh, oh. Here comes Freudenthal. Duck in here. No need to talk to him. He's carrying a package. To the post office? Why doesn't he let his secretary do it for him? Maybe he doesn't want her to know. He sends a bundle to Israel every month. Ham says so. Ham ought to know. Freudenthal innocently strolls down the avenue. Wearing sacred black skullcap of his tribe under expensive Panama. International. Protocols. Zion will be redomed. An ancient people. A credit to his race. Crafty.

Abie Freudenthal, King of the Jews,
Wipes his ass with the Babylon News.

The father of his tribe. THE LIFE OF OLD FREUDENTHAL. *The Wandering Tinker and How He Became the Father of His Craft, With New and Valuable Anecdotes Exemplary to the Young.* Like Father used to read to us. Before he went away. Stories written by enterprising ministers. Did they believe them themselves? Maybe. We believed what you read, Father. But the world didn't turn out that way. Damn it, it didn't! A swindle. It didn't pay off on the combination. We had faith in the Lored. But the Lawed didn't keep His promise to the Pennymanies. Life is real! Life is earnest! Industry will be rewarded. Everything should be like the stories. Like THE LIFE OF OLD FREUDENTHAL.

■

As *crafty* Captain Dreyfus was about to board the bark bound for *evergreen* Guiana, he espied in the sea of spectators a person certain to be a Yankee because of his well-favoured frame and noble bearing. The *celebrated* betrayor called out with what would be almost his ultimate breath in his own native land, "Oh, Yankee Doodle, how fares thy fellow countryman, my friend *Freudenthal?* And his seed, like the sands of the shore in your *prospering* Nation? Full fair is his fame, I pray. *Prosperity* shall praise his deeds, while my name shall live in evil fame!"

Who, then, was this *Freudenthal,* celebrated even by a contrite man without a country? The whole world acclaims *Abie Freudenthal*—and yet no one knows the real man! So we will now delineate for you *Freudenthal,* the dutiful son, the affectionate brother, the studious scholar, the friend to those in distress, the widows' support, and THE FATHER OF HIS CRAFT. Antiquarians have assembled the relics that remind us of the phenomenon of *Freudenthal.* But we will attend solely to a relic considered too inconsequential for inclusion in the rich array of *gifts* of state. We speak only of an ordinary— cooking kettle! And the time of which we are writing was that

56

fulcrum in *Abie Freudenthal's life* when he balanced between manhood and boyhood, between innocence and selfless *Service* for his brethren.

One bright and brilliant morn Little Abie decided it was time to set forth from the succouring *estate* where he first saw the light of day to seek simple *Service* in the virtuous village of New Salem. He *shrewdly* indentured himself to a miserable tinker by the name of Minkel the Miser in the expectation that that *penurious* patriarch might *profit* by his Example and be ushered down the shining road to *Service,* which will save our *precious* souls when they come before Almighty Providence. What a model Youth set for Miserly Age! Little Abie commenced his craft each morn with the first gleam of Dawn's beam, and he laboured lovingly long after dark, his *industrious* digits illumined only by flickering firelight. Never did Little Abie complain about his short rations, the bed he shared with vermin and a nigger, the lack of *pay,* and other inconveniences.

We now pause to enumerate the ancestors out of whose *lusty loins* Little Abie had sprung. These then are the nations and generations of *Freudenthal.* Hecht of Baltimore took to wife Lann of Baltimore and begat Belker of Cleveland, who begat Kaufman of Philadelphia, who begat both Abraham and Straus of New York, the latter of whom begat Saks of the same settlement. Saks begat Wanamaker of Philadelphia who then begat the mighty Filene of Boston who, during the dark years, begat *Gold*water of Phoenix. *Gold*water begat Flak of Albany and his brother Neiman. Neiman married into the house of Marcus of Dallas and the *fortunes* of the fine family of *Freudenthals* rose once more. Neiman begat Garfinckel of Washington who begat on May of Los Angeles the Saks of Miami, who begat Gimbel of New York, Strouss-Hirshberg of Youngstown, Hess of Allentown, and Burdine of Miami. Burdine begat Bloomingdale of New York, who begat Bamberger of Newark, who begat Lazarus of Columbus, who begat *Rich* of Atlanta. Those were the days of giants in the earth. Then *Rich* begat the Belk Brothers of Charlotte, the eldest of whom begat Rosenblum of Cleve-

57

land, who begat Schwarzschild of *Rich*mond, who begat Hertz-
berg of San Antonio, who begat Levy of Tucson, who begat
Renberg of Tulsa, who begat Neusteter of Denver. Neusteter
begat Brandeis of Omaha, who begat Lowenstein of Memphis,
who begat Schuster of Milwaukee, who begat Genung of
Mount Vernon, who begat *Little Abie Freudenthal of New
Salem!* And his brother as well, who took the easy road and has
not been heard of since.

One sultry day in September Little Abie laboured lovingly
while the Lord smiled fulsomely on his *favourite* village of
New Salem, basking in all its splendour and order. The corn-
crowned fields waved before the wanton breezes. The happy
kine, fattening to furnish food for fall, whitened the hills. Old
Sol sent his bright beams bouncing off the *polished* plough-
shares. The unostentatiously habilitated farmhands did yeoman
work in the perfumed pastures, singing the Blues playfully and
lustily in their labours, in rhythm to the resonant rings that encircled their ankles. Every man was content in his peace and
plenty.

On this distant day the New Salemites were startled to see
a stout *Stranger,* clad in black raiment, parade past down the
clean-kept lanes. The ravening *merchants* earnestly entreated
him to enter their lairs, but he looked neither to the left nor to
the right as he marched past the cabinetmaker, bootmaker, sad-
dler, cordmaker, broommaker, blacksmith, clockmaker, store-
keeper, tinsmith, hogreeve, periwig-maker, gunsmith, glass-
maker, locksmith, and wheelwright—not to mention those with
literary *aspirations,* such as the miller, mason, mastersman,
tanner, tailor, turner, cooper, hooper, draper, porter, potter,
paineter, sawyer, stower, weaver, hay dealer, ward heeler, frost
worker, crane operator, cablemaker, coffin-maker, chapman,
and garlander.

An unceasing hissing arose as Yinkel first accosted the
Stranger, and then Wrinkel and Zinkel, Blinkel and Dinkel.
Pinkel sang out his *wares* and Linkel put out for *purchase* his
trade blankets. But the *Stranger* paraded past the predacious

shopkeepers, their doors ajar like hungry jaws, to the Sign of Minkel the Miser, in which there *laboured* a youth of exceptional virtue, yclept *Little Abie Freudenthal.*

Minkel humbled himself like a twisted string before his precious *cash*box, on which was emblazoned the motto, "I've Trusted Many To My Sorrow—*Pay* Me Today, I'll Trust Tomorrow." But—NO!—the imposing *Stranger* would speak solely with Little Abie, for he sought the Truth of Youth. The repute of the good lad had already burgeoned beyond the boundaries of New Salem to reach the ears of the *Stranger.* So Minkel summoned Little Abie from the attic, where he lunged and lurched in a game of tickle-my-toe to divert the nigger, to stand in the presence of the stout *Stranger.*

"Little Abie?" inquired the *Stranger* in a reverberating voice which shook the very *coffers* with a boom and a bang.

"Yours to serve, my lord, if I have found favour in your sight and *might,*" affirmed Little Abie, a bright blush adorning his downy cheeks.

"Child, I have here a cooking kettle that wants mending," stated the *Stranger.* "Can you fulfill this *service* by sunrise?"

Did Little Abie's thoughts linger on the long *labour* required for the repairs, the fierce fire he would have to feed, or the resonant rings of the hammer required to remove the flaws? *No!* Little Abie sought only *Service!* "Yes, kind sir," Little Abie affirmed with ardour, fully aware that not a nod of sleep would he know before dappled Dawn adorned herself. The noble personage nodded, blew his nose noisily, and, of a certainty so torn by tears at the tenour of Little Abie's devotion, inadvertently overturned a package of *precious* chinaware as he issued from the shop.

The stout *Stranger* no sooner shut the whorled and worn oaken door, which shook with a shudder three sheets of glass from the window, than Minkel the Miser in his misery unknotted himself from his subservient stance. His face reflected the fire like a salted salmon held over a flame. "Fool! Fool!" he stated with some warmth to Little Abie. "You have been the dupe of an outrageous imposition! No man on earth could discharge this *obligation* by morn!" But Little Abie was not a man —he was an innocent lad! And a boy's *will* is the wind's *will*.

Little Abie squandered not a second before setting to work. All afternoon passersby heard the resonant ringing of *industry* as Little Abie directed his devotions to the dents in the cooking kettle in his care. The setting sun tipt with fire the dying day. But never did Little Abie Freudenthal falter. As the wise Abraham to his true son Isaac, so Little Abie's father had inspired in him the need for honour in labour's endeavours. Even though Little Abie's father had disappeared on an adventurous voyage of *enterprise* to some distant domaigne, he had already sown good seed in the womb of virtue, and the harvest was bountiful. Oh, how loved is a child who has learned these lessons well! How his sprightly schoolfellows seek to duplicate his dearest deeds! How other parents view him enviously! How the virtuous lasses dote on such a lively lad!

Old Sol bid adieu to New Salem for another happy day. Every man peaceably bent to his *groaning* board in the bosom of his affectionate family. Every child—save one!—placed his future *fate* into the arms of Morpheus. Little Abie paused not to eat, nor did he rest. He had made his *promise* and he would take particular pains that it should prove *of value*. He laboured with alacrity, for could Little Abie fail or fault when the Blessed God had *made good* on His *promises*? A solitary light shone in New Salem through the endless night and it illumined Little Abie *at his labours*. As the beams of Dawn beckoned, Little Abie mended the last dent in the cooking kettle. His task was completed—and exactly *on time*!—for Little Abie was ever a *punctual* boy.

Little Abie washed *white* his hands and face—as is the wont of *conscientious* children to do—and put his tools trimly into their proper places. Rosy Morn shone upon a workroom shipshape in every particular and a lad passing proud of his accomplishment. That great and good God who delights in orderly labour would assuredly *reward* him! Little Abie stood rooted to the door before the mean shop of Minkel the Miser where he awaited the arrival of the *Stranger*.

The Orb basked in the Sun's beams, but still the *Stranger* made not his appearance. Surely he lies stricken with some indisposition, surmised Little Abie, or else he is worn through from his large-hearted acts of *charity*. The Sun zoomed to the Zenith, but still the *Stranger* was not seen. Surely he is otherwise occupied with *commerce*, but he will arrive this afternoon, affirmed Little Abie. By evening it was evident to the entire village that the *Stranger* would not return to *reward* our hero. The elders mumbled and muttered, and they uttered cautions against the *credit* of outsiders. All that loving labour for naught, they asserted, to satisfy a *Stranger* not soon to be seen again.

But nary a tear did Little Abie shed upon the saddened soil! Not once did he wince at the slings and stones that fickle *Fortune* had hurled at him! For he knew in his heart of hearts that the *Stranger*, clearly a man of great *enterprises*, had simply let slip from his memory the trifling cooking kettle. Despite the demands of sleep to sustain and maintain a happy and healthy disposition, Little Abie was determined to set out and seek the *Stranger*. He suspended his apron properly from its hook and shed *abundant* tears in bidding adieu to the nigger Glngkinkel, with whom he was compelled to *share* a bed. Sturdy Little Abie marched straight into the starlit night in quest of the *Stranger*— whose name he did not even know!

In his arms Little Abie cradled the cooking kettle made whole again through his labours. He shouldered also a pack containing his paltry possessions, which consisted of clean linen—for Little Abie was ever a comely boy—and a balanced library of books which might serve as moral *fodder* to nourish him on his travels. The *treasured* tomes which he elected to transport, despite their bulk and burden, were *A Divine and Supernatural Light Immediately Imparted to the Soul by the Spirit of God, Sinners in the Hands of an Angry God, God Glorified in Man's Dependence, The Wonders of the Invisible*

World, Magnalia Christi Americana or The Ecclesiastical History of New England, The Day of Doom, Christian Experience, Conversations with Children on the Gospels, Milk for Babes Drawn Out of the Breasts of Both Testaments, Christianity as a Purely Internal Principle, Full Vindication of God's Flood and His Wisdom in Destroying the Wicked Human Race, God's Revenge Against Carousing, God's Revenge Against Sodomy and Solitary Pleasures, The Old Sinner's Dirty Looking Glass, The Onanist's Looking Glass, Hazardous Voyage to the Land of Pervertia, The Decline and Fall of Pederasteria, Lost in the Depraved Domaigne of Sodomia, The Damned Boy's Apology for His Private Pastimes, The Public Pleasures of a Good Boy, Uses and Abuses of Buggery, Know Your Own Brother, The Damnation of Onan the Semenite, The Double Damnation of Miss and Master Bates, Fingertip Tales, The Manual of Handshaking, Handbook for Boys, Masturbatory Idiocy as Described by the World's Leading Scientists, and *The Rules of Solitaire.*

Chance occasioned Little Abie to leave New Salem by the right road, for he soon spied an indigent Indian whose lepered limbs confirmed that dirt is their preferred way of living. "Pray, good mister," said Little Abie—for he respected all of God's creation and would make no more hesitation to address an Indian as "mister" than he would a nigger—"did you spy a black-clad *Stranger* depart this day?" The sullen spawn of the American soil pulled back a portion of his dirty-and-diseased blanket to reveal a black-and-blue bruise. "Kick me," responded the Redman, who could communicate, like all savages, only with gutteral grunts and verbs in the *present* tense.

"Oh no, mister, you are of a certainty confused, for the *Stranger* would not be so rude as to kick you, unless of course he were riled or ruffled," asserted Little Abie in staunch defense of the *Stranger*. Nevertheless the savage persisted in his certitude, and so Little Abie made believe that he believed the Indian's mistaken belief. Note, dear readers, that we draw a definite distinction between prevarication, which is abhorred by all civilized *society*, and Little Abie's simply making believe, which is the way one must *treat* savages to defeat their bred-in-the-bone doubts. At last the Redman revealed the *Stranger's* route down the long, long road. "Thank you very much, mister," avouched Little Abie, who was *polite in all particulars.* And he was happy to *win* this information, for he knew that Indians have a sixth *sense* of direction.

No sooner had New Salem become to Little Abie a shadow in the shallow hollow of the meadow than a horrendous hailstorm arose. He was sorely pelted and welted and no shelter could he spy, for the virtuous villagers thereabouts had *industriously* decapitated the trees in their brave battle to *win* out over the wilderness. As all things must, the storm at last abated and Little Abie witnessed the desolation it had caused. Mothers and children, ruing the ruination of the harvest, complained that they would consume bitter bread that year. One tear-sotted dame wrung her hands and wailed, "Oh, why is there so much suffering in this world of ours?"

"What an easy question to answer!" *volunteered* Little Abie, who suspected that the good woman had grown old before she grew wise. "Divine Providence gave you a *gift* of these afflictions that you might learn humility."

But the woman waywardly refused to accede to the clarity of Little Abie's logic. She inquired further, "You mean He wanted these *precious* little children to suffer?"

"Of course," Little Abie said sagaciously. "He desired to discipline the children."

"Peradventure, you mean He desired to discipline the adults at the *expense* of the suffering of *precious* children?" she persisted.

Little Abie was becoming increasingly irritated at her irrelevance, but nevertheless he professed politely, "Oh no, that discomfiture of yours was probably for another purpose. It must have been *proffered* you as punishment for some sin or other."

"Are you saying, young sir, that every one of us committed some sin or other?"

"Well, everyone knows that the righteous must roast along

with the wicked," Little Abie affirmed *brightly*. But, wearying of the woman's catechism, he once more set his spry steps after the *Stranger*.

As Aurora rubbed the repose from her bright eyes, Little Abie approached an unprepossessing but *picturesque* structure that stood—or shall we say staggered?—near a wide wallow. He *discovered* that there dwelled inside—rent *free!*—a *favoured* family of fifteen black persons, including an ailing and aged grandmother who appeared prepared to find that *unencumbered* felicity which the Providential Parent of us all has readied in heaven for those who stride down the *strait* path. "I reckon she is dying," reflected Little Abie, without wishing to mention such an embarrassment out loud.

"Oh, lil massa, effen onny she had sum uv dat speshal yerb medicine, den her life kould be spared," said her son.

Little Abie hoped that he had approached in time to prevent her passing. "May I obtain for you those *valuable* herbs from the kind people who inhabit that big *white* house on the hill?" he asked, anxious to assist these persons who had been transported from faraway Africa *at no cost to them* to come under the civilizing influence.

Instead of acceding to Little Abie's *offer* with alacrity, the suspiring woman's son rolled his eyes to signify some aversion to the suggestion. "Naw, naw, ah begs yu, lil massa. Tread not toward de house on de hill. Effen we disturbs Major Molineux, he lash us till we nearly dead."

The son seems sufficiently sincere, speculated Little Abie, but what a foolish Major to manage his *material possessions* in such a manner. Why, thought he, if I *possessed* slaves, I would not let them lie in the idleness of sickness until they die. I would furnish them with goodly garlands of herbs that might *further* their *fecundity*, in that way declaring *dividends* on my original *investment!* But, ever respectful of other people's *rightful* peculiarities, Little Abie forbore further reflections about hieing to the house on the hill. As the Reason which *reigns* over us all might have foretold, the woeful woman quickly coughed her last and closed her orbs on all mortal *things*. Little Abie had naught to do but pick up his pack and the cooking kettle confided to his care and eschew the shack where lusty ululations were let loose upon the *radiant* day.

Whistling a merry tune, Little Abie soon passed a wagon of teetotalers and found himself on the road to the rollicking twin towns of Hohokus. He passed through the hamlet of Pigtown and the town of Patterson where a comely child babbled to his father. Shortly he *overtook* an Indian who shuddered and shook at every step, as he alternately limped and loafed, lunged and lurched. At first Little Abie assumed that the Indian was under the *influence* of a spirituous decoction, to which their bodies are known to be singularly susceptible. But then his keen vision *noted* that the Indian's visage showed pitted ravages of some blemishing affliction. "Oh, mister, if you can manage the *mother* tongue, tell me the terrible misadventures that befell thee," inquired Little Abie, feigning attention, for in truth he had of late listened to enough hard-luck lamentations to *last* him a long while.

The Indian, who had *received* our blessed language from *ministering* missionaries, *conveyed* to Little Abie an anecdote whose length we have taken the *liberty* to abridge *on behalf of* brevity. "I am Old Chief Chingachgook, begot of a long line of chiefs and scion of Wundawucker, Broken Promises, White Man Bribed Him, Bloody Drawers, Smashed Testicles, Dropped Nut, Fallen Rock, Pried of Loins, Rash in Crotch, Burning Organ, Short Count, Cholera's Child, Mother Works on Backside, Cracked Ribs Didn't Heal, Trouble Follows Him, Smells to High Happy Hunting Ground, Daughters Stolen from Him, Black Cloud Overhead, Dirty Breechcloth, Spoiled Rations, Didn't Read Treaty, Hawks Shit on Him, Forgot Where Buried Gold, Looked into Loaded Rifle, and Swindled by Great *White* Father. I hadst ventured forth from my ruinèd village of Reck-awakes, where it came to pass that a stout *Stranger,* clad in black raiment, *sold* us divers blankets which we learnèd later —alas, to our loss and lament!—he hath obtainèd at *an excellent price*—for him!—from the smallpox hospital!"

"The smallpox hospital!" averred Little Abie.

"Yea, verily, the smallpox hospital!" responded the remarkably pockmarked Old Chief. "That was but the penultimate outrage of the *profusion* perpetratèd by this person upon our *trust*. Despite the *gifts* of feathers, quivers, shells, and the private parts of beasts we *presentèd* to the *Stranger,* he led my innocent sons into debauchery and violatèd my *comely* and virtuous wife. Verily, I solely survive the insidious *strategies* of the *Stranger*. Peradventure, I no longer dwell in a domicile, for after the disease had decimatèd us, the *Stranger* and his supernumeraries seizèd my *estates*. I cannot return to the land where I laid to rest my lovèd ones, for the *Stranger* hath sworn a solemn vow to shred me with a salvo of shot, such an animadversion for me he haveth. He fracturèd in a few places my feet, which thou can see have mendèd poorly. Sundry *coppers* on my person were stolen several leagues back by a bright-eyed boy, in which act I was struck a severe swat on the sconce which I fear hath vitiatèd my vision. And I am famishèd, for I *possess* no provisions."

Little Abie *paid* patient attention to these constant complaints. But, always one to peer around adversity's corner and contemplate the brighter side, Little Abie was overjoyed to observe how even a savage could *possess* the firmness of a *soldier* and the philosophy of a Christian. The *charitable* Little Abie let slip from his back the pack of *precious posséssions* and he withdrew his sole copy of *The Onanist's Looking Glass,* an appropriate tome for a tippling savage. "Chief Chingachgook, I *bestow* on thee a *boon* to be more esteemed in your present *estate* than even a *copper coin,*" asserted Little Abie, making a pretty bow at the appropriate place in his *presentation* speech. It was Little Abie's fervent hope that the savage should soon take hold of himself by *his own* bootstraps. For the Indians' problem, he averred, was that they lived in the present tents.

Little Abie identified in the distance a vision of delight—the twin towns of Hohokus, set proudly in a plain encircled by a verdant swamp. In happy Hohokus he anticipated that he would *find* a gale of laughter, a lot of realtors, a goggle of tourists, a fund of charitable organizations, a horde of misers, a score of musicians, a handful of onanists, a slew of homicides, an embarrassment of witches, and a peck of bad boys. As Little Abie approached, he was alerted to a turn of events, for his nose scented the acrid smell of smoke and his eyes espied a consternation of people. He perceived the populace flying to and fro, vying to fill vessels with water from the *free*-flowing swamp. A blaze-blackened fellow implored Little Abie Freudenthal to fill with fluid the cooking kettle he carried and to follow the fire fighters to the conflagration. Little Abie entered into the endeavours of the townspeople with energy and enthusiasm.

He helped them battle the blaze in the *princely palace* of Hohokus's most *opulent* landholder. Then he got his fill fighting the gourmandizing flames which bid fair to gobble up the *free*-holds of the *prosperous* lords of manors. Next the *mansions* of the industrious *merchants* were preserved, and thereafter the *neat* hovels of the hard-working artisans, and so on in sequence, as is suited to a settled *society*. Weariness *won* out over the fire fighters before they might extinguish the last vestiges of the conflagration, and so a *hundred* hovels went up in purifying smoke, thereby having a *beneficial* influence on the twin towns, for very verminous creatures were consumed, as were a few pestilence-prone persons, plagued by rickets, scurvy, malnutrition, and other dread diseases, who might have polluted the rest of the population. All smiled upon Little Abie, for they *speculated* that a Succouring Spirit had hastened him to Hohokus with his cooking kettle, so opportunely had he arrived to assist the embattled residents.

"Good elders of these enchanting twin towns," averred Little Abie, "on some other occasion I would have been honoured to enjoy your *hospitality*, but by Jove and Jehovah a long road still unwinds before me. I wend my way in quest of a stout *Stranger*, mantled in dark raiment, whose kettle I have mended and on whose *munificence* I rely to *reward* my labours, yea though I *lavish* a lifetime in looking for him." Before Little Abie could proceed with his pretty peroration, an auditor in proximity *bestowed* a well-positioned blow upon the side of the skull of the cheery chap that sent him sprawling.

"Gracious *Stranger* be d – – – ed!" roared the ruffian. "He's the one that fired this town!" Little Abie could barely believe the evidence of his ears. "Yes, fired this town! He came through here *selling* his wares and making various *promises,* but he never *paid off* on one of them. His reputation got so tarnished that no one *trusted* him, so he fired the town. Used that hayloft yonder for tinder. *Belonged* to Lancelot's wife who turned back to *save* it, but the fire felled her." Sundry survivors of the disaster, some of whom had lost cherished children or kith and kin, and some even their *possessions,* nodded in sorrowful *certification* of all that he had said.

Even so, Little Abie elected to persevere in his search, for he judged no one by hearsay alone. The friendly folk of Hohokus, though, entreated him to tarry for a time and restore himself in one of the enchanting inns which had received *rich* praise in *plenty* of periodicals. They commended the cardinal qualities of the Dew Drop Inn, U Kan Kom Inn, Kan-Tuck-U-Inn, Gid Inn, Peri's Swish Inn, Dontravellinn, Cliff's Inn (Drop Over & See Us), Welcommin, We-Ask-U-Inn, Suitsme Contemporary Courts, King Arthur's Kourts, Kumhavarest Kottages, Hatetoleavit Hotel, Holmes Sweet Home, Last Course Restaurant and Resort, Honest Inn and Out, Full Measure Cafe and Rooms, Ma's Rheum & Bored, Pa's Place (Plain Provisions), Uncle Tomahawk's End of the Trail Lodge (Reservations Restricted to Redskins), and various others which boasted one virtue or another. But Little Abie stood firm to forge on, despite the drizzle of the day, and so the saddened citizens waved him fond farewell. He again packed upon his back the sack of *precious* books (less the *treasured* tome which he had *contributed* to the uplift of the bloodthirsty Old Chief) and the mended cooking kettle, and fared forth on his peregrinations afresh.

Little Abie soon sighted Saugus where he was in the nick of

time to witness a triple hanging and quartering, an event capped by the glare and the blare of a *festival* to which a *free* invitation was courteously *conveyed* to him. He approved this polite protestation and participated with good *grace* in a patriotic pageant in which female parts were *taken* by male parts. Blessed by the throng and bloated by the *banquet*, Little Abie *repaid* with a postprandial peroration that pointed attention and perpension to the three separated heads, already basking upon *sturdy* stakes, as admonishments to all who might be tempted to ramble down the low route to deceit. He *took* his leave of Saugus after learning that the sconces of the three scapegraces had been separated not so much because of deceit as because they were servants of the *Stranger* whom he sought. Oh, thought Little Abie, if only I had sighted Saugus sooner! I might then have learned from their *very own* lips, which now are stilled upon sunlit stakes, where I might seek the *Stranger!*

Undaunted, Little Abie again *took* up the trail of the *Stranger*. At Seekonk he fell in with a freckle-faced fellow a few years his senior, a little man with turned-up pantaloons and merry whistled tunes. They agreed to lighten the way by travelling together and *trading* tales, as merry lads are wont to do. And so the two young gentlemen set off down the winsome and winding byway, as perfect a pair as seen in Christendom.

After saying their prayers the good lads retired into repose, *secure* under the starlighted skies. Arising to greet Aurora and gently rubbing the slumber from his sleepy eyes, Little Abie noted the absence of his cheerful companion. Absent also was the backpack which had *possessed,* aside from a change of linen and his grandfather's *gold* timepiece, all his uplifting and *enriching* books. Little Abie hurled himself upon the sweet-smelling soil and wept sorrowfully into the smooth bosom of nurturing earth. But, gentle reader, think not that he cried his *copious* tears for his *precious possessions*. No! Little Abie lamented only that the freckle-faced and feckless fellow should by this act of absconsion have so imperilled the salvation and *evaluation* of his soul!

Little Abie again detected the trail of the *Stranger* at Skaneateles, and he followed it faithfully through Keokuk, Meleke, and Agawam. At Chicopee he lamented the wretchedness of the land, induced surely by insufficient *industry*, for in the Eden of America all blossoms *bountifully*. Little Abie wended west to Atchafalaya where he learned that the *Stranger* had hurriedly hastened from hence after by happenstance sparking a fire in the powder factory. At Appalachia Little Abie viewed a virtuous village *surfeited* by ten feet of water, induced, it was courteously communicated to him by a survivor who shouted from atop a tree, by the *Stranger* when he inadvertently deflected the wrong lever on the levee. At Shawangunk it was readily declared that a gentleman delineated as the one described had leaned too *generously* against the *bank* door, and in that way accidentally encouraged the timbers, which probably had furnished a *free feast* for termites, to tear asunder. Although the good burghers were busy as beavers ascertaining the bank's *assets*, they troubled to *tender* to Little Abie information that the *Stranger* had embarked downriver in a barge for the beckoning lands of The Great West.

A lad less scrupulous than Little Abie might have thought he had searched sufficiently for the *Stranger* to have fully discharged his *debt*. But *No!* Little Abie thought, How could I in the future face my dear *Mother* in faraway New Salem if I do not *expend* my uttermost breath to seek the *Stranger* who committed his cooking kettle to my care!

Little Abie was not able to arrange accommodations on a river-*worthy* craft whereby to seek the *Stranger*, for all of the barges had been bespoke by The Great *White* Father to furnish *free* transport for the red heathens to the beauteous and *bountiful* oasis of Oklahoma where Flora with a wanton hand had *dispersed* her earthly delights. A contemptible tribe of Indians, looking as maculate and mendacious as they have been oft delineated in the chronicles of our Nation, had newly arrived at the waterway. They were escorted by sturdy soldiers, resplendent in their regalia, their sabers shiny and sharp, a conspicuous contrast between the blessings of civilization and heathen hope-lessness. Little Abie thrilled in his heart of hearts to be an American when he saw with his *very own* eyes how his Nation's ungrudging *munificence* was succouring these surly savages.

"D – – – ed savages!" exclaimed one enthusiastic gentleman who was ensconced alongside Little Abie. "Them d – – – ed injuns got the impewdence to object to bein transported *free and clear* to Oklahoma—to a *paradise!*—to *God's Country!* I've spoke with folks that been there and they tell me there ain't no blizzards, hurricanes, tornadoes, earthquakes, or hailstorms. Somethin can be planted most any time of the year and har-vested *at your leisure.* I hear you plant corn and afore you're all the way down the row you look back and the plants are already sproutin up! You eat homegrown July vegetables in January, and they say the fish in the rivers and lakes is available *with no effort.* I hear the whole country is civilizin rapidly and land *prices* are *risin* fast, so you can get in on the ground floor of a very *fast-movin investment.* And the taxes is so *low* you can take them out of your tobaccy *money* and still have *lots of cash* left over. Anybody can become *rich* enough in a year to travel around in the *best society.* The constant sea breezes from the Pacific Ocean make for cool summers and warm winters. They say Oklahoma is so peaceful you can sleep with your doors and windows unlocked with no fear of your *property* sufferin any. And all agree that because of the uncommon *purity* of the air people rarely die, except from murder or accident or old age or complaints. Yessir, folks comin back from The Great West say they don't have to prove none of these things—they just admit them! It's *God's Country!*"

"Sir, your countenance may be cut sharp like *expensive* crys-tal," exclaimed Little Abie, "but your words ring as true as the bright bell atop the belfry in New Salem village! I now clearly comprehend the concern that the civilizing influence be per-mitted to perform its *wonders* upon those heathen hordes brought low indubitably by their own debauchery. I had re-cently in my *possession* pious books which I would have promptly passed into their lying and looting hands, but the *treasured* tomes were separated from me by a freckle-faced fellow while I *surfeited* myself with sleep."

Because the indolent Indians had appropriated all the craft for their own carefree *cruise* to the lands conveyed to them *free and clear* in The Great West, Little Abie was forced to face the wilderness on his lively limbs. His determination, though, had not abated one whit and it still *grew bountifully* like a green bay tree or well-invested *greenbacks*. Little Abie marched into the western wilderness with neither musket nor *money*—armed only with his own true heart!—in search of a *Stranger* of whose peregrinations he knew no more than he knew his name. Little Abie still protected the *precious* kettle, and he let no opportunity pass to polish it so that it retained the radiance which he had diligently rendered it. Putting one leg in front of the other, he reached Defeated, Tennessee, but found a plague in *possession* of the place, the origin of which was an embroidered handkerchief the *Stranger* had inadvertently let drop from his pocket. Colonel Sellers, a natural enthusiast, *selled* him a ticket on a *luxurious* railroad line through Slouchburg, Doodleville, Belshazzar, Catfish, Babylon, Bloody Run, Hail Columbia, and Hark from the Tomb. Little Abie was fully *fortunate* to have obtained, *at good price*, the right to ride this railroad on its inaugural schedule, as soon as the *kings of fortune* had stockpiled sufficient *capital* to drive the first *golden* spike. But it is what we might have expected, for good little boys are always finding exceptional *fortune*.

Little Abie faced his frisky feet toward Kokomo, Kankakee, and Kaskaskia before setting his steps in the direction of Shakakko. He tarried only a short time in the last-listed locale because he could scarcely stomach the stench, for they were hog butcher for the world. At Shakakko, though, he was again *treated* to tidings of the *Stranger* who, he learned, had taken dignified departure after he accidentally rammed a hole in the dam, the result of which was loss of life and the ruination of much *property*. He tarried upon the *Stranger's* trail again at

Wounded Knee where he watched the *persevering* pioneers extirpate by antiseptic fire an Indian settlement that posed a threat to the *progress* and *plenty* which is *owed* to every *property owner*. At Loco, Arkansas, he acknowledged that the *aspirations* of the Indians were in the ascent, for they were energetically *employed* in honestly hunting the boundless buffaloes that the tasty tongues might be *exported* eastward to tempt the table of many a *hustling* and bustling *businessman*. So stimulated was the Indians' *industry*, impelled by *promises* of *currency* and quality beverages, that the shaggy beasts were promptly being expunged as impediments in the path of *Progress*.

Little Abie almost encountered the *Stranger* at Bowlegs, Oklahoma, for that industrious gentleman had tarried there to outfit himself with a *select* passel of slaves. Little Abie missed him once more at Nip and Tuck, Texas, where the *Stranger* had been delayed by the duty of *meting out* justice to a slave family, *fortunately* a small one, which up to their last moments enthusiastically debated the efficacy of the established institution of *indenture*. The plucky lad lost the scent again when the *Stranger* veered north to the village of Disobeyed, Oklahoma, but thereafter Little Abie travelled fast and light in his quest, inquiring for the *Stranger* in Poker Flat, What Cheer, Righteous Ridge, Despond, Scratch Gravel, Pinchtown, Hazard, Last Chance, War Whoop, Bloody Run, Lick Skillet, Buck Snort, Fair Play, Truth or Consequences, Steal Easy, Jacks Wild, Winner Take All, Necktie Party, Sinful, Tarnation Trot, not to mention Stone Dead, Hanging Tree, Tight Noose, Massacre Valley, Bloody Valley, Verdant Valley, Ambush Gulch, Poverty Slant, Rope Collar, Dead Injuns Gulch, Hidden Guns Hollow, Sixshooter Draw, Last Card, Posse's Success, Loser's Rest, Dirty Water, Troublesome, Hopper's Banquet, Sodville, Dust, and Squabble, as well as Skinout, Greasy Spoon, Hog Eye, Niggerhead Hollow, Last Mile, End of the Trail, Dissension, Sporting Life, Revenge, Grand Chance, Golden Dream, Honest Policy, God's Country, Opportunity, Justice, Mercy, Dear Heart, Mother's Memory, and several other towns that had been erected with whip and spur in the western wilderness. God be blessed, thought Little Abie, for He has assuredly made of us a great Nation.

And now, patient reader, we reach that moment in the life of Little Abie we have long anticipated with bated breath. Our scene is set upon the stage of the *bounteous* plain of Kansas, where Fauna has wantonly set an *abundance* of animals to disport around the spanking-new settlements. Here, where the American Dream is fated for fulfillment, Little Abie finally fetched up at the stopping place of the *Stranger*, his *select* passel of slaves, and their overworked overseers who nodded not at all the night through in order to shield and shepherd their childlike charges. During the years of discharging his duty, sturdy Little Abie had sprung up until he stood as straight as if a rod had been rammed down his backbone. His clothes, we will concede, were a trifle tattered, but he had not spared spotless soap and cleansing water, which are always the allies of a fastidious fellow. A bashful blush still decorated his downy cheeks, and he exuded good will from every pore. Here, at *Promised* Acres, Kansas, Little Abie at last came upon the camp of the *Stranger,* the object of his obstinate search.

"Oh, sir," began Little Abie—for he was forever as polite as if he were still his Mother's son in the virtuous village of New Salem—"Dear Sir, Kind Sir, Good Sir, Merciful One, Shepherd, Source of Comfort in Adversity, Watcher in the Sleep of Night, Light of Life—"

"Yeah?" inquired the solicitous *Stranger,* curious about this lanky lad with the cooking kettle.

"Wonderful, Counseller, Mighty, Everlasting, Prince, King, Prime Mover, Heart of Our Hearts, Fingernail Parer, Be-With-Us-Yetter, Hope of Our Salvation, Providence, Thee, All-Knowing, All-Seeing, Unspeakable Name—"

"Hurry it on up," quoth the *Stranger.*

"Beneficent, Terrible, Angry, Wrathful, Forgiving, Demanding, Omnipotent, Omniscient, Omnipresent, Eternal, Creator, Preserver, He of Our Fathers of Old, Ineffable, Immutable, Insubstantial—Him!"

"Stop grovellin, boy, and git on with it. Yer holdin up my *select* passel of slaves," the *Stranger* admonished Little Abie who, we must admit, indulged himself under a full head of steam.

Little Abie bent his body in another bow and resumed his address of the *Stranger*. "Dear Sir, how might I adequately avouch the adventures I have had and the wonders of this wide Nation that have been my education in my persistent search for *you!* Oh, Kind Sir, the obstacles I have overcome in my quest for a *Stranger* whose name I did not even know! But, Good Sir, let me dally no longer. You had sought and selected me to do you good *Service*, and I was neither loth nor wroth to give my oath. Without procrastination I now discharge the *debt* of my *obligation*. Here is the object I have protected in preference to my own *possessions* or my own person! Here is your COOKING KETTLE!"

The *Stranger* relieved Little Abie's weary arms of the weight of the kettle. Then he remarked to the lad in an unruffled yet rebuking utterance, "You sure took your time gittin here."

The *Stranger* next ordered his overworked overseers to set the *select* slaves, who had naught to do but idle, stirring again. And so they parted, after which a lively Little Abie retraced his trail through all the *thriving* villages which he had visited on his adventures. By and by he returned to *nurturing* Connecticut where other bright-eyed boys and freckle-faced fellows had been *diligent* also, for Elias Howe of Bridgeport had invented the sewing machine, Samuel Colt of Hartford both laughing gas and the revolver, David Bushnell of Westbrook the submarine, Charles Spencer of Hartford the *repeating* rifle, Charles Goodyear of New Haven the wondrous rubber, Eli Whitney of Whitneyville the *productive* cotton gin, Joseph Ive of Bristol the *cheap* kitchen clock, Abel Buell of Killingworth a *counterfeiting* machine, John Howe the *straight* pin, Linus Yale, Jr., of New Haven the dial-and-combination lock, Hiram Hayden of Waterbury the kerosene lantern, Tom Sanford of Beacon Falls the *faultless* friction match, Eb Jenks of Colebrook the *steel* fishhook, and Alonzo House of Bridgeport the horseless carriage. Little Abie cared not a straw for the fame and *fortune* that might have been his had he stayed home and tinkered, for he was pleased as punch that he had done *what any good lad should always do!*

■

ALL CLEAR. There he goes into post office. Abie Freudenthal, king of the Jews, loves the coloreds and sings their Blooz, to Jerusalem he pays his dues, Abie knows he'll never lose. Dum-dum-dum-DUM. Last crossing. Wait. All right. Curbstone. Be careful. Up and over. Excelsior! Few more steps. Awning down. "Jim's Barber Shop" painted on its flaps. Phoney olde scripte. The E looks like an A. Jim the Bar-bar-Barbarian. Door always squeaks. He never oils it. Wastes his time talking.

— Well, hi there, Mistah Punman! You come right in. Jest be a shake.

Chair wobbles. Try another. That's better. Ease in. Backside itching again. Stop by Myer's later. Smart-aleck signs. "In God We Trust, But Customers Pay Cash." "We Fight Poverty—We Work." "If You're So Smart, Why Ain't You Rich?" I'm next. Only a few minutes' wait if Jim stops gabbing. Wiseacre. From Alabama or someplace. Mirrors reflect me. Bounce my image back and forth. They get smaller each time. Why? Don't mirrors reflect the same size? Does the image eventually disappear? Ask someone sometime. Whom could I ask? Not important.

Magazines. Sprinkled with other people's hair. Snippets of our community. The Great American Molting Pot. Look at my mail. No sender's name. Just a box-office number. In New York. Oh, oh. Looks raunchy. Throw it away. No, not here. Someone might see my name on it. Get rid of it later. Tear my name off the envelope first. How did they get my name? People say they buy them from reputable businesses. Whom can you trust nowadays? Jim's still gabbing. Takes him twice as long. Newcomer also. Someone left today's *Times*. Do the puzzle now? No, I'll buy the paper later from Pete. Do it as the usual nightcap. A solitary pleasure. No, why waste? A penny saved. The paper will only be thrown out. Parsimoney.

— Say, Jim, I wonder if you mind my tearing out the puzzle.

— Whass that, Mistah Punman?

— I said, Do you mind if I tear out the crossword puzzle from *The New York Times*?

— Help yerself, Mistah Punman, my pleashur. Don't spect none of the other customers will be wantin it. And if they do, they can jest buy their own paper fer a dime.

Where is it? Oh yes, book page. *The Group*. Still selling. The new Michener novel. Here it is. Tear down the edge first. There. Now across this corner. Oh, damn! Tore off the answer to Saturday's. Ruined it. Smudged. I had it right, though. I think. Well, do today's. Get ahead of the day. Have more time tonight. For what? The Black Book. Looks like an easy one. One across, "Green." Jade? It fits. Now, one down, "Hoodoo." Jinx. Voodoo will hoodoo. Two down, "Field." Area? Yes. Three down, "Out's partner." Tennessee's partner. Down. Answer to three down is "Down." Four down, "Involve." Entail. Back to across. Five across, "Kind of puzzle." Rebus? Yes, fits. Five down, "Needed." Required. Six down, "Blank de cologne." Eau. Mother loved Paris. Seven down, "Stick of a fan." Starts with a B. Four letters. Mother always had one. Brin? That's right. Eight down, "Say." Utter. Nine down, "Jewish month." Damn! How am I supposed to know that? They're even in my cross-word puzzle. Unfair. Stuck already. Well, maybe I can work around it. Let's see now. Oh, oh. My nose itches. The superstition is true. If the nose itches, it's a sign of nosey company. He finished at the post office fast. He gets good service. Big tipper at Christmas. Make believe I'm dozing. Close eyes. Let Jim gab with him. Finish puzzle tonight. Lower chin. Breathe regularly.

— Hello, Ben.

Don't answer. Snore. Gurgle. Hrmmph.

— Come on in, Mistah Fraudall. You're next, right after Mistah Punman. How's that fine house of yours comin?

— Coming right along, Jim. We're trying to finish the restoration before snow starts.

— By the sound of the bangin acrost the common, you're makin progress. You sure know how to get a day's pay out of the men, Mistah Fraudall.

— Have to stay on top of them, Jim. Otherwise they'd never do a thing. Lazy. They hardly speak English.

— Thass right. Eyetalians. Rather sip wine than work honest. Reason that they're always thinkin bout love-makin.

— I can't wait just now, Jim. Have to be back at the bank at three thirty. Important visitor from New York. I'll stop by first thing in the morning. See you.

Fine, Freudenthal, fine. A tribe of fine Fraudalls. A peculiar people.

— Mistah Punman! Ah say, Mistah Punman! I'm ready fer you now. Jest step right up to the big ole chair. Thass right. No sense rushin yourself and perhaps takin a fall. Jest let me settle this towel round your neck. Thass it. It sure tickled me to see you fakin sleep when Mistah Fraudall was in here.

— Pardon?

— Now, don't you tell me different, Mistah Punman, cause I seen you. Yessir, when folks with different customs come round, kindest thing is jest to make believe you dozed off.

— I guess I did drop off for a moment, Jim. I didn't sleep well last night. I wouldn't be intentionally rude.

— Neither would I. None of us wants nasty things gettin out where they can pollute the fresh air.

— He is a little forward sometimes, though.

— Thass my feelin too. He ain't backward bout bein forward. Fancy dresser too. Bet that sharpskin suit cost two hundred dollars.

— I don't know.

— Might even cost more. You know, my nose itched afore he come in. My daddy always said it's a sure sign of nosey company comin. The tribe of Big Noses. A feller wunst told me their true Savior is the plastic surgeon. Haw-haw.

— Well.

— Anyway Mistah Fraudall got enough pushin to do to keep them lazy Eyetalians workin.

— Not all of them are lazy, Jim. My new secretary is Italian. She's very conscientious.

— You're lucky. You get a gem. But I bet she ain't too smart.

— No. I guess not.

— See? Anyway, Mistah Fraudall's tribe sure is smart with a dollar. They got the inside track on business, so you got to skin them afore they skin you. But you think Mistah Fraudall ever gave me a tip on the stock market? No sir, plays his cards mighty close to the vest. Well, like I was sayin, sumtimes the best thing is jest to avoid unpleasantness with folks that is different in customs from you. Thass what Jake Lord did, and everyone in New Canaan knew he was the smartest feller they ever did see. Thass where I hail from, you know, Canaan County in middle Tennessee. Down there we was all B.V.D.s— Baptist and Very Democrat. That was afore the Tee-Vee-Ay Dam flooded out the town and I started my wanderins. Sure appreshate the way you folks in New Salem let me set up here. I mean, my bein a newcomer and all. I'm right proud of the way my business been goin here, and I can tell you my feelin is mutchal toward all you folks. Yessir, New Salem is my home now. Anyway, I bet we done more cuttin up in New Canaan than in any town its size in the whole Yewnited States. Course a lot of it was due to Bubba Lord. Thass Jake's brother. Bubba sure used to keep the whole town in stitches. He was as sociable as a basket of kittens. Every Satiday night reglar, while all the fellers was round the barbershop sittin and spittin, ole Bubba would stop by my shop after he finished huntin and ask fer a shave and a lil touchin up round the ears. He'd start off the conversashun with me by sayin sumthin like, "You still clippin your customers, Jim?" or "Jim, you're gettin mighty uppity fer a mere shaver." It don't sound real funny when you

79

ain't got Bubba right in front of you, but if you was there I bet you would of laughed more than watchin a barrel of monkeys. Bubba sure was lighthearted. He'd screw most anythin on two legs, ceptin maybe kangaroos and newborns. Now, Jake Lord was tirely different. Jake was always proper in his bearin. Nobody ever saw him cut up none or spend his earnins on frivolities. Played his cards close to his vest. And he was so tough you couldn't stick a fork even into his gravy. That was how he hung on to his territory durin the hard-luck times of The Great Depreshun when most folks had to scrounge for their three squares. Yessir, steady as a ruler he was. Jake was a drummer and most of his trade was them lil Bible communities up in east Tennessee. Jake sure knew how to handle them hillbillies right and proper. He acted like he was their kissin cousin, jokin with the menfolk and speakin right courtly to the ladies. They thought he was real city, what with his hair so greased you could see your face in it. Ole Jake made his rounds of them hillbilly communities jest workin them over like a mower goin over a hayfield. Aside from fancy cloths, he also sold them thimbles, messerin tapes, brass buckles, pins, needles, needle cases, hooks, eyes, awls, wire, buttons in all assorted sizes, slates and chalk, pens, ink, pocket combs, spectacles, soap, shavin soaps, razors, brushes, shells from Floridah fer the windersill, nail files, fiddle strings, colored string, fancy braslets fer the young girls and brootches fer the old ones, Jew's harps, whistles fer the children, fancy belts, hat plumes, frocks, shoes, straw hats, gloves, yarn, shawls, bandanna kerchiefs, antimacassars, Bibles, loaf tobaccy, snuff, smellin bottles, astringents, stimulants, ungents, pungents, emetics, laxatives, cathartics, diuretics, yerbs, bitters, ferment, essences, wintergreen, corn plaster, castor oil, mustard, elegant pills, green tea, gum drops, honey, balsam, elixir, wormin powder, lozenges, comfits, mints, chinaware, sieves, tallow, scales, weights, tin messers, gill dippers, friction matches, dyes, whetstones, shears, steel traps, cages, birdshot, skinnin knives, kitchen knives, throwin knives, candle molds, workbaskets, pastry stamps, wooden bowls, mortars, colanders, graters, dustpans, jars, porringers, churns, pitchers, pepper boxes, lanterns, reprodukshuns of famous picshurs, the End of the Trail bronze statue fer the mantelpiece, B.V.D.s, personal products fer women, the Haldemann-Julius Little Blue Books, and a few notions I don't reklect now. Well, ole Jake was mighty sharp in all his dealins, not at all like Bubba who weren't very bright. Jake and Bubba came out of their momma fightin with each other worse than two crows on a tree branch. And they never laid off afterwards, them bein so different and all. Hardly a day passed that ole Jake didn't trick sumthin out of Bubba. Bubba was so dumb he'd spend his last dollar to buy a wallet to put it in. Like one time I remembers real well when Jake tells Bubba that he has a yewnique opportunity to purchase a live mountain-roarer from one of the folks up in his territory. "A mountain-roarer?" asks Bubba, cause even with all his experience as a hunter he hadn't never come upon such an animal. "Yessir," replies Jake real smart, "a livin and healthy mountain-roarer, possibly the last one of its generashun. Undoubtedly you has heard tell of this beast under another one of the names it sometimes goes by. Like rumptifusel? Or luferlang? You ain't? How bout hodag? No? Well, a mountain-roarer is bout the size of a weasel, only much bigger, and like a hunred in feroshus meanness. His food primarily is the livin flesh of other animals, though occashunally he takes birds and snakes. He's so wild that none has ever been able to tame him, though a few has tried, them havin only a stump instead of an arm or leg to remind them of the experience. His skin is uncommonly fine and coats made out of it would probably fetch you bout hunred, two hunred dollars—each one! But nobody would be so fool as to destroy a live mountain-roarer jest to get its fur!" Jake laid it on so thick you'd think he was goin to rupture his story. But it held the strain. Well now, Mistah Punman, you and I are smart enough to know there jest ain't no such beast and never was. But Bubba never learned that the safest way to double your money is to fold it over and keep it in your pocket. Bubba was mighty het up bout ownin this here animal.

Jake tells Bubba that he'll try to negoshate fer the beast, but he'll need the money in advance. So Bubba rushes to their daddy and tells him he been offered a yewnique opportunity to go into business and better hisself. Now, daddy was always one out to make a fast buck hisself, though he weren't partikly successful at it. In fact, bad luck followed him round like a stray dog. So the daddy rushes down to the Cornhuskers Bank & Fidushary Company and borrows all the money he can. When it came to shrewdness that daddy was jest as blind as the nails in a coffin. Bubba then hands over his birthright money to Jake and tells him to rush off to his kissin cousins and negoshate fer the mountain-roarer. Afore he leaves, Jake says to Bubba, "While I'm off negoshatin, you start talkin the mountain-roarer up round town and at the barber shop. In a few days you won't have no trouble sellin tickets fer two bits each, half price fer children, coloreds, and feeble-mindeds. Since I'm troublin to act as your finanshul agent in this endeavor, it peers to me like I am entitle to a small percent of whatever you takes in. Agreed? Good. Now, Bubba, you tell folks that next Thursday evenin, long bout seven sharp, you is goin to put on exibishun a beast never seen by human eyes afore, least not in middle Tennessee. Thass when I'll be back with your animal." Jest like Jake told him to, Bubba puts up a tent and gets some boards fixed up fer seats. Come Thursday, by only six o'clock in the evenin everyone in town who could walk, crawl, stagger, or be carried was in that tent waitin fer Jake to arrive with the beast. Long bout seven comes the sound of Jake's panel truck rattlin up the hill. And out of it folks could hear the loudest roarin that ever attacked your ears, sumthin like a trumpet bein blowed by a bull moose. Jake parks the truck behind the tent, and I admit that some of us had strong apprehenshuns to hear that roarin so close by. But Jake is calm as a newborn calf and tells Bubba he is now the proud owner of a genyewine mountain-roarer. He also reminds Bubba to hand over the small percent of the money taken in fer the exibishun—which percent Bubba later figures out came to slightly more than half. So Jake goes back into the truck to put some heavy chains round the feroshus beast, and soon we hears rattlin and bangin and a fearful roarin. All of a sudden Jake comes rushin into the tent bloody as a butcher. "Run fer your very lives!" he yells. "The feroshus mountain-roarer done escaped!" Well, the folks flew off in every direkshun and course none of them took the time to ask fer their money back. Sum of the folks expected that Jake was torn limb from limb and all thass left of him might be his leather belt and shoelaces which were too tough to eat, plus of course his heart which was even tougher. But the smarter ones come back to the truck the next mornin. Now, I won't say these folks was suspicious, but they did remind me sum of the sick man who receives a get-well card from the undertaker. One of them says, "I wonder if ole Jake, now that he is the victim of the feroshus mountain-roarer, would mind if we jest took a peek inside that truck." So they opens the doors to the truck and, sure nuff, there were some of the heaviest chains you ever saw, although I admit they was a bit rusted. There was a hunk of steer meat on the floor that the feroshus beast might of been gorgin hisself upon, though it looked to me like the blood been drawn off first. And down at the end of the truck was a victrola with a record on it entitled "The Fearsum Sounds of African Animals." Yessir, ole Jake sure pulled that one off and got away slick as a snake out of its skin. Jake sure conned Bubba out of his birthright. But of course now Jake had to find hisself a new town to settle in, since he figured he had everythin to live fer and nothin to die fer. So he went back to his territory in east Tennessee and there he fell head over heels with a cute lil girl, so serious an afflikshun that he even wanted to marry her. Her daddy was a right crafty feller and he said Jake'd jest have to make up fer the loss of purty lil Rae by puttin in sum time workin at his store, like six seven years, without the divershun of gettin a salary. But love sure does confuse a man as to where his best interests lie, and so Jake agreed without dickerin more than ten fifteen minutes. Jake fulfilled his part of the bargain by givin honest labor to her daddy, skinnin all his neighbors fer him, cheatin all the widders and starvin all the orphans, cuttin the moonshine with water and the flour with chalk, and in genral ways givin devoted service. After bout six seven years, which time passed so fast it was only like days, ole Jake reminds Rae's daddy of the bargain. "Yessir," the swindler says, "I well recklect my promise. Since you have discharged your obligashuns fair and square, I am goin to give you in sacred marriage my ever-lovin daughter—Lena." Now, I tell you, Mistah Punman, that girl was so runty she could fall through a flute and never stop a note. Not to menshun she had a complexshun like a potato. Jake was real taken back, but he stayed cool as a melon in the summerhouse. He tells the daddy that he was under the distinct impreshun that he had been laborin fer the purty lil daughter Rae and not her sister Lena. "Rae!" says the ole cheat. "Why, I never understood no such thing! I couldn't give away that preshus lil girl merely fer six seven years of shopkeepin. I'd say you got a bit more time to spend behind the counter afore I give you *her!*" Yessir, ole Jake sure was conned for wunst. So he went back to workin some more, lyin and cheatin and paddin bills and shortweightin and in genral ways carryin out his part of the bargain honestly. Well, all this time the years was flyin by and Rae weren't such an eye-grabber like she been at first. To tell the truth, she was puttin on a little flesh round the ankles and her skin was peppered in sevral places. Yessir, Jake finally did get to marry Rae, even though by then she had gotten a bit micey. By this time Jake was pretty well satisfied that he had enjoyed all the attrakshuns that east Tennessee had to offer, which was mostly thorns and gullies and stomach poisonin and an occashunal mad dog fer divershun. So he decides to seek out his fortune in The Great American West. He and Rae take off to get one of them farms sumone said the goviment was givin away, not neglectin to carry with them whatever chickens and tools and anythin else portable they could steal off the daddy-in-law. But Jake wasn't never the kind to ferget that he came out on the short side of a swindle. All the time he was in Kansas, eatin that dust and

84

divin into the cellar every few hours to escape from twisters and shakin centipedes out of his bed, he never fergot bout them thirteen fourteen years of his life he gave to daddy-in-law fer free. After Jake's farm takes off one day and blows to another state, Jake concludes that Kansas got more troubles than Heinz got pickles. So one night he and Rae sneak off, leavin enough unpaid bills to wallpaper the state capitol, and head back to east Tennessee. Well now, Jake left Kansas in the most beatup automobile I spect anyone ever seen allowed on the nashun's roads. At the first town he comes to he swaps it fer a slightly better automobile, though that fact probably weren't apparent to anyone else but Jake. He keeps swappin his autos at every town he comes to, each time makin a slightly better deal for hisself, until by the time he reaches east Tennessee he's drivin a spankin new Pierce tourin car with all delucks equipment. When they is only a few miles away from Rae's town, Jake shines up the Pierce real good. Then he gets Rae to fix herself up in the fancy dress she got left over from the saloon-and-cowboy hospitality center Jake set up in Kansas known as Frere Jock's. And he drapes round her neck some flashy stones which he took off a nigger and he wraps one of them fancy blankets round her shoulders that he stole off an injun. They arrive at the store still bein run by Rae's daddy and right off Jake observes that the place, which used to be dirty as ditchwater and bout the size of a dog kennel, has been painted and a new extry room nailed onto the back. Seems like the daddy-in-law done coaxed prosperity out of hidin while Jake been gone. But that don't beat Jake down none. He steps out of that Pierce delucks like he was the lost Dauphin hisself, and he helps Rae out too, her nigger jewels flashin fit to blind you. After all the kissin and huggin is over, Rae trots off to boast to her friends what millionaires they become. The daddy-in-law of course wants to hear how Jake made his pile, and so he fixes to close up the store early. He calls inside to where the clerk has been workin like a hiveful of bees all day and he asks, "Asher, are you finished yet with waterin the moonshine?"

"Sure am," the bright-eyed lad replies. "And you done addin sand to the brown sugar?" "Yessir, I done that already." "Very good. And did you get round to squeezin that widder fer her bill—you know, the one that got those five children that look uncommon thin?" "Yessir, I did that too." "Well, thass jest fine, Asher. I guess you can leave fer prayer meetin now." So Jake and his daddy-in-law sits down on the front porch and you can jest bet that somebody is mighty ankshus to hear what opportunities is like out West. But Jake jest heads him real easy, like a butcher tryin to work the hog into the chute. "Yessir," Jake says like he was reflectin, "I sure is homesick already fer my estate in Kansas."

"Estate! Ha!" says his disbelievin daddy-in-law.

"Thass right. My estate. I feels mighty poorly in this climate, so I don't know how much longer me and Rae will be able to visit with you afore the bad air gets us. I spect we'll have to jump into our delucks tourin car and head back to the County of Immortality."

"County of Immortality?"

"Thass right. Thass what we calls it. Course I'd appreshate if you didn't tell that to none of the folks hereabouts. We wants to keep strangers away, else all the bennyfits of The Great West gets divvied up too thin. I can tell *you*, though, it's really sumthin when folks never die, cept by bein killed."

"Never die!"

"Thass right. We lives till we die. It's an impossibility to die premashur because the dryness and uncommon purity of the air prevents any germs from growin. Well now, I wasn't really one hunred percent truthful when I menshuned no one died cept by bein killed."

"Ha! Thought I'd catch you!"

"Well, you did, and I'll try to pay more attenshun to details. You're right. There is one other way fer a person to die. Thass if he was ever blowed outside the state of Kansas. Then the foul air of the territories that surround Kansas might cause his premashur demise. I myself got to head back with Rae real soon afore all our allowable time outside of Kansas gets used up."

"Used up?"

"Thass right," says Jake. "In fact, if anyone plans to leave the state of Kansas fer more than two three months, he got to inform his legal execyewtors whether he wishes to stay dead or whether he wishes to be hauled back to Kansas to be revivified."

"Now, why should any man want hisself dead if he can help it?"

"Cause," Jake explains pashently, "you folks here in miserable east Tennessee jest can't imagine what a weight and responsibility it is to have to go to a lugshurious office two three mornins a week to manage all them portfolios. You jest don't realize the terrible responsibility we has towards widders and orphans from other states what has entrusted their money to us fer investin in God's Country. You don't understand the heap of trouble it is to have to keep multiplyin the value of your possesshuns by two every month, or sumtimes by three durin the busy Christmas and Easter seasons. You don't know what it's like to live fer three four hunred years and get all worn out from the tribyewlashuns of high finance. I tell you, it is worth bein dead jest to get away from them phone calls from Wall Stritt bankers."

"You mean Wall Script bankers call *you*—direct?"

"Thass right. But I don't always talk to them aritocranks. Ushally I'm too busy managin my own portfolios to take on any new folks' investments."

"That sure takes bluff."

"Well, it's a charity when I does take them on, cause they makes their fortunes inside a year. As I was sayin, after a time some folks does want a release from this burdensome life of ours. So all they got to do is leave Kansas fer some other state fer two three months. I knowed a merry lad of two hunred sevenny who went to Oklahoma and inside of two months he crumpled up. Seein as he had no kin in Oklahoma, the offishals there jest shipped him back to Kansas where they interred him. Everyone was weepin to see such a young boy torn from the world. But no more than a half hour after the rejuvenatin effects of the Kansas soil acted on him, the spark of life was restored to his bones. Them gravediggers was mighty put out to see a cadaver they jest tucked in come diggin hisself out and bawlin fer his momma. No, hangin is the only way we got to keep a man kilt proper out in Kansas."

"Fer fact?"

"Thass right. And I'll tell you nother thing. You ever heard tell bout the freeze-dried process?"

"Nope."

"Didn't spect you did. Ain't sumthin we wants to get nosed about. Well, sir, it is a patented process that was developed by the Kansas Histerical Society."

"Tell me bout it."

"Sure will," said Jake. "Sum of the folks who already lived fer maybe three four hunred years and still couldn't see even the approach of middle age, who was fed up to the gullet with the responsibilities of high finance, well these folks endowed the Histerical Society to find a painless way they could be released from their cares. But of course they wanted to hedge their bets and stay alive at the same time."

"Of course."

"Thass right. Well, this Histerical Society hired sum of the best brains to work night and day till they found a way. And they did! So now all these folks got to do is carry theirselves to the Histerical Society offices where they is put in a speshal machine that chills them and gently draws off their moisture. Thass why it's called freeze-dried."

"That makes sense," agreed daddy-in-law.

"Sure does. Then the Histerical Society places each new acquizishun in a metal cabinet, painted on the outside with flower pictures done by Grandma Moses and other famous artists, labels the box with its own yewnique number, and gently tilts it up against the wall of the Liberry."

"Of the Liberry?"

"Thass right. Any time the acquizishun's kin wants to gossip, all they got to do is go to the Liberry. There's an ole lady there with a pencil stuck in her moley hair who helps you look up the number in a big catalog. Then you fills out a speshal form, makin three copies. It's a bit of a bother, but it gives you the security of knowin they won't mix the cadavers up."

"Sure does."

"Thass what I always figured too. Oh, I fergot to menshun one other thing. You got to pay a fee."

"Aha!"

"Only six bits."

"Oh. Sure sounds like it's worth it, though."

"Thass what I always say. And you don't pay this fee without gettin bennyfits in return. Included in the price is the expense of huntin up the box in which your kin is residin and transportin it to the Rejuvenatin Room. Thass where some fine gentlemen in clean white gloves open the box real careful and spray the cadaver with pure tepid water. By and by your kin comes to life reconstituted jest as natchral as life. Then after you've both had your fill of conversashun, the cadaver is froze again, the water wiped off him with a clean sponge, and the box tilted up against the wall."

"I can hardly believe it!"

"Well, it's jest as true as everythin else I been tellin you. And I'll tell you sumthin else. I wunst got to wonderin why none of the gold that the injuns stole off the Western Pacific in eighty-nine was never recovered. I learnt the injuns kilt every white feller on that gold train cept one that had, by coincidence, wunst been the owner of an estate I done purchased tween phone calls from Wall Stritt. So I decided to look him up—his name was Sam Slick, cept he changed it fer business reasons—and do him the kindness to let him know how his estate was gettin on."

"Mighty white of you."

"Always happy to do a turn. So I went to the Liberry and found him filed under the catalog number LC 63-5724." Ole Jake then draws his chair up confidenshal to his daddy-in-law and whispers, "I got sum informashun to impart, if I can rely on your good judgment."

"Course you can. A man don't want to get the name of an idle gossip."

"Well, since you'll never be fortunate enough to get to Kansas, I can tell you with no fear of givin away the secret that LC is a speshal code the liberrians use. It signifies to them what knows that the feller bearin those letters in front of his number is one that was hung afore bein freeze-dried."

"Declare!"

"Thass right. Well, I filled out the forms proper, paid my six-bits fee, and had ole LC 63-etcetra thawed out. After the polite formalities was over and I had given him all the news bout how his estate was gettin on, not to menshun all the gossip bout the butlers—"

"Butlers!"

"Thass right. Two of them, cause one gets off evenins so's he can manage his own estate. Well, soon ole LC 63-etcetra got to confidin to me that he stole the gold back from the red savages hisself and stashed it away in a mighty tidy spot on his estate— which, in case you lost the track of the story, is the very one I own. Said he didn't have no need of the gold now that he had found peace and contentment in the freeze-dried condishun."

"Hell fire! You mean you was damn fool enough not to dig that gold up right away?"

"Jest hold your horses, daddy-in-law. That gold is good as money in the bank. Cause no one can get to talk to ole LC 63-etcetra cept the bearer of estate deed 57-46-35-24."

"Is that the estate deed I seen you jest glance at in your inside pocket?"

"The very one. But I wasn't expectin you'd catch me checkin to be sure it was still in my possesshun. Wanted to be sure it didn't get misplaced when the butler changed my clothes fer me. I'd be mighty indebted if you'd keep this confidenshal."

"Sure will."

"Much obliged. Anyway, price of gold is skyrocketin every

day. The longer you lets it lay in the ground the more it's worth. Jest like fine French likker in the cellar. I don't spect I'll have any pressin need for this gold in my lifetime, what with my Wall Stritt operashuns and all. I'll jest let my grandchildren or some cousin—*or whoever got this deed in his posseshun*—wait till they needs some tobaccy money."

"You mean—*anyone* who got that deed?"

"Thass right. I never said this deed natchrally got to stay in my blood line. I got so many investments all over Kansas I can't be troubled none by such a small thing as this."

"By God, you mean to tell me you would consider lettin that deed to your estate get out of *our* family! *Our* family! My preshus daughter what you took from me! No sir, a million times *no!* I would do most anythin to prevent your committin the sin of leavin your descendants without adequate gold reserves. And I could never stand the humiliashun—thass what it is—of havin strangers inherit my own daughter's birthright. No sir, not in a month of Sundays!"

"Golly, daddy-in-law, I jest didn't realize the seriousness of my decishun. I'm mighty obliged to you fer pointin out to me the error of my ways. But there's still a problem I got to study." So Jake puts his hands deep in his pockets and paces back and forth on the porch, lost in powerful deep thought. Then he mutters, as if talkin to hisself, "Oh, where would I ever find a person kind enough to relieve me of the responsibility I got towards that estate, and towards its previous owner, Mister LC 63-etcetra?"

"Son-in-law, I couldn't help but hear what you was, in your desperashun, mutterin to yourself. Seek no further! Paul traveled to Damascus and Peter to Rome. I spect I can make it to Kansas. *I* would be willin to assume your obligashuns toward that estate."

"That sure is white of you," replies Jake. "Course I wouldn't think of makin a profit out of your kindness."

"Mighty kind of you. Spoken like a grateful son-in-law."

"Don't menshun it. But I spect for your own personal reputashun in the community you would want to meet a few of the minor expenses attached to the estate."

"Such as?"

"Well now, lemmesee if I can think of any. Oh yes. I ought to be reimbursed fer my visit to the Liberry to see ole LC 63-etcetra. That makes six bits."

"Fittin and proper. An obligashun I will gladly discharge."

"Well, lemmesee if there's anythin else. Oh yes. In addishun to payin the six bits, I lost my pencil fillin out the forms, so that makes another—. Now, let me reklect since I don't want to Jew you. Was either three pennies or four pennies. Can't remember which."

"Don't matter none bout a penny, son-in-law. Make it four cents. Get on with it."

"Much obliged. Then of course I'll have to send the state the fee fer transferrin the deed, jest to make sure you got clear title. Thass two dollars. Costs another dollar fifty fer gettin an offishal copy made, plus the registrashun fee of twenny cents, and the thirty cents postage cost of mailin it first class to the state house—you wouldn't want to send it no other way than first class. Then also I think there was—"

"Come, come, Jake, jest give me a round figure."

"Lemmesee. There's a county tax of a dollar ten and a town tax of sevenny-six cents. Then there's the estate management firm in London, England, whose bill I jest paid fer a month in advance, which means you owe me nother four dollars. Well worth every cent, cause they sees that your butlers ain't swillin none of your fine French likker. Now, in addishun the owner of the estate is obliged to make sevral contribushons, such as two dollars to The Seminole Widow and Orphan Asylum. The Society fer the Convershun of the Hebrews gets a buck fifty. Then there's the Farmer's Union, the Boone and Crockett Club, Kansas Entomological Society, Clean Rivers Committee, Kansas Museum of Natchral History—each of them been promised a buck."

"By God, Jake, I am at the end of my pashence. I hope that does it. There can't be nothing else!"

"Guess not. Oh yes, I fergot. There's also contribushons to the Urban League, American Cancer Society, Liar's Club, Friends of Italian Opera, Linnaean Society, Humane Society, American Red Cross, Presbyterian Children, Salvashun Army, UNICEF, Fund fer the Concerned Photographer, Wycliffe Bible Society, Community Fund, Boys Clubs of America, DuBois Clubs of America, Internashunal Rescue Committee, Children's Blood Foundashun, Project Hope, Nashunal Council on Alcoholism, American Theayter Wing, Child Guidance Center, Women's Nashunal Council of the American Foundashun on Religion and Psychiatry—"

"Hell fire!"

"As I was about to say, each of them gets six bits. Now I can't ignore the solicitashuns of the Society fer the Prevenshun of Pauperism, the Magdalen Society, Society fer the Relief of Poor Widows with Small Children, Orphan Asylum Society, Hunred Neediest Cases, Welcome Wagon, Home fer Wayward Children, Associashun on American Injun Affairs, Lyin-In Hospital, Nashunal Audjeebon Society, Nashunal Rifle Associashun, Wilderness Society, Sierra Club—and of course the Metropolitan Opera, American Psychoanalytic Institute, Associashun fer Academic Travel Abroad, Americans to Free Captive Nashuns, League fer Mutchal Aid, Dramatists Guild, United States Chamber of Commerce, Mayo Clinic, Associashun of Producin Artists, Institute of American Injun Arts, NAACP Legal Defense Fund, Master Institute of United Arts, Philharmonic Society, Livin Theayter, United Jewish Appeal, Esalen Institute, Menninger Foundashun—"

"No more, no more!"

"But you can't slight your estate's faithful retainers, so you got to pay fer the Christmas Club, penshun fund, Blue Cross and Blue Shield, workman's compensashun, major medical inshurance, accident inshurance, soshal security, unemployment inshurance, liability inshurance, bonding, and your contribushon to the coffee break. Then in addishun there is—"

"Please stop this very minute!"

"Can't stop now. I got a runnin start like a country mule. There's also the Jewish Labor Bund, East Harlem Jaycees, Lee Onn Dong Associashun, Mental Health Associashun, Associates of the Smithsonian Institushun, Muscular Dystrophy Associashuns of America, Nashunal Foundashun fer Neuromuscular Diseases, Hospital fer Joint Diseases, Tuberculosis and Health Associashun, Nashunal Guild of Community Music Schools, American Histerical Associashun, Girl Scouts Council, Boy Scouts Council, Cub Scouts Council, Council on Unwanted Pregnancies, Associashun on Voluntary Sterilizashun, Actors Equity, American Foundashun fer Tropical Medicine, American Legion, Veterans of Foreign Wars, Blue Star Mothers' Associashun, Young Men's Christian Associashun, Young Women's Christian Associashun, Young Men's and Young Women's Hebrew Associashun. Plus I already sent in pledge cards in the name of the estate fer the World Relief Committee of the Nashunal Associashun of Evangelicals, War Resisters League, American Friends Service Committee, Veterans of the Abraham Lincoln Brigade, Student Nonviolatin Coordinatin Committee, Rosicrushan Anthroposophic League, Poetry Society of America, Athletics fer the Blind, Colonial Dames of America, Fresh Air Fund—"

"Hell fire, Jake, stop! Stop!"

"Gettin near the end now, daddy-in-law. Police Veteran Associashun, Regional Plan Associashun, Mutchal Benefit Associashun, Hadassah Medical Relief, Police Athletic League, Myopia Research Foundashun, Geological Society of America, American Institute of Biological Sciences, Ecological Society, Daughters of the American Revolushun, Nashunal Campin Associashun, Pulaski Memorial Committee, Educashunal Film Liberry Associashun, American Civil Liberties Union, Protestant Teachers Associashun, Huguenot Associashun of America, Nashunal Associashun of Manufacturers, Polish Institute of Arts & Sciences in America, Federashun of French War Veterans, Jewish Nazi Victims Organizashun, Junior League of America, Keep America Beautiful, Layman's Nashunal Committee, Catholic Near East Welfare Associashun, Hampton Institute, Southern Christian Leadership Conference, Bide-A-Wee Home, Estonian Educashunal Service, Foundashun fer a Better America, Catholic Actors' Guild, Freethinkers of America, League of Women Voters, Educashunal Guidance Council fer the Mentally Retarded, Congress of Racial Equality, Esperanto League fer North America, Friends of Poor Reeko, Infantile Paralysis Foundashun, Conservative Baptist Home Mishun Society, Credit Union, Tom Dooley Foundashun—"

"Gawd above!"

"Jest a couple more. Archaeological Institute of America, Near East College Associashun, Institute fer Glaucoma Research, American Psychological Associashun, Campaign to Check the Populashun Exploshun, Damon Runyon Memorial Fund fer Cancer Research, Anti-Nazi League, Nashunal Wildlife Federashun, Associashun fer Children with Retarded Mental Development, Negro Actors' Guild, Sino-American Amity, Women's Bible Society, Council fer American Unity, Diabetes Associashun, Associashun of Catholic Trade Unionists, Nashunal Committee fer a Sane Nuclear Policy, Holy Name Society, Cystic Fibrosis Nashunal Research Foundashun, Assembly of Captive European Nashuns, Heart Associashun, John Birch Society, Students fer a Democratic Society, Internashunal Committee fer Breakin the Language Barrier, Oral Health Committee, Paderewski Foundashun, Society fer the Prevenshun of Blindness, Pollushun Control Foundashun, Defenders of Wildlife, Nashunal Liberry Associashun, Internashunal House, Parents Associashun, Alcoholics Anonymous, Greek Orthodox Charities, Cerebral Palsy Associashun, Society fer the Propagashun of the Faith, Sons of the American Revolushon, Irish-American Histerical Associashun, Nashunal Kidney Foundashun, Bible Society, Speech Associashun, Society of Mayflower Descendants, Eyetalian Histerical Society—"

"I beg you, Jake! I can't suffer no more!"

"These was only the domestic institushuns what the estate owes an obligashun to. In addishun, in the past year I pledged two bits to each of the foreign cartels what asked me. As I reklect offhand, there was Aalborg Historiske Museum, Academia de Ciencias, Academia Sinica, Academiae Scientarium Hungaricae, Afrikanistische Abteilung des Seminars für Semitistik, Albert-Ludwigs-Universität, Anatomický Ústav Lekařskè Fakulty, Andaman and Nicobar Stashun, Anthropologisch-Erbbiologische Begutachtungsstelle, Archivic Internazionale, Ateneo de Manila—"

"By God, I won't listen to no more!"

"I only been through the A's so far, daddy-in-law. In addishun there is the Baessler-Archiv, Bamenda Museum, Berliner Gesellschaft—"

"Enough of them foreign entanglements! I'll pay them all! But you got to stop this very minute!"

"I think," Jake said slowly, squishin his words round like gargle water, "that bout does it. I mean that covers all the *recent* obligashuns. But there is some the estate has fallen in arrears of. Lemmesee, there is the Automobile Club of Kansas, Adventure-on-a-Shoestring Club, Afro-American Club, American Temperance Union, Beaux Arts Guild, B-4 Philanthropic Associashun, Big Club Political Club, Brotherhood of Painters, Decorators, and Paperhangers of America, Brotherhood of Sleepin Car Porters, Brotherhood-in-Action, Brotherhood of—"

"Hell fire, I won't listen to no more!" cried Jake's daddy-in-law like a baby.

"Since you and I got mutchal trust in each other, I spect I can jest give you the round figure. Comes to six hunred twenny skins, exact," says Jake.

Daddy-in-law whips his hand inside his shirt where he hides his money belt and out it comes stuffed with greenbacks that was a lil saucy from bein kept close to his miserly flesh fer so long. "Here! Take it, Jake! Take it!"

So Jake slowly starts countin it. "Six hunred leven, six hunred twelve, six hunred thirteen, six hunred fourteen—no, thass six hunred fifteen, cause two bills done stuck together—don't want to skin you none—six hunred thirteen, six hunred fourteen, six

hunred fifteen, six hunred sixteen—oops, couple more stuck together—want you to get a fair shake—six hunred fourteen, six
hunred fifteen—"

"Jake, stop countin! It's all there!"

"Well, if you says so. Don't want to dicker with you fer a
dollar here or a dollar there. As I always says, so long as a feller
comes close and is meanin you well, thass all that matters.
Now, there is only one more formality we has to pass through
afore I can hand you this valuable estate deed."

"Oh, no, no, no."

"Oh, yes, yes, yes. I spect you'll want to reimburse me fer
my original investment in the estate. Now, I'm not askin fer a
profit or even fer what the value has grown to under my judi-
shus management. Jest my original investment back. It were
two hunred thirty-eight dollars, includin all fees and charges,
which I will gladly enumerate fer you now. Lemmesee, there
was a buck twenny-five fer—"

"Jake, don't! I don't want to know!" So the daddy-in-law digs
under his mangy shirt again and comes up with two hunred
forty dollars. I reckon the mustard seed of charity still remained
in Jake's stony heart, cause he left off his enumerashuns of the
costs and took the money.

"Lemmesee now. I owes you two dollars fer change," says
Jake, always a stickler fer partiklers.

"Please, Jake, ferget it. Jest give me the deed!"

"Much obliged. Here tis." His daddy-in-law lunges at the
deed like a bear onto a butterfly. He rushes to the depot and
flags down the train headin fer The Great American West.
Course anyone could of told him not to trust Jake Lord in a
business arrangement, speshally since he had wunst cheated
Jake, who never fergets a slight. The daddy-in-law gets to Kansas all right, all the way holdin that deed careful as an egg. He
immediately hires hisself a buckboard to carry him out to the
estate which the deed had optimistically described as bein
right close to the railroad, not more than twice around a tooth-
pick. Well, his high hopes of riches starts droppin like a stone

in water when he sees he is ridin in a mighty pore wagon driven by a mighty hungry-lookin farmer and pulled by a mighty undernourished mule through mile after mile of the sorriest ground south of the badlands. At last the buckboard comes right up to the bank of the Missouri River and makes a dead stop. The farmer what drove him points to long bout the middle of the river and says, "Thass exakly where your estate stood. Well, not exakly. Bout ten fifteen feet closer to the middle. Thass it, near where the sandbar is. Must be near ten years since the river shifted and the estate floated down to New Orleyans." By this time the ole daddy-in-law has gone limp as a frog. "Course you might hire yourself a lawyer and claim you was entitle to farm some of the Big Muddy River itself. But I don't partikly recommend it. Don't know what you'd do with it. It's too thin to plow and too thick to bottle. Anyway, by the time the lawyers was finished with you you'd be plucked cleaner than Gramma's Sunday goose. Jake Lord done sold this estate four five times already. Guess he fergot to menshun that fact to you, which circumstance don't make no difference since he never owned it in the first place. Guess you've been swindled, mistah. That'll be twenty-five dollars fer the ride back, unless you cares to walk, which I don't partikly recommend, cause if the rattlers don't get you the coyotes will."

Well, Mistah Punman, I tell you we had more fun than a possum in a persimmon tree after hearin bout what happened with Jake's daddy-in-law. Of course Jake was long gone by the time the ole feller got back to east Tennessee. Jake came right back to Canaan County to settle down. All the folks had such a good laugh bout his estate in Kansas that they fergived him the trick of the mountain-roarer. Even Bubba stopped bein angry after awhile and they became friends like brothers should. Jake raised hisself a passel of boys, too, a dozen of them, each one as crafty as their daddy. I tell you, Mistah Punman, the fun we had in those days would of made a whole teevee series. But course thass all gone now, what with the town bein flooded out by the Tee-Vee-Ay dam and all. The whole town jest vanished under the water. Most important one in the county too. There weren't nothing left to mark that it ever existed at all. Jest gone. Feedin the fishes. Well, thass progress. I spect everybody's scattered over the land like quail out of a covey. But I'd sure give anything to hear from that ole bunch again. Yessir, I'd give the cash register receipts fer a week jest to see that door open right now and hear ole Bubba ask me, "You still clippin your customers, Jim?" Sure miss them all. Times change, and we all had to bend afore the winds of change. Thass the way our country grows. Only I wish. I wish. Well, can't nothin be done anymore. That bout finishes you up fer today, Mistah Punman. With that haircut you won't be givin the girls no rest, nosirree. Haw-haw. Now, might I recommend a singein of the cut hairs?

— No thanks, Jim, that will do it.

— A singe has been shown to keep the vital fluids in after the hair ends been nipped off. No? Well. Whoops, look at ole greased lightnin! You jest see our future First Selectman hurtlin past? Busy, busy Gladinski, no time to dropinski, fer a shaveski, from Jimski. Haw-haw.

— Gladinski? No, I didn't see him.

— Yessir, Mistah Punman. Gladinski jest this second went buckin past like he was carryin the ball fer New Salem High. A real select man, our First Selectman. Democrats still ain't been able to find a person to run against him. Ain't much pleashur, though, in winnin sumthin by default. Well, I always said Amuca is the land of opportunity and a Polish feller don't have to take no backseat here. Thass sumthin all these folks got to understand who extol the virtues of the Russkies. Here's your change, Mistah Punman. Well, thank you, obliged. Put four more combinashuns like that together and I'll have me a greenback. The eagles are really flyin today. Y'all come back and see us, hear? Meantime, don't take no wooden nickels. Okay now, you're next, Mistah—I don't believe I reklect your name. You're new here, ain't you? Well, step right up to the chair and let me show you what ole Jim can do. You'll never get a shearin any

other place. Haw-haw. Yessir, a fine ole gentleman is Mistah
Punman. Don't make them like him no more. Last of the breed.
Why, he wouldn't dream—

■

SLAM.

Three steps. One. Two. Three. Whee! Excelsior! This way or
that way? Dream-dream-dream-DREAM. Go left? Right? Do
right. Mistah Punman wouldn't dream. Dream. Life is but an
empty. Hair on glasses. Itches. Go back to office? Better stop by
Myer's first. Gladinski can wait a few minutes. Let him try to
talk to my secretary. The Italian torture. Go this way. Around
the square. Cross Main again. Careful of sidewalk crack. Now
in sun. Shadows lengthen, criss-crossed. I should have tipped
Jim more. A pourboire. Maybe in inflation should give more?
Well. Our tip—take it or leave it! Next time I'll raise it to a
quarter. Better remember. Why give him anything? He owns
the shop. I don't tip the grocery store owner, just Charlie the
delivery man. Insincere peapicker. Friendly on the outside,
fiendly on the inside. They're a violent people. Jim the Barberian.
   What was that he said? Mistah Punman wouldn't dream?
The American Dream. The Great American Dream of The
Great American Melting Pot. Only the alloys didn't melt. Can't
hear the pot bubbling any more. They're taking over. Everything, everything. Thing-thing-thing-THING. Long hot summer. The fire next time. Hail the King. New King for old. Black
kings on Pennyman Street. Was one of the three wise kings
black? I think so. Yes. Remember the painting. Three kings for
the King of Kings. Which king was black? Name the kings in
order categorical. Melchior. Gaspar. Balthazar. Which one
black? They worked magic. Word derived from Magi. Black
magic. Juju.
   Oh, oh. There he is again. Ingratiating smile. Droopy pants.
What wants in New Salem? Don't smile back. A world full of
mysteries. Astrologers. Wise kings. Too soon old. And too late

wise. It is not in our stars. Hitch wagon to a star. Careful. Car coming. All clear. Excelsior! Mistah Punman wouldn't dream. Behold the dreamer cometh. How did it go? I have a dream. The Great American Dream. I have I have I have. He said. Powerful speech. Wonder if he wrote it himself? I have a dream that a dream that someday someday. How did it go again? One day sons of sons of sons of former slaves. I have a dream that one day sons of former slaves and and and. Former slave-owners will will. Will someday. I have a dream I have a dream. That someday little black boys and girls will. Inspired oration. Perhaps he had a speech-writer. I have a dream that someday. Someday. Someday.

■

I GOT A DREAM that me and my husband was heading for The Great American West looking for the opportunities out there so's we could live off the fat of the land, and we had to keep stopping to ask directions and everyone we asked was colored or spoke funny languages, so I got hysterical with fear and made my husband drive back home to Vermont, which I refuse to budge from again even though my husband is on relief and we wants to get our share of the opportunities, but I just can't bear the thought of making that trip again and having to ask directions of all them foreign people. I was born into a loving and hardworking family on March 7, 1944, A.M., Eastern War Time. May I please have an interpretation?

Madame Potiphar replies: We are a nation of immigrants and each one of us is as good as anyone else regardless of race, religion, color, or national origins. It is unfortunate that an untypical minority of American extremists has taken it upon itself to hold necktie parties for people of a different hue and to desecrate houses of worship different from their own. But we must not indict an entire people because of the wanton acts of certain violent individuals. Any slight imperfections in The Great American Dream are being cured by education. It's the flaw of the land. The American people are truly one nation under God, indivisible with liberty and justice for all. (Next time take the Canadian route and you'll find a more select clientele.)

I have a dream a dream I have a dream that one day this nation will will rise up and will rise up and

Every night in my sleep I hear a riddle propounded for me to answer. I am told I will be endowed with a large reward if I answer correctly, but I find myself unable to find the correct solution, no matter how much I ponder. The riddle is as follows:

> *The old woman hiked her dress and took it,*
> *The old man shot it and shook it.*

Please send me an exposition, because I am the type of person who would put the reward money to beneficial use, instead of squandering it, as certain kinds of people might.

Madame Potiphar says that your unconscience has entertained you during the innocent hours of sleep with a delightful recollection of pastoral America in days of lore. The scene you describe was once a common occurrence in God's Country when the kindly old husbandman tried to shake apples out of a tree, while his good wife endeavored to catch them in her ample skirts. Tonight be sure to answer as I have suggested and you will receive your promised reward. Next problem.

I have a dream a dream. Of an oasis of freedom. I have a dream of

i am a full-bloodied american Indian and i don't know if i got a write to send you a litter, but i'll try anyway since i spent the for bits four your magazine and i figure i got the write four that. but if you don't print it that will be pretty much what i expect cause i never noticed before that your magazine ever printed nothing by a full-buddied american Indian even though we was here first and we got a raw deal all around as everyone knows. my dream is about this White man who's always going to come visit me on the reservation and bring all kinds of good things to make up for the raw deal, only he never comes, and i am sick and tired of waiting. may i please have a demythologization?

Since you failed to write bn only one side of the paper and did not leave a two-inch margin on the bottom, Madame Potiphar is under no obligation to reply to you.

I have a dream a dream a dream

One long and lovely night, in the innocence of my bed, with my winsome wife beside me, I dreamt a strange and unholy dream. The Lord God of Hosts visited me and, after sundry questions about my helpmeat, He betook in His gentle hands my ring finger. With a kingly bow, He addressed me: "I make thee a present of this ring. So long as it adorns thy finger, thy wife will not commit the sin of fornication without your knowledge." Lo and behold, I awakened to find my ring finger firmly entwined by the thing-a-me-jib between my wife's thighs. May I squeeze have a reconstitution?

Madame Potiphar replies: The reward of virtue is virtue.

I have a dream a dream that one day this nation will live out the true meaning. I have a dream that one day

I dreamed that I crept into the circle of Indian tipis with my knife clenched tightly between my teeth. I stole quietly into the tipi of Old Chief Wundawucker himself. His children lay asleep on the ground. I then slit their throats one by one. They didn't make a sound. Next my dream switched to Harlem where I crept into a tenement and knifed all the Negro children asleep in it. They squawked like crows. Tell me, do all Negro children squawk more than Indian children? May I please have an edification?

They do.

I have a dream about the red hills of Georgia a dream about Mississippi sweltering under the heat of injustice. I have a dream a dream a dream

My recurrent dream is that a sultry Jewess stands under my window at night and propounds a riddle: "Jesus, Jesus, King of the Jews, he got a prick smaller than—whose?" May I please have an elucidation?

Madame Potiphar never discusses personalities.

I have a dream a dream a dream of America

Let me ask from you something. Tell me, why am I always running? Why ain't I able settle down one place like Mister Pennyman? Why I always got to complain to Mister Pennyman who should pardon me breathing his air, for which I apologize? Why ain't my son classy enough be invited June Dance at Country Club even though I'm okay for Mister Pennyman to buy from me medicine for backside? My birthdate is twenty-fourth day of Shebat in year 5667, and my name is Jerry Myer in case you're interested. If you think I got problem, send real fast a judgment.

Modernize.

I have a dream of a nation of a nation of a nation. I have a dream dream dream

Every night I see before me the faces of all the old men whose teeth I knocked out for their gold and the swarthy women whose oil I melted down into soap. I try not to let these dreams disturb my equanimity because I realize that what is past is just so much water over the dam. Anyway, I'm willing to bury the hatchet and turn over a new life for myself in America. But I do have one question about these dreams. I am planning holy wedlock and wonder if these recollections will affect my sexual performance. I was born at latitude N 50′05″, longitude E 19′10″, into a well-organized family. May I please have a catharsis?

Madame Potiphar suggests that if your problem persists be sure to consult your minister or other religious leader.

I have a dream of this nation a dream of America of America, of little black boys and little white boys, a dream of America a dream a dream

My dream is that I have been transformed into a colored lad who lives with a white family in a big white house on a hill. I do everything they do. They let me sit at the dinner table with them and eat out of the same plates. They do not keep my silverware separate from theirs, nor do they wash it longer. I go to the same school they do and after school we all play games together. Nor am I always "it." When I am ill they call the doctor and he comes just as fast as he would for any white child. They even let me go to church with them and utter the very same prayers. They are so good to me! But I keep dreaming that this happy life will be ruined because I lust after the little blonde girl in the family. This dream is preposterous because I am not colored but a hard-working, honest white man who has a virtuous wife and two bright-eyed boys. May I please have a decipherment?

Madame Potiphar believes that your dreams expose your hidden anxieties about life today. You are obviously bewildered by the violence in the streets in recent years. So to protect your psyche from the horrible reality of what is happening to the American Dream, you have reversed roles. That way, in your dreams you can recount the numerous blessings Africans have received on our shores—the same food we eat, the same style of dress, the same churches, and the very same God! And another blessing they conveniently keep forgetting about is that we transported them across the Atlantic from Africa—at no charge to them!—to come under the civilizing influence. You are upset because you feel that no matter how generous you are to them, these people will never be satisfied until they have slept with every white woman they can. Everyone knows that their sexual needs are greater due to the influence of the African sun and, if they were not controlled by rigorous enforcement of the laws, they would give vent to their animal desires. And now, to make matters even worse, Martin Luther King is stirring them up and inciting them to acts of violence against our property and our lives.

Readers are invited to submit details of dreams or other intimate problems. Please state any feelings, or lack of them, about people and places and events. Do not send any money, at first, as Madame Potiphar's column is, primarily, a service to our readers. Remember—nothing is taboo in this column!

I have a I have I have I have

Nothing. I was made and not born. I came with nothing. And I leave with nothing. I am. I am. I am the last chapter in the Black Book. I am a shapeless life. An empty dream. A penny-worth of pity. Who am I? May I please have a sign? *You are Benjamin Pennyman, Esq., an outlaw, a Yankee Doodler, and a memory survivant.*

Signified.

■

DREAM-DREAM-dream-DREAM. Damn banging. Freudenthal's Folly. Comes all the way across the common. Which way? Witches way? Burn. Long hot summer. It was Gaspar or Balthazar. Cross through common? Shorter. No, here comes Freudenthal across common. Busy as a bee today. Lots of activity. Unusual activity is a sign of rain. Better go down the street instead. Tripod Camera Shop. Unblinking lenses looking at me. Dangling Conversation Pieces. People talk too much already. Left. Right. Do right. Fresh mums out. They say florists spray them with paint to make more salable. "Say It With Flowers." Arrowhead Hotel. Stop for tea? No, better go back to office. Don't forget Myer's. Oops! Almost hit me! Undisciplined children. No respect.

— You there, Georgy Amato! I saw you. You stop or I'll speak to your mother about this. You should not shoot a bow and arrow downtown. Don't you know you might hurt someone? You're more dangerous than the red Indians were!

Handsome child. But what they grow up into. Mafia. They stick a feather in their caps, and call it mac-a-ro-nee. Doesn't obey me. No one listens to Pennyman any more. Tom's Furnishings. Needs new stock. Business dying. New five-and-dime. What's a wail worth? Cheap merchandise for the new people. Paper littering the street. Unclean, unclean.

— Hello there, Charlie. Bit warm, hey?

— Yes, it is, Mister Pennyman. I think all that atomic-bomb testing must have changed the weather.

— Well. Maybe things will improve. The new treaty starts in a couple of weeks.

— If you can trust the Russkies.

— I guess you can't. But you never know. Well, see you, Charlie.

The way high-school quarterbacks end up. Clerking. Probably jazz the wives when they make deliveries. Reason my ice cream comes melted? There he is. The Wandering Jew again. Ingratiating smile. Go down, noses.

— Well, well, well, Virginia, and isn't he getting to be a big fellow! What a yelp! You're right, people do say that letting them cry makes the lungs strong. But he's not too big to give an old man a smile. There! You see, now he's smiling. My best to your father. Oh? I'm sorry to hear that. Don't worry, though. We old-timers have a way of pulling through.

She's putting on weight. Smells of whiskey. The white man's milk. Hear her husband's hard up since the accident. But too proud to ask her father. Proud but threadbare. Tribe of the Shabby Genteel. Too proud to beg, too honest to steal. John the Good wouldn't help her anyway. Last of the stern. Probably because he was such a hellion as a boy. She'll inherit soon. But not as much as she expects. Not much at all. Saw John few weeks ago when redid his will. I told her a white lie. He looked poorly. Better to lie and spare her feelings. Was it?

Left. Right. Do right. Rappaccini's Hardware. Pete's Notions. Magazines out front. *Playboy*. Shouldn't allow it. Has pull-out pictures. Do they? For the photographers? When they're naked? Pushovers. Unreal women. Shave the pubis. Theda Bara. Clara Bow. Isadora. Garbo. Dietrich. Lamarr. White slaves. False, false. The Myth America pungent. Smutty promise to reader never kept. Caught in coitus. Interrupt us. Annie Bell. I was a child and she was a child. Non, non, mon enfant, you must not. Irish Annie is too easy. When you grow older you will appreciate the fruit which grows highest on the tree. The flower inaccessible on a mountaintop. The blossom which could not be plucked. Qu'il t'y? I am quilty. A pun. Punish me. I admit it, humbled and low, dolorously, hazily.

City newspapers. SCHOOL STRIKE IS AVERTED. WALLACE TO LET SCHOOLS REOPEN. LATIN GRANDMOTHER BEARS QUINTUPLETS. War coming? REV. KING SAYS D.C. MARCH SUCCESS. Father of his people. The king. Copies of *New Salem Advertiser*. News of the new people. Mrs. Hannah Levy. Plurabelle. Is entertaining friends this weekend on her new patio. Mrs. Abraham Freudenthal will address the Historical Society on the subject of. HISTORICAL SOCIETY HOUSE AND GARDEN TOUR A SELLOUT. Soldout. Among the community's historic places to be visited is the Pennyman home. Come to pee in the Pennyman pot. MONSIGNOR O'HENNERRY TO VISIT NEW PARISH CHURCH. JEWISH RESIDENTS TO CELEBRATE HEBREW NEW YEAR 5724. What Jewish month has six letters? Ask Jerry Myer. Benjamin Punyman, Esq. Damn! Misspelled my name! Has announced he will close the historic law offices next spring which were founded in 1828 by his great-grandfather. Strong winds from the east last week toppled a tower at. SUMMER EXODUS TO MOUNTAINS ENDS. Exit us. The restoration of the historic Bellamy home on the common is proceeding rapidly, this paper was informed by Mr. Abraham Freudenthal who praised the workers for their industry. He further stated that. Gives us the word. Exit us.

— No, thank you, Pete. Not buying, just reading. Sure I know you're not running a public library. But it's cheaper than buying. Ha-ha. No, I guess I won't need my *Times* today. I only get it for the crossword anyway. A new puzzle magazine? No, I hadn't heard about that one. I'll look at it tomorrow. I ought to get back to the office now. Thanks. See you, Pete.

Left. Right. Do right. Slow down. Spare heart. Stop rushing. Mother dying stop. Come out, come out. Wherever you are stop. He didn't. Do right. I sent wire. He didn't come.

— Well, hello there, Owen. How's the old pony express rider? Couple of kids down the street are playing Indian. Look out they don't rob your mail stage.

— Thanks for the advice, Ben. But I'd rather take my chances on Indians than stick around the post office listening to Ham.

— I know. I saw him a while ago. You're right. When Ham gets in one of his moods, best thing is to excuse yourself.

— Ben, I think sometimes he's going off the deep end. I guess you know he's joined the Birchers.

— No, I didn't. But it figures. He told me he doesn't like wall-papering the post office with welfare notices. But then again, he'd object to anything. Plays the part of Old Integrity. He's harmless, though. My candidate for the town's unforgettable character. Well, see you, Owen.

Martinizing Dry Cleaning. Flavortowne Ice Cream. "Try Our So-Da-Licious." Comfit ye. Oops. There goes Freudenthal again.

Mofes was he,
Who Ifrael's Hoft,
Led thro' the Sea.

Wave to him. Smile. Byebye. Oscaleta Street. Wait. Last crossing. Me the wandering few. Through mine own town. Exit us. All of us. Me and my brooder. He. The man without a country. Our nation. Love it or leave it.

■

DEAR BROTHER BENJAMIN. Now that is a salutation calculated to startle the coon down from the persimmon tree. Yes, you still have, alive if not well, a brother. Or should I have given you warning, perhaps addressed the letter: To Whom It May Concern? And then about the third paragraph casually mentioned that your brother, flesh of your flesh and partaker of your memories, sends you his greetings? I may have handled the salutation badly, but here I am, for bitter or worse. I do not flatter myself that you are pleased to hear from me, but I do hope that your curiosity will command me a reading. So how are you, brother? How is that for an opening question? What do you answer when someone you haven't heard from directly in four decades asks how you are?

I suspect I sound somewhat bantering. Believe me when I say I have wanted to write you for many years. But I wasn't sure on what common ground to address you. My opinion of you alternated between poet and pleasant. I'm sorry if I sound bantering. Believe me. But I just can't get the tone right. This is the third start I have made at writing you this week. And so I have decided this time to begin a letter and write it straight through, not crossing out a word. It will be an adventure for both of us, because at this moment I am not certain how it will end. Or even if I will mail it to you. For I am what I am, and there's no hiding that. All right. Fresh start. Begin now, a Litter from an American Former. New paragraph.

How are you, brother? I mean that sincerely. I occasionally hear about you. In case you didn't know, I am one of the *New Salem Advertiser*'s few out-of-town subscribers. I try to picture you doing your nightly crossword in that big house on Founder's Street, with its atrocious mansard roof Mother brought her handsome protégé Pierre back from Paris to build. Probably you are now sitting in the library, for you were bookish even as a child. I remember the poems you wrote. Have you maintained your interest in this private transaction? And I well recall your childhood skill in memory feats. I used to envy you them. But not the way Mother made you perform before her ladies come to tea. Benjamin, the trained memory. "Memory Survives," Grandfather Samuel the Just ordered carved on his defective headstone. I suppose he intended something bland and sentimental by that phrase, but all he really did was describe the burden of the Pennymans. Nothing but memory.

I confess that your telegram telling me about Mother's imminent passing did reach me. You suspected as much, no doubt. But at that time I had no wish to return to New Salem. I held nothing against Mother. I knew beforehand that when I fled my sacred Duty to God and Country, Mother's rectitude would close the books on me. I would be a stranger in a very strange land. Officially nonexistent the moment I separated myself from the Army. Especially because I would not die for her beloved France. Good Americans, when they die, go to Paris, wrote old Oliver Wendell, Mother's favorite author—but I was determined to stay holme and live. I did not feel that I should proudly say, "Lafayette, we are heirs," and then chance my life in the trenches of France. Nor was it shame that prevented my return. Sure, I had been all over The Great American West and I was busted. But that isn't the point. I was unwilling to offer myself as an Example, on the hoof, of Youth Gone Wrong for the edification of New Salem's young. Because, Benjamin, I have no regrets that I ran away. Who is to define what is bravery and what is cowardice? You never had to face up to that question because your eyes kept you out of The Great War. I regretted that I had only one life, and I was determined not to lose it for my country.

We Pennymans always seem to be plumbing our consciences. If we're not applauding our own actions in the Black Book, then we're justifying them. It is a heavy burden, and perhaps that is why Father took French leave of our little famille. The idea of keeping those account books of the soul in the back of old Isaiah Pennyman's heavy black Bible is absurd! What a duty upon one's seed to condemn the males in each generation to write out in that damned Black Book their aspirations for the New Jerusalem, to be reread by each regeneration! I wish I understood why every Pennyman but Father—and, of course, myself—did his duty to the Black Book, although I believe that each must have found it ludicrous and even distasteful. Perhaps Father simply was not susceptible to the imperative of history. After all, the plagues on Egypt found the Hebrews immune.

All the other Pennymans were faithful to their links back to the past—and to the future of the American Dream, the founding of a New Jerusalem in the wilderness of our continent. I remember to this day what some of our ancestors wrote in the Black Book. Each one of them convinced himself that the Lord's cosmic plan would not unfold without him. The New World, as I believe one of our ancestors described it, is a flower opening from the budde to reveal the Grande Unfoulding of God's Designe for us. But, my brother, the budde was blasted on the vine, for these pious men first fell on their knees and then promptly fell on the Indians. That was the original sin, the loss of Eden.

Every Pennyman whose chronicle we read in the Black Book wore blinders to reality. The exception was Father, a man of good will. If his remains should ever be found, that is what you must carve on his headstone. Lord knows there are few enough men of good will in New Salem. I am a little your senior and so perhaps I remember things you were too young to notice. Mother once bought us some book or other about a good little lad, a barefoot boy with turned up pantaloons—I don't recall the title, perhaps it was the childhood of Abe Lincoln, but all those books were the same—and she made Father read us a little every night before bedtime. Finally he could stomach no more. Mother said he would continue the readings. He said he wouldn't. She threatened to burn the Black Book. Then he stuttered. The Blah-Blah-Black Book, he called it. He stuttered only on the letter B. Curious, wasn't it? So she won. As always. And when the American Dream was clobbered by the Panic of 1907, when Father simply found himself unable to believe in the Grande Unfoulding, he bolted. Like any sensible man would do. He ran away from memory.

I ran also. But you stayed, Benjamin. Why? Did you find in New Salem that designe that both Father and I overlooked? Someday you will make your contribution to the Black Book, if you have not done so already. You're the last of the Pennymans. You have to close the book. You are the only one who can tell what became of Isaiah Pennyman's dream of a New Jerusalem. Since you stayed to uphold the covenant old Isaiah made three centuries ago, you must have some sort of an answer. What did you see that I failed to see? I wish I could read your contribution. You are the custodian of a major American document, Benjamin. Leave it to Yale or UConn or some other university. Don't get in a black mood someday and burn it, for a black book burning in a moral desert will provide only little light and even less understanding. And this advice to participate in history comes to you from someone who always believed that history is bunkage. I do not compromise my conscience by offering you this advice. Because I know that there is no way you—or I—can erase history's mark. "Memory Survives," as old Samuel the Just said.

All those Poor Richard verities I tried to escape from! Honesty is the best policy, I was taught. But I don't like a man who operates from policy. Don't count your chickens before they hatch. But no one taught us not to gloat over our riches after they hatched. Temperance. Silence. Order. Resolution. Frugality. Industry. Sincerity. Justice. Moderation. Cleanliness. Tranquility. Chastity. Humility. Each verity is a post in a moral fence, The Great American Corral. No matter where the New Salemite has gone on earth, the verities have followed his trail like some stalking cougar. I learned that, Benjamin. At the very time I felt the freest, I was deluding myself that there was escape. For in the very act of fleeing I unwittingly became an instrument to disseminate these verities over the countryside. They are like some of those clever seeds which lock onto the leg of a bird who, without realizing it, carries the seed for perhaps tens of miles to colonize some new dominion. I was that bird, cleverly trapped into spreading verities across a continent, scattering all those righteous seeds that would grow upright and stifle the native growth.

Of course I didn't realize it at the time. I thought that I was as free as the wild goose. But I, too, was just another instrument in the unfolding of Isaiah's grand design. All the time that I was chasing down the American Dream, wandering in search of some Promised Land like a blinded Moses out of bunkage, I unknowingly transported the seeds of the New Salem verities.

Brother, let me tell you briefly of my wanderings since 1916, my forty years through the wilderness to God's Country. (I wrote that last sentence without thinking. We Pennymans have never been able to escape the reflex of Old Testament parallels.) At first I fled blindly, without reason or destination, across Connecticut and New York and Pennsylvania, fearing pursuit but not realizing that no one really cared, not the Army or Mother. I had many little adventures and some quiet moments of truth. In Pennsylvania I fell in with a cheerful companion of the road who subsequently, while I was sleeping, separated me from my possessions. I saw many acts of violence, and a few of kindness. But being an adventurous lad on my way to God's Country, I passed up no opportunitiy to engage in honest labor, as the books Mother bought for us encouraged me to do. I heard that the Kentucky coal fields were booming because of the war, and that is where I went. I labored honestly in the darkness of the mines, scratching out wealth from the underside of the earth, leaving gaping holes in the landscape, coughing out my lungs, and losing people I knew and sometimes loved in cave-ins due to economy in the selection of timbers. The dangers, though, passed over me.

The real wealth was not being made in those black holes, but above in the sunlight of Bonanzaland. The favorite pastime there was bringing suit for ownership of the mines. One might divert himself at any time of the day by strolling into one of the numerous courtrooms where causes were being pled for the delectation of the audience. The last thing anyone wanted was a verdict. That would call a halt to the fun. As soon as it appeared that one of the attorneys was forging ahead slightly in the argument, the judge might put up a few deadfalls or lead the testimony through brambles of quibbles. Or he might change the rules of the game from morning to morning, today following the elegancies of French jurisprudence, tomorrow sounding the depths of good old common sense. Or he might trot out some statute that hadn't been operative for fifty years for all to admire its parts and its deportment. Of course no case was ever settled. And so the final result was that the owners bled one another until the big coal companies, which had been standing on the sidelines encouraging everyone, walked in and scooped up the pot.

No, that was not God's Country, and so I set out wandering again. I went to Illinois, which its residents called "The Garden of the West," although the evidence of sight showed it to be mostly sand hills, scrub trees, and gullied farmland. But these people, like the Pennymans, had the delusion they were participating in some grand design. The southern triangle of Illinois is known locally as Little Egypt, and the sector numbers towns with such names as Cairo, Thebes, and Karnak. The prideful inhabitants told me the reason for the names is the uncommon fertility of the soil which someday will bring other folks to them for food, as the Israelites had to come to Egypt for grain during a crop failure. I arrived at an alternative explanation—the Egyptian darkness that lay over the mentality of these people. At the very time they boasted to me about their future granaries I witnessed with my own eyes that they were plagued by hordes of insects feasting on their crops.

So I left Little Egypt. I was working my way by stages down the Mississippi River just as the war ended. There was quite a celebration, although I observed that the denizens of the river were prompt to celebrate almost anything with equal enthusiasm, and should a specific occasion be lacking at the moment, they would celebrate an occasion that would come sooner or later. I found the river, the boats that plied it, and the shore frequented by single young gentlemen seeking their fortune, or, rather, someone else's fortune. No, the Father of Waters was not for me. It wasn't the way Mark Twain had described it. The types that Twain claimed he knew had long since fled its banks or had drunk themselves to death. Or perhaps they had never really existed at all. The ones I found were diseased harlots, quick-buck artists, confidence men of every description who changed the game with each play, and harried businessmen trying to bind up the wounds of cutthroat competition. The river was no longer a route of westward the course of empire. It was now a foul sewer, polluting the desperate and sullen people who were cast upon its shifting banks.

So I left the river and moved across to "The Wonder State," otherwise yclept Arkansas. It was true, as its promoters advertised, that there was an abundance of cheap land, but it was a stubborn land that begrudged every mouthful of food taken from it. At first I attracted considerable notice by laboring for my bread, a course of action guaranteed to throw you under immediate suspicion in Arkansas. I found the people of Arkansas the most conceited I ever met. They say of some dimwit, "He's real smart, even if he weren't born here." As to the boundaries of their state, they adjudged themselves to be confined on the north by the aurora borealis, on the east and west by the rising and setting suns, on the south by the Day of Judgment—and above them, the sky's the limit. But I really shouldn't be too harsh on them, for they are products of crossroads-school education, those that bothered to spend a year or two of their lives in them. Each of these one-room cabins, by the way, is called a "college"—or a "seminary" if it caters only to females—and every schoolteacher is addressed as "professor." The hinterllectual professors are not backward about placing the initials of academic achievement after their names. M.D. D.D. LL.D. For all I could tell, these initials signified Maresy Doats, Dosey Doats, and Little Lamsy Divey. Every year the scholars at the colleges and seminaries submit their essays to a contest on the subject "Why I Am Glad I Resid in Arkansas." That is not my misspelling, brother. It is the way the state education board announced the subject. When I pointed out to the professor of a local college that I detected a misspelling, he cogitated for a while, clucked his tongue, got a firm grip on his pencil, and then deftly put another K in Arkansas.

Arkansas wasn't God's Country either, so I turned west to partake of what I had been assured were golden opportunities where a man could still get in on the ground floor. I had read Kansas advertisements about beets two feet around, wheat so abundant there wasn't time in a year to winnow it, cabbages as big as barrels, and a single potato so large that ten people could have a filling dinner on it and still leave nearly half of it untouched. In my innocence I headed for Kansas, and the first thing I learned there was the reason for the conceit of Arkan-

sas. The beauties of Arkansas become manifold while you rec-
ollect them in your misery in Kansas, otherwise known as
"The Grasshopper State." I finally settled down in Wishes
Found, where the estate I purchased actually did belong to the
man who sold it to me. The settlers, by the way, called any
piece of property on which a sod shanty had been built an
"estate."

Yessirree, in God I trusted, and in Kansas I got busted. Because the land had no nourishment, the hoppers lacked the
strength to leap over the cracks in the field. Even so, they managed to eat everything but the mortgage. And the dust out
there was so thick that even the hoppers got catarrh. It was so
dry, you had to be primed before you could spit. One feller got
hit by a stray raindrop and he just keeled over. Yessirree, it
took a whole covey of quail huffing and puffing together to get
out just one "bobwhite" call. And the dogs were so weak that
to bark they had to lean against a fence for support. The earth
was so caked it took two men to plant—one pried the soil apart
with a crowbar while the other shot the seed in with a gun. The
cattle got so thin they climbed through holes in the chicken
wire and bedded down with the poultry for protection.

Those were some of the rueful sayings we had to comfort us.
I had given too much for my whistle. Nevertheless, my estate
was roundly admired by all my neighbors. The favorite pastime
of a Sunday was to drive from estate to estate, praising them
all indiscriminately, reinforcing the collective delusion that
prospects were bright and opportunities were golden. I decided
anyway to get in on the ground floor of the future prosperity of
The Great West, if energy and honest labor were really worth
anything at all. I tried to lift myself by my own bootstraps—
only to learn that violated a basic law of physics. At least I
didn't have to clear the land. That was a blessing. In fact, wood
was so scarce that pieces were carried about as if they came
from the True Cross. The first year I managed to plant some
corn and bring in a crop, which gave me some credit.

But the Lord gives with a loving hand—and takes with two.

By October it was time to sow wheat. I needed a wheat drill plus a lot of other machinery that the hardpan soils of God's Country seem to demand. I sent my money to Chicago, but my drill never arrived. Nor was my letter inquiring about my purchase ever answered. So I ordered another set of tools from a different company. They finally were launched in my general direction, that is, to a railroad freight office a hundred miles away, where the solicitous agent informed me that I owed shipping charges nearly as great as the cost of my tools. I wasn't the only one conned by the railroads, although that was small solace. In fact, it was a regular practice to gouge the dirt farmers, and we couldn't do much about it. The agent told me the railroad was willing to loan me the money to pay the freight charges at only several times the rate of usury. But we were a stiff-necked bunch. We paid, in pride, and maintained our contributions toward the well-being of the railroads, as if we Kansas farmers were really an eleemosynary institution. Yes, brother, I was a Yankee Diddled.

We went into hock to everybody—the railroads, the grain elevators, the farm-equipment salesmen, the water companies. They were borrowing money back East at three percent and allowing us to borrow it from them at twenty. But we owned our land, didn't we? So we thought, but we were really only tenants with a short-term lease. Whatever wheat we harvested was ultimately the property of the eastern banks. We fed their hogs for them and we broke our necks running their herds. We were ashamed to admit we were being swindled, so we acted like a gang of frontier roughs. But everyone knew our bullets were blanks. We plundered the land and we were plundered in return. We paid and we paid to the eastern bankers living it up in the fleshpots because they knew they had us. We didn't worry about the loans because soon beef might be up or hogs might become precious again, and anyway drought can't last forever. So slap another mortgage on the land, buy more seed, tear up the plains—and next year you'll be riding in a Pierce deluxe. Sure, the land might blow away, but let the next fellow worry about that. Yessirree, put money on your hunch, and with a little natural shrewdness and a lot of rain you might be able to get out before the next drought. But if you didn't get out in time—well, everyone in Kansas knew it took three bank-ruptcies to make a good farmer.

I broke my back on that unfriendly land. I fought the hop-pers and the hail and finally managed to raise some corn and wheat. Only I couldn't sell anything on the market because there was no market. Wheat that cost me over a dollar to grow was fetching sixty-six cents a bushel. Sacred covenants had been made by the Chicago Board of Trade and the Kansas City trusts to break the back of the dirt farmer. We were all busted, down to the last honest, sober, praying pioneer. Our neighborly banker was sitting there with the right to foreclose on every single farm in the county. And he did just that. Any conscien-tious businessman would have done the same. So we left, silent and sullen as a tribe of Indians who know when they have been licked, sneaking off into the night to avoid saying goodbye. Each of us headed for some new Promised Land in The Great American West we had read advertisements about. Westward again to golden opportunities, still in search of God's Country.

I headed for The Great Divide to match my luck against the mountains, trying all the mining camps, which mostly had been abandoned but which everyone claimed must be still chock-full of precious metal. What a mosaic of despairing names they formed! Roaring Camp, Chicken Thief, Gouge Eye, Dead Mule, Greenhorn Beware, Buyer's Luck, Poverty, Whallop, Bilked, Worked Out, Tombstone, Ragtown, Hungry, Steal Easy, Gone Home, Trouble, Slide Hill, Dust, Nineteen Dead Men, White Elephant, Burnt Offering, Hangtown, Grubby. I had been busted in Kentucky and busted on the Mississippi and busted in Arkansas and Kansas. But the good Lord was on my team this time. I went into the Rocky Mountains just a few paces ahead of a new era of prosperity. I made for Aspen, fi-nally, which had seen some good times and a lot of bad times. Still, you—

PROCESSION. Cars with lights on. Funeral. Byebye, Malachy. Goes right through the stoplight. Law-abiding entire life. Or nearly so. Now Malachy breaks law on way to burying. Though while alive he did push hard against the boundaries of the law. He'll probably bribe the celestial traffic cops. Exit him. Exit us. The law. Obey the law. A mountain of cloven-footed laws. Parteth the hoof. Cleaveth the cleft. Cheweth the cud. All right if parteth the hoof, but not if cleaveth the cleft and cheweth the cud. And such obedience will make ye a peculiar people unto the Lord. Obey the law. Stay In Line. Form Two Lanes. Cross Here. No Crossing. Park This Side. No Parking. Observe Minimum Speed. No Speeding. Turn Right Only On Red. Turn Left Only On Red. No Commercial Traffic. Is a funeral commercial? Pass Left Only. Keep To Right. No Stopping. Stop At Line. Go. Stop. Exit Only. Entrance Only. No Turns. Turn Here. No Traffic. All Traffic This Way. The law. Obey the law. Slow down at slippery crosswords. I command thee. I order and disdain. Do this. Do that. Blow Your Nose. Comb Your Hair, Benjamin. Tie Your Shoelaces. Do Not Forget Your Rubbers. Obey. The law of our house. Speak Only When Spoken To. Clean Your Eyeglasses. You Must Not Cry In Public. Stop Your Mumballing. Do Not Disobey. Do Not Pity Yourself. Don't. Or else. Fire and brimstone. Grasshoppers and frogs. Dust and flood. Imperil your future felicity. Says who? Big One. Big man in the ski. Old Chief. The King. The Stranger. All say. Obey the law. Prisoner, you are accused of flirting with the law. Have you got your lawyer? Sho nuff got mah leer, jedge. Law and behold.

COULD SMELL the boom in the air. I had arrived in a land flowing with bilk and money. I invested my last fifty dollars in the

Promised Land Mine just before other nostrils detected the sweet fragrance of profit. But once it filled the air, it was like a prairie fire. In bonanza country the stampede is not of bison or cattle but of the wandering herds of hopefuls at the end of their grubstake. Once the fever of Speculation attacks, it spreads rapidly through the ranks of the righteous, and even those who once had it and have recovered suffer a relapse.

Bonanza times came to Aspen again. Everyone heard on good authority that the price of metal was going up, up, up. Pay whatever they ask for a mine, because the sure-fire rise in price will guarantee you a profit. Any time two people met, and if they could sober up a lawyer, they entered into a deal at once. Some real-estate agents knew how to salt a mine to spice up its appeal, and those who didn't specialized in forged deeds instead. The hopefuls—as our own Connecticut resident, Mister Barnum, once told us—don't mind being conned so long as it is accomplished in an artistic way. I heard grown men, otherwise of proven sanity, calmly discuss the virtues of my mine, a mine which neither they nor I had ever worked or even so much as entered. I was introduced to each new hopeful as the owner of the Promised Land Mine, one of the most potential on the western slope, and an astute fellow to boot, who wouldn't sell, but just sat there watching its value go up and up every day, no one knowing when it would stop rising. In some weeks my mine appreciated as much as five hundred dollars. It probably didn't contain more than ten dollars of metal, and even that was by courtesy of a kindly real-estate agent to compensate for the lack of any natural endowments.

Marvelous accounts had gone forth about the riches in the mountains and emigrant autos were grinding westward. Newcomers found those who had gotten there first reluctant to part with mines, a reluctance that could be overcome only by trebling the price. New companies were founded almost every day to exploit the natural endowments, still unproved, of the surrounding mountains. Each company issued stock certificates by the mile from a printing press that worked night and day and still was months behind. A dozen shares were loaned for one, and that one usually was borrowed anyway. Prices rose like autumn smoke, and the only thing that remained cheap was money. To qualify for a loan a debtor needed only to show his clear-cut distress for funds.

Since money could be borrowed so freely and whatever was bought with it was likely to rise in value, people unaccustomed to wealth spent it recklessly. Even one who had amassed a tidy sum by the sound business practices he had learned back home —his skepticism, his firm policy of never trusting anyone and certainly not contributing to any charitable enterprise, his habit of searching all employees before he closed shop for the night, his relentless pursuit of widows and the aged who might have fallen a few pennies in arrears—all these time-tested business principles he threw to the winds that blew through the land of Speculation. A new arrival, bringing with him his life savings of $10,000 in specie, might reasonably be expected, if no ill fortune befell him, and he was not overly fond of gambling with those more expert than he, if he stayed clear of fancy women and didn't order French brandy, to hold out solvent for as long as a month. These infusions of real money from the constant arrival of new hopefuls kept the banks going and sharpened the scythes of Speculation. We all lived freely, for it was a time of great abandon, and we spent freely, because no one wanted to appear illiberal to his neighbors. Everyone required credit from someone, and in turn he had to give credit to someone else. So when—

■

—WELL, hello there, Rebecca. Getting ready to go back to college? You're not? To Alabama instead? Yes, I know the law is being flouted there. But why not get your education first? It's the most important thing you can do at your age. Our country was built on education. I know they've been deprived of an education. But now the Negroes will get their fair share. You can love your neighbor as yourself, Rebecca, without sacrificing your own education to go up and down the country for something that is inevitable anyway. You don't have to tell me that! Our people were fighting this battle long before it became fashionable. Jonathan Edwards founded the Anti-Slavery Society as far back as 1790 right here in this state. Of course I realize the situation today is different from slavery. But you might find yourself in the position of the good-natured lady who put a frozen rattlesnake inside her bodice to warm it. When it thawed out it bit her. That's the same kind of thanks you'll get for losing precious years of youth. No, no, you misunderstand me. Of course I know you're not looking for thanks. I didn't mean that at all. Of course they don't have to thank us for righting old wrongs. Now, now, Rebecca, your father and I have been chums since we were boys and I feel I don't have to be backward about speaking frankly to you. It's hard to undo the prejudices of centuries overnight. You're building castles in the air. You first have to put foundations under them. Don't forget that the roots of the Harum family go deep in this community. You Harums have a responsibility to New Salem. You're not some little secretary who can go running off to Alabama on a lark. It would be a shame to—

Walked off. Foolish girl. Excitable like her father. She'll do what she wants. She should have been spanked. Instead of spocked. Adolescent girls are irritable. Non composed menses. Probably sleep with some black boy there. Mingled seed. Gender with a diverse kind. White girls curious about them. Worship their molten gods. Our faults. We made too much of Negroes' sexual drives. Some people say it's due to the heat of the tropical sun. Overstimulates their sex glands?

■

THE BUST CAME, whole segments of the populace that had endorsed each other's notes collapsed at once. The bankers who had been so friendly during the bonanza days were now vultures squabbling over our poor, exposed flesh. The only real question they had to work out among themselves was not if they should feast on us, but which of them should have the choicest morsels. Once again I saw my neighbors and friends scatter to the winds. As for me, after the bust I was left with a fortune of $50,000—four bits of it in negotiable coin of the realm and the rest in experience.

Some, so recently owners of promising mines, applied to the bankers for help in putting together another grubstake to join the hopefuls in other parts of God's Country. But the bankers with their hardened hearts were indignant that we, proven failures, should consider ourselves worthwhile investments. "A loan, you say? A healthy man like you, no more than sixty years of age, with a limp that is scarcely detectable and a missing hand that no one would notice if only you would remember to keep the stump behind your back! *You* need a loan! A man like you who could raise himself up again by his own bootstraps! Why should there be need to borrow? Not if you would use some blank de cologne to prevent yourself from smelling like a compost heap. Is there no longer work for stokers on steamships? Do they no longer need people to break horses? Are the trees nowadays being felled by the wind? Are there no peddling territories left? Does the Alaskan frontier no longer exist? For shame! For shame!" No, there was no reprieve for any of us. Our mines had never produced a pailful of real metal. It was all a dream, and like a dream it evaporated in the clear light of reason. Someday, I suppose, people will return to Aspen and start selling the land back and forth again in search of some new promise they imagine is hidden in the mountains.

I, who so recently had been the envied owner of the Promised Land Mine, wandered hungrily from boom town to boom town, for I still thought America was a young nation full of opportunity. I was on my way to God's Country again via Pisgah Prospect and Edom and Jericho Corners, with stops along the way at Bonanza, Zenith, Grand, Sheba, Branch Mint, Empire,

Solomon's Throne, Golden Reward, Verdopolis, Garden City, Shiny Weather, and Crown of the Valley.

So I headed for Texas, which is where my Kansas farm had blown anyway. An old couple who had just lost their only son to typhoid took me on as a hired man. Their farm wasn't much to boast of, a run-down place near the town of Opp—named after Opportunity, which had never come along. No manna or quails dropped on us from the heavens. We brought forth crops by the sweat of our brows. When the old folks died I learned that they had left the farm to me, since there was nothing else for them to do with it. Within a year the bank told me it had a buyer willing to pay three dollars an acre for the place. I had had enough of wandering, and so I refused the offer, saying that I wouldn't sell for less than ten dollars an acre. That was an impossible price in those days, and I intended they refuse it. But a telegram came right back from Fort Worth saying the bank accepted my price and was buying at ten. For the first time I knew what it was like to possess hard cash instead of notes of credit or promises. After all the years of being cheated in God's Country, of being led to the brink of false opportunities, the bank played it fair and square, paying right down the line. Next thing I knew, though, that land was sprouting a good crop of oil wells.

I had been honest, mostly, during nearly forty years of wandering through The Great American West. And hard-working. No one can say I ever shirked. I had been loyal to my neighbors, friends, and the local and state governments under whose sovereignty I was residing at various times. I had never killed anyone. I did not drink to excess and I rarely played games of chance. I kept the commandments as much as the next man. I treated all honest men alike, regardless of their race or religion or color. And what had it gotten me? A wealth of experience, mostly. And a grubstake from the sale of the Texas farm. I had been to all the Promised Lands and not one had honored its promises to any decent comer. But I had learned important lessons. That a sharp bargain is better than an honest one. That there is no better relative than a buck. That the thief is the one who got caught. So I took my grubstake and my new set of verities to California for one last try at God's Country. And there I prospered like a green bay tree. I simply sold houses for more than people could afford to pay.

So now I sit here on my terrace looking down onto an irrigated valley, keeping track of my investments and worrying that my butler may be sneaking snorts of my French brandy. Forty years ago I set out in search of God's Country, and my envious neighbors think I have found it at last. But that is not so. God's Country is The Great American Swindle. God is not in our country. He abandoned it long ago. Perhaps he was with Isaiah Pennyman at the beginning. But then, while the Pennymans were extolling the glories of His grand design, He up and sneaked off, leaving his covenant unpaid. I had learned at last that God's Country is not the place you are always going to and never reaching. It is the place that you look back to. That, for what it is worth, is what life has taught me. For whatever instructive value this letter might have for future generations, please feel free to append it to the back of the Black Book as my contribution.

I must at this point be abrupt, brother. My request cannot wait, because daily the discomfort grows. Despite the beneficial climate of California and its uncommonly good soil, I shall very soon succumb to that indisposition known as cancer. Soon I will enter God's Country and I hope it is not as great a swindle as the other places I inspected in my wanderings. It would please me to know that I will be buried in New Salem alongside all our other Pennymans. At the very end I too must admit that I am a captive of history. Anyway, they say that being buried near a church improves your odds of salvation. And one more anyway: if there is room in that plot for Mother's Pierre, who died for une grande romance, then there is room for me, who died simply in pain. Please, brother, forgive me many things, spoken and unspoken, and honor this stupid and sentimental request of an old fool. Please.

PETITION DENIED. Thou shalt not. Sully again. Our soil. Thou shalt not disturb. All, all sleeping on the hill. Thou shalt not return. Forbidden. You chose another earth. Now sleep in it. You man without a country. Exit you. Exit us. Thou shalt never. Enter mine own promis'd land. Die on your mountain. While we carry on. Bury you yes on the lone pray-ree. No thirty days of weeping and mourning for you. Begone. Lay down no laws. Do this. Do that. Here. There. Leave me lie, Levi. While I number my blessings. Enumerate my privileges. Count the cost. Gauge the value. Add the joys. Compute the rate of half-life. Number. Number my life.

Age, 67 years, 4 months, 8 days. How did I get so old so fast? Domiciled at 1 Founder's Street. Home telephone, 683-5757. Office address, 12 Pennyman Street, 2nd floor front. Office telephone number, 683-1720. ZIP Code number? Don't remember. Something new to aggravate us. Post office box number, 1244. Get new one higher up. Bank vault number, B009. New Salem Library card number, 2574. Safe combination, 24L-75R-44L. Excelsior! Grave plot at New Salem Protestant Episcopal Church, 1. Soon, soon. Number of books in home, 1,764. Number of books in office, 396. Plus the Black Book. Artifacts of a life. Realicts. Number of books read for edification or enjoyment in past 12 months, 125, more or less. Eyes weakening. Number of theatrical performances attended, 0. Number of films seen, 0. Number of poker games participated in with cronies, 0. Number of athletic events witnessed, 0. Number of television programs watched, on an average day, 0. Number of radio programs heard each day, 2 or 3. Number of cigarettes smoked per diem, 0. Number of cigars and/or pipefuls consumed daily, 0. Number of cocktails imbibed per day, 0. Number of hours spent on hobbies other than daydreaming, puzzles, or reading, 0. If you consider reading a hobby, number of hours spent each day, 4. Mock Twain and American jokelore. Testymeants. Highthorne. Funnomore Keeper. Lungflow. J. Grimlife Whiter. Wilt White Man. Immersed Son. Edgar Allan Poetry. Pennyman wanted to be a poet. Bret Hurt. Ezra Punned. Rejoyce! Puneers! O Puneers! Homeowner's insurance policy number, 26H-5724. The Great American Accident Company policy number, 242457. Stock brokerage account number, 7542775. My stock went down. All others go up. Better sell. Number of teeth in situ, 14. Number of suits in reasonably good repair, 2. Maybe 3. No, only 2. I'm no Yankee Dude. Number of pairs of shoes not in need of resoling, 2. Number of shirts with collars attached, 4. Neck size, 14. Number of shirts with detachable collars in good repair, 4. Number of collars stained by repeated washings in caustic soap, 6. Pairs of socks not in need of darning, 5½. Find the other one. Pairs of socks in need of darning, 9. Miss Dickinson is too old. Switch to commercial laundry? To Ah Sin, the Chinee? But Miss Dickinson needs the money. She took care of Mother. Retire her? Hurt her pride? Maybe not. Number of wives now living or deceased, 0. And their present states of health? Meaningless. Number of children born in or out of wedlock? What father knows? Probably one. Number of old chums still alive, 2. Only 1 after John the Good goes. Number of people who might come to your aid were you viciously attacked on the streets by a Negro inflamed by the tropical sun, 0. Number of times voted in presidential elections, 11. Number of times your party was victorious, 5. Number of times cast ballot in state or local elections, 36. Number of times party was victorious, 32. But not recently. Number of times elected to an office, howsoever minor, 1. A freak. They wouldn't select me twice. Number of charities to which contributed in the last taxable year, 3. Average hours of sleep in each 24-hour period, 5½. Number of nights in past week in which sleep was a challenge, 7. Average number of bowel movements per week, 4. Constipated. Stop by Myer's now. Number of years you would wish to live longer did you incredibly possess the magical powers to make such a decision, 1. So I could see Paree. Fully attested this day, 9/9/63. Makes

three nines. Magic. Who was the black king? It was. Don't remember. My memory failing. Benjamin, the trained memory.
But there were three kings. Three a magic number. Black
magic. Numerology.

Eerie, meanie, miney, more. One-ery, two-ery, eckeery, Ann,
phillisy, phollisy, Nicholas, John. Queebe, quarby, Irish Annie,
you are out! No, no, count it again! All right, poor sport. Monkey,
monkey, do not fear, How many monkeys are there here? 1, 2,
3, you are HE! You're it again, Benny! No, no, try it another
way. No! Yes! Aw, let's go home. No, don't go. We will. Please
don't! All right, Benny, we'll stay, but this is the last time. Try
it injun counting. Don't know how. I do! I do! Are you sure you
know, Johnny? Yeah. But you better do it up to twenty, Johnny.
Why? Because it's fair. No it isn't, Benny. It is. Isn't. All right,
Benny, but this is the last time. Okay, Johnny. Een, teen, tether,
fether, fip, satra, latra, ko, tethery, dick. Eendick, teendick,
tetherdick, fetherdick, bump, eenbump, teenbump, tetherbump,
fetherbump, jicket. You lose again, Benny! You're it! You're it!
Now you got to say this over again as fast as you can. Six slick
slim saplings. Okay, start now, Benny. Six slix slimp saplings.
No, Benny, faster! Slix slix slix sliplinx. Blah-blah-black blook.
Aw, you're too young, Benny. I'm not, Johnny. Yes you are. We
don't want to play with you anymore. We think you stink. Go
sink in the drink. Haw-haw. Yeah, you got no toys, Benny. I
have only words to play with. No, that's not rue. Yeah, you
write poems. Pretty pretty pukey pukey poems. I do not.
Teacher says you do, Benny. Yeah, and you play with girls!
He plays with Irish Annie! Grab him by the bells! Haw-haw.
And you got four eyes. We'll break your glasses, Benny. Yeah,
and we'll go home and leave you by yourself. Yeah, go up and
cry to your mother, Benny. Ha-ha. You can't, cause your mother's in Paree. What's your mother doin off in gay Paree, Benny?
She's. She's. Bet she won't bring you back no present! I bet she
will. No she won't. She will! She will! She'll bring me back a
gold Eyeful Tower with a little hole you look into and see a picture of Paris. No she won't! Yes she will! And where's your old

man, Benny? Yeah, where's your old man? Ha-ha-ha-HA! He went away. Ha-ha-ha-HA! Where did he go, Benny? He went. He went. To explore secret islands where no white man has ever been before and he's going to bring back a black king with him to work as our butler and do whatever I command him to and he'll have a big scimitar to cut off the hands of anyone who hits me and his name is King Mumbo-Jumbo. Yeah, yeah, yeah! It's true! And my father will come home rich and famous and you'll read all about his adventures in the newspaper. Ha-ha-ha-HA. I'll get my big brother after you, Johnny, if you don't stop laughing. We won't. I'll hit you, Johnny. I'll hit you back, Benny. I'll stop if you stop. All right. But you're still it, Benny. No, count it again. All right, Benny, but this is the last time. Ena, mena, mona my. Panalona, bona, stry. O, U, T spells OUT! You're it again, Benny! You're it! Now you got to play what we want. I'm going to count, Benny, and you got to re- peat what I say. Only you got to make the number one higher. Understand? Yes. Are you sure, Benny? Yes, I do, Johnny. All right, here goes. I one it. Now, Benny, you got to say, I two it. I two it. I three it. I four it. I five it. I six it. I seven it. I eight it. Haw-haw-haw-HAW. You said, I ate it, Benny! Now you got to eat the dog shit! No, I won't, Johnny! Yes you will! No I won't! We'll make you! Count it again, Johnny! Count it again! Count it!

■

— BEN, if I didn't know you better, I'd think you were casing my bank.

— Oh, Don. Just counting. I mean. When did you get back?

— Last week. Peggy and I had a grand time in Italy. Just grand. They're not like our Italians at all. Those over there are all charm. Something must be lost in the Atlantic crossing.

— Well.

— Ben, when are you going to give Europe a fling?

— Guess I never had the time, Don. I mean, there was Mother.

And then getting her affairs in order after she passed on. Then clients. Winding up their estates. Anyway, as Thoreau said, I have traveled a good deal in New Salem. But if I had my druthers I'd like to go to Paris. Mother always loved the French. Maybe I'll take a vacation there this spring. I don't know.

— You'll find the time, Ben, you'll find it. But look out you don't go during the rainy season. Europe is a place everyone should see. Only learn a little of the language first. They no capitch the Henclutch very well, I can tell you that. We found one of those picturesque villages with a big, empty beach just off the Italian Riviera. Strong undertow, though. Peggy damn near drowned. I got to her before she went down for the third time. She said her whole life passed before her. No one knows about this place yet. No Americans, thank Gawd. Everything was splendid except our room. Noisy. So we tried to switch rooms. But they only spoke Italian. Talked to them right out of my Berlitz Phrase Book. Tried my best sign language. They just shrugged and showed me a mouthful of brown teeth. Finally, in desperation, they sent for the local schoolteacher. All smiles and gums, celluloid collar and cuffs, black string tie. Was I happy to see him! "So you speak English!" I said with relief, reaching into my pocket and slipping him a poor bar. He smiled and showed me his gums. "A leetel." So I told him the whole story of how we reserved a room facing the beach but they had given us one facing the street where whenever two people want to talk they first go to opposite ends of the street and yell. The more I spoke the more glassy his eyes became. When his smile evaporated I knew we were in deep difficulty. He just stood there. Desperate. Then he said, very slowly, "Let—me—understand. You say. You say—you wanna—buy—a—fat—duck?"

— Ever get your room changed?

— No, we didn't. It started to pour like the flood, so we wanted an excuse to get out of our reservation anyway. We went up to the Black Forest instead. Met some grand people there. Even the little milkmaids know how to speak English. The Germans are great organizers. But we'll go back to that

Italian beach someday. After they catch up a little with the modern world. Say, I've got some Kodachromes here I just picked up at Tripod Camera.

— You know I can't, Don.

— Oh.

— Almost achromatic. I see only black and white.

— I forgot, Ben. Sorry.

— Doesn't matter. It's always been in the family. It's inherited by the males in the line, like hemophilia.

— What are you up to, just standing here, Ben?

— I was thinking about something, I guess. I don't remember now. Getting old.

— Aren't we all, Ben, aren't we all. I'm retiring this January. Not much left for us old-timers to do except count our blessings.

— I think that is what I was just doing.

— But, Ben, the blessings are getting fewer and fewer every day. Talk about times that try men's souls. The days of this republic are numbered. I can tell you that, Ben. I can tell you that.

— Well.

— Letting that nigger take over our capital city like that. What was his name again?

— King?

— Yes. John Calvin King. You wouldn't have that black King inciting to riot if you didn't have a sympathetic administration in Washington. The minorities are running the government now. The great unwashed are in the saddle! And we're just their ponies to be whipped! That man doesn't even deserve to be in the White House. He wasn't elected fair and square. Everyone knows the Illinois ballot boxes were stuffed.

— Well.

— Would those people rather be back in Africa? Read the newspapers and see what's happening on that continent now. Barbaric. And why should they go back when they can stay here and get their checks without working? They never learned that what the mouth eats the hands ought to work for. Someday our children will have to pay off on these mistakes. But does the President care? He won't be around then. And that brother of his! He speaks like Bugs Bunny.

— Well, Kennedy's not my man either, Don. But he's my President. I guess we're stuck with him.

— The people still have the right of impeachment. I tell you, Ben, some of the stories I've heard about the President and his women are a disgrace to the office. Makes Harding sound like a Methodist circuit rider.

— Well.

— Something has got to give. You can't keep raising taxes to pay colored women to have babies out of wedlock. You can't send youngsters to college free who couldn't even hold a job cleaning out cuspidors. This used to be Gawd's Country, Ben. But those people are destroying it. Did you notice that all those welfare cases suddenly had enough money to travel to Washington a few weeks ago for their march? And a friend of mine with the New Haven says a lot of them traveled parlor car too. There's big money behind them, Ben. You know where it's coming from, I'm sure.

— Coming from? No, I guess I don't.

— The rich Long Noses are behind the coloreds. Always have been, and that's a fact I can show you in print. You ever read *The Passing of the Great Race* by Madison Grant? It's all there in black and white.

— That was written fifty years ago, Don.

— What does that matter? Facts don't change. I tell you, we're seeing the passing of the greatest race mankind has known. The white race has done more than all the others put together. They're the ones who invented automobiles and airplanes and everything else. We better start counting our blessings or this country will become nothing more than a colony of Old Jerusalem. The Jewnited States of America. Change all the names! Jew York. Kike's Peak. The Mocky Mountains. Change the songs! Yankee Yiddle Went to Town.

— I don't know. That's pretty rough talk, Don. Things aren't always as bad as they seem. Not to change the subject, but listen to that banging! He doesn't even give those men time to take a pee.

— Freudenthal? He's got the new money on his side. That's for sure. And he'll mortgage property we wouldn't even touch. I have to admit, though, it's paying off for him. It's unsound banking, but in these times soundness takes the back seat. Bad money drives out the good.

— Guess we all have to modernize, Don.

— I'm not one who's just sitting back and taking it. Ben, if solid people like you and me give in to chaos, then it's all over. Finished. The end of the line. I wanted to speak to you about this anyway. Glad the opportunity came up. I meet with a group of people in Stamford who feel the way we do. It's part of a nationwide movement.

— Not the Birchers?

— No, of course not. It's not the Liberty League either, or anything like that. No, no, it's perfectly respectable. We're not a bunch of extremists. We're mostly a study group. We have friends in Washington. They have to tread lightly because of the kind of administration we've got down there now. They know it would ruin their careers if they spoke out. But they're with us one hundred percent. They're just waiting for the winds of public opinion to shift. They're handing us secret testimony and revealing a lot of behind-the-scenes stuff that never gets printed in the liberal papers. I tell you, our group will soon begin to throw a scare into those politicians. They'll act a lot differently when they know every time they give in to those spades, someone is keeping score. You can count on that.

— I'm not a political animal, Don.

— That's not true at all, Ben. You were a good First Selectman once.

— That was twenty years ago. There was a war on. Wasn't anyone else to select from. I ran unopposed.

— Like Gladinski. Still, Ben, you really showed this town. They weren't expecting you to be so tough when they elected you.

— Well, they didn't make the same mistake at the next election. Most people can stand being bitten by a wolf. But not by a sheep.

— Ben, you're still the same man you were then. What are you planning to do with your time after you shut down your office?

— Haven't decided yet. Just winding things up now. The University at Storrs wants the family papers. I might give some of the more important ones to the Yale University Library. I have to get them in order first. After that, I just don't know. I'd like to see Paris.

— See what I mean? You can find the time. Come to our meeting this Sunday. We'll show you we make sense. Drive down to Stamford with me.

— Well. I'll let you know. By the way, I was just chatting with Rebecca. She tells me she's dropping out of college. To go to Alabama.

— She's a great disappointment to Peggy and me. I can admit it to you, Ben. She always was headstrong. I told her she's making a big mistake. Not to mention the embarrassment she's causing us. But when she learns the truth about those people in Alabama, she'll come back. The door is always open. She may be headstrong, but she's also sensible. The most she'll lose is a year, and I'm sure the experience will have some value. She might even do a term paper or something about it. We'll get her back into college. After all, it's Peggy's college too. Her grandmother's also, for that matter. The Harum girls have always gone there. They're not going to keep Rebecca from coming back just because she got her head turned for a while by this Reverend King's oratory. I wonder who wrote that speech for him, the one about having a dream. No colored man can write like that.

— Well.

— Anyway, I wish you'd think about coming with me on Sunday.

— I'll let you know, Don. I was going to stop by for a moment to look at the ticker. I've been thinking about getting out of a stock. Although, I don't know, it might go up.

— I'd sell. That's for sure. Don't be fooled because the market hit a high last week. The underpinnings are weak. The market just reflects the general psychology of the country. Confusion. Right now all the signs are pointing to a selloff this autumn. I'd get out now, Ben. It's not worth trying to squeeze out a few extra points. Don't be penny wise, pound foolish, Ben.

— I don't know. I saw an article in the *Times*. It said business is confident.

— When everyone starts talking confidence, that's the time to get out fast. It means they're just whistling in the dark. Confidence is all they talked before they started jumping out of windows in Twenty-Nine. No, Ben, a bull can make money in the market. A bear can make money. But not a hog.

— Well. I'll just come in for a few minutes. Ought to be getting back. Gladinski called a few times. Said he wanted to talk to me. Then he never came. He keeps telling my secretary it's important, and then he never shows up for the appointments.

— It may be nothing but stupidity, Ben. You know the one about a Polish crossword puzzle? One box.

— Better be careful who you tell that to, Don.

— Don't I know it! In this town nowadays you've got to be circumspect. Anyway, Ben, let Gladinski find you. Don't rush back for him.

— Well, I don't want to be rude. He'll think I'm doing it intentionally. They're touchy.

— It's good you mentioned Gladinski, Ben, because I've got something to talk to you about. I was just visiting John Purcell and—

— Is he any more comfortable?

— No, he's doing poorly, poorly.

— I saw Virginia a while ago. She told me. Smells as if she's become a daytime tippler.

— It's hard having a father like John the Good. He ought to help her and her husband out. But I guess she'll inherit soon enough.

— I'm not at liberty to say, Don.

— You mean? Who else could he leave it to?

— Well, he's got a sister out in California. And trusts are apt to skip a generation. There's no way to change John the Good at this late date. He's the last Puritan. Anyway, what did he say to you? About Gladinski, I mean.

— When did you see John last?

— I stopped by his house a few weeks ago, when we talked over his will.

— Guess he didn't know about it then. Or maybe his mind is wandering now and he's imagining things. Still, we'd better discuss it, Ben. Come on inside. People will wonder what we've been gossiping about so long. Throw a panic into the whole damn town.

Granite front. Iron doors. Safe. Reliable. Probity. Tiled floor. Click of heels. Tattoo of efficiency. Deposits and Withdrawals. Deposits and Withdrawals. Deposits and. Savings Accounts Only. Inquiries. Worshipers at the temple of finance. Jeu ave at the First Bank & Trust. They give everything a number. Add up the figures. Count the blessings.

— Here, Ben, this chair is a bit more comfortable. You can look at the ticker. I'll be back in a moment and we can talk.

— Thanks, Don.

IS PLANNED IF GIVERNOR XXXXXX GOVERNOR DOES NOT BOW TO COURT ON SHOOLS XXXXXX SCHOOLS.

WASHINGTON, SEPT 9—PRESIDENT KINNEDY'S BROTHER SAID HE IS WAIT-ING UNTIL TOMORROW TO SENSE WEATHER THE GIVERNOR WILL ALLOW OMISSIONS OF NIGROES TO SCHOOLS IN BUMINGHAM AND MOBIL.

TURKKU XXXXXX TURKU, FINLAND SEPT 9—VICE PRESIDENT JOHNSON, LOOKING SUBDUED, PAID A QUIET VISIT TO THIS POOR XXXXXX PORT CITY TODAY. MR. JOHNSON'S DEMANNER CONTRASTED WITH HIS BUBBLING GOOF HUMOR YESTERDAY WHEN

SALEM, ASS., SEPT 9—THE MEDICAL EXHUMINER STATED HE WAS NOT STUCK ALTHOUGH THE POLICE WERE WITHOUT A GLUE IN THE TENTH STRUNGLING DEATH IN EASTERN MASSACHUSETTS IN

SEPT 9—THE OAK BELIEVED TO BE THE TREE THAT INSPURRED JOYCE KILLMOR'S POEM "TREES" WILL BE XUT DOWN ON SEPT. 18. THE HUGE WHITE OAK, WHICH IS ALMOST 300 YEARS OLD, HAS BEEN DYING OF

WASHINGTON, SEPT 9—PRESIDENT KENNEDY SAD TODAY THAT "IT WOULD NOT BE HELPFUL AT THIS TIME" TO REDOUCE UNITED STATES ADD TO SOUTH VIETNAM

300 NIGROES IN HIGH PINT, NORTH CAROLINA, ARRESTED DURING

ATHLETICS TURN BACK YANKEES, 7-6

TWINS VICTORIOUS OVER INDIANS. BRAVES TAKE TWO

COFFEE F U T U R E PRICES, WHICH HAD BEEN QUIET FOR SUM TIME, PERCOLATED TODAY AND LEAD OTHER COMMODITIES ON THE JEW YORK EXCHANGES

MOST COTTON PRICES

FALL.

BRITISH PUND SHOWS DECLINE. BROKER SAYS HE IS CONCERNED BY

FALL IN PURCHASES.

CLOSING NYS PRICES. AMERADA 78⅜ —¾ AM AIRLINES 28¾ —⅛ AM BAKING 19¼ —⅛ AM CAN 46½ —⅛ AM CEM 10⅞ —⅛ AM CYAN 600½ xxxxxx 60½ —1¼

All down. Americans all down. Amer Dist. Down. Am El Pow. Down. Am Enka. Down. All fall. Down. But the others. Guinness Breweries. Up! Israel Bank Leumi. Up! Instituto Mobiliare Italiano. Up! Saarlandische Kreditbank. Up! Dreyfus Fund. Up! Joy Manufacturing Company. Up! Up! Excelsior! Oh. Just remembered. Better throw away that letter. Use Don's wastebasket. Tear my name off envelope first. Oh, oh. He's coming back. Put in pocket. Get rid of it later.

— Ben! Oh my Gawd, Ben!

— Don, what the?

— I knew it! I knew sooner or later he'd find us out. It was too good to believe that New Salem would be spared. Our luck has run out! He's coming!

— Don, talk sense. Who's coming?

— Who? Who? Only Josh Levitas, that's who! I might as well say only a tornado or only the Russian army!

— You mean the Wall Street operator?

— Could there be two of them? Oh Gawd, he's coming. He's invading. He's on his way! Start covering, boys, we've got to camouflage everything negotiable! Levitas's raiders are on their way! Lock your doors! Shutter your windows! Because Josh Levitas is coming! Increase your insurance! Cover your margin!

— Don, stop it. What has Josh Levitas to do with us?

— Everything! Blow the walls down, it's all over for us! Josh Levitas is coming!

— Don, what could he do to us?

— What could he do? What could he do? Let me tell you about Josh Levitas. Let me tell you how years ago everyone thought that he was only the small-time operator of European Remnants Corporation. That was long before his reputation got nosed through the country. His first plunge was buying up a shipload of timber that had become split beyond any use on the Atlantic crossing, not because he needed it for anything in particular but because it was so cheap it was almost free. Then he got the idea of making the chips into flat-sided toothpicks without points to hurt the tongue. That's when all the hayseeds in the country stopped sucking on grass blades and switched to toothpicks as if they were gumdrops. With the millions Levitas made on that deal he bought into The Last Trumpet Musical Instrument Company and Gehenna Constructing Company, and by switching assets back and forth, calling in preferreds, issuing new debentures, and such manipulations, he was able to make both companies appear profitable. He pulled in his sails at the top of the market in Twenty-Nine, and when the bust came he was just sitting there with his vaults filled with cash for new acquisitions. That was when Josh Levitas added to his holdings Millennium Mines, Jericho Land Company, Gilgal Gargle Products, Celestial Credit, Psalms of Bethlehem Lyres, and Hebron Devices, Inc. He merged them all into a new corporation, Hallelujah Investments, which he later combined with Sky City Futurist Furnishings and New Jerusalem Land Exploration Company. After that he lay quiet for a while, like a bobcat digesting its kill. Then he started making the newspapers a lot. Maybe you recall all the stories about him? Noted financier climbs a mountain. Wall Street wizard shoots the rapids. But Josh Levitas doesn't climb mountains or risk his neck in rapids unless he has something in mind. Oh no, not him! Because all the time he was climbing those mountains and breathing the uncommonly pure air of The Great American West, he wasn't out to improve his lungs. He was climbing to measure how many board feet of timber he could hew! He was shooting the rapids to calculate how much water he could draw for electric power! People should have guessed that—but they didn't, and so they lost everything. They learned all right after Levitas had raided Dream Land Improvement Company and Apache Power and Light, which, because of interlocking directorates, also controlled such promising western corporations as Bunkum Mines, Penny Express Transport, Red Man Distilleries, Slick Snuff, and Fairplay Army & Navy Stores. For a while he lay low, but then he emerged again in a new personality. A philanthropist! Pictures in the papers showed him at charity balls and patting little colored boys on the head. But Levitas does nothing unless there's a reason. With his good name for philanthropy, he was able to set up a whole new assortment of companies. F. D. Roosevelt Fidelity. Cradle-to-Grave Fiduciary. El Dorado Loan Company. Golden Opportunities Investments. Lone Eagle Loan. Longlasting Life Insurance Company. By the time the Second World War ended he controlled more companies than the financial community could keep track of. But still people hadn't wised up to his way of working. They watched for the big moves when they should have been keeping their eyes on the subtleties. As when Josh Levitas was heard to remark casually one day that he was going to modernize his operation. That should have been a tip-off to those who could read the signs! The signs that Josh Levitas was coming! One after another he bought up Standard Satellite, Kinetic Nuclear Electronics, Subtle Devices Corp, Heuristic Concepts, Basic Strategies, Adomic Research, and a dozen others I don't recall just now. After a few spinoffs, exchanges of stock, and other manipulations, he put the whole thing together into a conglomerate known as Monumental Investments. Yessir, he's just sitting pretty with hundreds of millions, ready to pounce whenever new prey comes within range. Wherever you turn, there he is! So, Ben, you can understand now why I'm worried.

— But, Don, all that has nothing to do with New Salem.

— Oh, it doesn't, does it? Do you know who I just learned called the New Salem Boosters & Commerce Association last week? Do you know who asked them for a copy of our zoning laws?

— Not Josh Levitas?

— Of course not, Ben. He's too crafty to use his own name. The inquiry came from Mister Dollod McDog, vice president of New England Monument Memorial Company.

— There's nothing suspicious about that.

— Not unless you know that New England Monument is a wholly owned subsidiary of the Paradise Casket Company of Valhalla, New York, which is—a—Josh—Levitas—company!

— Well, still.

— No, Ben, you've got to know how Levitas works to see his game. Oh, he's a crafty one! Just look at that name—Dollod McDog.

— Well. It is a little unusual.

— Unusual! You know how the Hebrews read from right to left. So the "Dog" part means "God." And you know what "Mc" means, of course.

— It usually means "son of."

— That's right, Ben! Son of God. They're always rubbing it in about being the chosen people. But I'm not finished. "Dollod." Just look at it! What does it tell you?

— Well, it could be a palindrome.

— A what?

— You know, reads the same backwards as forwards. As in A MAN, A PLAN, A CANAL, PANAMA. Or, MADAM, I'M ADAM. Or the word DEIFIED. There are lots of them.

— Hmm. Didn't think of that. They're always leading you around in circles. No, I was thinking it meant "dollared." Rich. Mister Rich Son of God. Oh, they're a boastful people all right! Who else could that be but Levitas not wanting word to get out that he's ready to pounce on New Salem?

— Don, it's a little farfetched. It could be a perfectly legitimate request. It could even be that some youngster has to write a high-school report on zoning and asked his father to help him. Or maybe an employee of New England Monument wants to buy a house here. It could be something completely innocent.

— You're wrong, Ben. I've got an instinct where Josh Levitas is concerned. I just called Missus Lowell at the Boosters & Commerce myself. She was the one who took the phone request. She chatters a lot. She'd bend the ear of the Lawd. Anyway, from what I could make out, she thought it was mighty suspicious. First a secretary told her to hold the wire a moment. Then there was a clicking of buttons and finally Mister Dollod McDog got on. Missus Lowell said he purred very apologetically for bothering her, for taking up from her valuable time, but could she maybe do by him little favors and send along maybe the zoning laws, maybe specialist delivery? Missus Lowell said he spoke with—a—faint—accent!

— That may not mean anything. Not everyone was born in America.

— I tell you, Ben, it's a raid by Levitas! But there's still a fighting chance. I don't know what he's after in New Salem, but we'll stop him! Yessir, we'll stop him! Edna! Edna! I want everyone from assistant vice president on up to come in here. Right away! Oh. Wait. All except Mister Goldgarten. Tell him. Tell him I heard his wife hasn't been feeling well and we can dispense with. I mean sacrifice his help. He can go home early.

And, Edna, tell the switchboard operator she'll have to stay late. Maybe the whole night. We're stopping the clocks! We'll get to the bottom of this! I want all phone lines kept open. And better tell a few of the girls to stay in case we need them. We're going into full mobilization. All right, fellows, to work! First, Reggy, I want you to get the best private investigation firm in New York City looking into what New England Monument is up to. Right away! Now, the rest of you, I want you to start thinking creatively. Give me any ideas, no matter how foolish they may sound at first. We'll brainstorm this thing through. Yes, Whitey, do you have an idea already?

— I sure do, Mister Harum. Do you remember O'Hara?

— O'Hara? O'Hara? Oh, you mean that drunken Irish embezzler?

— No one ever convicted him of it. Being Irish, I mean. Anyway, he claims to have handled a stock option for Levitas. He might know something.

— Phone him! Right now!

— Great idea, Whitey.

— Sure, Whitey, phone him.

— Good thinking, feller.

— Ye-ah!

— Thataway to go, guy.

— Hello. Hello. Yes I would like to speak to Bill O'Hara. Whitey Alcott here. Yes of course this is a business call. Oh, damn! Got disconnected. I'll try again. Hello, miss, you cut me off. I'd like to speak to Bill O'Hara. Yes, my name is Alcott. A-L-C-O-T-T. That's right. Yes, I'll wait. Hello. Yes, miss, this is Whitey Alcott, A-L-C-O-T-T, of the New Salem First Bank & Trust. No, there's no trouble at all. I just want to speak to Mister O'Hara. Yes, it's important. No, I do not care to write him a letter! I'm an old friend. A very old friend. You don't? Well, miss, I wouldn't expect you to know all his very old friends. Oh, I see. You've been his confidential secretary for twenty-two years. Well, we're not exactly the closest of old friends. But he'll remember me. We met at Hos Biglow's wedding in New Salem. Two years ago. Yes, that's right. Yes, that was the time he was arrested for disorderly conduct. No, he didn't do anything that terrible. He just put ice cubes down the women's dresses. No, I don't know why he was arrested if it wasn't so terrible. I'm not the New Salem police force! No, I don't care to tell you what my call is in reference to. Miss, please just connect me. I'll only take a moment of his time. Ah, I think she's doing it now. Oh damn, cut off!

— Good try anyway, Whitey.

— Not your fault, guy.

— Ye-ah.

— Good thinking anyway, guy.

— Sure was. Too bad.

— Yes, what is it, Willy?

— Just a crazy thought, Mister Harum, but you don't think Middlesex Fabrics could be involved, do you? You know he bought up that outfit just before homosexuality came out into the open.

— Might be. Who knows what he'll pull? It could come from any direction. Why do you ask, Willy?

— It's just that I saw a couple of new faggots promenading around town. Looking for property, I guess.

— Oh, Gawd! Them too! Now we've got a bunch of fairies pirouetting around the maypole on the common. That's going to finish us for sure. That's the end.

— Well, it could be worse, Mister Harum. Most of them are so afraid of the law that they don't cause trouble. Never complain about anything, not even an overcharge on the bank statement. Like Peri and his friend. You never hear a sound from their house. I don't have their habit myself, but there's a lot to be said for them.

— Still. Damn freaks walking around town. Not a good influence. Why does everyone who moves to New Salem nowadays have to be faggot, colored, Puerto Rican, or Mediterranean? Don't white people buy houses any more? Yes, Reggy? Which private investigator did you get?

— I'm afraid I struck out, Mister Harum. I first called Seeing Eye Investigations. They're the biggest. Handled that nasty divorce Stormy went through last year. After I told them what we wanted they said they couldn't take us on as clients. Conflict of interest.

— Conflict of interest?

— That's right. So then I called Undercover and got the same answer. Ditto at Ace and Eagle. Well, you can bet I was getting suspicious all right. So I tried them all—The Vulture Agency, Hawk Eyes, Deceive & Retrieve, Sleuth & Snoop, Oui-Non Whodunit, Swiss Confidential, The Original Swiss Confidential, The Bank Dick, Adams & Thieves, The We-Never-Slip Agency, Monsieur Dupin's Ruse, Stanley & Levenstein, Lone Wolff, The Third Legree, Injun Joe's Trackers, Buck's Privates, Baker Street Irregulars, The Think Man, Spillane Guts, Sam Spade (formerly The White Hunter), and Flat, Foot, Flugie & Floy. Not one would touch our case. And they all clammed up as soon as I mentioned New England Monument.

— Josh Levitas must have every damn one of them on retainer. No doubt about it! Oh Gawd, he's closing in!

— Just thought of something! I know the attorney in Bethel who handled the closing of a dairy farm one of Levitas's men bought as a tax shelter. He might know what's going on at New England Monument. At least he could tell us who Dollod McDog is.

— Thataway, Tommy.

— Righto!

— Good thinking, guy.

— Ye-ah!

— Call him!

— Hello. Simpson, how are you? This is Tommy Aldrich. I'm just great. Couldn't be better. Wife and the little chappies? Swell. Oh? Your mother? Gosh, Simpy, I'm sorry to hear that. I didn't know. Sure I'll tell Patsy. She'll be upset to hear it. Too bad. Golly, I'm sorry. Wish there were something we could do. Say, Simpy, I wanted to ask you something. It's about Josh

Levitas. But. But. All I want. I only. Oh, well. Thanks anyway.

— What did he say?

— Conflict of interest.

— What happened to his mother?

— Ran off with a French painter she met in Paris, France.

— Oh, oh. The artistic temperament can't be trusted.

— He wasn't that kind. A house painter.

— Oh.

— Twenty years old.

— Oh.

— Mister Harum! Mister Harum!

— Now, Billy, what do you mean by busting in here like that? Can't you see the executives are having a meeting? You can water the plants tomorrow.

— It's not that, Mister Harum. I heard Edna talking about Mister Levitas. I think I saw him!

— You did! Where?

— Right down the street. This afternoon. There was this little old man in sort of droopy pants. He kept smiling. He was looking at some of the streets near the common. He made notes in a little book. I think he was Hebrew.

— Say, Don, I think I saw him also.

— You did, Ben?

— Yes. Ingratiating smile.

— Now, Billy, I want you to think very carefully. Did you see him go any place in particular?

— Yes I did, Mister Harum. I saw him go into Rappaccini's Hardware.

— Get Rappaccini on the phone! Right now! Billy, if you're correct about this, you'll be promoted to head office boy. Yessir, we still reward ambition and initiative around here. Why hasn't anyone called Rappaccini?

— I have, Mister Harum. His daughter is getting him to the phone right now. Here he is.

— Hello, Rappaccini? This is Mister Harum down at the bank. Just fine, thank you. And all your children? Healthy and loud?

Ha-ha. That's what I like to hear. Oh, another on the way? The doctor thinks it's twins? At that rate we'll have to enlarge the school. Well, as the Good Book says, be fruitful and multiply. Ha-ha. Listen, Rappaccini, I wanted to ask you. Oh no, your bank balance is fine. No, I just wanted. No, no, the mortgage is fine too. No trouble at all. Of course we appreciate your patronage. I realize you have customers in the store right now. No, I can't call you at home tonight! No, I have to know something right now! I don't care! Now, just a minute, Rappaccini! I know very well you can take your business to Freudenthal's bank like your friends have! No, I'm not trying to sell you anything! Stop being so suspicious! I'm not the Mafia!

— Oh, oh.
— Oh, oh.
— Bad show.
— He shouldn't have.
— Said that.
— Yes, I apologize, Mister Rappaccini. It was just my little joke. Yes, I'm sorry. It was in bad taste. Of course I don't belie·e that everyone of Italian extraction belongs to the Mafia. Yes, I know that Columbus discovered America first. Yes, I'm sorry. Yes, you can get back to your customers in a minute. I just wanted to ask you a quick question. Billy Bee, our head office boy at the bank saw a little old man, droopy pants, smiled ingratiatingly, a slight Hebrew accent. Saw him go into your store. I thought I might have known him from some place. I was only wondering if you remembered his coming in. You do? Good! Do you recall his name? He didn't mention it? Well, did he ask for anything unusual? He didn't. Did he buy anything? Oh, he did! Are you sure? Well, thank you very much for your time. Sorry to have bothered you. Bye now.

— What did he buy?
— Oh, Gawd! A screwdriver.
— Nothing wrong with that. Anyone could buy a screwdriver.
— He said he needed a long one. To test for termites.
— Oh, oh.

— Cooks us.

— We're scuttled.

— That's the end.

— We better call Hilda right away! Now that Malachy is dead, she's the only agent who handles town properties. She'd know if anyone who looks like Levitas has been nosing around.

— Oh, damn! No answer.

— Call her sister. She might know where Hilda went.

— Hello, this is Reggy Howells down at the bank. How are you? Oh, just fine, thank you. No, not Mister Freudenthal's bank. The New Salem First Bank & Trust. Yes, that's the one. Oh, you've switched your account out of our bank? Well, we feel we don't have to give out dishware to depositors. We like to think that our service is a better incentive than any free merchandise from Hong Kong other banks may give out. Oh? You weren't satisfied with our service either? I see. Well, let's talk about it some other time. I tried to call Hilda but there was no answer. I thought you might know where she is. Oh, she has? I see. Well, thank you very much.

— What did she say?

— Hilda was out with some prospect from New York. And then she went with him—to—Freudenthal's—bank.

— Oh, oh.

— I knew it! It's Levitas for sure!

— Don, you just can't jump to conclusions like that. Eight million people live in New York City.

— Yes, Ben, but not all of them own New England Monument, request the New Salem zoning laws, wear droopy pants, have Hebrew accents, and are seen on our streets.

— Well.

— By golly, Mister Harum! I just thought of something! I've got an acquaintance at Dreyfus & Company who handled that last stock issue Levitas floated.

— Will he talk to you?

— He better! He's trying to get his boy into my prep. He needs a recommendation. Been brown-nosing me for the past two years like my fanny was made of maple syrup. He'd tell me the color underwear his rabbi wears.

— Call him! Call him!

— Ye-ah, feller, go to it!

— Sure, Chrissy, call him!

— Thataway to go, guy!

— Hello, Nathan? Yes indeedy. This is Chrissy Adams. Righto. Golly, good to speak to you after all this time. And how is that bright little son of yours? You don't say? Straight A's? That's topnotch and foursquare. All through junior high? Aha! One exception! Oh. A-plus in mathematics. Golly, I guess he'll soon be applying to some real fine prep. He won't? Oh. Andover accepted him right off. But you turned them down? Because you prefer Choate? You're driving up next week to enroll him? I see. I was going to recommend him for my prep. Well, it doesn't matter now. But say, my wife's on the board of Sarah Lawrence College. Do you have any daughters? You don't. Too bad. No, there wasn't any special reason for calling. Just wanted to say hello. That's all. Of course we'll get together some time. No, I can't make it then. The Country Club Dance. No, not then either. Church committee meeting. Lunch? Golly I don't get to the city very often. No, no, I wouldn't want to make you come all the way up here. I'll tell you what. I'll call you real soon. That's right. Nail down a date. Swell. Topnotch. Bye now.

— Well, that's that.

— Too bad.

— Good try anyway, Chrissy.

— Ye-ah, good try.

— We've got to think of something.

— Sure do.

— Wish we knew what.

— We're stumped.

— Up against it.

— Backs to the walls.

— Sold out.

149

— Hopeless.

— Yes, Edna? I told you I didn't want to be disturbed.

— I'm sorry, Mister Harum. But there's a call for you.

— I said I'm busy.

— It's Mister Freudenthal.

— I'm twice as busy.

— He says it's important.

— Tell him I'll call him back later. All right now, fellows, let's put on our thinking caps. Let's examine this step by step. First question. Why does Levitas want a copy of our zoning laws?

— That's easy. He wants to know where we're vulnerable. He wants to know if he can plunk down a synagogue on Pennyman Street.

— Ha-ha.

— That's rich.

— Fat chance.

— Let's stay serious, fellows. You're right. He wants to know what he can get away with in our town. So now we come to our second question. Why is he working through New England Monument instead of one of his other companies?

— Search me.

— Because it has something to do with New England Monument. It's just common sense.

— Good thinking, Mister Harum.

— Sure is.

— Thataway, Mister Harum.

— Ye-ah.

— Thank you. Now, the next question. What resources do we have here that could interest New England Monument?

— There isn't any good rock for headstones within a hundred miles. So it's not that.

— Maybe he'll have the stone shipped here and then put up another factory in New Salem.

— No. The New Haven is nearly bankrupt. They wouldn't lay down new track for him.

— I've got it! A graveyard! The two hundred acres on the

north end of town. Been tied up in litigation, but it was settled last week.

— Rusty, you're off your rocker. That's mostly swamp. I wouldn't sell that land to my worst enemy. In fact, I wouldn't take it if you paid me. Go one step off the path and you sink in up to your privates.

— But Levitas wouldn't know that. It's been a dry summer. He wouldn't know it's a lake in the spring. And Hilda would conveniently forget to mention it.

— Haw-haw. Wouldn't it be something if Levitas got took?

— Serve him right.

— I'll say. He could go in the mud-pie business.

— Haw-haw.

— I'll call Junie Wharton. His firm handled the litigation. He'll know.

— Great idea, Mister Harum!

— Thank you. Hello, Junie? How's the old ambulance chaser? Couldn't be better. Say, have you found anyone to stick with that old Nebo place? You have? It was sold? Oh, Gawd! Just today?

— Oh, oh.

— Oh, oh.

— Lord preserve us! He's got a foothold here!

— Of course I'd like to know who you hated enough to sell it to. You did? Well now, isn't that something! We'll be having fresh faces in the community. Of course we welcome new people to New Salem. Haw-haw! Boy, when you stick it to them, you really stick it good! Well, thanks a lot, Junie. Bye now.

— Who did he stick it to, Mister Harum?

— He didn't sell it to Josh Levitas for a cemetery. But Hilda did find a buyer for him. It was bought by the Episcopal Church for a retreat!

— Whew! That was close!

— I'll say.

— Poor Episcopalians.

— God help them.

— There's no other land available I can think of. Say, Ben, you've been mighty quiet. You're not thinking of selling off what's left of the old Pennyman lands, are you?

— Of course not, Don. You know it's promised to the town parks commission.

— Only joshing, Ben. Anyway, in times like this everyone becomes suspect. But you did develop part of it once.

— An unfortunate chapter in the life of Benjamin Pennyman. Malachy Murphy and Freudenthal cured me of trying that again.

— I warned you at the time, Ben, not to get mixed up in a deal with those two. Especially since it was your land. What did they contribute besides blarney and craft?

— You warned me, Don, I know. But they asked for only a small percentage of the profits, which seemed reasonable enough.

— And which turned out to be—?

— Well, a little more than half. Of course, there wouldn't have been any profits if they hadn't pushed the transaction in the first place.

— They tried to swindle you, Ben.

— Not to hear them tell it. Guess I was a Yankee Diddled.

— Still. Oh, well, once burned, twice wary. All right, fellows, we still have to figure out what Josh Levitas is after.

— Maybe a shopping center?

— No, I don't think so. Josh Levitas is big, but not big enough to take on Safeway.

— Well, there's one other possibility. Now, I don't want you fellows to start laughing. I know it may sound ridiculous on the face of it.

— Come on, Whitey. Stop beating around the bush.

— Well, I'm almost embarrassed to mention it. It seems so foolish at first. But I wonder if Josh Levitas isn't going to—

— Excuse me for interrupting again, Mister Harum. But Mister Freudenthal says he has to speak to you. He says it will only take a moment and it's important.

— Oh, damn! All right, Edna, switch the call in here. Excuse me, fellows, while I shake this sheeny. Hello. Hello there, Freudenthal. The world treating you right? Yessir, I'm right as gravy. And all the fine little Freudenthals? Wonderful! Now, what can I do for you that's so all-powerful important? Can I attend a luncheon? I'm very busy right now. Do you have to know this minute if I'll attend? Oh, I see, you have to set it up with the others. What others? Oh, those who will be honoring our community's newest benefactor. Doing it up real brown for him, hey? And who might our mysterious benefactor be? Ye gawds and little fishes! Josh Levitas! Oh, Gawd! He already put his John Hancock on the deal? Gladinski already made out the policies? Hilda was the agent on the sale? Oh, Gawd!

— Poor Mister Harum. He can't talk.

— It must be terrible news.

— Gee, he looks awful.

— I'll say. Think we should call a doctor?

— No, just let him recover for a moment or two. What were you about to say, Whitey, before the call interrupted you?

— I was only going to say that if Levitas built a big old-folks' home—you know, one with all modern contraptions that would make a big splash in the papers—then he could sell their families the monuments when they kick off. It sure would give Levitas an edge over the competition.

— What? What did you say?

— Oh, Mister Harum is coming to. Mister Harum? No, fellows, he's closed his eyes again. Better let him rest.

— Whitey, that's a screwy idea.

— Come off it, Whitey.

— Yeah, what you been drinking today?

— Better stop sniffing the stuff. Crazy idea! An old-folks' home!

— Mister Harum looks better now. Mister Harum! Can you tell us what Josh Levitas is building?

— What? What? Old-folks' home? Levitas Home for Aged Hebrews?

— Did Mister Harum say The Levitas Home—??
— For Aged Hebrews???
— The Levitas Home for Aged Hebrews!
— The Levitas Home for Aged Hebrews!!
— The Levitas Home for Aged Hebrews!!!
— I think Mister Harum is coming around again! Did he say what street Levitas is building it on, Mister Pennyman?
— Pennyman? Pennyman?
— Did Mister Harum just say Pennyman Street?
— I think so!
— Pennyman Street!
— Pennyman Street!!
— Pennyman Street!!!
— The Levitas Home for Aged Hebrews on Pennyman Street!!!!

■

EXIT US. All over. Walls come tumbling down. Blow the man down. The Harums. Old people. Reliable people.

> *Ohhhh, Cap'n Harum was a Yankee slaver,*
> *He traded in niggers and praised his Savior.*

Better leave. Ought to get back. Shouldn't be rude to Gladinski. Don is resting easy now. He's too excitable. He might have picked up a bug in Europe. Leave quietly. Inquiries. Savings Accounts Only. Deposits and Withdrawals. Deposits and Withdrawals. Deposits and. Iron and glass doors. Double doors in place now. Bank empty. Guardian at the gate.

— Thank you, Mister Petichek. You don't have to search me. I'm not taking home any samples. Ha-ha. They'll probably be staying in Mister Harum's office for a while, though.

— Say, Mister Pennyman, if you've got a moment, I just want to ask you something. We got a little problem.

— If it's a legal matter, Mister Petichek, you'd better call me at the office.

— It'll just take a second, Mister Pennyman. You could probably answer it right off.

— Well.

— You see, my wife tripped on a cracked curb. You know, the one that got broken two years ago when the truck skidded and was never fixed.

— I'm sorry to hear it. I saw her a little while ago coming out of Freudenthal's bank and she seemed fine. Your wife enhances our landscape.

— Well, Mister Pennyman, she seems all right now. But who knows what trouble might crop up later? And then, you know, the mental anguish. And the pain and suffering. We spoke to some town officials about compensation since it seems plain to me it's their fault. But the town won't pay a red cent. Some of the fellows think I got a good case.

— I'm afraid it's more complicated than a few seconds, Mister Petichek. You'd have to prove negligence. It's a messy sort of suit. Sometimes it doesn't pay to be litigious. I don't handle cases like that. But if you insist on pursuing it, there's an attorney in Danbury who would take it. By name Aaron Lustvogel.

— Thanks, Mister Pennyman. Let me write it down.

— He'll charge you a pretty penny, though.

— Well, I always figured you got to pay for shrewdness. And as long as he gets me something, I don't mind splitting. Those people are sure crafty. They know the ins and outs.

— I've got to leave now, Mister Petichek.

— Thanks again, Mister Pennyman. I'm going to call him first thing in the morning.

Granite front. Not impregnable to Levitas's raiders. Gone are the days. New settlers. They settle for thirty cents on the dollar. It's theirs. They're heirs. Lafayette, we are heir. They win. Sing glory to the House of Levitas, the house that Jake built. Dollod McDog. DOG AS A DEVIL DEIFIED, DEIFIED LIVED AS A GOD. Longest palindrome. Possibly I could make up a longer one. Some day.

Still banging. Freudenthal doesn't even let them stop working at five. Pillar of the community. Perspicacious. Parsimonious. Pridenthal. Psame psong psings. Sing-sing-sing-SING. Exalted shall he be. His name. Evermore. Forever. And ever. And ever. Greet the new eerie. Sing praise to the Levitas. Prisoner, air you represented by a lawyer? Yes, jedge, ah done brought my lyre with me. Sing! Sing! Psame psong. I hear America zinging. Praise. Be the waters of. We wept. Praise ye. Give me that ole-time religion. It was good for your momma, it was good for your poppa. Psame ole psongs. Psalm psongs.

■

WELL, how-dee, folks! How-dee! Yessiree, good tu heah y'all yellin an stompin. Thass what ah like—enthewsiasm! Wellcum, one an all! Yessiree, we got an inimable program fer yu tonight. Rod Foney, Ray Hiccup, Jolly Rogers, Ernie Tube, Hunk Womens, Cousin Miney Purl, The Prayree Rumblers—all yur favrites an mine. But fust, as aways, we open with a few words uv praise tu the Good Lawd what watches us. So less heah y'all give a big greetin tu Billy Joe Highcock, the singin preacher uv Fine Bluff, Arkkansaw! Take it away, revrend!

> *Shepherd, Shepherd, show us*
> *The straight an narrow way.*
> *An if we fail t' follow*
> *Someday we'll have to pay.*
>
> *We'll eat when we're hungry,*
> *We'll drink when we're dry,*
> *If bad times don't kill us,*
> *We'll live till we die.*
>
> *Shepherd, Shepherd, show us*
> *The path that is so straight,*
> *The cup that runneth o'er.*
> *For Heaven we can't wait.*
>
> *Oh, Shepherd, Shepherd, we do not moan.*
> *We're sleepin neath the fallen stone.*

> *Because we know we dwell with you*
> *In the House of Twenny-Three Skiddoo.*

Yessiree! How yu like that, folks? Less show our appreshashun tu the Revrend Billy Joe. A true son uv the puneers! Thataway! We'll be hearin from Billy Joe a lil later, but now we got a real treat fer yu out uv the heartland uv Amuca—Cactus Sam Witlock, the singin hogpuncher! He's corn-fed an home-bred! Now, y'all be real quiet while he sings, an keep the lil ones from fussin, cause we ain't fixin tu ask Cactus Sam tu raise his voice an bust his golden chords. Allrightee, Cactus, stick it tu em!

> *Those blood-drunk injuns sprung on the dead*
> *An wounded boys in blue.*
> *Three hunred bleedin scalps ran high*
> *Above the fiendish crew.*
> *The death groans uv the dyin braves,*
> *Their wounded piercin cries,*
> *The hurlin uv the arrows fleet*
> *Did cloud the noonday skies.*
>
> *Come, injuns, come, an listen to my noise.*
> *Don't you bother the cavalry boys.*
> *Fer if you do yer fortune it will be*
> *Bloodied limbs an gallows is all you'll see.*
>
> *The heathen savage's dead,*
> *Bullet clean through the head.*
> *Singin—oh, death an lead,*
> *Oh, singin death an lead.*

How d'ja like that, friends? How d'ja like that! Cactus, yu knows by the yellin and stompin that the folks preshate yur comin all the way heah. Nother big hand fer Cactus, folks! Thataway! An now it's ballad time. Hang on tu yur seats, gurls! Yu got em real good? Well, heah is Handsome Harry Warlock, the gurls' favorite. Greet im, folks, greet im!

> *The ole lady pitted it an patted it,*
> *The ole man down with his britches at it,*

157

When it goes in it's stiff an stout,
When it comes out it's floppin bout.
Ohhhh, sing—
Big at the bottom an lil at the top,
An a lil thing in the middle that goes pippity-pop.
Ohhhh, sing—
Bout six inches long, a mighty pretty size,
Ev'ry lady in the county takes it tween her thighs!

Thass enuff! Thass enuff! Whoa! Stop right there, Harry! Ah guess we all gits the idea. Ah see yur style changed a bit, hey? Well now, folks, as a comic relief we got yur faithful servant an mine, the Limpin Darky from Darktown, Tennessee—Barefoot Hyde Freeman! Even though he's diffrent from us, he's gonna dance someday afore the Lawed. Tickle our toes, Barefoot!

Torn fum de world uv tyrants,
Beneath dis western sky,
We formed de new dominion,
De land uv libertiy.
An nashuns ober oceans said,
Dey shall obey, obey,
De sons, de sons, de sons
Uv Virgin-i-ay!

Thataway, Barefoot! Keep em comin! Yeaaaaah!

When de boatman blow his horn,
Look out, nigger, yur hog is gone.
He steal mah sheep, he catch mah shoat.
Den put em in de bag, tote em to de boat.
Oh, de ribber is up an de cotton is down,
De white man, he run dis town.

Singin—
Dey cut him up into sausage meat,
An Sambo was his name.
Dey whistled to dat sausage meat,
An Sambo he came, he came.

Thankee, Barefoot! A man after mah own hurt! Now, yu folks might uv observed that Barefoot got a compleshon a bit diffrent from ours. Let me tell yu a story Barefoot confided in me bout how he counts fer the misery uv colored folks. Seems that long, long ago the good Lawd let down from the heavens two bundles. Well, Great Emperor Blooz, who was the fust nigger, an Adam, the fust white man, raced tu git tu them. But Emperor Blooz tripped up Adam an so the nigger gits there fust. He falls ahead uv the giant bundle, leavin the white feller with the itsybitsy bundle. Well now, the nigger opened his tremenjous bundle, an he sure found out why it was so big! Cause inside were shovels an hoes an picks an even a plow. When Adam opened his itsy-bitsy bundle, he found inside a bankbook an a supply uv slips tu make his deposits with. So thass why today yu aways see the nigger workin out in the hot sun an yu see the white feller takin all the cash tu the bank. It were all the nigger's own fault in bein so hoggish in the fust place. And it all happened way back at the beginnin uv the whirld, so we can't do nothin tu alter it any. But folks what know Barefoot can tell yu he is a diffrent breed. Yessiree! Barefoot, after all the nice things ah been sayin bout yu—yu stand up an take nother bow! Thataway! Yessir, our Barefoot didn't let his compleshon hold hisself back none. He conquered over aversity.

But we got tu keep movin right long, folks. Got lots more guests tu entertain us this evenin. Whoops! Haw-haw! Don't worry none bout that spill Barefoot jis took. Probably jis nother one uv his comedy acts tu keep us all cheerful. Hand him back his crutches. Thataway. Whoops! Y'all see the way he done it agin? Haw-haw! Jis lookit him actin like he's tryin tu crawl offstage. Ah tell yu, that Barefoot is somethin! Yu see the way he got that ketchup on his head tu look like blood without us noticin how he done it? Haw-haw! Well, got tu keep the program movin right long, folks. Our next guest come all the way from Kansas! So less heah yu yell real good fer—Tummy Akin!

> *The farmer is the man,*
> *Begs credit if he can.*

The banker every fall
Gits it all, gits it all.

Got no cotton, got no meat,
Poor man got nothin to eat.
Flour is high, crops is low,
Can't eat if ain't got dough.

Poor gets poorer round here,
Babies come near every year.
Ain't got chickens, ain't got corn.
Oh, I wish I was never born.

Oh wait, you will eat by and by,
In that holy land way up high.
Work and pray, live on hay.
They'll feed you pie—
> *In the sky—*
> *When you die.*

Folks, ah'm sorry tu be bustin in heah on Tummy Akin's ballad, but ah have jis learned that Barefoot's trick fall weren't yet purfected fer yur enjoyment, an it misfired a lil bit. In fact, Barefoot is dead. An in the very act uv entertainin all yu nice folks. It sure does take a lil uv the edge off the fun we been havin heah. Yessir, the accommodatin Barefoot is dead. How art the mitey fallen! Well, let me jis say that Barefoot was a micey nice feller. He had redeemin qualities. He weren't no Olympic speed star, but leastwise he tried tu limp along on them crutches swifter than a tortoise. An he could bray louder than a hog's call. Challenges didn't scare him none. He'd lay down an sleep right longside the biggest uv them. How art the mousey fallen! So in tribute tu the best darky we ever had heah, ah myself will sing Barefoot's favurite ballad. It's mah way uv thankin him fer the years durin which he never gave us one bit uv trouble. Ah'd preshate it if yu folks what remembers the words joins in. An it'd be a mighty nice jestshur if y'all took off yer hats. Yu won't catch cold none, an anyway 'tain't good tu keep wool close tu the scalp fer tu long. As mah Granmother Shincock—she was bout ten years younger than Methusla—always said, wool dissipates the will. Ah think that is a good thing tu remember. Wool dissipates the will! Why, Granmother Shincock was filled with a million uv those sayins, some uv which her folks brung across the ocean with em from Englung. Well now, some uv the things Granmother said was true an some wasn't. Of course we'd believe what was true an disbelieve what was untrue. Only problem was you couldn't tell the parts what was true. And tu make it wurst, somethin that weren't true was often easier tu believe than what was true, so if we believed what we thunk was true, but really was untrue, then we was disbelievin the truth. Ah remember one time Granmother Shincock advised all us lil tykes with nother one uv her famous sayins. Wit in a woman kin never replace looks. Now, we was too lil at the time tu unnerstand the philosophy in it. But, folks, ah sure unnerstood it after ah got married! Haw-haw-haw-HAW. Not tu say mah Sally Jo don't try tu play her strong suit uv wit. She ain't like most womenfolk, aways wantin to go out uv the shack an sniff round everyone else's front porch. No sirree! Not mah Sally Jo! Why, ah remember oncet Sally Jo's cousin Phil Paincock—he was the slick preacher down in Risin Gorge—the kind when he left yur house after callin fer Sunday tea, you'd step out back real fast an count yur poultry—but yu won't find no Risin Gorge on yur maps no more cause the Tee-Vee-Ay dam done swallered it up under the reservoor. Risin Gorge used tu be a mighty nice lil town—had four churches, one fer each Sunday in the month, but the biggest uv them was the Southern Baptist—only it never had its steeple built on. That was cause the lumber yard was owned by Sammy Joe Sincock—not to be confused with Granmother Shincock, which has an aitch in it—Sammy Joe was kin tu the Sincocks down in Black Bottom—but even so, Sammy Joe was the stupidest white man ah ever met. Why, put his brains in a jaybird's head and it would fly backwards—on top uv which he was the stingiest, which he come by rightly, cause he got it from his granddaddy on his momma's side—she was a Frumcock—an everyone knows the Frumcocks aways been that way, even when they wasn't yet the best society an was still farmin those mighty impovrished lands they bought from Sut Lovincock—now these mighty pore acres was right close tu Hallowed Hollow—which is a place folks never knew how it got its name—that is, not till ole lady Saycock did some askin round fer the hysterical society uv the old folks that was left—folks like Charlie Purcock who ah don't suppose yu really could believe since he'd rather tell a lie on credit than the truth fer cash—but that didn't prevent Charlie from fightin so gallantly in the war up in Virgin-i-ay—his regment was the Fifty-seventh Cavalry—maybe yu heard tell uv them? Iffen yu didn't, yu kin bet the Yankees did! Why, I oncet met a Yankee peddler down heah by the name uv Fraudall—he was a Saks on his momma's side—he was also slick as a greased eel—an he told me even up in Connycut he'd heard bout the famed Fifty-seventh from a northern gineral—ah didn't quite catch his name, but it sounded if it might uv been uv foreign extracshun, though uv course his chilluns is all Amucans now. Well, anyway, this northern gineral was the friend uv a polished politishun who had the shrewd instinct when tu pay fer a constituent's drinks—he lived in a town up in New Englung some folks thereabouts call Righteous Ridge—though its rightful name on the maps was New Salem—thass where bout twenny-four years ago, when they'd had lots uv rain, an the fog was so thick yu could hardly spit—well, this stranger comes tu town one day, all dressed in black like his professhun was mournin at folks' buryins—but this stranger was—

■

LET FREEMAN RING. Mine lies have seen the gory of the clinging of the flawed. Mumbo-Jumbo will die in the jungle. Let us now sing your song.

Mass' got no hooks nor nails,
Nor anythin like dat,
So on dis nigger's nose,
He hang his coat an hat.

By the rivers of babble on. We dismembered Zion. I hear
Amucka clinging. Slame sleet slongs. Psame psongs. Lostfound-
land. Better get back. To office.

— Well, well, well, Mister Pennyman. And what was that infectious melody I heard you humming?

— Oh, Doctor DuMont. Just some old psong. I mean song.

— Looks as if summer doesn't want to call it quits, does it?

— Guess not. Pretty humid.

— Well, the bees are active, so that's a sign we'll have some
rain tonight to cool us off. I notice, though, that the squirrels
are putting on a heavy coat of fur, which might indicate we'll
have a hard winter.

— I suppose so.

— That's right. What will be will be, whether it happens or
not.

— Well.

— How fortunate to meet you by chance this way, Mister
Pennyman. I had been intending to be very forward and call
you. We have noted your absence for some time. I hope we will
see you on Sunday. We miss the mint to flavor our soup.

— I don't know. I might be driving down to Stamford with
Don Harum.

— Ah, yes, Mister Harum. We miss also his mint. Or I might
say pepper. I fear he still has not forgiven me. You know, for
my unflinching position.

— Position?

— Yes. You recall, I'm sure, my matter of conscience about the
Country Club affair.

— No, I guess I don't know about it.

— Oh, Mister Pennyman, I was certain everyone had heard
of my little crusade. You haven't? Indeed. As a result of it there

163

has even been a bit of talk about my being honored when all the priests come together at the next convention.

— A mass of priests.

— Pardon? Oh, very good. Hee-hee. I must remember that one. Well, a most unfortunate event occurred at the June Dance of the Country Club. One of the maids of honor invited a delightful young man, a resident of this town and an honors student at Yale, to be her escort. But the powers that control this annual ball judged him unacceptable as an escort because of his Jewish parentage, despite the clear facts that, one, he has forsworn the creed of his fathers, and, two, his parentage is unrecognizable in his physiognomy. I myself baptized him last year at the font in my church. Well, after wrestling with my conscience for several weeks, I decided to take a forceful stand. If I recall rightly, the sermon I preached was along the following lines. Ahem. "As a priest of your congregation, I realize that I am treading on shaky ground when I intrude into a very complex issue. But my conscience does not permit me to remain silent! I must speak out when a dignified young man, whose every known act in this town has been the epitome of prudence, propriety, and piety, and who is now a Christian and a member of my congregation, is excluded from the Country Club. The injustice cries out! I cannot remain still! The exclusion of such a promising lad is morally reprehensible to the Christian principles which he has fully accepted by the act of baptism. I am not blaming the Country Club. But I am blaming members of my parish who, despite their claims to being Christians, are not acting as Christians should. As your pastor, I must take firm action in this regard. Any persons responsible for the rudeness to our attractive young maid of honor and her chosen escort, the pious young man whom I myself baptized, is no longer welcome to receive Holy Communion at this altar. This suspension will be lifted as soon as the transgressors have worked out their own peace with God, either by using the General Confession in Morning or Evening Prayer, or by making their confessions to me or to any other priest of the Protestant Episcopal Church.

And I personally add that I would hope that those responsible should eat humble bread and apologize to this dignified young man." Ahem. That, Mister Pennyman, was, as I recall, the substance of my little sermon.

— What does that have to do with Don Harum?

— Mister Harum! Why, everyone knows that he dictates the policies of the Country Club. I consider it an indication of his guilt that he has not taken Holy Communion since I hurled that challenge at the congregation.

— Don Harum quit the Country Club a year ago. He had a messy squabble with them. I think they towed away his car when he left it blocking the driveway.

— Oh.

— Anyway, he's been in Europe all summer.

— Oh.

— What if he had a hooked nose and swarthy skin?

— Mister Harum?

— No, your delightful young convert.

— Oh. But he didn't. Well, Mister Pennyman, as I said, this was a nasty incident. This young man has suffered rudeness and embarrassment. But our community will be the better for it. The young, you know, are resilient. The incident will leave few scars. But you and I are not so young any more. Increasing age is the time for increasing reliance on our church. Time runs out, Mister Pennyman. Tomorrow is what today was yesterday.

— Well.

— Seek not grapes on the thorn tree, Mister Pennyman.

— Well.

— There are verities that we feel in our heart of hearts. Like the wise Solomon, we have been given a wise and understanding heart—if only we used it. I have just been at the library doing some research for my next sermon. No sooner finish one than begin another. I fear I measure out my life in sermons. My sermon this Sunday will be concerned with the misconceptions people have about Solomon. You know that he was a man who, as the Bible informs us, could lecture on everything from the cedar tree that is in Lebanon unto. Unto. Unto the lilies that springeth out of the field. The very latest archeological scholarship supports everything the Bible says about him. Unreservedly! Did you know that Solomon's Mines have actually been unearthed at Ezion-geber? Did you know that his city has been found at Megiddo?

— No, I guess I didn't.

— Yes, my sermon on Sunday will be about the archeological confirmation of Solomon's wisdom. Archeology is proving that the Bible gave us factual reporting as well as direction for our lives. Particularly important work is going on now on the post-Solomonic kingdoms. Jeroboam. Nadab. Baasha. Elah. Zimri. Omri. And. And.

— Ahab?

— Yes, Ahab. And, you know, all those other wicked kings of Israel before the disappearance of the ten tribes into Assyria.

— And the appearance of the ten tribes in America.

— Pardon?

— The Indians. Some people think the Indians are descended from the ten lost tribes.

— A delightful myth. Of course there is no evidence in scripture one way or the other. Did you know that when America was discovered, the pope had to ponder the question of whether or not the Indians were truly human?

— I imagine Columbus's sailors proved that before he made up his mind.

— Pardon?

— Syphilis. The sailors brought back syphilis with them. The syphilizing influence of discovery.

— Oh? Yes. Well, getting back to the Bible, nowadays archeologists dig into the mounds of biblical cities and uncover their history layer by layer. Each layer is like a page in a book—a book we can read! We must dig and dig! Speak to the earth and it shall teach ye! Any fool can prove the Bible is untrue, but it takes a wise man to understand it. Yes, today archeology is uncovering—

FROM the Early Epicene and Muddled My Sin to the latest Quarternary dividend in the Groan Rover shill fumation, artifactials are the daughters of the earth and realicts are the sins of heaven. Today I speak of the manyfacturers of Coca-Cola and the petrifaked Newlithic formation. Arkologists till us that this formation is fund in varyous kinds of rock—shill, gyp some, grunt, base all, slight, metaphoric, and of course limestone. (For an altardating, see Midders and Evens, 1963 B, biased on everydense deduced from the fact that the half earth resolves on its own assel.) The sequestered object which will today be the subject of my sermon is the folklife artyfix known as the "Coke" buttle.

Copyous samples of Coke bottles exist and provide empathology for analcyst of evilition of types and variants. Because of the changeling prettans of taste, seekwhence dating is possible. Styles range from prymerry "Mae West" shape to the trademucked Coke biddle of the Puppsy Gineration. Appended blow is the botteler's licksycon. Each bottle is composed of parts variously assignated "mouth," "lip," "neck," "front," "backside," "bottom," and so on and so froth. Continuing with the erratic connytonations, "bum" is a bottle that can be refulled but looks disraped. "Scuffle" is a bum that is scruffled. "Crock" is a bum with a chipped bottom. Arkology must endear smut.

The treatymarked Coke bottle is found in all tips and varyants, each marked with a U.S. patient numbher, and each is found littered with assosited artiflux, such as chewing-chum rapers, peer cans, candrums, lingstuck, car tricks, and ciggies on a darklighted thoroughfear often known to the Puppsy Gineration as down Mammary Lane. Bussketry and pettery are sometimes, but not all ways, present.

Intense analysis of manyfacturer's his story reveals burgeoning size of bottles and demeanishing contents of flood ounces. Crafty designer of the very foist Coke bottle is Mister A. Samuelson of Terre Haute. A satisfactual sample reveals that the bottle bares the leg-end "Patted Nov. 1915" and is funned in shill straighther 1916-23.

At the depressive debts of the Great Wheepression in 1937, a new bottle makes its appoorance, with a significant loss of capacity in the battle to 207.0 c.c. The umpty weight of the bundle is 14.01 ozs., dispute all adtempts to hide the fact that .01 ozs. are being saved in the broadlines. This variant disapproves in 1951 when data from other dizzyplins indicates contents of 6 fl. ozs., down from previous 6½ ozs., which may ripresent an unclean hound's tooth.

Conscious stricten in 1957, the compaignie's adverting agency restories capacity to 6½ ozs., after missive advertising campaigne. But the umpty wight is now oweny 13.80 ozs. and capaciousty has been secretely decreased by 4.2 c.c. Further fraud comes to late in strata 1958-60 when the manyfacturer reduces the impty weight to an alltime lo of 13.65 ozs., and carryacity fills a gain by 0.7 c.c. to 202.1 c.c. Rectitude later rites itself and compacity rises 2.2 c.c., although containts remain only 6½ ozs. and empty wheet plummpts still more to 13.26 ozs.

■

HE DRONES on and on. People arrive early at his church to get the best seats. In the rear. Wish I could slip away. He was wrong. It was hyssops that springeth out of the wall. Not lilies out of the field. On and on. Lectures on all things. He's. He's the little fixer who spills the whine. Proverbial wisdom. Farmer's Almanac mind. The Book of Comeon Prayer.

— And, as I was saying, Mister Pennyman, many of the proverbs attributed to Solomon have been documented by modern science. You recall that in Proverbs six, six through eight, Solomon said, "Go to the ant, thou sluggard; consider her ways, and be wise: Which having no guide, overseer, or ruler, Provideth her meat in the summer and gathereth her food in the harvest." For centuries it was common belief that Solomon's wisdom had failed him in this case. Because there was not a shred of evidence that ants gathered seeds during the harvest and stored them for use in the winter. In fact, so many people doubted the wisdom of Solomon's proverb that—

There is no better friend than God, and no better relative than a buck. Even nuns are screwed in their coffins. There's no market for nice girls. Waiting to be hanged is the most uninteresting period of a man's life. Someday the lion and the lamb will lie down together, but meanwhile I'll put my money on the lion. The thief is the one who got caught. The knife doesn't know

—the famed Linnaean Society of London undertook to investigate the matter. One member, J. Traherne Muggridge, went to the Mediterranean where he finally discovered—

its owner. Good whiskey is good in its place, and the mouth is the place for it. A buck is worth more than a hundred promises. Dogs don't bite at the front gate. The rattlesnake doesn't mind

—that ants were actually carrying seeds. Well, you can imagine the consternation of the unbelievers who—

being skinny. Watch out when you gittin all you wants, cause fattenin hogs ain't in luck. A man who farts in church sits in his own pew. Do unto others what they do unto you, only do it first. You can lead a horse to water if you've got the horse. A poor man's proverbs don't travel far. All work and no play make Jack so sharp he'll cut himself. A man must

—had been attacking Solomon's wisdom. But he who allows himself to become an ox will ever lick the yoke. So for final proof Mister Muggridge returned to the Mediterranean and there he—

make his own arrows. Hungry dogs run faster. A man is known by the Company he raids. All the poor people don't weigh as much as one mortgage company. Dirty hands make clean money. When the eagle grows old it becomes a mouse-catcher. Trust your red brothers, from ten miles away. Try to

—took up his investigations once again. Lo and behold, he found that the ants not only carried back seeds that had fallen to—

be on friendly terms with everyone and they'll take advantage of you. Think twice before you speak to a friend in need. Liquor talks loud when it gets loose from the jug. Whiskey can soothe
—the ground, but they also collected them from—
an Indian, but I'd rather try a revolver on him first. Tell me where a man earns his bread and I'll tell you his politics. You'll never skid if you stay in a rut. The desire to
—the plants themselves. And nowadays we—
shit takes priority over any order. When you eats de white man's pay you shure gonna suffer in de stumack. Don't look for pure water to
—know that harvesting ants, as they are called, are widespread around—
put out a fire. If you wanna know how much folks is gonna miss you, jest stick yer finger in the pond an peer into
—the world.
the hole.
— Well, well, I fear my enthusiasm got the better of me, Mister Pennyman. I am sorry to have been going on at such length. But by all means attend on Sunday and you will hear the rest. I certainly hope we will see you there. After all, what is the Protestant Episcopal Church in New Salem without a Pennyman in attendance? It is unfortunate that we have never really gotten to know one another better. To think I have been in New Salem for two years and we never had a nice long chat. Perhaps some evening?
— I wish I could, Doctor DuMont. But I usually take work home. There's lots to do. Clients must be served.
— Perhaps when your burden becomes lighter. Then we can spend a leisurely evening. Really get to know each other. I never knew your dear mother either, I am sorry to say. When did she pass on?
— Nineteen forty-five.
— Nevertheless, I feel that I know her by reputation and by her lasting imprint on New Salem. I am reminded of her every time I walk past your house and note its unusual mansard roof.

— Yes, she had it done after she returned from her trip to Paris. She brought the artist back with her. He later killed himself.

— Ah, yes, the fragile artistic temperament. Of course it might have been due to the French diet. Their bubbly champagne does make them lightheaded.

— Well, Mother loved Paris.

— Did she go there often?

— No, actually only that once. She was there only a few days and she had to rush back. Because I became ill. It didn't turn out to be serious, though. But she never got back to Paris again.

— You have no other family?

— I had a brother. He died five years ago.

— Oh?

— Yes. He's buried in California. He wanted it that way. No children. Someone who was out there said his wife ran off with her swami.

— There must be other Pennymans somewhere.

— No, I'm the last of them. The rightful ones anyway. There's another Pennyman listed in the New Haven directory. But it wasn't his name originally. He changed it from Pensig. Change the name, change the game.

— And when did your father pass on?

— I don't know.

— Pardon?

— He disappeared in 1907. I was only eleven.

— Oh?

— Yes. He was an eccentric. Not everyone understood him. When the historical society campaigned to display coats-of-arms on some of the older houses, Father said our family tree had only one limb. It stood out at a right angle.

— Pardon?

— A gallows.

— I see. Hee-hee. I must remember that one.

— And when lightning hit the church steeple, Father refused to contribute to rebuild it. He said he wasn't man enough to undo God's will. After they got that crank architect from New Haven to rebuild it, Father said it looked like a witch's hat. The name stuck.

— Yes indeed, your father's appellation earned us favorable mention in *Reader's Digest*. I see more and more tourists at the church taking away photographs.

— Taking *away?* You mean it takes something from the church?

— Come, come, just a figure of speech, Mister Pennyman. Why do you ask?

— No. It's just something I was thinking about today. I don't remember.

— Well, as the scion of a founding family of this town, you should allow us to enlist your interest in church affairs. You know, reason sometimes makes mistakes, but the spirit never does. What we sometimes need is un-common sense.

— I'm too old for committees, Doctor DuMont. Seems to me they keep minutes and waste hours.

— Hee-hee. Another very good one, Mister Pennyman. I can see that when we have our leisurely chat it will be a very amusing one for me. But I would assuredly like to see you again on the vestry. It is in your traditions, Mister Pennyman! The fox runs from habit but the man from character.

— No, I'm afraid not.

— Now, now, Mister Pennyman. We can find something for you that blends inclination with talent. We all know that the strength of the eagle is in the air.

— I don't think I can.

— Mister Pennyman, we have in this community so many services to perform that we hardly know where to begin. We must show charity to our own barnyard fowl as well as feed the wild birds. We are surrounded by a backlog of worthy cases. Poverty is keen enough without our sharpening its edge by neglect. One case recently earned my attention—an inspiring example of Christian steadfastness. I refer of course to our dusky brother, Barefoot Hyde the handyman. You must have heard about his spate of bad luck?

— No, I guess I didn't.

— You didn't indeed? Why I thought everyone knew about Barefoot, his inviolate flesh destroyed piecemeal by a succession of calamities that would test the faith of a Job.

— Job feels the Rod, yet bleffes God.

— Pardon?

— Primer. It's from the New England Primer.

— Oh. Well, as I was saying, Barefoot was a good man, God-fearing and evil-eschewing. But everything is born to trouble, particularly man. Barefoot stands before us as a mute testimony to the—

■

LITTLE NOTICE was paid when Barefoot Hyde contracted a case of chicken pox which left his face with all the mountains, ridges, gaps, bottomlands, and valleys of the Appalachians. But it was the harbinger of greater indispositions to come. One day, while he was mowing a patron's front lawn, the machine mal-functioned and took off Barefoot's foot, thankfully in a clean cut. Nevertheless, handymen are in short supply in New Salem and therefore many people winked an eye at his deficiency. Barefoot did not fear machines for naught, since while operating a chain saw, a jinx in the design, later rectified at great expense by the manufacturer's research department, caused an erratic motion which took with it Barefoot's arm, fortunately below the elbow. Not long after that he damaged himself again. One eye, thank God it was only the left one, closed up from some infection or other. Then a mild case of influenza developed complications which left him unable to control his bowels. I suspect that his life was not completely an open book because it was determined at the time that he was also suffering from crabs, yaws, syphilis, gonorrhea, and Saint Anthony's Fire. Ca-lamities multiplied as he gathered momentum down the road to disaster. His remaining foot was soon attacked by septicemia. In the general hubbub of the surgical procedures, slightly too much flesh was removed, in fact the entire leg. But Barefoot, clever fellow that he was, got through these troubles by the skin of his teeth. He built a little cart whereby he might roll himself along. Did he complain? Not our Barefoot! An inventory at this point revealed that he was generally of one piece except for the loss of one and a half legs, one half of one arm, the left eye, a tendency toward bowel accidents, a poor complexion, and sundry other complaints. There was, however, the definite prospect of his destroying himself in his entirety, so the insurance company had no choice but to exercise its option and cancel his accident policy. The company took the trouble to warn him that the guilt for any further violence he did to himself would lie squarely in his own hands. Perhaps the gift of this good advice shocked him into being more conscientious in his dealings with his environment, because for the next few weeks Barefoot courted no further difficulties, aside from piles. But I fear that gloves are a poor gift for a man with no hands. He soon stopped paying heed to the advice. The storm broke and sheets of calamities rained down upon him. A virulent case of mumps deprived him of his manhood, and the subsequent loss of testosterone caused his hair to fall out in fistfuls. Barefoot's remaining asset, the arm in its entirety, was crushed when he fell from a ladder while trying to hang wallpaper. Then his skin began to peel from herpes. Lazarus also had sores, but he had dogs to lick them. Bitterness, however, did not seep into his heart. They are such a laughing people that even reduced to his stumps he managed to find a happy philosophy. "Well, de Lawed give an den he takes. Guess de bargain's bout square," he is quoted as having remarked cheerily at the time. By now he was down to a mere two-sevenths of his natural endowment and he was careening toward his fate out of all control of himself. Of course medical technology is clever nowadays at concocting artificial limbs, glass eyes, and wigs that give you another throw for your money. So in one way or another this fragment of a human being strove with all his might to get by. But being limbless, hairless, and maleless, he found not all doors to opportunity standing agape before him. In fact, he had nothing to fill his belly with but the east wind. However, be it said to the everlasting credit of the New Salemites, he was never refused work because of his color, religion, or national origins. So he idled away the day by preaching outside the door of an evangelical church on the other side of town where some kindly folk used to tote him each morning and prop him in the sun. He understood that we kneel to pray but we must stand to praise. He had a set piece about the tribulations and subsequent redemption of Job that attracted favorable comment. And the tide of his extraordinary battle to pull himself together did indeed seem to be turning! But then he let his resolve wilt again, and he left himself undefended against attacks of amoebic dysentery, hookworm, pinworm, and trichinosis. He also developed a cataract in his remaining orb which obscured his vision. But fortunately blind people develop a sixth sense to guide them. By now he was totally unemployable, even though he retained general use of his faculties except vision. Which confirms the old adage that no man is poor save by his own fault or circumstances. These latest indispositions left him at loose ends, a dog without a master. You might think that at last he was surfeited with the attention he had attracted, but not Barefoot. One fine morning he rolled out of his litter, causing a concussion which left him with frequent fainting spells, despite the fact that their skulls are known to be thicker than ours. By now most people had given up on him. He was no longer a man but a vegetable who might become a suitable patient for the ministrations of a tree surgeon. And it was clear that he intended to string out his life for all it was worth, even though emphysema, galloping consumption, hypersensitivity to penicillin, and a diagnosis of lung cancer made him a martyr to ill health. He was stubbornly sticking it out, even though he attracted cases—most, thank God, mild ones—of botulism, German measles, regular measles, whooping cough, asthma, bronchitis, scarlet fever, diphtheria, ague, pneumonia, and tonsilitis. His body became a vessel in which all sorts of corruption festered in security. His inoculation protected him against poliomyelitis, but he was waylaid by yellow fever, ulcerated colon, kwashiorkor, coughing spells, paratyphoid, trench fever, encephalitis, hepatitis, constipation, flatulence, diarrhea, muscular dystrophy, acne, carbuncles, Chagas' disease, abscessed teeth, elephantiasis, leukemia, boils, chronic vomiting, biliousness, heartburn, colic, enlarged prostate, hives, rheumatic fever, warts, diabetes, seizures, apoplexy, paresthesia, and anorexia. And still the indispositions did not cease. I fear that Barefoot became a valetudinarian through his contraction of migraines, neuralgia, ulcerated duodenum, gastroenteritis, rheumatism, palsy, epilepsy, mange, ringworm, pustules, and urticaria. Not to mention hypochondria and narcissism, a selection of fits, paranoia, anxiety reactions, schizophrenia, obsessions, fixations, infected gums, scrofula, deafness, la turista, tularemia, plague, and other distressing complaints of the skin, scalp, bones, glands, joints, muscles, brain, nerves, blood, arteries, veins, heart, bronchial tubes, lungs, spleen, kidney, liver, stomach, and intestines which kept him on the sick list. Finally all that remained of Barefoot was a hoarse voice that lay upon its pillow and screamed night and day. Even a small mouse has anger. At last he capriciously allowed his voice to succumb, this last holdout choked off by some infirmity or other. You might feel that he should have slit his own throat at an early age and avoided causing everyone such concern. But he chose a different policy. He went at it bit by bit. He had opted for the slow way, to kill the hawk by starving the chickens. Just because he did things differently from us is no reason for us to display any prejudice against him. It was his life and he lived it as he wanted.

■

— Yes, Doctor DuMont. That is an unfortunate case. But it figures.
— Pardon?
— Well, we violated everything else about them. We den-

egrated them. We were bound to get around to their flesh sooner or later.

— Yes, they are a people plagued by adversity. Oh. The half-hour bell. It is getting on, isn't it? I didn't mean to keep you so long, Mister Pennyman. But I fear I am a sleepless fisher of men. I do hope we can lure you back to our net. Please give it some thought.

— I will, Doctor DuMont. By the way, I was trying to recall today. But I couldn't remember. The three wise kings who visited Christ. Wasn't one of them black?

— Oh, dear me, Mister Pennyman. Does anyone still believe those myths of our most holy Roman friends? The Bible never stated anything of the sort. Let me recall. See. See John, chapter two, one through twelve. The three kings were concocted hundreds of years after the birth of Our Lord. It was strictly a political maneuver on the part of the Catholic Church. They wanted to stress the point that gentiles as well as Jews came to worship the infant Jesus. The kings were not named in the Testament of course, but tradition refers to them as Gaspar, Melchior, and. And.

— Balthazar.

— Yes. Thank you. Belshazzar. It was all a trick of Rome. But one of them black? No, I don't believe so. Perhaps it is some new maneuver to convince our American Negroes that they are children of Rome. It may be a sop to that fellow who organized that agitation in Washington a few weeks ago. King. He hasn't yet learned that all creatures are better off in their own element. I don't recall that myth about blackness, though. Oh, oh. Let us step into this doorway, Mister Pennyman, and avoid that unfortunate woman.

Shameless. Jazzybell. Lurches down street. Wreathed in clouds. Of alcohol. Reason town drunks live so long. Makes them immune to infection. Hair electric. Scarlet woeman. Unpardonable. I once. I. I was a child and she. Years and years ago. In a kingdom by. I tried. To ring the bell. Caught us. Interrupt us. After all, mon petit, Annie Bell is Irlandaise. And you are both too young to understand une grande romance such as Pierre felt and who died for a love I could not requite. Someday you will search out the flower that grows on the highest mountaintop. Non, mon fils, she is not for you. She is lo-lee. Qu'il t'y? Dolorously. Hazily. Humbled. She's almost past. Look away.

— Poeu! The woman reeks of spirits! Mister Pennyman, the town really should take measures that Irish Annie not be allowed to roam the streets intoxicated. I am afraid she worships at the altar of the pagan god Alcohol. It is her enemy and it has found her out. She should be looked after. There are public institutions for such people. I predict she'll be run over if she goes around like that. Now, what were we saying? Oh, yes. The black king. I can try to look it up for you if it really matters.

— No. I guess not. Excuse me. I have to drop in here at Myer's Drugs for a moment. Before he closes. It was nice chatting with you, Doctor DuMort. I mean DuMont. I will try to come one of these Sundays.

— Please do, Mister Pennyman. We need your mint.

Mumbo-Jumbo. Died in the jungle. Of boredom. He puts the congregation to sleep. Doctor DuMont. Double Dee. D. D. Doctor of Drivel. I forgot about Gladinski. I'm an hour late. I'm a Yankee Daddler. He probably didn't come anyway. Better stop by Jerry Myer's now. Only take a moment. If he doesn't chatter. Constant complainer. A man of contention.

— So! And how are you, Mister Pennyman?

— Fine, Mister Myer. Yourself?

— Mister Pennyman, are you asking from politeness or from curiosity?

— Well.

— If you are asking from politeness, everything is from the best. Hunky-dory! A-number-one! Happy times here again! Two chickens every pot! God bless America! But if you asking from curiosity, is different story altogether. By me every grape in bunch is sour.

— Well.

— If you got a minute, no, two minutes, I can tell you. I ain't
no prophet, but listen a minute from Jerry Myer and I promise
it ain't complete waste time. What else could you be doing?
Make more money so the government grabs it? Write letter the
post office loses in five minutes? Make phone call that the crooks
disconnect you and steal dime? Sit by front porch and get from
fumes lung cancer? Put out seed for wild birds and watch starlings eat all up? Work fingers to elbow for charity until find out
fund raiser grabs eighty percent? Go drive in car and get killed
because manufacturer saved two bits from cheap bolt? Read
newspaper about murders, bankruptcy, income-tax evasion, embezzlement, graft, fraud, perjury, burglaries, muggings, arson,
riots, rapes, diseases, starvation, earthquakes, hurricanes, sunk
ships, wrecked railroads, automobile smashups, plane crashes?
In five seconds Jerry Myer is telling you more what's wrong
than you'll hear from college professor what wrote ten books but
ain't looked out window. You listen from Jerry Myer.
— Well.
— By me every day in year is one big aggravation. Is enough
set teeth on edge. I can't get no one type out orders, and if maybe
I did, typewriter would bust into thousand pieces first touch. Or
envelopes wouldn't stick. Or post office would be shut because
now government works by appointment, which is only for give
out ZIP numbers, something new for aggravating us. And kids
won't walk packages next door by post office no more but you
got negotiate with their mothers maybe chauffeur them. The
last kid I am hiring was smoking in storeroom and that was almost finish Myer's Drugs, which twenty-five years come next
February I been building up, we should all live to see the day.
And I'll tell you from something else. You see that cash register?
Two years old and already is genuine antique. It sits on counter
like was cut from glass. They get rockets fly into air but nobody
can't get draw on Myer's cash register open. Greatest minds in
world could all have meeting in Myer's Drugs to look cash register and all agree the diagnosis—impossible to fix. Sure, sure, I
called company what made it long distance—twice—but who is

coming? So I'm calling again, am connected with wrong number, and so I call operator for credit. She is apologizing, not something made up out her heart but something they are giving her read to angry customers. So she is connecting me again—you guessed it, with another wrong number! For which I know I am being charged because all calls I write down, how else you going straighten out bill every month? By me is one mistake being made top the other. So finally Myer gets company and they puts on man with voice like from Harvard who says I should watch front door cause they are sending over repairman. So after two, no, three months getting cross-eyed from watching front door, someone is finally coming. He asks me, "You the one in need service on cash register?" Service! Get that! It's something to laugh! So I says to him, "Must of been the guy what owned this store before me. He died five years ago come next April." Did I say he was repairman? No, this man is like surgeon of cash registers. Instead uniform he got two-hundred-dollar suit. Gold rings on three fingers. Smells from cologne water. He pokes around my antique with lifted pinky and then looks at me like he was world's greatest brain surgeon I called over for consultation how to cut toenails. He says absolutely ain't nothing defective my machine. The trouble, thank God, is very minor. There is busted tiny screw on underside. Rappaccini sells hundred ninety-nine different kinds screws in his store, but screw for Myer's cash register is special. It got to come direct from factory, which used to be by Pittsburgh but now is moving by Alabama so it can get away from strikes. It's something to laugh! So he writes up bill which is for $39.75, which if you don't believe I will show you, and tells me I should keep watching mailbox for special screw. So I'm watching until cross-eyed from spring to summer and ain't no screw coming by mailbox. Bills and complaints I get, screws no. So I'm calling the company again long distance and they switches me one to another up down hallways, everyone in company liking I suppose the sound Jerry Myer's accent, they got take opportunity to chat while I'm paying phone bills. So when bill is maybe up to twenty, no, thirty dollars, I am being connected to nice little girl who sounds like she shouldn't be working from such crooks. Miss Vivaci says she is checking computers immediate and calling right back soon as she finds out what happened special screw I am watching mailbox should come direct from factory. So—what you expect? —she is never calling back. It figures. Can black man change color his skin? Since I'm related to Rothschild on my mother's side, but distantly, I act like millionaire and call back. So again her nice voice is apologizing, but she explains me everything ain't her fault. She says if she were president from company my special screw already would be in mailbox. But she ain't, she is only programmer for computer. To check one computer she got to program different kind computer to kibbitz over its shoulder and nudge when it makes mistake. One computer they got can't talk language of other computer they got. It's something to laugh! She says she is calling back in one, no, two weeks after giving them elocution lessons so they learns to speak like graduated with honors by Harvard. So miracle like quails dropping from heaven, she calls back like she just is winning medal at Bunker Hill battle. Her fancy computers are finding trouble! She says I ain't been sent screw because I ain't yet paid $39.75 bill for consultation from brain surgeon of cash registers. Get that! Always I am paying bills on first the month so don't lose credit rating, which is another aggravation I'll tell you sometime when you ain't in such rush. I takes out canceled checks and tells Miss Vivaci I got proof would win me unanimous the Supreme Court. Poor Miss Vivaci now is getting upset I been having such troubles. She says she wonders what I must think her company. I tell her they make plenty mistakes for one thing, for another their product ain't so hot. She explains they is having lots problems in accounting department because by Alabama they got unions too. Everybody is threatening strike every Tuesday afternoon regular. So she asks, Suppose what I give her opportunity check and call back? She got to talk computers again. I tells her, look, if it help any, I got night-school-professor uncle in Bronx who can learn computer to talk the accounting department in jiffy, and for friend mine he'll make special price. So in month she calls back excited like she won battle San Joon Hill before Teddy Rosenfelt even got on horse. She says positively I is right, I did pay bill prompt, but somebody forgot give it the computer between threats go strike every Tuesday afternoon regular. She thanks me for being always such prompt payer and she is hoping I keep doing business with company, which rarely makes mistakes, but when it does, all is made for Jerry Myer. But regarding my screw, that model register been discontinued and the screw ain't made no more. It's something to laugh! So instead from being fixed, now I got cash register is an heirloom only two years old. I could be getting it gold-plated for what cost the brain surgeon coming all the way New Salem to make acquaintance, not to mention phone calls, not to mention aggravation. So what I going do with it now? Donate it the Smithsonian Institution? I been looking around give it away, but I ain't yet found somebody I wants to ruin that way. It would bankrupt him in three, no, two months. So now I'm making change from pocket like they done in Dark Ages.

— Well.

— Not well—rotten! Nothing works. Nobody does nothing. Nobody pays, everybody is charging. What we need money for? All we doing with it is feeding parking meters, which is latest idea from New Salem thought up by some genius. Problem number one with parking meters is most time you ain't got car to park because it is spending more time in shop than in garage. Problem number two is if maybe your car is working, where you going find empty space? Problem number three is if maybe your car is working and maybe you find empty space, the meter ain't working. Things is better riding to town on pony. And suppose what I complain to selectmen about busted meters, they tells me they been trying to get manufacturer send them special screws for six months, but that model meter been discontinued. So now I'm saving myself trouble and walking from store in blizzards and hurricanes, which means at my age maybe I'll hold out one more winter before pneumonia gets me. And if I get pneumonia, what happens? Physician tells me come by office during regular hours—which is between two fifteen and two forty-five every other Wednesday except first week every month which is on Thursdays. Suppose what Jerry Myer is smart enough catch pneumonia on Thursday afternoon on first week every month, then he is allowed, no, invited sit in Turkish bath waiting room with twenty other people all wanting swap diseases. And if sun is really shining on Jerry Myer, if he is really one the blessed, physician finds maybe time to see him before he closes down office at two forty-five, which he just is opening at two fifteen, if he ain't late, which he is, usual. So when nurse finally calls and I crawl inside examining room, what does physician do? He gives tip on stock market. He talks about weather. He asks how business is. I tell him, look, if I want to invest I call Dreyfus, if I want know weather I read newspapers, on top of which my business is dying from my pneumonia. So he finally catches hint, puts me on scale for weighing, which is busted, tries to look in ears but light is gone out from instrument, apologizes he can't fix stethoscope because for six months special screw is coming direct from factory. It's something to laugh! So I shouldn't feel trip to office wasn't pleasure equal to going up to Jerusalem, he writes prescription for miracle drug in penmanship his medical school hired special a Chinaman to teach. He's big man, doctor from medical college, but I got to argue him and tell him last month government is calling back all bottles that drug which is defective miracle. Soon as government learns something makes miracles, they call back. Any prescription I am filling nowadays means it got to be worthless, junk. Look, customer was just in and left prescription for gall bladder which I can fill because it ain't been called back. Four bucks it costs bottle with fancy-pants label. "Aqua destillata, 62%; aqua fontis, 19%; eadem repetita, 9%; nil aliud, 7.6%; iteram eiusdam, 2.4%." Who knows, maybe it helps? The customer maybe feels little better from it, not much but little. Who knows? Doctor Froid said sometimes people helped by pleasebo. So for troubles I am getting walks in snow to physician, exchange communicable diseases, free Turkish bath, tip from stock market, weather forecast, and bill for ten dollars. So I go home and wife is putting on my chest mustard plaster, which, thank God, ain't defective and don't get busted. Maybe at last fever drops down only 103 and Jerry Myer can go store before receivers arrive. But what pleasure I got here? All I got is customers waiting yell at me because aspirins come crumpled or toothpaste got sand in it. Is my fault? I ask you? When I was boy in old country, and so poor I ain't got what to eat with, much less what to eat, all we are hearing is about God's Country, America, where everybody is rich and honest. Honest! It's something to laugh! Let me tell for you how one day salesman from biggest company comes here with all different kinds fancy order forms for new product being advertised from *Reader's Digest*. I says to him, "Sidney, by me you are like a brother. With my whole heart and whole soul I wish you well. So tell me, entry noose, is this colored distilled water like last miracle drug you said to order?" He swears me on mother's grave it is greatest product of American ingenuity. But who can believe him? Suppose what he ain't the one lying to me. Suppose what he is being lied to by his company who is guaranteeing him good product. Suppose what even the company makes it ain't lying, but maybe some other company what sold different kinds ingredients for it was lying. So everybody got somebody else to blame, all except Jerry Myer who ain't got no one to blame and who customers treat like he was drunken Indian. And I tell you something else. Another company sends me salesman, such thief I never seen in twenty-five years business come next February, we should all live to see the day. So I call long distance vice president from this company and tell him such salesman from ethical company shouldn't be sent on road without policeman watching him like eagle. This vice president with fancy-pants voice tells me, "You are right, Mister Myer. You are beyond doubt correct your appraisal this man. The scoundrel is disgrace whole profession salesmanship. But what possibly I can do?" Get that! What can he do! I tell him for one thing, just for start, he can fire that salesman. So now vice president is getting angry with me. "Speak harshly by him, you say, Mister Myer! Do you realize what you suggesting? If I even hint to him his work ain't up par, he'll become demoralized and resign! Customers I can get easier than salesmen!" It's something to laugh! Who can argue with him? Don't I know how impossible is to get people work for you? I can't get no one type out orders, and if maybe I did, typewriter would bust into thousand pieces first touch. Or envelopes wouldn't stick. Or post office would be shut because now government works by appointment. And I'll tell you from something else. You see that cash register? Two years old and already is genuine antique. It sits on counter like it was—

— Excuse me, Mister Myer, but I can't stay any longer. Someone is coming to my office and I'm late now.

— All right, all right. Listen, Mister Pennyman, if I didn't see you was in rush, I could tell some things would convince you world was coming to end. Peace, peace, I'll tell you where it is. When I'm tucked away in burial plot, which is only real estate I own. Say, maybe you do by me one little favor? There's this lady you write about personal problems and she answers them for free in magazine. Maybe she can tell me how help my son Manny who is doing everything honors by Yale but ain't doing so hot getting by front door Country Club. Is probably big gyp, but what I got lose? If I lose postage stamp, so I lose it. But my English ain't so fancy-pants. Maybe you spare me five, no, only two minutes look my letter and fix up words a little. A touch here, a touch there. Look, it says in magazine, "Readers are invited to submit details of dreams or other intimate problems. Please state any feelings, or lack of them, about people and places and events. Do not send any money, at first, as Madame Potiphar's column is—"

— No, excuse me, Mister Myer. I can't do it now. I have to get back to the office. Maybe some other time.

— All right, so I'll ask again when I see you. Another few days ain't going kill me.

— I meant to ask you something, Mister Myer. I almost forgot. Could you tell me what month in the Jewish calendar has six letters? It's for my crossword puzzle.

— For puzzles you got time. Well, not to boast, could be my month, Shebat. I was born twenty-fourth day Shebat. But could also maybe be Tishri. That comes this month, right after Elul. It got six letters. So does Kislev. Or maybe also Tammuz, which sometimes only got five, depending from how you spell it. Or else maybe—

— That's all right, Mister Myer, I'll try them all. I have to get back. Someone has an appointment with me and I don't want to be rude. I really came in just for a tube of Preparation H.

— What makes you think I got, just like that? Nowadays to order medicines you got to have appointments personal with president the company what makes them. Preparation H is precious, like pearl of great price, like blessing. Three months I been waiting order to come. First the jobber tells me was lost from mails. Five, no, ten times I call him and now he says they forgot send out. I should watch mailbox. But still it ain't come. All week I been trying call but nobody picks up phone. Maybe I should do signals like Paul Revere. One by land, two by seashore. But, look, I got different kind product here just came out. I can't guarantee, but maybe it'll give relief. Who knows?

— No, I'll wait for the Preparation H. I'll try again in a few days.

— With luck, Mister Pennyman. With luck like you never believed possible in craziest dreams from Madame Potiphar. With luck like got Moses across Red Sea. With luck like—

Slam. Slam-slam-slam-SLAM. If he doesn't like it here. Let him go back. To where he came from. Zion will be redeemed. When? When the tongues of the dumb shall sing. He makes mountains out of hills. Exalts every valley. Because he feels himself despised, rejected? Still, he acts as if he's better than we are. Holier-than-thou. Complainer in the wilderness. Back to office. Almost there. Oh, oh. Barking. Smells me from here. The mongrel. Get away fast. Don't try to outstare him. Made it! Excelsior! I was gone too long. It's late. Don't rush up stairs. Three.

Four. Five. Six. Seven. Eight. Nine. This step squeaks. Didn't this time, though. Thirteen. Fourteen. Fifteen. Excelsior! Oh. I'd better first. Down the hall. Should have gone at the bank. Made my deposit. It's quiet. Everyone gone home. You can hear a. Murmuring piss. Antiseptic smell in here. At least they keep it clean. Do number one. A long one. Overstretched. Not good at my age. Be more regular. Ah. Excelsior! Please Flush After Each Use. Please Adjust Your Clothing Before Leaving. The law! I was overdue. Gladinski ever come? Pee on poles. Nasty dog down there. Speak to its owner. There. Shake off last drop. Try a movement also? Been two days. No urge. Don't want to irritate. Should have bought substitute for Preparation H. Brand loyalty. Accept no substitutes. I'll eat more lettuce. Serutan. Spell it backward. Pull chain for gurgles of bubble on. Damn! Doesn't flush. Broken. Leave it. They'll see when they clean to-morrow. Please Turn Off Light. The law! Go back down hall. Miss Maggiore forgot to turn off light. She shouldn't waste. A penny saved.

BENJAMIN PENNYMAN, ESQ.
ATTORNEY-AT-LAW

A tourney! Outlaw! Prisoner, air ye ripresented by a toney? Yes, jedge, got mah key right heah! Damn, she left door unlocked. Forgot that also. Everything on her mind but my office. Nice girl, but not smart. She forgot.

— Oh. Miss Maggiore.

— Oh, Mister Pennyman. I was getting concerned, so I waited. You said you would be back by four thirty. I called you at Jim's, but he said you left long ago. And then I tried your home. I thought you might have gone there.

— I kept meeting people. They talk so much you can't get a word in sledgewise. It took time to get back. I couldn't be rude.

— No, of course not.

— I'm sorry you stayed so late, Miss Maggiore. It was thought-ful of you. But you didn't have to. You must have a family or a boyfriend waiting for you.

— Yes. But that's all right. I watered the plants while waiting. I don't know why they don't grow better.

She blushes. Probably someone in Little Italy. Black shiny hair. Wears zoot suit. Spaghetti stain on shirt front. And calls it mac-a-ro-nee. Maybe he works for Mafia. Numbers racket? But she's a nice girl. Polite. Not everyone would have waited. For an old man.

— Well, it was thoughtful of you, Miss Maggiore.

— That's all right, Mister Pennyman.

— No need to have worried, though. Still bounce left in the Pennyman. Did Mister Gladinski stop by?

— No, I. He. No, he didn't.

— The First Selectman-to-be probably had sufficient reason, Miss Maggiore. I heard he was busy this afternoon writing a policy for our community's latest eleemosynary institution. The Levitas Home for Aged Hebrews. On Pennyman Street.

— Oh? You did get one call, though. Missus Freudenthal.

— To invite me to the luncheon for Levitas?

— No, she wants to ask you to write an article for the Historical Society Newsletter. About your great-grandfather and the founding of the law firm.

— Why the sudden interest?

— She said now that you're going to close the office, they would like to have a record of it.

— White of them. Did she say how long an article?

— Yes. Very short. Just for the record.

— I see. A newslitter. Well, it's nearly six, Miss Maggiore, and I'm sure you have to leave. I'll be staying a while. I have something I'd better do tonight. It was nice of you to have waited.

— It wasn't any inconvenience.

— No, I'm sure it was. I'm sure you had other plans for this evening. If I might ask just one more favor of you. I wonder if you would mind stopping by Flavortowne and asking them to send over a sandwich. I believe you pass by on your way home. American cheese on white toast. Dry. No mustard. But I'd like lots of lettuce.

— Yes sir. A Coke or tea?

— Tea, please. Hot. Weak. Don't forget about the lettuce on the sandwich. And better leave the door unlocked so the delivery boy can come in.

— Mister Pennyman?

— Yes?

— I have to speak to you about something. I've wanted to mention it all week. I decided I just have to get it off my mind tonight.

— Oh? You waited tonight because you—?

— It wasn't only that. I mean. I would have waited for you anyway.

— I see. What is it you want to talk about?

— I. I'm leaving. Not right away. I mean. As soon as you can find someone to replace me.

— But you just started working for me a month ago.

— I'll stay until it's convenient for you. But I would like to leave soon.

— Well, I admit that it's a moribund law firm. Not much excitement for a young girl. I'm afraid I have no incentive to offer you to stay on until I close the office in the spring.

— That isn't the reason at all, Mister Pennyman. I've been very happy working for you. It's just that I'm going down south. To Alabama. To help with the voter registration drive. You know, for the Negroes.

— Oh?

— Yes. I volunteered. It was arranged through the Church of Our Lady of the Lame. Monsignor O'Hennerry is coming to New Salem to bless us. Before we leave. A lot of the girls from the church are going.

— It's a bad situation in Alabama. Disregard of the law. It's nice you should want to help.

— Thank you, Mister Pennyman.

— Don't worry about me. There's not much activity around here. You can see that for yourself. Of course you're welcome to your old job again if the office is still open when you come back.

Until you get yourself situated in something else, I mean.

— That's very sweet of you, Mister Pennyman. I appreciate it. I'll. I'll send you a postcard. From Alabama.

— Yes. I'd like to hear how you are getting on. They are a violent people down there. Please be cautious. I hear they've been imprisoning and maltreating whites who join the Negroes in protest marches. Especially the young girls. Take care.

— Yes, I will. Well. Good night, Mister Pennyman. I'll stop by Flavortowne. I'll ask them to send your order right over.

— Good night, Miss Maggiore.

Gently closed. Left unlocked. Considerate. Will she come back? She has nothing to lose. Just delay her marrying some wine-drinking husband and bearing ten kids. But Rebecca Harum. Rebecca is sacrificing. An education. Her rightful place in New Salem. Her own kind of people. Maybe not. The college will probably let her back in. Her mother. And grandmother. Don Harum contributes every year. She'll be wiser for the experience.

Umghmpph. Hemorrhoids bothering. Chair uncomfortable. The stuffing shifted. Not worth repairing. Hold out a few more months. Squeaks as it turns. Whee! Lied to her. No work to do. All clients gone. But have to finish the Black Book. The end of it. Gone are the Pennymanies. Finish it tonight! I'm tired. Close the book! Books. And books. Contracts. Blackstone. Torts. Old wrongs. Right wrongs. No, some other time. Tonight! Do it and forget it. Get rid of it. Give it to Yale University. Bury it in their library. To be opened five years after my decease. Surcease from sorrow. It lies there, gathering dust. Pushed farther and farther back on the shelf. Some conscientious young scholar finds it. A hundred years from now. Becomes curious about it. Stays awake night after night reading the musty pages. Understands its great importance. Writes learned dissertation about it. Publishes Black Book with copious footnotes. Hailed by fellow scholars. Favorable reviews. People talk about it. Judged most important book of decade. He's promoted to full professor. Then chairman of his department. Fame. Money. Prestige. Love. Marries childhood sweetheart. Even though she is lo-lee. And he is humble.

All from the Pennyman memories. Or maybe people will laugh at us? We'll sound quaint, look foolish. So? It was America, lads. Take it or leave it.

Finish it, now! Right here, after what Grandfather Samuel the Just wrote. He read too much Whitman. All the leaves except the fig leaf. His style too much influenced. I am the man. I suffered. Demoncratic visitors to our shores. *The neat white-painted houses. And the glistening sinlight. And the free men walking arm in arm to church on a Sunday morn. And seeing the apple trees cover'd with blossoms and the fruit afterward. And the sable vaults.* And the etceteras. Biblical catalogs. Period piece. Will what I write seem funny later? Don't write. Do write. Do right. Later. It's warm. She closed the window. Because of the banging. She forgot to open it again. No air. Sticky. Damn! I can't. Don't push too hard. Don't strain. It won't. Maybe leave it closed. Rain starting. Distant thunderclap. Hear the wonder of God's thunder. Car lights reflecting on wet street. Evening rush. Exodus from the city. To our promis'd land. Weary businessmen. Coming home to pizzas, bagels, Guinness. What do Poles eat? Heavy food. That's what makes them slow and stubborn. Oh. Hearse coming back. Empty of flowers. Funeral corsage. Malachy Murphy all tucked in. Pushing daisies. But can't keep a good man down. The kind who would frame his death stifficate. Probably selling real-estate lots already. Boost, don't knock. Malarkey's in the cold, cold ground. Priest intones. Tears shed. A wake. Will he wake again? Byebye, Malachy. What is it like, Malachy? Is it what your saints told you to expect? Or did they swindle you? Let there be no moaning. He's set out to see. What wonders did you see, Malachy? After crossing the bar. Sunset and evening star. Tell us, tell. Give us the old Malarkey.

■

OI TILL YOU, there air prospicts in that place. Iv coorse oi haven't bin there more thin a short toime. But if you've got a sharp oiye, that's enough t' look th' prospicts over. Now, Bin Pinnyman, oi don't want you t' hold me sthrictly t' anythin' oi till you 'bout the place 'cause oi'll have t' chick lather t' confoirm th' pitty ditails. But oi'll stake me riputation that it'll turn out 'bout th' way oi'm goin t' discribe it t' you. Th' foist thing you nothice is it isn't at all what you bin led t' ixpect. F'r one thing, you don't floiy around. Oi met lots iv people right off an' niver was one iv thim with wings. No sir, if you ixpect any eerial acrobathics you'll be dhisappointed. Which is foin if you suffer fr'm fear iv heighths. You don't? Well, it's a bennyfit anyway, an' it don't cost no more t' have it. Yes sir, there's good solid ground there. Maybe it's bin a little too much worked over. Oi'll till you honesthly, oi saw some irosion in a few places. But this isn't raley anythin' that a few loads iv thopsoil an' some ground cover wouldn't hoide. Why, jus' be fixin' it up a little with some showy shrubs you kin raise th' value iv the pro-pirty be 'bout twenty-foive pircent. Another advanthage many people don't realize is there airn't any angels 'round or any iv that pomp an' ceremoney. Which means it isn't a dhressy neighborhood where you always got t' be on your guard not t' offend conventions. An' it's rale quiet. No blowin' iv trumpets. Th' fellers who write th' idiotorials f'r th' newspapers is all wrong 'bout that too. It's another advanthage in case you're th' kind iv pirson that noise bothers. Oi jus' don't have th' toime t' till you all th' other advanthages. F'r ixample, they don't make any partiklar fuss 'bout you whin you arrive, which is a bennyfit 'cause oi know you're th' koind that gits imbarrassed easy. Another thing is that you'll be mixin' in th' bist society. You'll be rubbin' elbows with a lot iv foine people you wouldn't otherwise have th' opporthunity t' meet. An' th' things you'll loin! Oi jus' had a brief conversation with a feller named Suckrathes, an' th' things he told me air thruly exthraordinary! That man has got a surefoire scheme t' mannypulate th' proice iv grain in Shakakko, which means you'll be dealt in on busyness opporthunities. An' thin oi had th' privilege t' chat a little with Moses, which oi thought was rale white iv him, me bein' iv a diff'rent faith. Well, th' same God made us all, oi always say.

He's someone you kin walk roight up t' an' start off a conversation 'bout inflation. Oi'm sorry t' riport, though, that he's not doin' too well there. He has a little novilty shop that dheals in magic thricks an' sich, but th' gossip is that he's lost his touch an' he's not prosperin'. Anyway, if you're any koind iv a mixer at all, you'll soon foind yoursilf meetin' all the roight people. You'll git ahead. Iv coorse they're a little nosey at foist 'bout your accomplishments so, as Capthain Soimon Suggs wonst said, it's good t' be shifty in a new counthry. But that wirs off an' they're plinty happy t' till you their throubles. Now, as oi said, oi only had toime f'r an initial impression. But one thing that sthruck me roight off is that these people haven't bin takin' advanthage iv th' prospects iv th' place. They're doin' a poor job iv managin'. Well, their loss kin be your gain if you handle your pro-pirty roight. Th' main thing is t' git a good location, which most iv these people weren't smart enough t' do. An' thin t' dhress it up a bit as a come-on. A pirson with half a moind on his busyness would prospir there. But most iv them airn't. In fact, most iv thim air mis'rable 'bout their fate. Thim what was bifore hayroes in th' armed forces iv our deemocracy or staitsmen or authors iv litherachore now foind thimselves bein' stuck with what they did or said in th' other loife. An' thim what may have made foolish statemints in an oidle momint have got t' display it at their place iv busyness roight above th' cash rigister. You'll foind that many iv the folks there air sorry they didn't listen more an' speak less.

Oi got t' see Goige Washintown who is called Fahthir iv His Country be all th' pathriotic Americins there. But his busyness is so slow that he's bin obliged t' increase t' a quarther inch th' thickness iv th' gold coatin' on th' bricks he sills.

Thomas Pain plays th' ouija board t' git out iv th' mess *Commin Sinse* made iv his loife.

Bendyourmind Frunklin is doin' poorly an' he's iniligible f'r welfair paimints 'cause he wonst said, "God hilps thim that hilps thimselves."

Daniel Whipster, who wonst said "Liberthy an' Union, now an' f'river, one an' insiperable," was found guilthy as charged iv fixin' th' jury in th' Misther Scratch case.

Join Brown is moighty harried bookin' seats on th' Undherground Railroad, which oi hear has gone into ricivership.

Honest Abe Lunkin is moighty uncomforthable livin' in that log cabin he always boasted 'bout.

Harriet Belcher Stew inf'rmed me proudhly she was th' little ladhy that stharted a war. She now runs a small boardin' house f'r mutilated sojars, but oi hear th' ambiance is not viry appitizin' an most iv her rooms air impty.

Jiffyson Davis foinds hisself shunned be th' bist society, an' his only chums air some coloreds named Countee Cullen, Jaimes Whilldone Joinston, Doubleyou Ee Bee DuBoys, Marcus Gravy, an' some other gintlemin whose monickers oi didn't catch. No one ilse had heard iv thim either.

You would think that all th' authors iv litherachore would live close be one 'nother, since they air in th' same loine iv work, but that ain't thrue. Fillup Freneau, who has justhly bin called "Th' Po-it iv th' Americin Rivalution," has bin diddled out iv his royalthy. William Cullin Brunt has grown deaf thryin' t' undherstand th' "varyous languages" Nathure spoke t' him who hild communion. Headgear Hellion Pew, the famous po-it, foinds that families tind t' keep their little goils away fr'm his kingdhom be th' sea, ivin though he promises "Nivirmore." Nathaniel Highthorn has sold his soul t' th' Divil, but he didn't git a good price f'r it. Idward Iveritt Hale, the pathriotic author iv th' famous *Man Without a Counthry,* oi found hell an' hearthy. Hummin Mullville is a whale iv a complainer. Hinry Winceworth Lungflow is a booster an' not a knocker, oi was glad t' see confoimed. Join Grimleaf Whiter, oi loined, is tone deaf an' can't whistle th' mirry thunes iv th' bairfoot boy with chicks iv tan. Joimes Funnymore Keeper is an Indhian agent. Oi spotted that old faker Ralph Dildo Himersin standin' be a rude bridge that arched a flood. 'Cause he was wonst foolish enough t' say that "Th' only riward iv virtue is virtue," you foind him pritty much grubbin' 'round f'r three squares an' a flop.

Thin, iv coorse, there air a whole group iv inventhors that has brought fame on Amirica an' made this th' cinchery iv pro-griss with their modhern masheens. But much as they moight iv bin a whizz in th' other loife, in this new place they air findin' that masheeniry did ivirythin f'r thim but help thim. Thomas Halfer Eddyson niver spoke a thruer woid thin "There is no substithute f'r hard woik," but he took a plunge in th' stock markit that didn't woik out. An' Hinry Fraud, who said that histhory is bunk, is now writin' a histhory iv Zion in 5,724 volumes.

Jim Frisk, Conn Vanderwilt, Jay Pee Morgan, Ee Haitch Harriedman, Henry Gray Flick, Andhrew Connigie, Samwell Insult, Join Dee Rockyfeller, Thomas Doubleyou Lament, an' th' other kings iv forthune oi found livin' in a neighborhood where th' smoke poors out iv the chimbly iv th' workin' glass. They sthill air selflessly workin' t' keep th' money movin' through th' iconomy, mosthly into their own pockets. They air all partnirs in a dhiscount istablishmint that's prisintly plagued be inventhory problims, although they tries t' keep up a good front an' not sill Amirica short. Oi found thim very injoyable company an' rale upsthandin' men, if you were not in their way.

Th' main topic iv conversation iv the kings iv forthune was that thrust-buster Tiddy Rosenfelt. But oi didn't git t' see that famous man. He was ristin' indhoors with a catarrh he got fr'm leadin' th' Sthrenuous Loife.

Horeass Mann is sthill lookin' f'r th' two goldhen hours, each sit with sixty dimond minutes, he misplaced 'tween sunup an' sundown. Only now th' skinflint is offerin' a riward, which moight improve his prospicts.

Oi hear Pee Tee Bunkum was taken f'r his whole roll be his lady high-thrapeze arthist.

Boss Treed oi found a very able man. He had t' be t' succeed like he done. He was in office only a few years an' he was worth tin million dhollars. Only the masheen he built up is busthed an' th' t modhel isn't made no more.

Oi found Booger Tee Washintown ricoverin' fr'm a hernia he got thryin' t' lift hisself up be his own bootsthraps.

Oi always rispected Willyum Ginnings Bryan who said, "You shall not crucify mankind on a cross iv gold." He is now hawkin' silver crosses, but he is workin' a bad corner.

Oi'm dhisappointed in th' judgmint shown be Eugene Vee Dips, a faithful mimber iv th' international commonturn. He was th' one, you moight reklect, who boasted, "While thir is a lower class, oi am iv it." Now he foinds hisself unable t' roise out iv the muck iv poorverty.

Woodrow Willson still bilieves that "Amirica is th' only oidealistic nation in th' woirld," even though someone mugged him last week.

Gineral Blackjock Pushing, his head irect an' th' feelin' iv thrue pathriotism in his heart, binds your ear thryin' t' ixplain that he meant t' say "Lafayette, we air hayroes," but he got combombulated be th' ixcitemint iv seein' Madame Ovary an' her French goils.

Cal Coolitch is learnin' th' hard way that "Th' busyness iv Amirica is busyness." He's gone bankrupt 57,240 toimes.

Oi was happy t' see that Al Smith, daubed th' "Hoppy Worrier," sthill ritains th' good pints iv his singin' voice, an kin give a good rindition iv "East Side, Wet Side."

Hellbut Hoover sits with an addhin' masheen, oiyeshades, an' a quill pin thryin' t' balance th' books iv "Th' Amirican systim iv Rugged Individhualism."

Well, there air lots iv other people oi sthill got t' hear 'bout an' oi ixpect t' be meetin' more iv thim as toime goes by. Oi've bin invited t' sivral git-togithers nixt week, which oi thought was moighty white iv thim, me bein' jus' a rale-istate agint fr'm a small community loike New Salem. But they must iv loiked me hustle. Oi hear, though, these git-togithers airn't as loively as they moight be. Sooner or lather th' conversation always thurns t' the same thing. Seems hardhly anyone is contint with his loine iv work in this place. An' most iv thim feel that if they didn't git their riwards on earth, they air surely not goin' t' git thim here. In fact, some iv th' folks feel they've bin conned. But oi think it is a place iv goldhen opporthunities f'r a feller with go. Oi ixpect t' go boundhin' t' th' top iv th' laddher.

Well, that's 'bout all oi kin till you now. Oi missed your prisence today at th' festhivities in me honor at th' Soign iv Hopealong Chastity—which oi think is in bad taste iv you t' call it. Oi'll be waitin' f'r you, Bin Pinnyman. You'll foind your place iv busyness all riddy f'r you, includin' th' soign "Mimory Survives" above your cash rigister. You an' me will be parthners again. Only this toime, Bin Pinnyman, oi holds th' swag an' we dhivides up fair an' honest. You'll have lots t' think 'bout till thin. Haw-haw.

■

— SCUSE ME. Ah say, scuse me, Mist' Poorman. Fer bustin in on you. But you didn't answer mah knock. Ah tried twice.

— Oh. Yes? Oh, from Flavortowne. Daniel Hyde, isn't it? You shoveled snow for me last winter I believe, Mister Hyde.

— Dat's right.

— That was fast. I appreciate it.

— Thass awright, Mist' Poorman. Weren't much else to do. So they made it up right quick fer you.

— Still, I appreciate it. Well, it's not exactly Belshazzar's feast, but I am hungry. Just a moment, Mister Hyde. Here's something for your trouble.

— Kind uv you, Mist' Poorman.

— Don't mention it. I appreciate your prompt service. It couldn't have been more than three quarters of an hour since my secretary gave the order.

— No, suh, weren't even dat long.

— Well, I must say that certainly was prompt.

— Thass awright.

— Let's see. I did give you something already, didn't I?

— Yes suh, ten cents.

— Well, I appreciate your service.

— Gonight, Mist' Poorman.

— Good night, Mister Hyde. Oh, damn! Daniel!!

— Suh?

— Daniel, this isn't my order! I wanted an American cheese on dry toast. White. With a lot of lettuce. Not a hot pastrami with a pickle.

— Oh, oh.

— And I wanted tea—weak. Not a celery tonic.

— Oh, oh.

— Well, Mister Hyde, it's not so bad that it can't be corrected easily enough. Please just go back and bring me my correct order.

— Ah mene. Ah mene to say.

— Yes? What's wrong with that suggestion?

— Ah couldn't study de writin on de bag too good. Ah must uv switched your order wid Mist' Fraudtall's at de bank. Iffen ah could read writin good, ah would uv gotten me better work. Now Mist' Fraudtall gone be angry wid me too. Oh, oh.

— Mister Hyde, please just get me my correct order. I don't care how you do it. But I want something to eat. I have work to do tonight.

— Yes suh, ah shure will. Jest let me shovel dis salami back on de bread an fold it up real nice so Mist' Fraudtall won't notice nothin. Dere! Ah'll jest whistle dis order ober to him an pick up your rightful one, Mist' Poorman.

— But by the time you get back my tea will be cold.

— Oh, oh.

— Mister Hyde, I'm sure Mister Freudenthal has already opened my order, just as I opened his. I don't think I'd care for that sandwich any more. Can't you just go back to Flavortowne and start out from scratch on my order? That's an American cheese on dry toast. White. A lot of lettuce.

— Mist' Magnificent gone make me pay fer de mistake. Oh, oh.

— Damn! All right, bring this order to Mister Freudenthal and exchange it for my sandwich. Then bring mine back to me. I'll eat it anyway. But that doesn't solve the tea problem. I still want my tea hot. So on your way back from Mister Freudenthal please stop by Flavortowne again and tell Mister Magnicenti I'm unusually thirsty and want another tea. Weak. Be sure it's weak. All right? That works it out for everyone. Mister Magnicenti won't know about the mistake, and it doesn't cost you anything. I'm the only one who is out of pocket—fifteen cents for the second tea. Mister Magnicenti will put it on my bill. There! Everything is solved.

— 'Tain't.

— Why not?

— Tea's gone up. It's twenny cents now.

— Oh, damn! All right then.

— Still 'tain't right.

— Why not?

— Dat still don't square me wid Mist' Fraudtall. He gone say all de pop gone out uv his tonic while ah been jabberin heah wid you. An he ordered a hot salami. It's gone be cold by de time ah git dis to him. Oh, oh.

— Well, Mister Freudenthal will just have to endure life's irregularities.

— Suh?

— I mean. Never mind. Please just go ahead and do as I asked.

— Ah think it best ah don't do nuffin, Mist' Poorman, iffen you don't mind. De salami is mighty good, an it costs more dan de cheese. Iffen you keeps dis order, you is ahead.

— But I don't want pastrami. I don't like the smell of it. I never eat it. I don't like greasy food.

— No, suh, guess not. Elsewise you would uv ordered it in de fust place.

— Yes, that's right.

— Oh, oh. Mist' Magnificent gone be turrible angry wid me.

— Well, I'm sorry, Mister Hyde. You should have taken more care in reading what was written so you could deliver the correct orders. It's your own fault.

— Ah knows ah is in de wrong. Dat makes it wurst.

— Well, there's no problem that can't be solved.

— But Mist' Magnificent gone take it out mah pay whether ah knows ah is wrong or not.

— Mister Hyde, just tell him it was an honest mistake. Especially late in the day when people aren't alert.

— You don't know Mist' Magnificent. He act real cosy wid de customers, but he is a terror in de kitchen. Ah ain't havin much luck wid work. Ah got fired fum de last job an ah gone be fired fum dis one. Ah can tell.

— I'm sure Mister Magnicenti won't be that severe.

— Yes suh, he will. An he'll make me feel mighty small afore he fires me. He'll cut me down to de size uv de cockrich insect. An den he'll say he scrapped de bottom uv de barrel afore he found me.

— Mister Hyde, just explain the whole mix-up to him. It's an honest mistake. Tell him that. That's all you have to do.

— Please suh, Mist' Poorman. You call Mist' Magnificent fer me.

— I call! It's not up to me to explain it! After all, I'm the one who has been inconvenienced. I'm the one who got the pastrami instead of the American cheese. And the celery tonic instead of the tea. And who has to pay an extra twenty cents to hide your mistake, Mister Hyde.

— Ah jest don't know how to splain good. Speshally when Mist' Magnificent git in a fit. Ah loses mah tongue.

— That's ridiculous, Mister Hyde. Just talk to him.

— 'Tain't. Ah neber been to school where dey teaches you to talk back to folks. When ah tries, ah gits pimples all ober. Please. Ah'd do most anythin rather than have to splain to Mist' Magnificent.

— I'm sorry, but I can't help you any further, Mister Hyde.

— Oh, oh.

— Anyway, this whole matter is taking entirely too long. And I want my sandwich. Please do as I ask. Just bring this order to Mister Freudenthal and exchange it for mine. Then pick up some fresh tea. Weak.

— Can't.

— Now what's wrong?

— Mist' Magnificent closes up at seben. He washed de teapot out awready.

— Well, he'll just have to make some fresh.

— Oh, oh.

— I'm sorry, Mister Hyde. You'll have to explain it to Mister Magnicenti. He'll understand that it was an honest mistake.

— Oh, oh.

Shuffles off. He Pooribus Unum. Damn! Left door open. What hope for them? Uneducated. Backward. REVILED, DID DE-LIVER. Superstitious. Voodoo. Inconsiderate. Damn! I have to get up. And close the door. Slam! Oh. He remembered to close it. Came back. Freudenthal is all over the place today. First in my hair, now in my food. At least the hammering on his house stopped. He finally let the workmen go. But he's working late. Adding up his profits. Planning new conquests. They say he's a very charitable man. Makes a contribution each leap year in four. Mister Facing-Both-Ways. How can we ever stop them? They're all over the place. How can we rewin New Jerusalem? From those Roamans. We need a new crusade. The MacAbies again. Retake the holy places.

■

IT's EASY, mon fils, it's very easy. You don't need a great multitude. For who is like to you among the strong? All you have to do is listen carefully and follow my instructions. First thing tomorrow, Benjamin, remove all your bonds from the vault. Sell them, down to the last certificate, and divide your pile into two equal parts. With the first, launch a speculation against those mortgages Freudenthal has been playing hot and heavy with. Don't forget to earmark a small part of this pile to bribe a federal agent to open an investigation of Freudenthal's income-tax returns for the years 1958–62. The agent probably won't find anything that can stand up in court because Freudenthal is a crafty one, but this diversionary sweep will serve its purpose of making him edgy. He will post his sentries against this agent while you are marshaling for an attack from a different quarter. That's where your second pile comes in, mon enfant. It has not been idle to no eventual purpose. Strike with it now to purchase shares in Freudenthal's bank, which you will find are traded over the counter. Bien entendu, your interest might cause the price to rise somewhat, but that can be kept to a minimum if a crony of yours keeps selling back a little of what you buy. Now you will be in an excellent position to demand seating on his board of directors, in which stronghold you will soon find you have allies, for these men cannot fail to be impressed with your esprit. But don't be greedy of the spoils now, Benjamin, for you will soon take enough to satisfy the lust of Dives. Your position is now fortified, whereas Freudenthal is in a panic to jettison assets, discount mortgages, retrench his vulnerable position. Your attack begins! Buy up whatever you can! I know as well as you that these mortgages are mostly on the property of the minorities who deal with his bank, but their money crinkles just as loudly as ours. A quarter of New Salem will feel your might before anyone awakens to what your game is. You will have a death grip on stores, homes, lake-front acreage, a cemetery, toute la ville. Even the Levitas Home for Aged Hebrews. Josh Levitas will be shrewd enough to recognize the terrible swift sword of his enemy and retreat to easier pickings in some other town. But you will not merely sit there with those mortgages, Benjamin. Oh, no! You'll squeeze them until the eagle screams by threatening, bribing, bearing false witness, foreclosing, holding auctions with your confederates among the bidders, and in general ways creating havoc and stripping the owners down to their nether garments. Your power has now so magnified that you can strike out to the fortified villages the aliens have made their own in Connecticut—Sharon, Danbury, New Canaan, Bethel, Bethany, Bethlehem. Oh, how the news of your might has been nosed about! Oh, how loved is my child who has learned his lesson well! How the other mothers will look on enviously! How the other gentlemen will try to emulate your deeds! You have emerged as a magnetic leader to whom reinforcements flock. You will pursue the dollared sons of God and hurl them backward! LIVE EVIL! Do not fear to attack at night and to ambush on the sabbath. The workers of iniquity will flee in panic, tossing their Swiss bankbooks to the winds. But if any make a stand, give no quarter! Plunge in all the way until they fall to their knees and cry to their bearded prophets for mercy. Dread of you will fall upon the nations all around. It is now a holy war against the infidels. You will be le bel homme sans merci.

— Oh no, Mother. I will try to be merciful. I have integrity.

Only if they agree to being baptized by Doctor DuMont and giving you forty percent of their usurious profits, Benjamin. Otherwise, scoop up every realm, for you are a conqueror. Be like a lion's whelp roaring over its prey. You can now meet the mercantile forces head on for a showdown. These crafty ones will expect you first to raid the flanks of their suburban branches. But your strategy will outwit them! You will persevere, Benjamin! Allons, my little Christian soldier! But first, please stop scratching your derrière. No conqueror in the anals of empire ever let on that he suffered from that disgusting malady.

— May I ask a question, Mother?

Ask and learn.

— Do I stop there?

Au contraire! Rien ne réussit comme le succès. How can you be so lacking in ambition, Benjamin? You have now won a position whereby you can penetrate to la coeur de la coeur, their sanctuary of Mammon. Make battlefields everywhere of Dreyfus, Hirsch, Oppenheimer, the brothers Lehman, Goldman, Sachs, Bache, Kuhn, Loeb, Godnick, J. Ezra, Vogel, Lorber, Pressman, Wertheim, the brothers Salomon, Frohlich, Hentz, Lerner, Scheinman, Hochstein, Trotta, Cohn and Ivers. They are yours, yours!

— When do I start on the usurious banks, Mother?

No, Benjamin, you will touch not a hair of yon gray heads, for the bankers are our true allies, except for Freudenthal, whom you have already sent to his fathers.

— Well then, can I go after the electric utilities which have exceeded the TVA yardstick by several feet?

Au contraire, Benjamin, for they are all our own true people, loyal to the last man.

— The railroads, then? The railroads which no longer give Service while they stoke their boilers with profits?

No, no, Benjamin, we already possess those.

— I know! I can go after the airlines, those high-fliers!

I must disappoint you again, Benjamin. They also are in our camp, true-blue and foursquare.

— Then the automobile manufacturers! I hear they wax in riches from saving two bits on cheaper bolts.

Benjamin, tu ne comprends pas. We already control those industrious tinkers which have put America on wheels.

— How about the construction companies which house well two-thirds of a nation?

Non, non! Leave them in peace to harvest the timber of a nation.

— I've got it! The yeomen farmers who feed well two-thirds of a nation.

Oh Benjamin, you grow more fanciful with every word. They are the very ramrod of our crusade. Leave them in peace to bring forth bounty from the American soil where Flora has wantonly spread her riches.

— Could I attack the telephone companies?

Not our closest allies!

— The coal companies?

No!

— Then the ship-building companies?

No! No!

— The Olympic Committee?

Unspeakable!

— The yachting clubs?

Unheard of!

— The foreign service?

Unbelievable!

— The oil companies?

Impossible! They fuel our military-industrial allies.

— The corporation lawyers?

Grotesquerie! No, Benjamin, now you will turn to the powerful entertainment industry. Hit hard at Goldwyn, Mayer, Selznick, Zukor, Zanuck, Schary, Hurok, and the other impresarios. Lob a few blockbusters into them! Onward to the heights!

— When can I decimate utterly their resorts where they replenish themselves?

Fire when ready, grisly. Start with Charles & Lillie Brown's. Then advance rapidly to Kutsher's, Concord, Granit, Pincus Pines, Waldmere, Nemerson's, Kiamesha Lake, Nevele, Sacks Lodge, Fallview, Copake, Ackerman's, Green's. After this display of your might, Grossinger's will sue for peace. Your terms will be unbearable, yet they will be forced to bear them!

— Will they include permission for me to read at the pool?

No, you have important work to do. You must forge ahead. Allons, mon enfant. The fruits of victory will be yours to pluck later. Because you want to avoid unfavorable publicity, you must now destroy their propaganda machines. Extirpate Simon & Schuster, Atheneum, Viking, Geis, Grossman, Random House, Knopf, Pantheon, Crown, Schocken, Stein & Day, Abrams, and Farrar, Straus.

— Mother, can I censor their smut?

Of course you can, Benjamin. The works they publish are alien ideologies. Literature is the mirror of a nation's soul and honest heart. Our nation is mirrored flawlessly in the collected works of Longfellow and Whittier. It is certainly not the same nation that is despicably portrayed in the books these people hawk.

— When will I be ready for a crack at *Reader's Digest, Life, Time, Look, Playboy,* and *The Saturday Evening Post?*

Oh, inept pupil! No, it is time now to make a diversionary sweep through the art dealers—Wise, Janis, Perls, Rosenberg, Fischbach, Hirschl & Adler, Kornblee, Wildenstein, Saidenberg, Schaefer, Gerson, Fried, Emmerich, Krasner, Stone, Frumkin, Deitsch, and Feigen. If only Pierre had lived to enlist in your cause, for he loved art. C'est dommage. Now, hold your breath while I tell you your next move. You are going national! Every one of those counties across the nation with suspect names will feel your might. They're yours already! Levy, Florida, will fall first.

— How about Emanuel, Georgia?

That too. Go on to Kaplan, Louisiana. Head north and then strike west to Pitkin, Colorado. You'll get every one. You'll be victorious on every battlefield! But remember that we have been waging a solemn jihad. We are now ready for the grand deliverance itself—the retaking of Jerusalem! Scion will be redeemed!

— Blessed day! I will rebuild Solomon's Temple with a cross on the top painted cleverly to look like silver. Oh, oh. I just thought of something. What will I do for food in those deserts? I'll perish.

I've taken care of everything as usual, Benjamin. You will have manna and quails dropping from heaven.

— But aren't those Jewish foods?

You won't mind them. They are served with very little horse-radish. Now, Benjamin, you are sitting pretty. You are monarch of all you survey. It is time to institute a new Bill of Rites. You must get a piece of the action at the money-changers' tables in the Temple. And then you must redistribute the alien property.

— Mother, I make you a gift of everything. Everything! I want only to sit under the fig trees and do my crossword puzzles.

Your gift is fitting and proper, Benjamin. Your speech delights the ear. Thank you, Benjamin. Merci beaucoup. You are a son any mother can be proud of. Not like that brother of yours who is a man without a country. Thank you again. It's all over. You are the victor. It's the end of them. Good night, laddies, good night, swart laddies, good night. They're dispersed. Die, spoor! Babble on! Exit you. Exit us. Excelsior!

■

RLLLNG. Rlllng. Must be wrong number. Rlllng. Don't answer. Rlllng. After office hours. Rlllng. Who would call me? Rlllng. Keeps up. Oh, well.

— Hello. Yes? What? You must have the wrong number. Who? Can you please speak more distinctly? Wait a minute! I can't understand you! Yes, this is Mister Pennyman. Please calm down! Oh! Mister Magnicenti? Yes, of course, of Flavortowne. What do you mean what did I say? To Daniel Hyde? He what? Please speak more slowly. He hung up his apron and left? How do you know he's not coming back? Oh, I see, he asked for his pay. No, I did not advise him to quit. In fact, I suggested he discuss something with you. He didn't? No, I will not go into it with you. If he decided not to discuss it himself, then it's not up to me to do so. Yes, I realize I've had an account with you for nine years. But a charge account isn't the same as revealing a private conversation. Of course there's nothing to be secret about. It really isn't that important, Mister Magnicenti. No, of course I'm not keeping anything from you. No, no one is spying on you. I'm not the. No, I definitely was not going to say the Mafia! Please calm down. I was going to say, I'm not the FBI. Yes, I know Columbus discovered America first. I told you before that the misunderstanding really isn't worth all this discussion. I'm sorry about Daniel, but it's not my fault that he's leaving. I know he wasn't perfect. I'm glad to hear, though, that he had redeeming features. Yes, I know a lot of them steal. I'm glad he didn't. And that he's not on dope either. And not diseased. Yes, I know most of them have a case of it. Yes, I know they do it a lot. The effect of the African sun on their organs? I don't know, you might be right. Yes, a lot of them do get into trouble. Yes, I did hear what his brother Barefoot did to himself. Yes, destroyed himself piecemeal. Well, I'm sure you will find someone else. Even if he was the bottom of the barrel, you'll find another one. Please don't worry so much. Fine. Good. I'm glad you see it that way. You're right, never run after a bus or an employee. Right. Yes. What? My bill? A mistake? Wait, let me see. Yes, Daniel did leave it. It's here on my desk. I can hardly make out his damn writing. Oh, I see. It's your writing. What's that? You didn't charge me enough? You wrote American cheese but you sent me a hot pastrami? But. But. I thought it was Daniel's error. Oh. You packed and addressed the orders yourself? You always do it yourself to insure no mistakes? I see. Of course I know a hot pastrami costs forty-five cents more than an American cheese. But. I. Oh, damn! All right, all right. Yes, add the forty-five cents to my account. Yes, I'll pay it. No, I won't argue with you when the bill comes. This damn sandwich has taken too much of my time! No, I'm not getting excited. Damn, I did say I'd pay for it! Yes, and the extra five cents for the celery tonic instead of the tea. Right. That makes a total of fifty cents. Yes. I said I'd pay it. Yes, I'll remember. All right? Goodbye. Fine. Of course I'll continue to do business with you. Yes. Goodbye. What! You found out about the error of fifty cents from? From Mister Freudenthal? He called to say you over-charged him? Charged him for a hot pastrami instead of an American cheese? Oh, I see. You'll deduct fifty cents from his bill? Damn! No, of course I'm not angry. No. All right. Oh, wait. Hold the phone a minute, please. Come in, Mister Gladinski. Have a seat. I'll be off the phone in just a moment. Hello, Mister Magnicenti. Someone just came into my office. I have to hang up now. Yes. If I see Daniel I'll tell him you'll take him back. Yes, I'm sorry also for the mix-ups. Yes. Goodbye. Yes. Fine. What! It would simplify your bookkeeping if I gave Mister Freudenthal the fifty cents? Then you wouldn't have to add to my account and deduct from his? No, damn it! What? I'm not swearing at you! Of course you're entitled to respect. Yes. I said I'm sorry. I'm going to have to hang up. I have someone in my office. Yes, I know you have problems. All right. Yes. I will. I'll give it to Mister Freudenthal. Yes, fifty cents. No, I won't forget. Good-bye. Yes. Of course I'll continue to do business. I told you I would. Yes. Goodbye. Yes, I know there's nothing more left at the bottom of the barrel. You're getting excited again, Mister Magnicenti. I'm sure you won't go bankrupt just because you don't have a delivery boy for a few days. Yes. My hot pastrami sandwich was delicious. Yes, it was. Topnotch flavor. Yes, a su-perior cut of meat. And juicy too. I'm glad you buy from a new supplier. Yes. He does supply you with first-class meat. Yes, he does. What! You've switched to a kosher supplier? No, of course there's nothing wrong with that. Of course I'm not prejudiced! Of course I know many of our citizens are of that faith. No, there was no prejudice in that remark. Just because I can't abide garlic bread doesn't mean I'm prejudiced against Italians. Now, wait a minute, Mister Magnicenti! Please calm down. There was absolutely nothing in bad taste about my remark. There wasn't an ounce of prejudice in it. I. I. Please try to understand. Yes. I said. I meant. It was only a passing remark. I know if someone pricks you you bleed like anyone else. Yes. But. I mean. I. Boom-lay. Boom. Damn! He hung up!

Well, Mister Gladinski.

■

THE COMING-AT-LAST OF
FIRST SELECTMAN-TO-BE GLADINSKI

SCENE: *Law offices of Benjamin Pennyman, Esq., facing the common in New Salem, Connecticut, on the evening of September 9, 1963, at about seven o'clock.*

At the left is a door leading to the hallway with the legend

BENJAMIN PENNYMAN, ESQ.
ATTORNEY-AT-LAW

painted on it in somewhat flaked gilt. This is the aspect it presents to passersby in the hallway, but to those inside the office, as we are, it reads as a mirror image. Perhaps because Pennyman stares at such an image during much of the day, he is particularly alert to reflections in words, scenes, and events. At the rear of the office two large windows reach nearly to the floor. There can be seen, despite the darkness and the storm, the trunks and lower branches of some elm trees, blighted by a disease that came from Europe.

Against one wall is an elaborate mantelpiece, on which rests an End of the Trail bronze statue depicting a forlorn and defeated Indian, his lance lowered. Above it hang two large pe-

*riod portraits: Pennyman's grandfather, fondly remembered as
Samuel the Just, who died in 1910 when Pennyman was fourteen, and his great-grandfather Gideon, who founded the firm
on the services that occupied a legal counselor in a homogeneous
and bucolic Connecticut village in the simpler days of 1828,
such as drawing leases and deeds and bonds for deeds, examining claims, attending arbitrations, recovering estates, making
out partnership agreements, searching for wills, writing wills,
taking depositions, searching land titles and water rights, arbi-
trating turnpike-toll disputes, waging suits over the support of
paupers and former slaves, breach of promise, stolen property,
and courtroom defenses against charges of Sabbath-breaking,
profane swearing, lascivious carriage, failure to contribute to the
support of the ministry, fornication, abuse of an apprentice, de-
struction of property, defamation, contempt, libel, trespass, as-
sault and battery, drunkenness, vagrancy, smuggling, extortion,
gambling, sodomy, molestation of a minor, bestiality, adultery,
desertion of a spouse, theft, embezzlement, fraud, tax evasion,
perjury, arson, riot, kidnaping, mutilation, lynching, conspiracy,
treason, rape, manslaughter, and homicide. There is no portrait
of Pennyman's father. The walls are paneled with wood, somewhat too somber, which reflects the heavy sheen of generations
of conscientious waxing. Set inconspicuously in a corner on the
wall are Benjamin's baccalaureate and law diplomas from Yale,
framed simply. The walls are further adorned with framed letters written by people locally famous but now long forgotten.
Also framed is a poem written by Benjamin and published in
the New York Evening Sun in 1919, which he denigrates to visitors but of which he is secretly proud.*

> *Fairy book, fairy book,*
> *Friend of my childhood days;*
> *Fairy book, fairy book,*
> *That told of ogre's ways.*
>
> *Oh, these short and stirring tales,*
> *That banished childhood cares;*

Somehow like quiet, peaceful vales
They calmed the heart's despairs.

From out my little pent-up home,
They took my pent-up heart to roam;
To life—adventure—fascination,
The capers of imagination!

Man's cares and trials go on forever,
Just like the poet's babbling brook;
But now I'm older I must never
Read the children's fairy book.

The room appears insulated from the maelstrom of contemporary events. It conveys probity, integrity, and discretion, the safety of too little rather than too much. A conscientious secretary has attempted unsuccessfully to make the room less forbidding by placing six or seven plants on a windowsill, but their leaves droop, unresponsive to the watering. Life seems to find it difficult to flourish in the oppressive air of the memories bottled up in this room.

Two glassed-in bookcases are on either side of the double windows. The smaller contains law texts, bound in buckram and leather, worn at the tops where they have been pulled from the shelves to settle knotty problems; but not recently, for Pennyman has no clients with knotty problems these days. The larger bookcase on the opposite side of the windows is the favored one, its volumes attentively oiled and dusted. They are works of literature—the mirror of a nation's soul and honest heart, as Pennyman's emphatic mother used to tell him—and exclusively by American authors. The most accessible shelves are devoted to favorite authors: collections of Indian folk tales, William Bradford, John Winthrop, Michael Wigglesworth, Cotton Mather, the New England Primer, Jonathan Edwards, St. John de Crèvecoeur, Benjamin Franklin, Thomas Paine, James Fenimore Cooper, David Crockett, Seba Smith, Nathaniel Hawthorne, Mason L. Weems, Edgar Allan Poe, Harriet Beecher Stowe,

John Greenleaf Whittier, Oliver Wendell Holmes, Henry Wadsworth Longfellow, James Russell Lowell, Ralph Waldo Emerson, Walt Whitman, Thomas Bailey Aldrich, Sarah Orne Jewett, Joel Chandler Harris, T. C. Haliburton, Josh Billings, Artemus Ward, Mark Twain, Finley Peter Dunne, Vachel Lindsay, John P. Marquand, Robert Frost, and Eugene O'Neill. Whether these books possess an honest heart or not, Pennyman's soul is their mirror.

Near the hallway door stands a secretary's desk, on which rests a neat pile of law portfolios tied with frayed ribbons. The typewriter has been covered with plastic for the night. A large desk of hand-hewn oak stands in front of the windows and dominates the stage. The desk is nearly bare, but seen on it is an ornate penholder Benjamin's mother brought back for him as a gift from her trip to Paree in 1908 instead of one of those gold-painted models of the Eiffel Tower popular at the time as gifts for little boys. She is present also as a propped-up memory, a small silver frame holding a photograph of her in middle age. One other object is on the desk—a large black book, a treasured family Bible, unmistakably very old, the kind in which generation after generation has chronicled the births, deaths, and major events of their lives. Two deep chairs, their leather arms scuffed badly by several generations of fretful clients, are positioned on one side of the desk. A revolving chair, also covered in leather, but showing considerably more wear, is on the opposite side.

As the curtain rises BENJAMIN PENNYMAN, ESQ. is seated at the desk in the revolving chair. The motion of his hand reveals that he has just replaced the telephone receiver. He exhales slowly. The day has exposed him to a succession of petty annoyances which he would rather have avoided if he had had his druthers. He is sixty-seven, of medium height but appearing much shorter because of his slight frame. In a different age he would have dressed in New England homespun. Instead, he wears the modern equivalent, a shapeless gray suit, serviceable, tailored for long wear rather than for fashion. He would never *think of giving away a suit of clothes before it had reached its limit of usefulness. He joins with Thoreau in the caution: Beware of all enterprises that require new clothes. One flap of a side pocket has a slight tear and his shirt collar is poorly ironed, perhaps by an aging day laundress. His attire shows the lack of a woman's attention. Light from the desk lamp plays upon his thick glasses, silver-rimmed. His features are thin and pale, framed by a full head of white hair streaked with remnant black. A wart with a tuft of hairs rises near his left nostril, and one ear lobe is interestingly longer than the other; his aristocratic nose is streaked by prominent veins in a trellis pattern. His lips are sensitive and they wear a persistent speck of dewy saliva. His motions are quick, as if he did not want to be caught in the act of doing anything definitive, such as scratching his derrière, plagued by piles. His fingers are long and tapering, magnificent hands that required centuries of careful breeding to produce, but they would be enhanced by a manicure. If he had the habit of tugging at an unlit briar pipe, some people might make the mistake of considering him deep. But he does not smoke. He is clearly not the attorney one would select for the courtroom or for a negotiation with attorney Aaron Lustvogel of Danbury. His value to clients, the very few paying ones who are left, is the reassurance of the Pennyman name and his vague reputation for integrity—a reputation which, by the way, he has successfully avoided putting to a test.*

First Selectman-to-be Gladinski is deep-chested, with a strong neck, unmistakably the build of a peasant, despite his attempts to hide it by careful tailoring. As the curtain rises he has just entered from the hallway door, but he is still in the shadows, an unresolved presence, as he has in fact been all day to Pennyman. He walks confidently forward, almost without effort, and we get a better look at him. He is wearing a summer linen suit, actually a clever synthetic fiber, ivory-colored, with a bright but not ostentatious tie. He is all spit and Polish, thinks Pennyman. Despite the rain, which has been pelting the windows, he is immaculately pressed. The handkerchief at his breast is well folded, his shoes shined. He shows the attention of a woman.

It is difficult to tell Gladinski's age. He is either an older man who has kept his youth or a young man who has grown wise before he grew old. Most probably he is in his thirties. In any event, the two men facing each other might be father and son, although the play's director should not make this point too insistent. Gladinski's features are not handsome—his ears are a trifle too large, his hooked nose is more Jewish than Roman, his hairline is too low. Yet, assuredly, the health and well-being that he conveys make him not unattractive. He is stolid, nerveless, a man who would expect to knock and find the gate opened to him. He is quick, perhaps too quick, to smile. One suspects that under his exterior charm there might be a vulnerable spot. But who really knows?

PENNYMAN (*Not rising*): Well, Mister Gladinski. That was an annoying call. A stupid matter. Not worth the time it took. I see you escaped getting soaked by the rain. Make yourself comfortable. (*He joshes insincerely.*) And what glad tidings do you bring?

GLADINSKI (*Advancing to shake hands and breaking into an automatic smile*): Mister Pennyman. How are you? I saw your light burning and decided to give it a try. It appears we have been missing each other all day. It's a miracle, but we seem to have gotten together at last.

PENNYMAN: Yes, I'd been expecting you this morning, then early this afternoon. And I hurried back at four thirty.

GLADINSKI (*The smile remains effortlessly on his face*): Yes, I'm terribly sorry. There were a few unexpected duties to perform. And then I had to rush off to Malachy's funeral. Almost missed it. I didn't see you there.

PENNYMAN: No, I was occupied. Had to make some urgent long-distance calls for a client.

GLADINSKI: I hope my failure to appear this afternoon did not inconvenience you.

214

PENNYMAN (*Dryly*): No. It was a busy day for me anyway. I almost caught you when I came out of Jim's Barber Shop. You had just rushed by as if you were carrying the ball for New Salem High.

GLADINSKI (*Ignoring the hint of sarcasm*): And I was on the next block when I spotted you standing in front of the First Bank & Trust. I was about to come over, but by the time I looked up again you were in earnest conversation with Mister Harum. I didn't want to break in.

PENNYMAN: Considerate of you. But you could have.

GLADINSKI (*Searchingly*): Oh?

PENNYMAN: We were just chatting.

GLADINSKI (*Unconvinced*): You seemed to be in deep conversation. I didn't think I should interrupt you.

PENNYMAN: I believe we were talking about Mister Levitas. Or maybe that came later. I don't remember.

GLADINSKI (*In his brisk insurance-salesman manner*): Oh, yes, Josh Levitas. He purchased some property today. I wrote the policies. He is wise in these matters and knows it's always best to have a local broker.

PENNYMAN (*Dryly*): The Levitas Home for Aged Hebrews.

GLADINSKI (*His failure to comprehend appears genuine*): Pardon?

PENNYMAN (*Speaking slowly and distinctly*): I said—The Levitas Home for Aged Hebrews. That's what he bought the property for. On Pennyman Street.

GLADINSKI: That simply isn't true. I wrote the policy. It's non-commercial, noninstitutional.

PENNYMAN: That wasn't what I heard. I was at the bank when—

GLADINSKI: I swear, as God is my witness.

PENNYMAN: God, unfortunately, is a witness who can't be sworn.

GLADINSKI: Mister Pennyman, you know as well as I that he never could get a variance for a place like that on Pennyman Street.

PENNYMAN (*Still not convinced*): Sometimes people are not above paying a little extra for privilege.

GLADINSKI (*Ignoring at first the intimation of a pourboire*): Well, it's simply not true. It's his retirement home. He's past seventy, you know. He is the only aged Hebrew who will ever live in that house. I wonder if I didn't detect in what you just said, Mister Pennyman, the intimation of conflict of interest. Well, let me state for the record that after I am elected I plan to release myself from any active solicitation of new insurance business. I realize I can't serve two masters. I'm putting Whit in full charge of Gladinski Insurance. He's young, but he's a natural enthusiast.

PENNYMAN (*Noncommittally*): He's a promising lad.

GLADINSKI: He's got a bright future with me, that's for sure. It's good to see a blue blood not afraid to dig with his silver spoon.

PENNYMAN: But back to Mister Levitas. I guess Hilda stuck him good for the property.

GLADINSKI: If you mean that he wrote out a big check, yes he did. But most of that was for maintenance.

PENNYMAN: Pardon?

GLADINSKI (*Speaking with the confidence of someone who knows that he has the advantage of information*): Yes. He offered it himself after he heard about the historical interest in the house. Upon his death the house goes to a trust for the New Salem Historical Society. The maintenance fund guarantees that not one of our tax dollars will have to be spent on upkeep. That's the reason for the big luncheon next week. To thank him on behalf of the town. Abe Freudenthal is setting it up. I'm sure he'll be phoning to invite you.

PENNYMAN: I don't know. Haven't heard from Mister Freudenthal yet. Depends on how busy I am that day. You know, clients must be served. Still. Don Harum said. Of course Don may have misunderstood. He fainted—a germ he must have picked up in Germany—around the time one of the fellows was joking about an old-folks' home. I don't know.

GLADINSKI: Well, it's true. I would certainly know if it weren't.

PENNYMAN (*With just a tinge of sarcasm*): Yes, you would. I expect as future First Selectman, you're getting a running start on your job.

GLADINSKI: Unless the Democrats decide to enter a candidate at the last minute. I wouldn't mind if they put up someone. It's not a little humiliating to win by default.

PENNYMAN: The Democrats probably thought it would be misinterpreted if they opposed you too heartily. Might look like prejudice rather than issues. Everyone wants the various minorities in the town to unite. It's a sign of the times. Bless the peacemakers.

GLADINSKI: I suppose that is why I was selected. Anyway, times have certainly changed. My father used to tell me that when he came to New Salem all the job listings stated, "No Irish or Poles Need Apply." I was the first-born and I remember how he slaved to support us. He was a good man. Hard-working and honest through and through.

PENNYMAN: I'm sure he was. By the fruit we know him.

GLADINSKI: Thank you for the compliment. But nevertheless he couldn't find work here.

PENNYMAN: Yes, I remember the situation when I was a boy. Except the Poles didn't have it as bad as the Irish. The Irish were accused of being heavy drinkers, but other people said their diet was so poor they had to drink to keep up body heat. My mother didn't let me have any Irish playmates. There was one girl. She passes me on the street now without recognition. Wreathed in clouds of alcohol. Doctor DuMont is recommending that she be taken care of in an institution.

GLADINSKI: Oh, you must mean Old Annie Bell. She's harmless, although the flesh is weak. They say she was once involved in a scandal or something many years ago.

PENNYMAN (*Without show, or perhaps without possession, of emotion*): Well, whatever it was, she used it as an excuse for taking to drink. Anyway, it was many and many a year ago, and my Mother is dead. But you're right. Times have changed. And for the better. I wish you well. It will be quite a feather in your cap.

GLADINSKI: Thank you. I appreciate your support. (*He leans forward and speaks cautiously.*) I wish everyone felt that way.

PENNYMAN: I'm sure they do. Most of them, anyway. They may have their petty prejudices. But in the end they'll respond the fair way. America always does the fair thing, even though it may scare ten years off you in the process. It has taken the American a few centuries to cast off the prejudices and manners of the Old World.

GLADINSKI: But sometimes he gets new prejudices to replace the old.

PENNYMAN: We're still a young country.

GLADINSKI: After more than three hundred years? Well, I hope you're right. I mean about doing the fair thing.

PENNYMAN: I wouldn't worry too much.

GLADINSKI: But I do. There are some people in this community who would do almost anything to prevent my being elected.

PENNYMAN: Wherever there's a carcass, you'll find a few eagles. Some people just like to play the role of Old Integrity. They're the men of little faith. Don't take them seriously.

GLADINSKI: These men have an entrenched position. They're not going to give it up so easily. Especially not to a Catholic and the son of an immigrant.

PENNYMAN: That's looking for prejudice where it doesn't exist, Mister Gladinski. The old families are the very ones who have continually welcomed new people to the melting pot. Even the Pilgrims carried what they called "Strangers" with them on the *Mayflower.* And one of my ancestors wrote that George Washington was proud to enumerate the national origins of the men who were his closest aides—England, France, Ireland, Germany, Italy, Spain, Portugal. And yes, Poland also. They included Protestants, Catholics, and even Jews.

GLADINSKI: Then that changed. They weren't welcomed any more.

PENNYMAN: That's because the new wave of immigrants broke

the compact. Instead of coming here to build a new country, anarchists and socialists came here to destroy it.

GLADINSKI: Well, I still think you're an exception among the older families, Mister Pennyman. You're fair-minded.

PENNYMAN: Thank you. But you're imagining more than the situation warrants. You won't have much difficulty.

GLADINSKI (*Slowly*): I already have.

PENNYMAN: Pardon?

GLADINSKI: Yes. Mister Harum is one. But my real problem is John Purcell.

PENNYMAN: Poor John the Good is nine-tenths dead. Cancer.

GLADINSKI: But with his remaining one-tenth he'll try to stop me. (*He pauses.*) I confess that the subject of John Purcell did not come up accidentally this evening. It is the reason I stopped by.

PENNYMAN (*Defensively*): I didn't imagine you had nothing better to do with your time than gossip with an old man.

GLADINSKI (*Quick to reassure*): I didn't mean it that way.

PENNYMAN: Well.

GLADINSKI: Mister Pennyman, I want to speak frankly to you. But I seem to have a bit of difficulty in getting started. Almost anything sincere I might say sounds like campaign oratory. But I mean these things. My father was an immigrant. He followed a dream when he came to this country. I wish he had lived to see his son become First Selectman in a community where he was once refused work because he was Polish and a Catholic. I pulled myself up. I will be proud, if by being elected First Selectman, I can play some small part in unfolding this dream for others.

PENNYMAN: Well.

GLADINSKI: But it won't unfold if bigoted old men pull my name through the gutter.

PENNYMAN: I haven't seen anyone doing that.

GLADINSKI: You're not being completely honest with me, Mister Pennyman.

PENNYMAN (*Annoyed at having his statement challenged*): I mean that. There is no reason for me to lie to you.

GLADINSKI: You really have heard nothing?

PENNYMAN (*Still irked at having his word doubted*): I said that once already.

GLADINSKI: Yes, you did. Still. It's amazing that you haven't heard.

PENNYMAN: There's nothing amazing at all. I have few friends left. I don't socialize. And, frankly, I'm not interested in petty gossip.

GLADINSKI (*Pauses, still in doubt*): Didn't Mister Harum say anything to you?

PENNYMAN: Don? Oh, yes. That's right. He did mention this afternoon that he wanted to talk to me about you. But we never got to it. I remember now.

GLADINSKI: Mister Harum is a prime mover in trying to keep me and the office of First Selectman apart.

PENNYMAN: Harum? How could he? He just got back from Europe.

GLADINSKI: He's been home long enough for him and John Purcell to put their heads together. For the blind to lead the blind.

PENNYMAN (*Looking off and reminiscing*): Poor old John. We used to play together as boys. He was the only one who knew how to count Indian style. At least we thought it was Indian style. Of course we found out later it wasn't. I remember John once tried to make me eat dog manure after I lost a counting game. Whoever thought we'd end up calling him John the Good? Anyway, he's fading fast. Halfway to heaven.

GLADINSKI: I'm sorry about his illness. But still, am I supposed to bless those who curse me?

PENNYMAN: John's problem is a little too much Old Testament righteousness.

GLADINSKI: Well, his righteousness has lost some of its savor for me. I don't recall the Old Testament saying anything about it being righteous to be bigoted.

PENNYMAN: You have to understand John. He got it from his father. The family always kept to a straight path. It's hard to break away from one's upbringing. To John there's no incense quite so smelly as that from goodness tainted.

GLADINSKI: Mister Pennyman, please don't play with words with me about incense and all your other puns. I know already of your skill in this area. But I think you are using it as a defense against being frank with me. The least I would appreciate is frankness.

PENNYMAN (*Under his breath*): Frankincense and more.

GLADINSKI: What? Oh, another one!

PENNYMAN: Sorry. Couldn't resist. Penny wise, punned foolish.

GLADINSKI: Mister Pennyman, we're not talking about a strict upbringing. Or about going to church on Sunday. We're talking about destroying a man's reputation to serve bigoted ends.

PENNYMAN: If John the Good does something it is because he believes it. He'd rise up from the dead if he thought a penny of tax money had been improperly spent.

GLADINSKI (*Sarcastically*): And we're not talking about fiscal management.

PENNYMAN: Perhaps, Mister Gladinski, you had better tell me exactly what we are talking about.

GLADINSKI: Yes, I suppose so. Since you say you don't know. (*Pauses, not certain how to begin*) For some years now my wife and I have not been truly husband and wife, if you understand what I mean. (*Quickly*) Oh, it's nothing that would affect my qualifications for First Selectman. It's just one of those things. A mismatching when we were both in college. Then a lifetime to regret it. You know how marriages are sometimes.

PENNYMAN: No, I don't. I never married.

GLADINSKI: Still. You must have run up against situations of this sort in your practice.

PENNYMAN (*Stubbornly*): No. My great-grandfather believed marriage was sacred. Whether it was happy or not. He was the first Pennyman to leave the land and go into trade, as law was considered in those days. He retained the yeoman's conservatism. He believed what God had joined together, and so forth. Our firm never handled a marital case. And Grandfather Samuel the Just always said he was going to back slowly into modernity. I carried on the tradition. But we're getting away from the subject. You were speaking about your being First Selectman.

GLADINSKI: Not really away from it. The two things are interrelated. (*He pauses to reflect whether Pennyman is being intentionally obtuse. He decides to continue.*) Anyway, because of my relations with my wife I. Or. Or maybe that really has nothing to do with it. Maybe I would have anyway.

PENNYMAN: Would have—what?

GLADINSKI: Would have gotten involved. With a girl.

PENNYMAN: That's your private affair, distasteful as it may be to some people.

GLADINSKI: Are you one of those people?

PENNYMAN: I suppose so. But I try not to go around judging. It's your business so long as people don't make a to-do about it.

GLADINSKI: But someone is. John Purcell.

PENNYMAN (*He is still wryly amused by his recollections of John Purcell as a boy, unable to put himself in Gladinski's place and realize the threat Purcell poses.*): Poor old John. Even on his deathbed he knows more about what is going on in this community than the *New Salem Advertiser.*

GLADINSKI: Maybe so. Does he also know that his daughter Virginia is fast becoming an alcoholic, or even worse? Does he know that his son-in-law's accident wasn't covered by insurance?

PENNYMAN (*Seriously*): Yes, I suppose John does know. But it's not in him to help them any more than their pride allows them to ask for help. Anyway, John believes the poor have always been with us.

GLADINSKI: Well, his daughter will inherit soon enough.

PENNYMAN: Possibly.

GLADINSKI (*Growing angry at the thought of John the Good's callousness*): And meanwhile his daughter and son-in-law are supposed to scrimp and save? While he sits there with money he can't take to heaven with him—unless the undertaker sews pockets on his backside?

PENNYMAN: That's the way John the Good is. Anyway, he has laid up treasures in heaven already. It's too late to change him. He'll have an eternity to think about whether he did rightly or wrongly.

GLADINSKI: But before that eternity comes he'll do one last thing. He'll pull me down and tarnish a young girl's name.

PENNYMAN: Does anyone else know about your liaison? You know this town might go against you if too many people hear about it.

GLADINSKI: Liaison? That's an interesting word for it. (*Reflects a moment*) Father Riley used to call it philandering. I suppose one word is as good as another. Well, philandering, or liaisons, is a recreational activity of this town the Commerce & Boosters Association doesn't write about in its brochure. It's time someone cleansed the Country Club. But they're not the only ones. Even Tim the cop partakes.

PENNYMAN: What?

GLADINSKI: It's general knowledge.

PENNYMAN: I unconsciously always felt something about him. A ladies' man.

GLADINSKI: What?

PENNYMAN: A ladies' man.

GLADINSKI: No, not Tim. He has special tastes. He's the butch in our hive of homos. He was nicely bedded down with Peri's crowd when some new faggot moved to town. There was quite a row about it this afternoon. Right in Peri's Buttons 'n' Things.

PENNYMAN: I thought he. Well, it doesn't matter.

GLADINSKI: No, Mister Pennyman. I am not guilty of philandering. Under ordinary circumstances I would have married the girl months ago. But in the eyes of my church I still have a wife. Always will.

PENNYMAN: I must confess I have never understood your church's position on this. If you divorce and marry someone else, then you're guilty of the sin of adultery. That's what you're guilty of right now, without divorce. It reads like a palindrome to me. Well, that's for discussion some other time. (*Still refusing to be sympathetic*) But it seems to me that sometimes you just have to take what the world offers. If your wife had fallen and paralyzed herself, instead of just fallen out of love, you would have stuck with her.

GLADINSKI: Perhaps. But she hasn't paralyzed herself.

PENNYMAN: Love is like an automobile. It's not the initial investment, but the upkeep.

GLADINSKI (*Mockingly*): Well said. For a bachelor.

PENNYMAN: Sometimes one knows the right thing to do without having the problem himself. Since your—your philandering —seems to have been discovered, might I inquire who the other party is?

GLADINSKI (*With amazement*): You don't know?

PENNYMAN: If I did, I would not have asked.

GLADINSKI: Joy.

PENNYMAN: Who?

GLADINSKI: Joy Maggiore. Your new secretary.

PENNYMAN: Miss Maggiore! Why I! Damn! I don't even know what's going on in my own office!

GLADINSKI (*Quickly*): She's a marvelous person, Mister Pennyman. She's as loyal as they come. You know yourself how considerate and thoughtful she is.

PENNYMAN: Still. She's such a simple child. She's practically a minor.

GLADINSKI: That doesn't bother either of us. And she's very understanding.

PENNYMAN: I know she is. She has been very patient with an old man. But. It's not right.

GLADINSKI: I must confess I didn't come up here because I saw your light on. I met Joy after she dropped off your order at Flavortowne. I was waiting for her down the street in my car. That's the reason I didn't get soaked by the rain. She told me you were staying late tonight.

PENNYMAN: Poor little Miss Maggiore. Well, you've gotten her into a mess. I don't know how she'll stand up to the calumny. She's such a young girl.

GLADINSKI (*Brightly*): Oh, there's no difficulty. That part is all worked out.

PENNYMAN: I don't understand.

GLADINSKI (*Proudly*): She worked it out herself. She knows what's best for both of us. She's leaving for Alabama, where she'll be away from the whole thing. She heard that some of the girls from the church were going there. It gave her an excuse to go also. She can be far away for a good cause while I deny the whole thing. That is, if John Purcell persists in persecuting me. And if he dies before he can kick up a fuss, then she can come right back. She figured it all out. She's very smart.

PENNYMAN (*Bewildered*): I thought Miss Maggiore was going because she wanted to help the Negro minority. I thought she—

GLADINSKI (*Quickly*): Oh yes, that too. Of course. She's very interested in current events. She joined the League of Women Voters last year. And she reads a lot of magazines.

PENNYMAN: But. But it's not the same thing as reading. Law is being denied down there. Those Southerners are a violent people and she is likely to be in danger.

GLADINSKI: Oh, please don't worry, Mister Pennyman. She won't be taking any chances. She won't be protesting or anything like that. She only volunteered for office work. And, anyway, she won't be there too long. She'll come back right after the election. She's leaving in two days and—

PENNYMAN: In *two* days! I thought. Why, I clearly heard her say she was in no rush to leave. She said she'd stay until it was convenient for me.

GLADINSKI: Oh, yes. She did mention she was going to tell you that. But it's best for us if she leaves as soon as possible. I guess she didn't want to break all the bad news to you at once. She'll probably tell you tomorrow.

PENNYMAN (*Dryly*): I'm sure she will. Well, it appears that you and the clever Miss Maggiore have solved all your problems very nicely. There doesn't seem to be anything for me to do.

GLADINSKI: There still is, Mister Pennyman. We want your help very much. Joy and I have tried to head off the trouble. We can soften the blow of John Purcell's righteousness, but we can't stop it. And a complete halt to his plans is what we need. Believe me, we've thought of everything. I even thought of making a deal with him. I wouldn't say anything about his daughter if he didn't say anything about Joy. He can't pose as a judge without being judged himself.

PENNYMAN: About his daughter? You mean something about Virginia?

GLADINSKI: Yes. She and Charlie. The one who used to play football. You know, the clerk down at the grocery store. When he makes deliveries. His boss found out about Virginia and Charlie when some people complained that the ice cream always comes melted. I could have tried to make a deal with John Purcell. But I won't.

PENNYMAN: I'm glad you won't. You don't get yourself out of a mess by sacrificing other people. Poor Virginia.

GLADINSKI: Also it wouldn't have worked. John Purcell would gladly throw his daughter to the wolves for the opportunity to show that righteousness is more important to him than paternal devotion. No, I'd like to squelch this thing completely. Joy has nothing to do with my qualifications for First Selectman. It's just the old prejudices and bigotry coming to the surface—under the guise of righteousness. Mister Pennyman, I would like to ask your help.

PENNYMAN: You and Miss Maggiore seem to have figured everything out already.

GLADINSKI: No. There is something you can do. I would be forever grateful if you spoke to John Purcell. I'm sure he would listen to you. I'm not asking him to alter his moral views. But nor am I going to turn the other cheek. I merely want him not to mix up three things that have nothing to do with one another —Joy, my being the son of a Polish immigrant, and my running for First Selectman. Because he doesn't like people of foreign extraction doesn't mean he has the right to intrude into my private life. Nor that he has the right to keep me out of office if the majority of the people want me. And it seems that they do.

PENNYMAN: Maybe he's looking at the whole man. Maybe John Purcell thinks one qualification for the office of First Selectman is an orderly domestic life.

GLADINSKI: Maybe. But what does my being the son of a Polish immigrant have to do with my qualifications?

PENNYMAN (*Slowly and emphatically*): You started it, he didn't. Every time you make a speech you're introduced as the son of a Polish immigrant who pulled himself up. It was even in your statement when you announced for the office.

GLADINSKI: Oh, *that*. Everyone knows that's just campaign oratory. It's an American political tradition. Didn't Abe Lincoln do the same thing with his log cabin? Americans love to vote for someone who has pulled himself out of poverty. It shows he can work wonders for the country. Voters are always hoping for a miracle.

PENNYMAN: But when you campaign on a false issue you leave yourself open to attack. You're appealing to the prejudices of the new people in New Salem.

GLADINSKI: *Their* prejudices?

PENNYMAN: Yes. A Freudenthal will vote for you because he hopes someday a Freudenthal will be in your place. The same goes for Petichek and Rappaccini and all the others. Even the Negroes, because they hope that someday their grandsons can do what you're doing. So if you appeal to the prejudices of the new people, it seems to me that the old people have the right to attack you on it.

GLADINSKI: Abe Freudenthal's father was a peddler with a pack on his back. Josh Levitas wasn't even born here and he has become a benefactor to preserve a heritage he never knew. Malachy Murphy, may he rest in Heaven, started out in New Salem pushing a wheelbarrow. What I am saying to you is this. We all came here empty-handed and yet we share in the American Dream. Someday the Negroes will get their share also, if they will just be patient.

PENNYMAN: That's what I was trying to say before.

GLADINSKI: I don't understand.

PENNYMAN: How can you speak about prejudices when so many different kinds of people have received rewards in this country? People of all colors and persuasions and nations have made successes of themselves. Prejudice didn't keep them down.

GLADINSKI: But they worked harder for it. And many jobs and professions are still closed to them. Could Abe Freudenthal's son ever get an executive position with a utility or a railroad or an airline or General Motors? Can he join a yachting club or the Olympic Committee or even rise very high in the foreign service? It is time that the old people realized that America is not their country only, that it's no longer a sacred preserve for the Puritan godly. Times have changed. The torch has been passed to a new generation. The election of Kennedy three years ago should have taught them that. The old people have been appealing to the old prejudices for generations. I have the right this once to appeal to the same sort of prejudice. Leadership in America is passing to a new breed of men!

PENNYMAN: Come now, Mister Gladinski, save your oratory for public occasions. We've all seen the changes and a lot of us have welcomed them. After all, change is what my own ancestors came seeking in this country. Why, a few years ago my university—Yale—elected a Negro as captain of the football team and he was also tapped for the Skull and Bones society. His name was Levi Jackson.

GLADINSKI: If his names had been reversed he never would have made it.

PENNYMAN: Well, my people suffered persecution just as Negroes and Jews did. Anglicans were suspected during the Revolution of being pro-British. Even though they changed the name of the church to Protestant Episcopal, Anglican ministers were driven from their homes and churches were closed. Those were terrible times.

228

GLADINSKI (*Amazed*): But that was almost two hundred years ago!

PENNYMAN (*Irritated*): Well, we still remember it. Tell me, Mister Gladinski, what you want me to do about your problem. I have work I must do this evening.

GLADINSKI: Please speak to John Purcell. Tell him that a new order is coming. He can't stop it. All he can do is reopen wounds which have nearly healed over. Tell him to die in peace with our blessings.

PENNYMAN: Of all the people in this town, why did you come to me? You know I've been out of things for a long time. Since Mother died, I guess. Mister Freudenthal would be a much better spokesman for you. He's up on everything. Knows everyone. Serves on committees. His wife can put in a word with all the Historical Society ladies. Why me?

GLADINSKI: That should be obvious.

PENNYMAN: No, it isn't.

GLADINSKI: Mister Pennyman, I don't have to tell you that your great-great-great-and-so-on-grandfather was a founder of this town. We learn about him in school. Isaiah Pennyman, wasn't it? One of our main thoroughfares is named Pennyman Street. You're the scion of a distinguished family in this town. Do I have to say any more?

PENNYMAN (*Slowly*): No. I suppose not. I would have liked to think you came to me because I've tried to be fair to people, no matter what I personally might think.

GLADINSKI (*He speaks quickly, suddenly aware that he may have offended*): Oh yes, of course. That too. The Pennyman reputation for integrity is well known. Everyone says so. But also you know how to speak to John Purcell. You both speak the same language. It's not something they teach us in the public schools. You both went to the same college (*pointing to the Yale diplomas on the wall*). I went to Holy Cross, up in Worces-ter. Where people like Father Riley use words like "philander-ing." We don't learn your language up there. To us it's as strange as some Indian tongue. Maybe in a few generations my descendants will learn it. But I hope by then there will no longer be a need for it. I hope it'll be as dead as Aramaic.

PENNYMAN: If I understand you correctly, you appoint me your spokesman because I am one of "them."

GLADINSKI: Well, in a way, yes. Is there anything wrong with that?

PENNYMAN: There is. As much wrong as if. As if to get you to do something I were to seek out some other son of a Polish immigrant.

GLADINSKI (*Patly*): People always get on better with their own kind.

PENNYMAN: You are telling me that the merits of a particular case—whether or not someone is acting unfairly—aren't important? You are saying that the really important thing is to get the right person to speak to the right people? (*He rises angrily, and both men face each other across the desk.*)

GLADINSKI (*Bewildered by an anger he does not understand*): Well. I mean.

PENNYMAN (*With increasing effect, for even a small mouse has anger*): You mean that I can never say anything directly to some Negro handyman in Darktown, but instead I have to get some other Negro to do my talking for me? You mean that I can't talk to Mister Freudenthal, but instead have to find an intermediate of the Hebrew persuasion to represent me? Damn! You come in here spouting about healing wounds and all you're doing is keeping the old wounds open. You haven't come to bring peace to this town, Mister Gladinski, but dissension. If that's the way your new breed of men thinks, then I want no part of it!

GLADINSKI: Mister Pennyman! That's the last straw! I know you're upset and you're an older man—but that still gives you no right to make those crude gestures at me!

PENNYMAN: What? Oh. I didn't mean. Damn it, those are my piles itching! Anyway, don't you raise your voice to me, young man! You talk about prejudices blocking you from the office of First Selectman. Well, my Grandfather Samuel the Just was

First Selectman of this town, and, Lord knows, he had his prejudices. For some reason known only to himself he couldn't abide Negroes. But he recognized that as his own failing and he went out of his way to hire Negro servants, even though there were plenty of white people out of work at the time. He kept his prejudices where they belong—inside his own head. You haven't proved to me that your way of handling prejudice is any better. It's only different. (*Pennyman has grown increasingly agitated. Gladinski retreats backward, repelled by this outburst of power, as if he had been bitten by a sheep. He knows he has not gotten what he came for, but he does not quite understand at what point Miss Maggiore's clever plan went astray.*) What's new isn't always better, Mister Gladinski. Sometimes it may be worse. I don't think you're a turn for the better in New Salem. You're just a new wine in the same old bottle. No, I won't speak to John Purcell about you and your clever little Miss Maggiore. Save yourself, if you can. I try to be a fair man, so I will attempt to forget this disagreeable conversation. I may still vote for you —with the greatest reluctance—simply because there is no other candidate and I have always exercised my franchise. Now—good night!

Gladinski, meek as a lamb, turns and walks slowly toward the hallway door. He wears a vinegarish expression, as if he had just quaffed a beverage made from gall and sour apples. Pennyman appears to have grown in stature and self-assurance as, triumphantly, he watches Gladinski's slow departure. The hundred-piece orchestra, which has been silent until now, suddenly strikes up the victory theme from Beethoven's Fifth Symphony —dot-dot-dot-DOOM—which is followed immediately by the husky contralto warble of Miss Annie Bellissima of Dear Dirty Dublin who offers a ringing rendition of "He was despised and rejected of men" from Handel's Messiah, essayed with considerable bel canto embellishment which the assembled throng finds ably done. As the podium rises, a celestial light falls upon Maestro Powerman, Esq., transformed into a mighty man of war who beats out the infectious rhythms of the "Hallelujah Chorus,"

*shattering the chandeliers and showering the auditors with fac-
eted pellets somewhat like manna, while the Polack waxes in
wrath until, with a snarl, he becomes the scandal of the evening
by reverting to the peasant he is. His fine tailoring of sheep's
clothing, which has camouflaged his humble origins, now bursts
apart at the seams, and he stands revealed as a ravening wolf,
while the enthusiastic patrons pelt him with well-directed quart
containers of ice cream which Charlie, the grocery clerk, has
allowed to melt while he dallied indoors with Virginia. As crest-
fallen as Adam, he picks his way past the whited sepulchres of
Miss Maggiore's typing paper lying upon her desk, searching
perhaps for some word of illumination—but not finding it, he
drops upon the desk the keys to the liaison cottage in which he
had sought a new life. He stumbles out into the dark and forbidding hallway to make his way in New Salem, but in a final
act of rebellion slams the door behind him. Himself he cannot
save.*

SLOW CURTAIN, *while the bell atop the witch's hat of New
Salem's Protestant Episcopal steeple sonorously tolls the hour of
8:00* P.M.

■

MAYBE he got the idea. Maybe not. I'd better speak to John the
Good. Tomorrow morning first thing. Maybe we should stop Gladinski. Find out the story. Well, my night was filled with music.
Victory songs and cries of joy. A long day. A long night still to
come. My night is a long day's work. Better finish the Black
Book now. No. Calm down first. Finish my crossword. By the
light of the moon. See if moon is over my right shoulder. It'll be
a sign of no more troubles. Peace will come again. Everything
will be all right. Everyone is a moon, with a dark side he never
shows. Let's see where the moon is tonight. Oh, forgot. Hasn't
risen yet. I saw it this morning, walking to the office. By the
dawn's early blight. Do my crossword. It was probably Shebat.

232

Relax. Damn! Not in my pocket. Must have fallen out some place. Maybe at the bank. And Pete's is closed now. Should have bought the *Times* from him anyway. Penny wise. Damn! That letter is still in my pocket. Throw it away. Tear my name off the envelope first. Raunchy. Epistle to the Salemites. Look at it first? Why not?

HEBRON DEVICES, INC.
— A. J. Levitas Company —
P. O. Box 5724
New York, N.Y.

AT LAST! THE MANUAL YOU HOPED
SOMEONE WOULD DARE TO PUBLISH ! !

Surprise Your WIFE!   Use of the HANDS!
How to SCREW!   More Fun with NUTS!
Use of the JOINT!   POSITIONS of the FINGERS!

NO SECRETS WITHHELD! SATISFACTION GUARANTEED!
DIRECT TO YOUR MAILBOX—AVAILABLE TO MEMBERS ONLY!

Dear Friend:

Suppose *tonight,* right in the privacy of your own home, a beautiful young girl were to teach you *all she knows*—safe *positions,* interesting ways to get more fun from your *tool,* even all the exciting *hand grips* and hitherto-secret *finger positions*—right before your very eyes!

Well, it can happen—and to YOU! Not in the flesh, of course, but the very next best way—in *exciting* photographs! *Unretouched* scenes! . . . *vivid* words! Each and every position is *artistically and faithfully illustrated* in these manuals of ADVANCED TECHNIQUES!

If you act right now—by becoming a MEMBER—we will send your first illustrated manual—FREE!—with your very first selection. And none of your neighbors or friends will know—only your *wife!*—for your selections will arrive at your mailbox in *plain, brown wrappers!* In a few months you will have built up a complete library of techniques—everything from how to feel your "goods" with your fingers to *advanced tips* from French experts! We GUARANTEE you will achieve SATISFACTION never before imagined—*time after time*—or your money is *promptly* refunded. You will be more confident, more self-assured in the use of your EQUIPMENT—or your money back! See this material now, use it, and if it doesn't make your *evenings at home* richer, doesn't give you *complete satisfaction* on *the very first evening*—then return it for a prompt, full refund!

Yes, friend, the beautiful Miss Annie Bell—Miss Hardware of 1963 —has been photographed with *amazing fidelity* in every *conceivable position* to show you how to get more fun out of your home workshop—how to *reproduce* faithfully those early American treasures . . . needle cases, candle molds, pastry stamps, porringers . . . churns, gill dippers, antimacassars, colanders . . . your very own cast of the End of the Trail statue . . . all the things that made American ingenuity the envy of the world's craftsmen! You will even learn how to construct a scale model of the Eiffel Tower—and to antique it so well that none of your friends will know it was not *made* half a century ago! . . . And that's not all! The course in *advanced techniques* illustrates—also with *exciting* photographs of Miss Hardware, *taken just for you*—how to make a wonderful one-hoss shay. And—

DAMN! Another swindle. Unfulfilled promise. I'm a conned Yankee. Buds blasted in the garden of dee-li-lights. Sam's son fled. All gone. Many Pennymans. I'm the last of the Pennymany. Well, no more excuses for delay left at the bottom of the barrel. Onward, little Christian soldier. To the Black Book. Now comes my chance to be a conning Yankee. Now Yankee Doodler really goes to town!

The Blah-Blah-Black Book. It's the last word. From me. Formerly me. It's every Pennyman's genealesis. Read by each of their regenerations. Looking backward. Write finis to it. ti ot sinif. Bye, Pennymans. Good night, ladies, good night, sweet ladies, good night. Three hundred years. Old. Vellum mellowed, yellowed, and hellowed. Ink faded. Folio. Bible black. No ribbon to mark where they fell to sleep or drooped dead. Pennyman in gilt. I am quilty. The Great American Unfolding. The promis'd place. Do it now.

By the act of writing in this Black Book I today take advantage of my birthright opportunity to append some thoughts in the back of our commodious family Bible. In this way I keep nearly unbroken a tradition that originated with my ancestor, the ~~fanatical~~ visionary *Isaiah Pennyman, who first set down his words in this book in 1663 and at that time* ~~ordered~~ expressed the wish *that every male Pennyman thereafter might follow his example. And indeed, almost to a man, the Pennyman generations have inscribed in this book their* ~~desires~~ cherished hopes *for the new society that they helped plant on American soil. Each Pennyman of us has been a* ~~slave to~~ steward of *the* ~~biblical visions~~ dreams *of the founders of this New Jerusalem, a torch to whom the burning faith has been passed.*

All day I have been pondering a question: How can I best ~~justify~~ interpret *the America of my era to you young people who may perhaps read this Black Book many years hence? I have the choice either to set down for you my own reflections, which would constitute only my* ~~biased~~ personal

235

opinions, or, as I much prefer, to describe without ornamentation how I acted out a typical afternoon in a typical American community in the typical year 1963. As you will soon see, I have chosen the second alternative.

Let me first set the stage, as a playwright might do. I now sit writing in my law office, the same one founded by my great-grandfather in 1828, in which I have ~~hung on to~~ preserved for the future *many of the original accoutrements. It is a* ~~somber~~ pleasant *room* ~~haunted by~~ in which tribute is paid to *my ancestors by oil portraits on the walls and on my desk, and by* ~~old~~ treasured *pieces of furniture that evoke* ~~many~~ fond *family memories. As I glance up, I see the reverse image of my name on the office door:*

BENJAMIN PENNYMAN, ESQ.

ATTORNEY-AT-LAW

It is evening, and our village is quiet save for the occasional trucks that ~~rumble~~ carry commerce *through the town. The* ~~clatter~~ hum *of industry that has permeated our community throughout the day is now muted. The shops and offices are closed, the streets are nearly deserted. Peace and contentment reign.*

This afternoon I left my office for ~~several hours~~ a little while *to attend to some trivial personal errands, in the process of which I circled the* ~~blighted~~ lovely *common which lies at our town's heart. My first stop was the post office, where*

I found no ~~mail in my box aside from an ad~~ urgent correspondence. I chatted
for a while with our postmaster, Hamilton Holliway, a
man who has lifted himself out of his boyhood ~~squalor~~ deprivations
and has devoted four decades of selfless service to our
community and to our federal government. With him I
discussed the ~~demands~~ aspirations of our present-day ~~poor~~ deprived and
the many ~~schemes~~ programs which aim to ~~cure~~ ameliorate these conditions. He
raised the question, which of course concerns all
~~taxpayers,~~ people of good will, of how to tell the ~~cheat~~ slacker from the person in
legitimate need of ~~charity.~~ welfare.

I next ~~waded through~~ negotiated the traffic and was, I confess, somewhat ~~angry at~~ disturbed by the noise and smells of exhaust. But
upon further reflection I realized that these ~~pollutants~~ inconveniences
are but sure signs of growth. We have indeed come a
long way from the wonderful one-hoss shay! And none of
us would want the wheels of Progress to grind to a stop,
or even to slow down. I soon passed a historic New Salem
house in the process of being ~~ruined~~ restored to its past splendor by a banker in our
town whose father was ~~a Jew peddler~~ an immigrant with a pack on
his back. Ours is truly a land of opportunity! I was
reminded that among our community's merchants and
~~tradesmen~~ businessmen we number many whose fathers and
grandfathers came here from all corners of the globe—
French Canada, Ireland, Italy, Poland, Germany,
Portugal, Africa, and, most recently, Puerto Rico. It might

seem that such a situation could cause ~~prejudice~~ dissension, but no—all of these people have become precious alloys in The Great American Melting Pot. As it states on our coins, our Nation is truly "E Pluribus Unum."

I then paused for a few moments at the insurance office, where I learned something new (as I try to do each day) about how a compact with this ~~lottery~~ institution can remove many of the hazards of life. I passed several businesses which I patronize and spent a moment or two reflecting on their prospects. Almost all are thriving. One or two are not. I am thinking in particular of the glass, shades, and wallpaper shop now piloted by the son of its founder. The lad is ~~nearly bankrupt~~ in difficulties, but that is to be expected when Youth feels its way. Instead of accepting the humiliation of government ~~handouts~~ assistance, this young man is displaying daring and initiative in trying to make his own way under the full sail of Adventure. He knows that Youth ~~sometimes makes a mess of things,~~ has a God-given right to fail, and also how to profit from the experience.

I soon reached the barbershop, whose proprietor, interestingly enough, is an unusual type of immigrant to our community. He is a white Southerner—some might regard him as a ~~hillbilly~~ rustic—whose roots reach deep into our Nation's early history. He typifies the resiliency born into the American character. He ~~was dispossessed~~ left

238

~~from~~ his ancestral village in Tennessee after the
construction of a mighty dam to harness the benefits of a
river and, after some wandering, he finally selected
New Salem in which to ~~set up shop.~~ *practice his skill.* His amusing
anecdotes are indeed worth attending to, for they bring
to our village news of the length and breadth of our
Nation. He represents but one more facet of the
~~mongrelization~~ *diversity* of our community.

As I departed from the barbershop, a chance remark
led me to think about the ~~incendiary~~ *inspiring* "I Have a Dream"
speech delivered by the Reverend Martin Luther King
at a recent Washington ~~protest march,~~ *rally,* in which he
~~stated his demands~~ *articulated his dreams* for the American Negro to achieve full
legal ~~and social~~ status. Despite ~~considerable fears~~ *some anxiety* about
the rally, it was carried on without any incidents
of ~~violence.~~ *dissension.* It was truly an example of ~~a free~~ *an emancipated* people
expressing their ~~demands~~ *aspirations* in a free society. As I reflected
upon the ~~inflammatory~~ *stirring* words of the speech, I was
impressed that a Negro could ~~find talented assistance in writing~~ *compose* such a compelling oration. I was reminded of the
legend that one of the Three Wise Kings who came
to worship the infant Jesus was a Negro. Under the skin
we are all ~~brothers.~~ *equal before the law.* The affirmation of Youth confirmed
the justice of my reverie. Young Rebecca Harum,
daughter of ~~our most reputable~~ *another* banker, informed me

239

that she is ~~giving up~~ *temporarily suspending* her college education to aid in the voter-registration ~~agitation~~ *campaign* for the Alabama Negroes.

At that point something or other reminded me of my only brother, who trod a path different from the one I selected. While I was ~~content~~ *happy* to stay at home and aid in bringing to fruition the New Eden planted by my ancestor Isaiah, my brother was more ~~discontent.~~ *adventuresome.* He carried on his search for God's Country the length and breadth of our great Nation, working with ~~numerous~~ *all sorts and conditions of men,* ~~failures and has-beens,~~ and with his own two hands ~~fighting the elements, the pests, and the bankers.~~ *helping to bring forth the bounty of a Nation.* He found the unfolding of the American Dream three thousand miles and a continent away from New Salem. I, of course, found it right in my backyard. Both of us were correct, for everywhere this is God's Country, a land of limitless opportunities. His own wish was that he be buried ~~near our church,~~ *in California,* symbol of ~~salvation.~~ *our Nation's far-flung frontiers.* Unfortunately, I am unable to append his contribution, mailed me just before his death, to this Black Book, for his letter ~~about~~ *extolling* God's Country went astray in the postal service.

I then chatted with our ~~nervous~~ *conscientious* banker, Don Harum, who had summered abroad on the peaceful Italian shore, where he received surcease from the ~~anxieties~~ *tensions* of ministering to our community's financial health. I was flattered that he invited me to join ~~an organization~~ *a club* in

Stamford and to drive with him to attend one of its

meetings this weekend. Don and I have been chums since

we were boys together, and it is wonderful that we both

can in our twilight years participate in the same

~~organization's~~ *club's* activities to keep us ~~on our guard~~ *informed* about

~~liberal infiltration in Washington.~~ *contemporary affairs.* While I was chatting

with Don in his bank we were both ~~amazed~~ *delighted* to learn that

one of our Nation's ~~Wall Street operators~~ *financial wizards* has decided to

preserve for posterity a historic New Salem house. He is

an immigrant of the Hebrew ~~persuasion~~ *faith* who by ~~stock~~ *prudent*

~~manipulation~~ *management* has ~~raided~~ *accumulated* a wide variety of corporate

enterprises.

Emerging from the bank, I met Doctor DuMont, for

the past two years the faithful shepherd of our Protestant

Episcopal flock. The press of affairs on both our parts has

prevented us from having a leisurely interchange of ideas,

so we both welcomed this opportunity to chat. He is a

very ~~garrulous~~ *interesting* person, with a ~~Farmer's Almanac~~ *storehouse of fascinating lore.*

~~mentality.~~ He kindly showed an interest in my family,

and inquired particularly about Mother, a person of

compassion who had devoted her life to culture, and who

is known for her ~~support~~ *encouragement* of promising young French

artists. Doctor DuMont inquired also about my Father,

and I took the opportunity to ~~squelch~~ *clarify* several stories he had

241

heard. I informed Doctor DuMont that my Father had

gone off on a commercial expedition to remote isles,

where he ~~might have been~~ *undoubtedly was* lost at sea ~~after becoming a king over the blacks of the island,~~ as were so many of our

intrepid New Englanders.

While we were chatting, ~~the town drunkard,~~ *an unfortunate person,* known

affectionately as Irish Annie Bell, passed by. No one knows

what private sorrow has cast her to these depths. Some

of the older residents aver that many a year ago, when

she was a young beauty, she had an affair of the heart that

ended unfortunately because of ~~her lowly origins.~~ *the constraints of her religion.* I do

recall, though, that at one time Mother took a special

interest in this unfortunate person, and even gave her the

money for an ~~extended~~ *interesting* trip. Doctor DuMont assured

me that Annie Bell will receive public ~~charity~~ *assistance* in finding

~~an institution~~ *a pleasant home* where she can be cared for in her ~~declining~~ *golden*

years. Doctor DuMont also told me about the Job-like

steadfastness demonstrated by ~~a handyman~~ *an artisan* named

Mister Barefoot Hyde, who had never been deprived of

~~work~~ *opportunities* in New Salem because of his color. I think I will

in the future devote more time to church committees, for

the church is ever a steadfast rock in our society.

After pausing to make a purchase at Myer's Drugs,

where I listened to Mister Myer's ~~constant complaints~~ *amusing comments* the challenges

about ~~the frustrations~~ of doing business in a complex

society, I returned to my office. There I learned from my

considerate

also is aiding the Negro cause

~~clever~~ secretary that she ~~is getting out of town~~ and is

right wrongs against

nearly on her way to Alabama to ~~enforce laws in favor of~~

Negroes there. Her people were Italian immigrants

some

to our shores and ~~a few~~ of them have made their way in

~~legitimate~~ businesses. It is proper and fitting that she

people.

should so selflessly help less fortunate ~~minorities~~.

Shortly after returning I glanced out of my office
window and witnessed the funeral procession that had
interred Mister Malachy Murphy. Mister Murphy is
another refutation of the nay-sayers who have lost faith
in the American system. He arrived in New Salem as an

utilized to the utmost his native skills.

Irish immigrant and ~~finally found work as a common~~
~~laborer~~. He died a comparatively wealthy man,

an enthusiastic

~~a respected~~ real-estate agent, whose funeral at the

almost all

Church of Our Lady of the Lame was attended by ~~some~~
of our community's prominent citizens. The passing of
Mister Murphy reminded me that he and I, together with

energetic

one of our town's ~~crafty~~ bankers, a man of the Hebrew

an important venture

faith, had once shared in ~~a real estate deal~~ to develop what

venture

remained of the Pennyman lands. Although this ~~deal~~

foundered on the rocks of Chance, and earned me

only a pittance for my troubles,

~~much less profit than most people think,~~ the three of us—

an Episcopalian, an Irish Catholic, and a Jew—in ~~cahoots~~ ^{concord}
furnished the entire community with an Example of
Brotherhood-in-Action.

   My day was rounded off by a visit this evening from
^{the son of a Polish immigrant}
~~an ambitious young man~~ who is running ~~unopposed~~ for
the office of First Selectman. We do not as yet know
who his opponent in the election will be, but I feel
certain that very soon a reputable and stable person will be
nominated. I discussed with Mister Gladinski several
problems in our community and his aspirations to ~~cure~~ ^{ameliorate}
them. Because of the press of client affairs, I had fallen
somewhat behind in the news of our community, and so I
was grateful for the frank chat in which the candidate
brought me up to date. He told me that several people
in our community are concerned about ~~indications~~ ^{the possibility} of
~~liaisons,~~ ^{moral laxity,}
~~philandering,~~ and he assured me about his position if he is
elected. I wished him well in his campaign, but I fear,
in all frankness and more, that he will not be elected.
Perhaps fickle Fortune will go against him and an
opposing candidate with probity will be found. However,
it is salutary that ~~such an ambitious young man~~ ^{the son of a Polish immigrant} should
attempt this office, and, if he is patient, ~~it is possible~~ ^{I am certain}
that his opportunity to serve will come someday. After
all, the young are resilient.

   One final note before I conclude what I fear has been a

tiresome chronicle for you young readers of the future.
My sandwich snack and celery tonic were delivered
to me this evening by Mister Daniel Hyde, a Negro,
whose ~~genetic endowment~~ background and ~~upbringing~~ education qualify him
only for ~~menial work~~ less taxing endeavors. Yet I well remember that when I
employed him last winter to shovel snow, I was very
impressed by the straightness of the path he made. It
indicated tremendous skill and dedication to the task at
hand. I recall asking Mister Hyde how he managed to
do it. "Well, sir," he said to me, "long ago I came to the
realization that I lacked both the advanced education
and the innate ability for any cerebral tasks. So I became
determined to perform well the few tasks I could do at all.
I made shoveling snow into a diversion—each time
testing my skill to see how straight a path I could shovel.
While all the New Salemites pitied me for being exposed
to the hazards of cold and wet, I really had the advantage.
I was earning wages for playing a game. It is not
really hard to learn to shovel a straight path if you bend
all your energies to it!" ~~Daniel~~ Mister Hyde taught me a valuable
lesson: Whatever people do they should do well, even if
it is only shoveling snow. If everyone did his job
~~willingly,~~ cheerily, this would indeed be a more pleasant world.

Such were my actions this afternoon. Uneventful—
yes. Inconsequential—no. For we can learn much from the

casual meetings and idle conversations that make up the ~~undercurrents~~ passing parade *in a typical community. In many ways these events are more consequential than the publicized actions taken by our representatives in Washington. We should never forget that the national* ~~arena~~ stage *of Washington is really composed of thousands of little stages like New Salem. And we are the actors whose* ~~demands~~ recommendations *ultimately* ~~determine~~ play a role in *our national posture. I am confident that no national leader will* ~~long continue~~ choose *to ignore the* ~~will~~ Common Sense *of all the loyal little New Salems in our great Nation. Unimportant as my afternoon may appear, it reveals the human contacts and orderly transaction of business that are our* ~~will.~~ way of life.

I am the scion of a family that for generations has striven to plant our vision of a new world—a holy city, a New Jerusalem—on these shores. The only book my ancestors brought to the task was the book of Life. And they were faithful to their dream until death. They brought forth wealth out of the earth, encouraged advances in science and culture, and watered prosperity with the sacrifices demanded by that pale rider, Death. When necessary, ~~some~~ many *Pennymans have* ~~obediently~~ selflessly *gone off to defend the grand vision our ancestors had for this Nation. My ancestors are now resting from their labors, but their works have brought forth splendid fruit.*

They stood at the door of a new society and knocked—
and their knock was answered! Revealed to them was a
new heavenly city, the God's Country of America, ruled
over by a sovereign Common Sense!

Prophets of gloom and doom speak today about a
coming battle, an Armageddon, in which some of us will
be pitted against what are called "minorities," a
decisive battle that will rend our Nation. But I deny such
pessimism with all my heart and soul! Our "minorities"
are really part of our great majority—for they voluntarily
joined it when they freely migrated to this land to
make a better life.
find easy wealth. No one forced them to come here. In
the same way that the "Strangers" who journeyed with
the Pilgrim "Saints" put their signatures to the
Mayflower Compact and covenanted to obey the Pilgrim
laws and customs, so the more recent Strangers to our
shore arrived here under an implied contract to accept
the laws, customs, institutions, and language of America,
host.
their haven. I am pleased to state in this Black Book that
many have faithfully carried out their part of the bargain
and have subsequently been rewarded in their new land.
ornery folk
There will, of course, always be agitators who rebel
against established institutions for the simple reason that
they are born nay-sayers. They are the ones who glibly
call out "Freedom" to us the loudest. They say, for

example, that they want freedom from fear—yet fear of ~~extreme punishment~~ ^{the law} is what keeps people from committing crimes. I am a free man, yet I do not possess the freedom to careen down Pennyman Street at one hundred miles per hour. My freedom to swing my arm ends where the tip of someone else's nose begins. Today our ~~left-wing~~ ^{liberal} press informs me that I live in a time of turmoil, of dire threat, the beginning and the end of our Nation. They make prophecies about the coming battle of group against group, of rich against poor, of black against white. They even tell me that our American Dream has ~~turned into a nightmare.~~ ^{not been fully achieved.} Let me confide in you, my future readers, that in preparation for what I would inscribe on these pages, this afternoon I reread the contributions of my ancestors to the Black Book. The lesson of the Black Book, my unknown friends, is that things were never as ~~dangerous~~ ^{discouraging} as they appeared at the time. There has never been a period in our great history when certain people did not feel that ~~they were being swindled of the rewards of the American Dream.~~ ^{their wishes were not receiving all the attention they might.} With a little good will and fair play we shall easily enough ~~survive~~ ^{conquer} our current problems. In fact, I predict that you readers of the future will look back upon my own placid times and wonder amusedly how any of us could have been ~~fearful.~~ ^{concerned.}

As the last survivor of the line of Isaiah, I, Benjamin Pennyman, bequeath this historic document about the soul of a Nation to the Yale University Library, to be opened no less than five years following my death. It is my hope that some future scholar will chance upon this book and perhaps dip into it out of curiosity. Let him bring sympathy to it and take away understanding. Should he decide to bestow upon it the fruits of his scholarship, not the least of his rewards will be bringing to light the honest record of the fulfillment of the covenant Isaiah Pennyman made three centuries ago with this Promis'd Land. There is no more fitting way for me to conclude this testament of America than with the words that my Grandfather Samuel the Just directed to be carved upon the immutable granite of his headstone:

"MEMORY SURVIVES"